SOVEREIGN

The Books of Mortals

SOVEREIGN

TED DEKKER
AND TOSCA LEE

Faith
Words

New York   Boston   Nashville

FaithWords
Hachette Book Group
237 Park Avenue
New York, NY 10017
www.HachetteBookGroup.com

FaithWords is a division of Hachette Book Group, Inc.
The FaithWords name and logo are trademarks of Hachette Book Group, Inc.

The Hachette Speakers Bureau provides a wide range of authors for speaking events. To find out more, go to www.hachettespeakersbureau.com or call (866) 376-6591.

The publisher is not responsible for websites (or their content) that are not owned by the publisher.

Printed in the United States of America

Originally published in hardcover by Hachette Book Group
First mass market edition: March 2014

10 9 8 7 6 5 4 3 2 1
OPM

SOVEREIGN

THE BEGINNING

IN THE YEAR 2005, geneticists discovered the human gene that controlled both innate and learned forms of fear. It was called Strathmin, or Oncoprotein 18. Within fifteen years, genetic influencers for all primary emotions were similarly identified.

Nearly a decade later, in the wake of a catastrophic war that destroyed much of civilization, humanity vowed to forsake ruinous emotion and serve the way of a new Order. To this end, the first Sovereign unleashed a virus called Legion, which genetically stripped an unsuspecting world of all emotions but one: fear. As humanity forgot hope, love, and joy, it also left behind hatred, malice, and anger.

For nearly five hundred years, perfect peace reigned.

But a sect called the Keepers closely guarded the terrible secret that every soul on earth, though in every appearance human, was actually dead. The world was inhabited solely by Corpses. For centuries they clung tenaciously to a prediction that the viral code introduced by Legion would one day revert in the blood of a single child born to be Sovereign of the world. Humanity's final hope for life would be found in this single child. Also passed down by the Keepers: a sealed vial of ancient blood with the power to awaken five souls who would assist the boy and usher him into power.

In the year 471 a boy with true life running through his veins was born in the line of Sovereigns. The boy's name was Jonathan. His life was closely guarded by Rom Sebastian and four others brought to life by the Keeper's ancient vial, and then by twelve hundred Nomads brought to life with Jonathan's blood and empowered with vastly superior senses. They called themselves Mortals.

At first it seemed that Jonathan's blood was meant to return life to a dead world through the reawakening of emotion and enhancement of the senses. Those Mortals who followed and protected Jonathan celebrated their newfound life with passion, determined to set Jonathan in the Sovereign's seat of world power.

Desperate to experience the same kind of life through means of alchemy, Saric became the first Dark Blood through the design of Master Alchemist Pravus. Filled with ambition, hatred, and jealousy, Saric determined to rid the world of all Mortals. But in the end his half sister, Feyn, who had once saved Jonathan's life before her conversion to a Dark Blood at Saric's hands, thwarted them all. Forsaking both Jonathan and Saric, she seized her right to the Sovereign throne and began her rule with an iron fist. So betrayed, Saric killed Jonathan and then vanished into the wilderness, stripped of power.

Upon his death, Jonathan's blood no longer effected the physical advantages it once had, offering instead a new awareness of life characterized by knowledge and wisdom in those who injected the last remnants of his blood into their veins. The few Mortals who chose to follow Jonathan's teachings renamed themselves Sovereigns.

They are led by Rom Sebastian and Jordin, the woman who loved Jonathan during his life.

Those Mortals who rejected Jonathan's blood following his death in favor of vastly extended lives and heightened sensory perception now call themselves Immortals. They are led by the Prince of the Nomads, Roland.

Six years have passed since Mortals were divided into Sovereigns and Immortals and Feyn began her dark rule. She continues her campaign to purge the world of Sovereigns and Immortals both. Having been systematically hunted and killed, only thirty-seven Sovereigns remain, hidden under the city where they live in secret.

CHAPTER ONE

JORDIN CROUCHED atop the warehouse on Byzantium's eastern perimeter, dark hair lifting with the gust of an oncoming storm, eyes scanning the darkening streets below for any sign of Triphon. There could be only one reason why he would leave his watch at the door.

Dark Bloods. Hosts of hell.

More than eighty thousand of the vicious warriors hunted throughout the city, guarding the Citadel where their maker, Feyn Cerelia, ruled the world with an iron fist, determined to rid it of Jordin's kind.

Triphon had undoubtedly followed protocol and made an attempt to draw danger away from the provisions bank, one of only a few on the edges of the city from which Sovereigns "borrowed" food.

Jagged lightning lit the eastern horizon, baring the low hills a mere hundred meters distant. Beyond lay the wastelands, home to Roland's Immortals.

Immortals. They had rarely been sighted by her kind, and then only at a distance. They were lethal by any estimation, both to Feyn's Dark Bloods and to the few Sovereigns still living. Ghosts in the night.

Most Mortals had soundly rejected Jordin's appeal to

follow Jonathan in his death and had vanished north with Roland, defiantly embracing the promise of immortality. Only a handful had remained to seek new life—new wisdom—as Sovereigns.

But now, six years later, that life had been all but stamped out by the Blood War between Feyn's Dark Bloods and the Immortals, neither of which courted tolerance for Sovereigns. Jonathan's selfless love had spawned only hatred and the ruthless bloodshed that had held Byzantium in its grip for the last year.

Only thirty-seven Sovereigns still drew breath, hidden deep in the expansive caverns beneath Byzantium. Once over seven hundred in number, their ranks had been whittled down to a remnant in dire need of food and supplies. Under perpetual threat of death, they emerged only under cover of darkness and then only in pairs. Being caught alone was too dangerous; more than two presented the possibility of too great a loss if trouble found them.

Jordin turned and hurried along the two-foot-wide concrete wall bordering the top of the building in a crouch, her rubber-soled boots soundless on the asphalt roof. No sight of Triphon, no sound but the thunder rolling to the east.

She scanned the streets to the south. Empty. There was a Dark Blood post two streets over, beyond her line of vision, one of thousands positioned throughout Byzantium.

She twisted to the west. Five miles distant, the Citadel's ominous spires towered over the city. Heavily fortified rings of Dark Blood patrols had taken position, expanding out from the world's capital buildings to protect Feyn from the increasingly aggressive attacks of Roland's Immortals. But the Dark Bloods and the Immortals were not Jordin's only concern.

Well over two million Corpses crowded the capital, each of them loyal to Feyn's new Order. Although the Corpses possessed no emotion save fear, that fear included a holy terror of Jordin's kind. Feyn had seen to that. And though Corpses would never raise a hand in violence, they were quick to report any contact with a Sovereign. Anyone caught for not reporting a Sovereign was summarily sent to the Authority of Passing—to death.

Hiding from two million Corpses was no easy task. Though Sovereigns looked no different in appearance save their eyes, which had turned a brilliant green, Corpses could smell them. Apparently her kind gave off the pungent scent of incense. Sovereigns: Loving all, loved by none. Then again, they had no problem loving Dark Bloods with a sword. Hadn't Jonathan done the same?

Jonathan. She would yet die for him without second thought. Some said he was out there waiting in the flesh, others said he existed only in their blood. All she knew for certain was that the expanded Mortal senses she'd lost in becoming a Sovereign—senses presumably still retained by Roland's Immortals—would be a welcome gift right now. With them she would know the exact location of the nearest Dark Bloods with a single sniff of the air. She would hear the scuffle on any street below . . . even a mumbled word from a hundred meters.

Instead of Mortal perception, her kind held surety of true life and occasional precognition of the future, which, although intriguing, proved limited—they could only see a few seconds or minutes ahead, and even then inconsistently. The "seeing" that had become the inheritance of all Sovereigns couldn't match the sheer strength of the Dark Bloods or the wicked skill of the Immortals.

Their enemies were hunting them to extinction.

She reminded herself that they were as they were meant to be, transformed by Jonathan's blood. It was Jonathan's way, to bring life—how, they still didn't know. But there was deep mystery in their transformation, and they held that mystery with reverence along with the knowledge that Sovereigns were like Jonathan in ways Corpses and Immortals never could be.

She knew this, but it didn't keep her from lying awake at night, badgered by questions without answers—questions she could speak to no one but Rom, and then only when her frustration boiled over. She was their leader, side by side with Rom. The others couldn't know how deeply she suffered. To be Sovereign was to be brimming with love in a new realm—they all said it. Jonathan had said it. But saying it didn't change the fact that they lived like dying rats beneath the city while Dark Bloods and Immortals flourished in the sun.

Was it possible what Roland had said six years ago... that Jonathan had abandoned them all?

Jordin closed her eyes and let the ugly question fall from her mind. No. They lived to bring Jonathan's life to the world—a last vestige of hope for a world steeped in death. Thirty-seven Sovereigns left, and now one more of them seemed to have vanished. They couldn't afford to lose another, much less one of their warriors. Triphon was the only one who could wield a weapon as efficiently as she or Rom.

A cry cut the night to the east, and Jordin whipped around, ears keen. She heard a shout followed by an unmistakable grunt.

Dark Blood.

Jordin reached the fire escape ladder in three running strides, grabbed the rail with her gloved hand, and threw her legs over the low perimeter wall. Her feet landed on the fifth rung and she descended on the fly. She stood only an inch over five feet in boots, and her body was lighter than any of the large bags of rice she'd dumped at the warehouse entrance, but her speed and skill made up for her lack of heft in any fight.

She released the ladder from ten feet up, landed lightly on the balls of her feet, and then sprinted east along the southern wall, reaching for her bow.

"Jordin!"

Triphon's familiar voice rode the wind, flooding her veins with adrenaline. He would call out only if his situation was dire enough to warrant the risk of drawing Dark Bloods.

She rounded the warehouse to find an empty alley and then flew through the narrow way. Beyond the last building the street broadened into open ground that ran into the hills. The fact that Triphon's shout had come from this direction meant one thing: having been discovered by a roving patrol, he had led them toward the wasteland. The Dark Bloods were wary of the wilderness—not for the expanse of land itself, but for the Immortals who materialized from the darkness without warning. With their singularly acute eyesight, Immortals owned the night.

But those same Immortals posed as great a threat to Triphon.

She ran faster.

A sliver of moon peered out from beneath the clouds on the eastern horizon, giving Jordin clear sight of the street. The scene snapped into form in a single blink of her eye.

Triphon, sword drawn, was backed up against an unlit

streetlamp. He was dressed for the night in black pants, a short coat, and rubber-soled boots like her own. His hood had fallen back, the scant moonlight illuminating his green eyes, radiant even at a hundred paces.

Seven Dark Bloods were closing in on him, bold despite the knowledge that some of them would surely die. They weren't stupid. Sovereigns might not have the superior breeding of Dark Bloods, but by the way Triphon held his sword easily in one hand, tipped toward the concrete, anyone could see he was trained in the Nomadic way of the Mortals—the same Mortals who'd stood their ground only six hundred strong against Saric's twelve thousand Dark Bloods six years ago.

Jordin had killed countless Dark Bloods that day; she and Triphon could take seven today.

To a man they towered nearly a foot over Triphon, built like bulls—muscle and brawn. But they moved with uncanny speed and took blows as if made of ironwood. Whatever alchemy had created such raw specimens of brutality couldn't be undone. They could not be brought to life like a common Corpse. Only Sovereign blood killed them.

Most still wore their hair in dreadlocks, but they had evolved over the past several years. Their retinas were as black as their pupils, but rimmed now in gold. So well proportioned, they were specimens of perfection; loyal slaves, their insatiable lusts held in check only by Feyn herself. It was well known they abused common Corpses at will.

They hadn't seen her yet. She dropped to one knee, notched an arrow, and drew her bowstring.

The Dark Bloods pulled short, and the ringleader stepped forward, twirling his heavy sword as if it were a stick of balsa wood. His mutter was full of gravel—Jordin couldn't make out his words. She did, however, understand the meaning of the sudden approach by the two warriors to the leader's left.

They were going in for the kill.

She steadied her breath and released the bowstring. The wind had lulled, and her arrow flew straight. It slammed into the leader's head as she quickly notched her second arrow.

The Dark Blood she'd struck staggered back, bellowing a cry that momentarily arrested the others. Triphon moved while their attention was drawn away, lunging at the closest warrior, swinging his blade up to catch the unsuspecting Blood under his chin.

Jordin sent another arrow at a third warrior and then she was on her feet.

"Triphon!"

Four heads swiveled to the threat at their backs. Without pausing, Triphon swung his blade at the fifth's belly, missed, but arced the sword into the shoulder of one of those who'd turned.

Another arrow—this one sent quickly into the mass of Bloods where it struck one of them in the side. In the course of ten seconds they had cut down three and wounded two more. They had once fought by Roland's side with as much precision, before the prince had turned his back on Jonathan's legacy.

She raced at breakneck speed, flipping her bow over her back, palming two knives as she went in. Leaderless and stunned by such lethal attack from behind, the Dark Bloods suddenly found themselves at a disadvantage.

She threw the seven-inch blade in her right hand from ten paces off, sidearm, but the Blood she'd intended it for slapped it from the air. The three remaining warriors sprang back, more cautious now.

Three on two—they would fell these fiends where they stood. Outrunning them would be far more difficult, and they couldn't risk leading them back to the cavern. If Feyn learned where they lived, they would all be crushed in a single blow and Sovereign blood would be no more.

"We kill them," Jordin said.

"We kill them," Triphon repeated with the hint of a grin.

The Blood to Jordin's left nodded and slowly straightened. A sick smile crept over his face.

"All of us?"

"All of you," Jordin said.

His gaze lifted past her shoulder. Triphon's followed. His face flattened. Jordin threw a quick glance behind her. Three Dark Bloods had emerged from the same alley from which she'd come.

"Jordin…"

She twisted back. More. No fewer than ten Dark Bloods had slipped from the corners of both buildings at the end of the street. They were boxed in, cut off on either side by brick warehouses, to the front and back by Dark Bloods.

Her heart rose into her throat. She shifted to one side, all thoughts of an easy escape gone. A fresh gust of wind whipped a dusty dervish up from the knoll beyond the end of the street. If they could make a run for the wasteland, the Dark Bloods might not follow. But getting past the line marching toward them would prove difficult if not impossible—Bloods were anything but slow.

"I'm sorry, I didn't hear your response," the Dark Blood said. "Are you sure? All of us?"

Jonathan, where are you now?

The sentiment that accompanied the question had become more bitter than inquisitive as of late. But she hadn't always needed Jonathan to survive. She'd been his guardian once, when her skill as a fighter had been unquestioned even by Roland himself. Her veins flooded with new resolve, fueled by anger. Their quest to follow Jonathan and bring life could *not* end here, regardless of the odds.

The sword of a fallen Blood lay on the ground three paces away. She still had nine arrows in the quiver at her back. Two more knives were sheathed against her thighs. And if no way for escape presented itself, there was the sword.

The calm calculation that had served Jordin so well at Roland's side slipped for an instant as an image filled her mind: Jonathan spreading his arms wide, crying out for Saric to kill him as she screamed, powerless, from the cliff above. Saric's blade arcing down into the chest of the only man she had ever loved, before or since.

She swallowed, mouth dry. Was this her fate as well?

Then so be it.

She whipped the knife in her left hand underhanded and watched it bite deeply into the eye of the Blood who'd spoken. His smirk exploded in a spray of blood. With a full-throated scream, she snatched the bow and arrow from her back.

Triphon's roar joined her cry, and he flew at the Bloods who'd first attacked him. She spun to face the new arrivals, dropped to one knee, notched an arrow, and sent it into one of the three who were now running from the same direction she'd come. A second and a third arrow, in rapid succession.

Her arrows found bodies but failed to take down two of the Bloods.

Jordin faced a critical decision. They'd have to split the Bloods—surrounded, they stood no chance. She'd have to deal with the two approaching from the rear, but she also had to find a way past the line beyond Triphon.

She let a final arrow fly toward the two Bloods sprinting for her, already bringing their blades to bear. They seemed utterly oblivious to the threat of death—what was death to the dead?

Without waiting to see her arrow find its mark, she twisted and came to her feet. Five arrows left.

She strung one on the fly and started forward, angling left. Triphon had taken down one of two Bloods he had engaged and was lunging at the other like a bull. If she could break through the line of Dark Bloods between them and the wasteland beyond, forcing them into two fronts, they'd still have a chance.

The ten had become twelve, all at a full run fifty paces distant and closing, thinner on the left than the right.

"Split them!" she cried and tore forward, shooting as she ran. She sent four arrows into the three warriors farthest to her left without precision, only caring that she stalled them enough to break past them.

One arrow left. She flung her bow over her back and ran at a full sprint toward the two stumbling on her far left. She had to reach them. Get one of their swords, engage from behind. It was the only way.

But that way was cut short by a terrible sound behind her. A wet *thunk* followed by a sick *grunt*.

The *thunk* she knew to be a blade cutting deep into flesh. It was the *grunt* that made her start. She knew the voice.

Jordin twisted her head back. Triphon had killed the two Bloods he'd set upon, but a third had reached him from behind. Her arrow hung from the Blood's side, but it hadn't put him down.

Triphon's arms were thrown wide; his grimacing face tilted to the sky.

A sword protruded from his chest.

Jordin pulled up hard, stunned. The night stalled, ripped beyond the boundaries of time. Triphon was severed nearly in two, held up only by the Dark Blood whose sword was buried in his chest.

Jonathan had fallen to a similar blow.

The Dark Blood wrenched his blade free, and Triphon collapsed on the concrete street. Dead.

Time refused to return. Triphon dead. At the hand of one she'd failed to kill.

Jordin didn't know why she ran for him, losing the final advantage she had in breaking past the line of Bloods. Perhaps she could only see Jonathan there on the ground, dead because she had failed him as well. Perhaps in the deepest part of her soul she wanted to join Triphon in a pool of her own blood.

The Dark Blood standing over Triphon with bloody sword grinned wickedly.

Rage pushed reason from her mind. With a raw scream, she snatched her final arrow from her quiver, crammed it against the string with trembling fingers, pulled up five paces short, and fired at the Blood's head.

The arrow took the warrior in his mouth, knocking out his teeth and cutting clean through his spinal column. He dropped dead in Triphon's blood, eyes still wide in shock.

In Jordin's mind this was Saric. Saric, whom she despised more than Roland, whom she hated more than death itself for killing the man she loved.

Sounds of pursuit from behind had slowed. They were

close. Too close. There would be no chance of escape. Even with a bow and a dozen knives, her favored weapon, she could not fend off ten Dark Bloods alone. Nor could she outrun them.

She could only honor Triphon by taking his sword and killing as many as would join them in death.

Tonight she would be rejoined with Jonathan. Finally.

She heard the scuff of boots behind her. To her right. Her left. They were in no hurry.

She walked up to Triphon's body, took a knee, and kissed his bloody lips. "I will see you soon, my friend."

She eased Triphon's sword from his fingers and stood. To the Bloods she would only be one more victim among so many for their taking. They couldn't know that they now had one of the two Sovereign commanders in their grasp. All that mattered was that they had been created to vanquish the blood that flowed in her veins.

Jonathan's blood.

She turned. They had positioned themselves in a wide arc around her. *Calm now.* They were here to kill her, and that surety was as thick as the air they all breathed.

"You fought well," one of them said, stepping forward.

"I'm not done," she heard herself say.

"No, I expect not. It's honorable to die with a sword in hand. But in the end death is still death." A shallow smile toyed with his lips. "What say we make sport of it?"

"I'm not here for sport."

"It would be a shame to die without offering us some pleasure."

"The only pleasure I'm interested in comes at the end of this sword."

Several of them chuckled. Revulsion swept through her gut.

"Not all swords bring death," the commander said. "Can a small thing like you wield a sword as well as you fling arrows? Your weight behind it would be hard pressed to knock a dog down."

"And I see ten before me."

His grin broadened. "Well spoken. If you weren't the enemy of my Maker I might make some dogs with you."

His smile vanished, and he stepped forward. The men to Jordin's far left closed in. As did two more on her right. They had no intention of killing her outright. This was it, then.

Jordin took a step back, thinking that she might be better off making a run for it. She cast a quick look behind her. Two more Dark Bloods stood on the end of the street, eyeing her lazily. There would be no running.

Too many closing in. If she couldn't run, would she be better off cutting her own throat before they could overpower her? The thought seized her, profane and inviting at once.

She backed up another step and pivoted to face the commander. The glint in his eyes was unmistakable. Her earlier notion of taking as many with her as possible would only lead to more suffering. They would not let her die quickly.

"Drop the sword and we'll be gentle," the Dark Blood said. "By my Maker I swear it."

She lifted her eyes to the moon shining through an opening in the clouds on the horizon. She had danced beneath that moon once. Its face was cold and foreign now. The sandy knoll already looked like something from another land, another life, distorted and jagged on the horizon.

The knoll moved. Only then did she realize what she was seeing, and the awareness of it stalled her breath. A line of horses stood on top of it, silhouetted by the cold light of the moon.

Black horses. Seven of them abreast, mounted by seven hooded warriors dressed in black. Staring down at the scene before them.

It was the first time Jordin had seen an Immortal in years. Their faces were covered in black. Like wraiths come to collect souls before vanishing into the wasteland once again. The Dark Blood before her must have seen her eyes widen. He twisted around. It only took him an instant to know what he was seeing.

"Form up! Immortals."

As one, the Dark Bloods spun to the east. The line of horses began to descend the sandy slope, slowly at first and then breaking into a full gallop, riders bent low. Fearless. Silent.

The sight of such raw power and stealth was so compelling that Jordin didn't immediately recognize she had just been granted her means of escape. The Dark Bloods had forgotten their single prey, now clearly prey themselves.

She spun just as the two Bloods who'd taken up behind her rushed forward. One took a swing at her, which she easily sidestepped. Then they were past and scrambling for position on either side of the street with the others.

Jordin reached down, snatched Triphon's amulet from his neck, turned up the empty street, and ran.

CHAPTER TWO

THE STILL figure stood looking out the six-foot-tall window, a dark silhouette against the night. Her hands were folded before her. The flicker of a lone candle on a table ten feet away lapped at the folds of her gown. All the others had long burned out.

Black, the velvet. Obsidian, the constellation of beading upon it. Ebony, the fall of unbound hair to the small of that back.

White, the skin.

It itched sometimes, on nights like this, as though the churning sky called to the inky dark of her veins beneath. Her skin had always been pale, but the shadow in her veins was six years new. A gift of the Dark Blood by her half brother, Saric, who had been Sovereign and Dark Blood before her.

Lightning flashed on the horizon, to the east. For an instant, a jagged finger of light illuminated the capital of the world. Her world. A dominion of state religion and new Order. Of loyalty fearfully given because it was demanded by an all-seeing Maker who would, without qualm, send those who did not obey to Hades. For the common Corpse, that Maker was the source of life they believed they had.

But to her Dark Blood minions, she was that Maker.

Feyn Cerelia, the Sovereign of the world. Destined to it by birthright, she had once laid it down along with her life for the sake of a boy. Nine years later she had been forced to the throne by her brother's ambition. Today, the brother was gone and the boy was dead. Each had been the other's undoing—she had seen to that. Now she ruled by one will alone: her own.

Eighty thousand Dark Bloods patrolled the capital city, guarded her borders, and controlled her transport ways. They were not "children," as they had been to Saric, but minions. Lethal, rabid, loyal...and expendable. After all, Dark Bloods might be made anytime, at will.

Hers.

She instinctively touched the ring of office on her finger, straightening the heavy gold sigil, which had a habit of twisting. She found herself in this posture often at night, looking out at her realm from the palace tower, trying to understand what, if anything, she was missing. What did she search for through those windows that she didn't already have?

Saric?

No. She seldom thought of him since the day he'd staggered off into the wilderness, broken, defeated, abandoning his army and his power, either driven by madness or in a bid to find his own life. Somehow he had escaped with it. No matter. He couldn't have survived long in the wilderness, pampered as he had been all his years. They'd both been royal children once. In some ways, Saric had never become more than that. He'd grasped at the world as though a toy—and at her, as well. But he'd never been meant to rule. He didn't have the fortitude for it, despite his raging ambition.

She crossed her arms and paced along the curve of the window, looking past the walls of the Citadel and the spires of the great basilica beyond it, toward the west where the city met the wastelands.

Home of Immortals.

Irritation rose in her mind at the thought of the wastelands. The Immortals had become the bane of her rule and were too often on her mind. A pack of wolves that hunted her city, evading her traps and hunters. It both fascinated and infuriated her that her Dark Bloods had failed to take a single Immortal—had not even been able to recover one body so her alchemists might distill the secret to their lethal ways. The prince, Roland, had grown increasingly aggressive with each raid on the city—something she admired greatly.

But her admiration only strengthened her resolve to see her enemy and all of his followers dead. Any ruler who thwarted her rule would have to die.

She searched the darkness beyond the window, following the current of the shifting clouds by the moonlight, and then shifted her focus to the glass of the window itself.

A pale face stared back. Now she could see the fine black branching of veins creeping beneath the skin over her jaw. The dark vein, there, just above her temple. Her skin was perfect, paler even than the prized translucence of the royals, without the fine lines that might have belied her age.

Nine years in stasis would do that.

But there was one change in her. A brilliant color that had crept in along the edges of her irises, which had turned black from the dark blood Saric had injected into her veins. The color was so slight at first that she hadn't noticed it for months, but one day she'd seen it in her mirror: a thin ring of gold around the edges, so her eyes no longer looked like giant pupils but twin suns eclipsed by a dark moon.

She had commanded that amber seeds be sewn among the glittering beads of her bodice, along the sleeves that hung, full, nearly to her knee. Black and gold, they blinked over her hips and scattered toward the hem, a thousand eyes turned toward the world.

A thousand eyes looking for something as she stood by the window each night. Because that was the heart of it, the thing Saric had never fathomed and would never have the chance to grasp: that when one rules the world, one finds that it's not enough. An ancient ruler—arcane even by the Age of Chaos—had bemoaned once that there were no more lands left to conquer. Today, she understood the barbarian king of that age in a way that connected them through the millennia.

She'd heard the knock at the tower door some time ago. She had chosen to let whoever it was—and it could only be Dominic or Corban at this hour—stand and wait.

Now she turned from the window, hands still folded, and said, "Come."

The door opened immediately, and Dominic's slender form stepped into the dim light, admitted by the guard outside.

"My liege," he said, sinking to one knee, eyes on the floor before him.

Her gaze fell with dispassion on the former leader of the senate—a senate she had disbanded three years earlier under the strictures of her new Order. It had sent the world prelates spinning, leaving the cattle of the world population caught between loyalty to the Sovereign, who was the living agent of the Maker on earth, and the statutes of the old Order. A tension that kept them perpetually off balance and served her well.

"What is it, Dominic?"

His hair had grayed in the years since she had disbanded the senate and renounced many of Megas's statutes. He was a Dark Blood now, one of her own, genetically compelled to obey. But he'd been the staunchest guardian of Order before that. How many nights since his remaking had he tossed on his bed, prematurely sweating in the fires of Hades?

In the last year, his expression had grown more haunted. The furrows around his eyes had deepened into the pall of the damned—one who could do nothing to avert his eternal destiny. It had been interesting to watch at first. Now she found him a wasting vestige of an obsolete office.

"There was an engagement near a warehouse on the eastern end. Fifteen of your men were killed." In all this while he'd never once lifted his gaze. He knew better.

"Immortals, I assume." Sovereigns lacked the luster of their former selves. It seemed they had a talent only for dying these days.

"Yes. Though this incident was different."

"How?"

"We recovered a body."

Her pulse surged. Was it possible? One of the wasteland horde—perhaps even Roland himself? Strange, the pang she felt at the thought.

"Yes? Well?"

"A Sovereign."

She gave a snort of disgust.

He gestured, and a Dark Blood stepped in and sank to

his knee a stride behind Dominic, the mouth of a burlap sack gathered in one hand that was visibly trembling in her presence.

"This is nothing new."

"No, my liege. But we believe we may have recovered one of the leaders."

Rom's face flashed before her mind's eye. Not the Rom of today as she imagined him. He was here in the city somewhere, she knew. He must be nearly forty by now. No, not him, but the Rom of a former life. A naïve boy she'd met once when she had been a naïve young woman.

A boy who had thrown his life away for a dream. Soon his body would be presented to her, dead as well. And for what?

"Show me."

The warrior opened the bag and lifted the head by the hair.

She gazed at the gaping mouth of that head for a long moment. It was spread wide, as though surprised by some great, cosmic joke. She knew the face.

Triphon. Rom's right-hand man, one of the first to sample the original vial of blood that had sent Rom on his holy quest.

"I want no more Sovereign heads brought before me."

"As you wish, my liege," Dominic said.

"Bring me a living Sovereign or a dead Immortal...or nothing at all."

"As you wish. What would you have us do with this one?"

"Burn it, along with the others."

"Yes, my liege."

"Dominic, you may go."

The aging former senate leader rose, backed out of the door, and closed it behind him. When only the Dark

Blood warrior remained, she said, "Burn Dominic along with the body."

She waited until the Dark Blood had taken his leave before crossing the room and snuffing out the candle with her fingers.

A moment later, she stood before the window again, this time in utter darkness.

If there were no more worlds to conquer, then she had no choice but to subdue this one thoroughly and utterly, wringing from every living soul an obedience unseen and unfathomed by any ruler before.

CHAPTER THREE

JORDIN STOOD in the stone chamber beneath the city, bathed in torchlight, smattered with blood. Drenched in grief. Before her, Rom Sebastian paced in the pool of wan light. Shadows played in the hollows beneath his eyes, made more pronounced by hardship, lack of sleep, and loss.

He paused before the altar carved into the limestone wall. Neither one of them spoke. There was no need; the chamber told the story plainly: the Book of Mortals, propped on its wooden stand, somehow seemed more haggard with each passing day. A simple box containing the ancient vellum in which the first vial of blood had been wrapped the day it had come into Rom's possession, fifteen years—a lifetime—ago. Upon the box rested the amulet of the Keeper, dead now nearly a month. Jordin lifted her gaze to the cavern walls. The amulets of every Sovereign lost to date, hundreds in all, hung on the uneven surface, reflecting the light of the torch like so many fading stars.

And then there was the newest addition to their number laid upon the altar by Jordin herself: Triphon's amulet. The carving of Avra's heart was stained red not with dye but with true blood, as was the tree that grew out of the heart—the symbol of the Sovereigns. The chain hung limply over the altar's edge, coated in grime. Lifeless.

She turned away.

Beyond the ill-fitted door at the narrow chamber opening, the passage widened into a series of rooms that led eventually to the great chamber itself. There, Rom, the Keeper, and Jordin herself had often recited the teachings of Jonathan and the history of the blood, speaking in impassioned tones and sometimes with tears until the forms of those sitting in the subterranean theater's stone seats blurred before them. They did it for the sake of the surviving seroconverts—those who had taken the Sovereign blood and joined them—with increasing urgency as their numbers had dwindled. But they also did it to remember and cling to hope.

They called the labyrinth of these caverns that had become their home in the last year the Sanctuary. A place of refuge and relative safety. Little of the electrical wiring had survived the centuries, though many of its heavy tapestries and a few relics, including the random weapon and a small collection of books, had. It had been a crypt in ancient times—one expanded and fortified into a hideout during the Zealot Wars that had nearly decimated the world's population five hundred years earlier—a history attested to when the Keeper found a cache of ancient records in one of the smaller chambers. In similar fashion, the remaining Sovereigns had come here to protect and reaffirm the life within them, in these ancient arched passages. And yet, Jordin could not help but remember that it had once been a house of the dead. Could not help but notice the abandoned personal effects of the newly deceased—a cloak, a pair of shoes, the wall of amulets.

Or the fact that the shelves they were relegated to, like the altar Rom paced before now, had once been the final bed of a true corpse.

But if the thought wore on her, it wore more on Rom.

Though only thirty-nine years of age, the stress of living under oppression these last six years had reduced Rom to a shadow of his former self. He was haggard, with unshaven stubble on his cheeks and chin, graying hair swept back into a ponytail at the nape of his neck. He wore moccasins and soft leather breeches that rarely required cleaning—water was too precious to waste on such niceties. His stained tan tunic hung on a frame more wiry and less broad than it had once been. As the elder between them, Rom had assumed the position of primary spiritual leader, leaving Jordin to contend with the Herculean task of keeping their dwindling race alive beneath the city.

An undertaking that would now prove nearly impossible.

Triphon had played an invaluable role—other than Jordin and Rom, he was the last of twenty trained fighters who had served the Sovereigns over the last six years. All the others had been pedestrian Corpses seroconverted through the injection of Sovereign blood. Enlightened, yes. But not fighters.

Watching Rom now, Jordin held her tongue, but her mind was not silent. She knew that bitterness gnawed at the edge of her heart, but she couldn't afford to demonstrate any emotion raging in it. How Rom could be so stoic in such desperate times, she didn't know. His passivity would end in death. It was only a matter of time.

Rom stopped before the altar, reached out, and touched Triphon's amulet.

"He made a way for you," Rom said. "It's a sign."

"He's dead," Jordin corrected him. "As I would be if not for dumb chance." She moved toward the altar, her eyes misted as much in frustration as grief. "And the Dark Bloods wouldn't have killed me without ripping me to shreds first. Or worse."

"I'm not speaking about Triphon."

"Then who? The Immortals?" Jordin spat to the side. "They're as much our enemies as Feyn's monsters."

"Jonathan," Rom said.

A year ago, when the Sovereigns still numbered three hundred, Jordin would have readily agreed. She too had once attributed every turn of fortune to Jonathan's ever-watchful eye from beyond the grave.

But surety had evaporated with the passing of each Sovereign life—and all but abandoned her a month ago with the passing of the old Keeper whom they had called "the Book."

"This wasn't the Maker's hand," she said. "We were on the edge of the city—the Immortals could *smell* a kill and came in for it. If not for the Dark Bloods, they would have slaughtered me as well."

Rom drew the tips of his fingers along the altar's edge and lifted his eyes to meet hers. "And yet here you stand. Alive."

"And Triphon is dead." She turned her head away, blinking at the torch flame on the wall.

"Then honor his death. As you did Jonathan's. You were the first to take his blood. Do I hear regret in your voice?"

She hesitated. Too long. There was no hiding from Rom. With the Book's passing Rom had taken his place as Keeper—the last in a line of unyielding believers who'd given their lives over the centuries to see the day of salvation and life finally come. How could he remain so unshaken?

"No," she said, turning to him. "Not even you can pretend our end isn't near. We haven't seen a single sign of Jonathan's purpose. He gave us this Sovereign life—why? Only to see us die? What are we now but a cloistered relic of Jonathan's blood? We're facing extinction! The few left are mostly old and children. I can't hold the Dark Bloods off by myself for long. Open your eyes, Rom. It's only a matter of time—"

"Enough!" The echo of his voice ricocheted off the walls. Rom stood like stone, his emerald eyes blazing. "You loved him once. And now you doubt?"

"How *dare* you question my loyalty?"

"Then demonstrate it. Hold fast. The morale of the others depends on it. I was with Jonathan when he was a child. I watched him grow into a warrior. I heard him speak and saw him love before you knew he existed. You weren't the only one who wept when he died. I'll never deny the awakening I found by taking his blood."

Rom's gaze remained unflinching, but his voice softened. "He'll show us a way, Jordin. However mysterious, however yet unknown, Jonathan isn't finished. And by the Maker, he's not dead."

"No, he lives in our blood. But that too may soon be wasted on the ground."

Without a word, he took her elbow and guided her over to the far side of the chamber. There, on a carved shelf eerily sized just right for a child, stood a small, potted tree. Above it, a fissure through the bedrock allowed a sliver of light to reach the cavern during the day.

"What do you see?"

"Your tree," she said.

"Life where there should be none. Was there a tree at the head of Jonathan's grave when we planted him in the ground?"

She knew where he was going. "No," she said quietly.

"No. And yet you saw the large acacia tree at the head of Jonathan's grave when we last visited, two years ago. You fell down by its roots and wept. It was the tree of life, you said."

She recalled the day clearly. There were no other acacia trees on the bluff—just the one. Seeing the tree over his grave, she'd suddenly been sure: Jonathan was alive. Not only in their blood, but *in person*. Somehow he lived and was soon to show himself and finally give them the abundant life that would allow them to crush the Dark Bloods and put the Immortals to shame.

How much her sentiments had changed in the last year.

"Two years ago," she said. "We numbered in the hundreds then. Now we are only thirty-six."

"And we may only be one before we know the path, but that doesn't mean there is no path. Jonathan didn't die in vain—you, the one he loved the most, should know that. See to it that you don't mock the blood in your own veins, Jordin. He chose you. Have you forgotten so easily?"

"He chose us all..."

Rom's voice held a slight tremor. "*I* found him, *I* chose him, *I* served him and fought for him. But he chose you. And one day Jonathan will come to you and reveal himself in a way only you will understand."

His words washed over Jordin like warm water, quieting her heart...and then filled her with shame and regret for her doubt.

And yet, even now she couldn't dismiss that doubt entirely. Thirdhand rumors of strange happenings had filtered in from the wastelands for years. Storms where there should be none; a mysterious figure wandering the desert like a ghost, bringing food and water to starving Corpses. If such a ghost existed, it seemed to have no interest in the cause of saving Sovereigns.

Jonathan, my love, where have you gone? Tears filled her eyes. *Why did you leave us?*

There was an urgent knock on the ancient door. Word had no doubt reached the rest of the council—or what remained of it. A month ago they'd been seven. With the Book's passing, only six. Now, absent Triphon, only three remained alongside Rom and Jordin, and only two of those had known Jonathan before his death.

Gamil, made Sovereign in the days immediately following Jonathan's death, had once been a Nomad like Jordin, living under Roland's authority. He was one of the precious few Nomads who'd chosen this new life over loyalty to the Immortal Prince. Though not an alchemist, he was well trained in the ways of patching wounds and addressing illness, and so he had acted these years as their physician.

Adah had once been Rom's servant and cook. She now oversaw all matters related to their food and housing. She ruled the underground like a mother hen, with wisdom that extended far beyond her domestic duties.

And then there was Mattius, an alchemist recruited and turned Sovereign by the Book himself two years earlier. The eldest among them at fifty-nine, he was the only council member to not have known Jonathan. But his ardent loyalty to the blood that had brought him life along with his deep alchemy—in ways that surpassed even the Book, the Keeper had claimed—had made him a valuable addition to the leadership.

"Come," Rom said.

They entered like three ships making harbor, gliding in long robes that had once been white, stoic in the way of Sovereign leaders, their expressions quieted of whatever emotion stirred beneath. Having faced so much death, there would be no display of grief or anguish, even over Triphon.

She had accepted—even adopted, to an extent—the detached demeanor of their ways. Of this new, contemplative life as it should have been. But more often of late, it had only served to remind her of her own dead life before Jonathan's blood had awakened them to the full, rampant emotion of Mortality. Tonight, would Roland's Immortals celebrate as they all had once with Jonathan, dancing and chanting into the night around their fires? While intuition told her she had something *more* now than in those wild days, a part of her wondered if she had not also lost something.

"Thank you for coming so quickly," Rom said, stepping past her.

Adah glanced around the chamber. "Where's Triphon?" Her gaze came to rest on Jordin. "Please tell me you brought the rice."

They didn't know.

She found herself glancing in the direction of the altar but didn't allow herself to look at the bloody amulet on it. "We ran into Dark Bloods," she said, turning back. "Triphon is dead. If not for Jonathan's intervention, I would be as well." She could feel Rom's eyes on her, though she did not meet them.

For several breaths no one spoke. Scant years ago, the news might have caused them to fall to their knees and weep. But now ... what was death, but the order of another day? They stared, fighting, she knew, the same bitterness that had taken deep root in her own mind.

Gamil finally approached the altar. He touched the amulet gingerly, followed by Adah, then Mattius. In hours to come, the door to the chamber would be laid open to the others, who would come to express their sorrow. But for now they must decide what to say to those who had placed trust in their leaders.

"He died quickly," Jordin said. "A single blow."

"You call this Jonathan's intervention?" Gamil said.

I don't know what to call any of this.

"No. I call it his doing that I'm still alive."

Adah turned, robe swirling. "We'll be out of food in two days. We can't go on like this, Rom. The children need protein and starch. They're starving in their beds, under orders not to get up and expend unnecessary energy. And the older ones—Celinda, Rojert, Mekar—I have more than ten aged souls who will be too weak to walk if we delay any longer. This Sanctuary will become our grave."

"Ironic," Jordin heard herself murmur.

"Make the food stretch," Rom said, ignoring her. "Jordin and I will get the rice."

"When? These missions are clearly far too dangerous now."

"Tonight," Jordin said. "The Dark Bloods around the warehouse are most likely dead at the hands of the Immortals who saved me. Either way, they won't expect us to return tonight."

"Immortals?" Gamil said. "Why would they save you? These are the same hosts of hell who slaughtered so many of us a year ago and now keep us trapped in the city."

"They didn't mean to save me. But I can guarantee

you they made quick work of the Bloods that had me sur-rounded." She gave a curt nod.

"We can't afford to lose both of you."

"Then Rom stays and you come with me. You heard Adah. We need the rice."

"We need to get out of the city while the elderly can still walk," Adah objected.

Rom said in an even tone, "We've been over this before. The Immortals hold the wastelands to the north, south, east, and west. They'll smell us from miles away and hunt us down in the open. We have no choice but to stay deep, where our scent is masked by the city above us. Leaving isn't an option."

"I say we stand a better chance begging for mercy than being starved out here." Adah pointed a finger toward the chamber door and the chambers beyond. "Have you seen the state of those who remain? Please, we can't sit here and allow what's left of our kind to die. We do nothing here but waste away."

"I understand your concern, Adah. But we have done what we as a council agreed to be Jonathan's will since his passing. He will make a way; we have no choice but to stand fast."

"Adah's right," Gamil said. "We have fewer than ten able bodies who might hold a sword, none of them with any fighting skills. If we stay, we will die. We've done as we thought Jonathan willed, but now it's only a matter of time before the Dark Bloods snuff us out. We have to pro-tect the blood that runs in our veins. Jonathan came to us for a purpose, and that blood is his legacy."

Rom looked at Jordin for support.

She studied them, noting Mattius's silence. The older man with graying hair in his neatly trimmed beard wore an unyielding stare. Before the Book's passing, the pair of alchemists had been inseparable, at work day and night with their acolytes. They would bring life to all Corpses in one fell swoop, they had said. Jordin had placed no faith in such a drastic measure—nor did she want anything to do with involuntary conversions between the species. Sovereigns converted through choice, not force. But she had held her tongue in the face of desperation and missing answers.

"Rom's right. We stand no chance of survival in the wastelands—Roland's set on ridding the world of us, we all know that much. We're hunted through the city and out of hiding places. Our only option is to stay the course."

"To what end? Death? That isn't the worst of our fate. If we're found out—"

"Then we appeal to Feyn," Rom said.

Their calmness, so tenaciously held in place, visibly slipped. Gamil openly blanched.

But of course he did. How Rom could place any hope on the ruler who'd issued an edict condemning their kind was a mystery to Jordin. They had argued about it before, and the outcome was always the same. Rom had tricked her into drinking a portion of the ancient blood fifteen years earlier; she'd tasted true life for but a day, but that ancient blood still ran somewhere in her veins. There was not only hope for her, he insisted—she might very well be the key to their survival.

Jonathan had made a pact with her, Rom said. Was that not a sign? He wanted her to be Sovereign of the world, even as a Dark Blood. Never mind that the same pact had ended in Jonathan's death at the end of Saric's sword.

Feyn, Saric—they had been Jonathan's greatest enemies and were, by extension, theirs as well. Jordin would kill either of them without a second thought if ever given the opportunity, no matter what Rom said.

Adah sighed, shook her head. "From six hundred to thirty-six, and you still speak the same words. You're an obstinate fool, Rom."

He nodded. "Perhaps. But I am Jonathan's fool. I always have been and always will be."

"Soon to be a dead fool." Adah alone had the right to speak in such terms to Rom, and no one made any attempt to correct her.

Silence settled over them. There was little more to be said in such desperate straits. Triphon's amulet lay bloody on the altar, a portent of what awaited them all. There was never an end to discussions like these, both in the council and among the surviving body. In the end, they always ended the same . . . in silence.

"Jordin, your precognition didn't lend any assistance?" Rom suddenly asked.

"No."

The gift they'd presumably been given by Jonathan and expected to strengthen had only weakened with each passing year. In the beginning they might have been able to anticipate an opponent's move moments before it happened, allowing them to sidestep the swipe of a sword or duck out of sight before being seen. But these days the uncanny ability presented itself sporadically, as if it had a will of its own. What they had first heralded as a great advantage now made a mockery of them.

Was Jonathan abandoning the very blood in their veins? Rom had called out her doubt, told her to hold fast—to what?

If only she could *do* something, take matters into her own hands. But reduced to such numbers, hungry, trapped, the only options before any of them were insane.

"There is another way."

As one, they looked at Mattius the alchemist, as much for the fact that he had finally spoken as for the quiet in his voice.

"A way to preserve Sovereign blood as Jonathan intended without danger to our kind."

"Surely you don't mean the virus," Gamil said. "Book was clear that it was experimental at best and would take years to perfect."

The alchemist walked past them to the altar, lifted Triphon's amulet, and turned to face them, holding it delicately between his fingers. For a moment he stared at the pendant as though just noticing the blood, and then he lifted his eyes to Jordin.

"We have in our possession thirty-six living vessels of Sovereign blood." He looked in turn at Adah, Gamil, and finally Rom. "You might think us all human, fully alive, but I see vessels running with a blood that defies all I know as a master alchemist. I was a Corpse when Book approached me two years ago with a vial of blood—the same blood that runs in your veins. The same that spilled from Triphon tonight. Only after extensive examination did I come to understand the remarkable difference between the sample under my scope and my own Corpse blood. At first I thought the sample diseased and Corpse blood whole. When I accepted the truth that it was, in fact, the other way around, I gave myself to Sovereign life solely for the purpose of preserving it and ridding the world of the disease infecting its Corpses."

"You've told us all this," Adah said. "What is this way you're talking about?"

"It's important that you first understand my reasoning. Sovereign power is in our blood. We are but vessels. It is the most precious thing on this dead earth. On this we all agree." He acknowledged slight nods from the others. "We cannot, under any circumstance and no matter how high the cost, allow our blood to die. But out of the body, it lasts only a week before losing its power—no other vessel is able to preserve it, or else I would siphon every ounce of blood we could spare from our remaining number and send it to the four corners with the hope that someday, when we are gone, someone might use the blood to reawaken humanity as Jonathan intended."

Jordin's skin prickled. It had been the same mission of the very first Keeper five centuries ago to preserve life within a vial of ancient *"TH"* blood. She glanced at Rom. His jaw had visibly tightened—at the memory of that first vial that had come into his life and set all of this in motion? Was it even possible that this is what Jonathan might have intended all along—that his legacy be inherited not by those who had known his face, who had loved him and fought for him, but by those who might not even know his name?

Something like despair seized her.

No. That couldn't be what Jonathan intended—the fact that it wouldn't survive beyond a week was evidence of that.

"And yet, as you say, it's impossible," she snapped. "What's your point?"

"The cost of the solution I have found may seem high, but it's not too high if there's no other way. I have considered every factor, and I can now tell you that there is no other way."

He was choosing his words too carefully, Jordin thought. He was preparing them. Her eyes narrowed.

"Go on," Rom said, voice taut.

"Book was wrong about the virus. We have perfected it."

Rom's right brow lifted. Book had talked about it for months: a virus that accomplished what they had only formerly been able to do to one Corpse at a time. Mass seroconversion. They'd all written off such a possibility, thinking it only the play-stuff of alchemists who didn't know a better way to channel time and hope. It had been no surprise when the old Keeper had labeled the experiment a failure in the weeks before his death.

"Even if that's true," Rom said, "unilaterally changing Corpses to Sovereigns through a virus defies Jonathan's nature. It's no more ethical than kidnapping Corpses and forcing blood into their veins against their will."

"I said nothing about changing Corpses," Mattius said quietly.

A flicker of glances.

"Reaper is an airborne virus that will only give Corpses a common cold."

"Reaper?"

"The name I've given the virus, also called simply 'R.' When released into the air, it will spread on the winds and infect every breathing soul on earth within months. Beginning here in Byzantium, naturally."

"How does infecting Corpses with a common cold help us?" Gamil said.

"The virus has a three-day incubation period. It remains latent in its host for three days before the onset of disease. A cold in some. Death in others."

"Death? Which others?" Rom said.

Mattius looked at him. "The virus will kill all Dark Bloods."

Jordin felt her heart begin to pound. Kill all Dark

Bloods? Was it even possible? And if it was, why hadn't Mattius rushed in to tell them the good news immediately?

She glanced at Rom, his pale expression unreadable.

Gamil, on the other hand, appeared shocked. "You're sure about this? You've tested it?"

"Only on Dark Blood tissue, but yes, I am as sure as one can be without actually releasing the virus."

"And there's no way they can protect themselves?" Jordin demanded.

"No. It's contagious once contracted and kills Dark Blood cells with astonishing speed once past its latency. They won't have time to begin—much less complete—work on an antiviral. The death of all Dark Bloods will be rapid...and assured."

They stared at him, aghast.

"Feyn," Rom said. "She has the ancient blood in her veins as well."

Mattius nodded. "But not Sovereign blood. She too will die."

There had to be more. And suddenly Jordin knew what it was.

She stepped forward, intent. "Leaving Roland and his demons easy and immediate access to the throne. We kill one enemy only to strengthen another. Free to rule without adversary, Immortals will prove far more dangerous to Sovereigns than Dark Bloods ever did."

Even as she spoke, she knew by Mattius's calm gaze that he was ahead of her. "Immortals will prove no threat to Sovereigns. We knew at the outset that any virus we developed would need to deal with both species. Immortals will suffer the same fate as Dark Bloods."

"They will all die?"

"Yes. Not as quickly, perhaps, but yes."

Jordin's head swam. For the first time in a year she imagined uncompromised victory over their enemies. For a moment the room felt robbed of oxygen. Did she dare surrender to such a hope?

"Then it's no solution at all," Rom said. "To kill Dark Bloods is one thing. But to take the lives of Immortals—those who are Mortal and fully capable of finding life as we ourselves once did—that's absolutely unacceptable."

"They are our enemies," Jordin said. His hard glare did not deter her. "How can you dismiss it so quickly?"

"What makes you so sure that Immortals will die?" Gamil asked. He spoke with control but there was no hiding the enthusiasm in his voice.

"Because we know Mortal blood. It is our own with only slight—but significant—modifications. The virus will kill Immortals."

"But not affect Sovereigns?"

Mattius hesitated a beat. "Perhaps."

The physician blinked as if he weren't sure he'd heard correctly. "Perhaps?"

"We may lose our emotions, but we can't be sure. I'd say it's fifty-fifty. Even so, losing emotion might be to our gain. The strength of Sovereignty is in our wisdom and knowing, not in emotional ecstasy."

"No!" Rom snapped, snatching Triphon's amulet from Mattius's hand. He slapped it down on the altar. "Return to the life of a Corpse? I forbid it! Neither can we murder thousands of Immortals in a war to preserve our own blood. Or destroy all Dark Bloods wholesale. This is not Jonathan's way."

Jordin stared at him. And then she knew.

It was because of *her*.

Feyn.

"Then you would allow all Sovereigns to be butchered and eradicate the world's last hope for true life *as a matter of principle?*" Mattius demanded, his calm slipping. "This is what you call love?"

"I saw love while you were still concocting brews as a Corpse," Rom said with dangerous quiet. "I saw Jonathan spread his arms and die for those same Immortals you now mean to wipe out. Don't lecture me on love."

"Your *love* will get us all killed."

"So be it!" Rom's voice rang out in the chamber like thunder.

Adah gave voice to what was on Jordin's mind. "Rom, walk through these chambers and look in the faces of the children before deciding their fate. The Immortals made their choice and since have stopped at nothing to kill us. Maker in heaven—they've all but exterminated us!"

"The Maker's not in heaven; he's in our veins. And the Maker I know does not kill those he can save."

"But you would kill the Maker in your veins," she shot back. "I say if we have no other reasonable choice, sacrifice Immortals to preserve true Sovereign life."

Rom rounded on Mattius. "Burn it. If you don't, I swear I will."

"No. You won't."

"You would stop me?"

"I don't have to. I've hidden five samples where they can't be found. It will only take one to save Sovereigns from annihilation. And more than one of us knows how to release the virus. Even if you kill me, it will gain you nothing."

Realization crept across Rom's face even as it blossomed in Jordin's mind: Mattius hadn't come to propose his solution, but to inform them of a decision he'd already made. It was as good as done. For the first time, she faltered.

Rom drew a slow breath in through his nose. He glanced at each one of them in turn and finally at her.

"Does this ring a bell in your thick skulls?" he asked. "The irony of it? Five hundred years ago another alchemist named Talus created a virus. It was deployed by Megas, the first tyrant to rule the world unchallenged as Sovereign. Now you would release another virus as Megas's reincarnation? Talus gave his life to *bring*, not take, life. As has every Keeper since, including Book."

"A small price to pay to preserve Jonathan's life," Mattius said. "For us and for all Corpses. We need a true Sovereign on the throne. A *Sovereign*—not that Dark Blood imposter, Feyn." His lips curled as he said it.

"This isn't just about survival. You mean to kill her."

"With any fortune, Feyn will be the *first* to die."

Rom turned to Jordin, his expression devoid of color. "You lived with Roland when he was only Mortal. They took you in when you were a child before any of this. They saved you. And now you would stand by while Mattius slaughters them all?"

She knew he was pleading for the life of that Dark Blood witch.

"No one has seen the face of an Immortal since they left us," she said, her voice sounding cold even to her own ear. "For all we know they're mindless. Beasts that do nothing but kill."

But Mattius had acted without agreement or consultation, ready to decide for them all. Was she ready to accept such a decision? The Dark Bloods should die. The Immortals deserved to die. In her mind, they had betrayed Jonathan as much as Saric and Feyn. And yet...was this truly Jonathan's way?

Jonathan, where are you?

"The matter deserves further consideration," she said, sure of nothing anymore.

"Jonathan will show a better way!" Cords stood out on Rom's neck as he spoke. "You think they're only rumors, or that he lives only in your blood. He's alive; I know it to be true. Somehow—out there. He lives!"

"Then he'd better hurry," Mattius snapped. "If he hasn't shown himself within seven days, I will release Reaper to keep alive the hope of salvation. And if I'm wrong, Jonathan himself can take pity on my soul."

CHAPTER FOUR

JONATHAN, WHAT have I done? I followed you. I did everything you asked.

Be still, Jordin, and know.

What is there to know? You left me!

I never left, my love. See me.

I don't see anything.

Open your eyes. See me. Find me...

Jordin's eyes fluttered open in the darkness. She'd had the recurring dream for two weeks now, always the same, always the voice...always without him. She was no stranger to vivid dreams over the last six years. Some said that their dreams, like the unpredictable precognition and their emerald eyes, had been Jonathan's last mysterious gifts to all Sovereigns. What the dreams meant, she had no idea. The meaning of *any* of their dreams was beyond them. Perhaps they were nothing more than lifelike experiences devoid of the suffering they'd found beneath the city. Snippets of familiar faces, of things that might be and that sometimes did manifest. But mostly she dreamed of Jonathan. Perhaps because she'd loved him in a way none of the others ever had, as a woman loves a man. And perhaps because Jonathan had loved her as well.

But that love now left her heartsick and alone. What was love if there was nobody to love...no lover beyond the figments of imagination or the fabric of dreams?

The events of the previous night had interrupted her sleep. Mattius's ultimatum—seven days. A part of her felt relieved that they'd reached such a clear intersection. Waiting for death had never been in her blood, before or since it had become Jonathan's.

The worn curtain into her room moved. She tilted her head to see who was there, but the curtain was still closed. She'd only foreseen it, the gift most active these days in the residue of her dreams.

Jordin pulled her shirt on and shoved herself up to greet whoever was coming.

The curtain moved, pushed aside by Rom, who was framed by the eerie light of an outer chamber. Seeing her awake, he stepped in, his expression calm, determined. She knew the look well.

"Come in," she said wryly, leaning over for a match.

He stopped at the end of her pallet. "You were expecting me."

She lit the match and applied the flame to the wick of her lamp. The amber light only seemed to further illuminate the shadows in the ancient crypt. Filled with cracks and sooty depressions, the wall moved with darkness, its uneven surface stained with secrets.

"I saw the curtain open before it did. Not that foresight ever comes when I really need it."

"Then let's hope that changes. I've made a decision."

She blew out the match and looked at him. He was dressed in black as if he intended to travel aboveground. Was it still night? She'd gone back for the rice with Gamil and found it untouched. As anticipated, there were no

Dark Bloods near the warehouse—they'd found them lying on the street, cut to ribbons by the Immortals. If Roland had lost any men, they had taken their bodies. And someone had taken Triphon's.

For as much as she despised the Immortal Prince, she admitted her grudging respect. Their cunning and speed had proved the bane of Feyn's new regime—Roland was as cruel and driven as she.

She wished them both dead.

"And?"

"You'll lead while I'm gone."

"Gone where?"

"Gone where only I can go," he said, walking toward the bed. "Mattius must not be allowed to release the virus. I won't accept any victory that comes with the death of so many innocents."

"Innocents?" She narrowed her eyes.

"You know as well as I do . . . that is not Jonathan's way."

She returned his stare for a moment, then flung off her wool blanket and stood on the opposite side of the bed, dressed only in her long white nightshirt.

"You talk about Jonathan, but he's in the grave and now we've found our own. If nothing changes, they'll discover our bones in this crypt centuries from now. We might as well carve it here, on the wall: 'Here lie unknown bones draped in dried-out flesh.'"

"Then I go to the grave with him. But I won't deny the blood he gave me by doing what I know he would not."

"No? Then what will you do? Wait here to die and take the rest with you?"

Rom looked taken aback at the harshness of her tone. She told herself to stop, that venting her frustration wouldn't help anything, but she found herself unable to.

"If there were any other way, it would have presented itself to us by now. Mattius has a point. Sovereign blood must be saved at any cost. You know that Roland won't rest until all Sovereigns and Dark Bloods are dead, leaving only hapless Corpses to block his way. Never mind the Dark Bloods—the Immortals will always be our enemies, and they won't stop until we're dead."

He gazed at her, silent, eyes glistening in the firelight.

Jordin turned toward the chair and snatched her pants off the back. "I know that's not what you want to hear, but it's the truth. We have nowhere left to go. Even if we did, the others are too weak to even attempt to move. But we can't just wait here and let them slaughter us."

"You mean like they slaughtered Jonathan," he said quietly.

The words cut. "Yes. Like they slaughtered Jonathan."

"And yet he made no move to save himself. He knew what he was doing. He had a reason. Honor it, even if you don't understand it. Seek him. Find him."

She spun around. "How? Tell me and I'll do it. Show me where to find him. But no, you can't, because you don't know either. No matter how much we might wish it otherwise—and believe me, I've wished myself to the bone—we can't. We can't because he's dead."

"Is he?"

"I'm not talking about his blood."

"Neither am I," Rom said.

She took a long, steadying breath. "What do you mean?"

"I mean I dreamed the same dream you told me about a few nights ago. His voice calling from the desert."

"It's a dream, Rom."

"Is it?"

"Haven't they all been?"

"I pray you lead the Sovereigns with Jonathan's heart, Jordin," he said in a soft voice.

The ugly echo of her words hung in the air. How could he have such surety about the heart of the man she had loved more than any of them... while she felt only lost?

"I have to leave now, while it's still dark," he said.

"Where?"

"To the Citadel."

She wasn't sure she'd heard correctly.

"To the witch?"

He only looked at her.

"You'll never make it! Even if you do, she'll kill you."

"It's a chance I am forced to take. I hope I'm right in saying that you underestimate her. She hosts the ancient blood somewhere beneath her death."

"You're going to just turn yourself in?"

His gaze was quiet.

"It's madness!"

"I beg you, Jordin, never vacate your love for Jonathan or your vow to follow him. Tell the others that I've gone to Feyn to barter a way for our survival. Tell them Feyn will attempt to turn me into one of her Dark Bloods. If she succeeds, Mattius's virus will kill me as well. Tell it to every Sovereign—not just the council. Promise me that much."

"This can't be the way."

"It's the *only* way!" He turned and strode toward the curtain as if to leave. "If Mattius is willing to kill me, so be it. But the others will think twice. If it's true that we're all doomed, then I have nothing to lose. And neither do you."

She stood rooted in the dim light, feeling shame in the face of his commitment.

Rom turned back at the entrance. "You remember

what we discussed about Roland? If there were no other options?"

How could she forget? "That, too, is insanity," she said.

"They said that about Jonathan before his death."

She stared after him long after he had left, the waist-band of her pants still clutched in her hand.

"INSANITY!" Mattius's voice rang out in the chamber. The man's stoic face had gone red beneath his whitening beard. "How dare he attempt to take hostage our salvation by putting himself up as a martyr!" He paced, his robe sweeping the stone floor at his heels. He turned on Jordin, green eyes glaring. "No one must know of this. Not a word beyond this hall."

"They already know," Jordin said.

"Who knows?" the alchemist demanded, glaring at Gamil, then Adah.

"All of them," Jordin said.

"Insanity!"

"So you've said."

The moment Rom left, she had fallen onto her bed and wept with frustration until, frantic, she'd tried to chase him down, planning to restrain him if she must. But when she reached the tunnel to the surface, Stephan, the elderly man on third watch, informed her Rom had left ten minutes earlier.

It had been an hour and a half to sunrise. Three hours to the customary rising hour. She'd spent half the time pacing in her room, wrestling with madness. Only in an extended moment of clarity, with the image of Triphon slain before her in a manner so similar to Jonathan, did her course of action become plain.

She would do as Rom asked. For Jonathan. For Sover-eigns. For Rom. For herself.

Peace had come like a flood, and on its heels, absolute surety. She'd quickly dressed and made her rounds of the chambers still occupied by the living. With so few left, it took only moments to spread the message that Rom had gone to win favor with Feyn. She understood the widening of their eyes, the haunting look of fear: if Rom were taken, death would follow fast for them all.

"Trust him," Jordin had assured each of them. "Trust Rom to know Jonathan's heart. Even if Rom becomes a Dark Blood, he'll find a way."

In the space of an hour their whispers carried through the caverns with hallowed awe. *Rom has gone to save us. Jonathan will come again; Rom will make a way.*

Standing before Mattius now, she understood his rage because she had felt it herself—along with a grim respect for Rom's genius; in one move, he had outmaneuvered the alchemist.

And where did it leave her? With Rom or with Mattius? Both of them had made their play.

It was time to make hers.

Gamil strode to the high-backed chair at the end of the long table they reserved for the monthly feast and sat heavily. They celebrated Jonathan's passing at the new moon each month by eating the finest foods they could marshal for the occasion. Ancient wines from a makeshift cellar they'd found below the main chamber, meats and cheeses when they were available. It had been rice and beef stock as of late, though the previous month Jordin had brought a clutch of rabbits she'd borrowed from a small farm south of the city.

"So be it," Mattius snapped. "He's thrown his life away."

"Thrown his life away?" Jordin said. "Feyn won't kill him. Will you prove worse than her?"

His face hardened. "His fate is in his hands, not mine."

"We must assume Feyn will turn him," Adah said.

"His Sovereign blood won't have it," Gamil said.

"Do we know that?"

"No. But the virus will kill him," Jordin said, her stare fixed on Mattius.

"His decision."

"So you don't deny that the virus—this Reaper of yours—may kill Rom if he's forced to Dark Blood?"

His silence was answer enough.

"Then all Sovereigns will know that Mattius the alchemist—no, Mattius the *traitor*—killed the holiest among us. Rom Sebastian, the very man who found Jonathan when he was a boy and saved him from certain death so he could give us the blood that now flows in our veins. They will know, and I will make sure of it."

Mattius showed no sign her words had affected him. "Far better to bring death to one if it means the salvation of Jonathan's blood."

"Far better to trust the leaders Jonathan put over you," Jordin said.

He leaned in toward her. "Rom brought him to maturity, you let him die, but I will see his legacy live forever."

Jordin trembled with the effort not to shove him against the wall by the neck.

Adah, too wise by far, stepped between them. "What does a resurrected Corpse know of Jonathan's legacy? I was caring for Jonathan's scraped knees when you were still dead. I will *not* see his blood defiled, and I won't stand by while you kill Rom."

Mattius said with deadly calm, "Seven days—six now. It's already done, with or without me. Rom knew the stakes. I have done what I must, not to defile Jonathan's blood but to *preserve* it."

"So you hope," Gamil said from the end of the table, shaking his head. "You said we might lose some of our emotions. Your plan to preserve Jonathan's blood may in fact only reenact the very event that made it necessary!"

"Better muted emotion than the annihilation of our kind."

"As the alchemists no doubt said then!"

"And if you remember, I said that we may suffer no effects at all."

"Then take it yourself and show us," Adah said.

"We don't have time for the madness of old women or the antics of children! Call me a traitor if you must, but I will stand by what is right."

He strode to the door.

"I have another way," Jordin said.

Mattius grasped the door handle. "There is no other way." He swung the door wide.

"I will kill Feyn. Without her, the Dark Bloods are a serpent with no head."

Mattius hesitated and then cast a condescending look over his shoulder. "Don't be absurd."

"I tell you another way, and you won't even hear me out?"

The alchemist shut the door and turned back. He spoke as one does to a very dull child. "You follow Rom to folly. There *is* no other way."

"Your calculations have failed you. There is."

"You can't even reach Feyn, much less kill her. The old tunnels into the Citadel are far too heavily guarded for any Sovereign to pass." He paused. "Even if you could get in—even if you *could* kill Feyn—you would only be paving the way for the Immortals."

"Not if Roland is dead."

He gave a short laugh. "Kill Feyn and Roland both?"

He looked around with theatrical incredulity. "Have you hit your head?"

"If it were possible, Rom would have thought of it already," Gamil said with audible reluctance.

"He has."

"He would never approve of your killing Roland, much less Feyn," Adah said.

"He wouldn't approve. But Rom is no longer your leader, I am. If I say I can deliver Roland's head, then clearly," she said, looking meaningfully at Mattius, "I have a way."

"How?"

She lowered her arms and walked to a bottle of wine on the table. She poured some into a goblet and set the cork back into the bottle. "That's my concern." She took a sip, set the goblet down, and turned to face Mattius.

"But I need more than six days. Give me ten."

"You have six."

"Give me nine days."

"You have six."

Jordin stalked toward the alchemist. "I would throw myself into the jaws of death to save us all, and you refuse to give even a day?"

"How can I, when you won't share your plan?"

"I plan to cut off Roland's head and bring it to you in a bag with Feyn's. That's all you need to know. But what I need is time!"

A long measure of silence filled the chamber before he spoke. "So you'll fly into the Immortal lair, pluck off Roland's head, fly to the Citadel, and do the same to Feyn. Do we look like fools?"

"Do you want me to answer that? Because history will. What foolishness is found in attempting one last desperate option before throwing the world back into Chaos with alchemy? Before throwing away all that Jonathan came to bring!"

"They'll smell you coming and spill your blood on the sand before you lay eyes on them. It's not reasonable. It's not even sane."

The echo of Rom's parting words sounded in Jordin's head. *Insanity.* She gave a slight quirk to her lips. "It's a pity you never knew Jonathan. They said the same of him."

Gamil stood up from the table. "Jordin, please. In one thing I agree with Mattius. There's no way to get to Roland alive. How many lives must we lose? Take time to think."

"I have. And I know what I must do."

"Do you even know where the Immortals are?" Adah asked.

"No."

"Have you ever seen one unmasked?"

"No."

"How can you kill an enemy you can't see?"

"That's my problem. I just need more time." She fixed Mattius with a hard gaze. "Give me eight days. If I don't deliver both Feyn's and Roland's heads, assume that I am dead and the fate of all Sovereigns will be on yours."

Mattius flicked a glance from Adah to Gamil, who both appeared at a loss for words.

"First Rom walks to his death, and now the fearless Jordin," Mattius said. "Suicide abounds."

"Better than genocide. Eight days."

He spun and strode for the door. "Seven. If at that time either Feyn or Roland is still alive, Reaper will be loosed."

CHAPTER FIVE

EYN'S FATHER, Vorrin, had sat in this very chamber. At this dining table not ten strides from the claw-footed desk that dominated the far end of the room. In her father's day as Sovereign, it had been covered with documents, newspapers, reports. But today it was meticulously clean, leaving bare a stone surface that reminded her at every glance of a sarcophagus lid or altar.

She was intimately familiar with both. For nine years she had lingered in stasis in a sarcophagus, until the day Saric brought her painfully back to life on an altar.

She held a plate of warm venison on her lap, leaned back in the wing-backed chair. Her bare foot rested atop the head of the lion still attached to the hide that sprawled beneath the table, the hem of her dark shift pooling on the floor. The curtains were thrown wide to the rare, late-morning sun—in fact, they had never closed. No one had seen her glide down the Citadel hall to her chamber in the hour just before dawn or return through the back passage a scant three hours later.

She rarely slept—her physical needs had changed since the day of her resurrection.

There had been another raid, late in the night, just south

of the Citadel. Eight of her warriors had gone missing.
Their bodies had turned up early this morning, on pikes
just beyond the city. The sight incited a panic in the first
morning commute. Seth, her new captain, had begged to
reinforce the city perimeter. He was chiseled and handsome as a god, having been personally designed by and
for her. And so she had named him after the ancient god
of Chaos. He was devoted as a lover and feral as a wolf—
one that would die to protect her... or slit his own throat if
she but asked it. He had no choice; it was in his chemistry.

She had calmly pointed out that to bolster perimeter defenses would lessen the concentric ranks of Dark
Bloods around the Citadel itself. The very thing, no doubt,
that Roland wanted.

The Immortal was either preparing for a major offensive or frustrated by his inability to reach the Citadel.
Feyn could have commanded twenty thousand men to
sweep into the hills, but she would only be throwing her
Dark Bloods like so many stones into a ravine. The day
would come when a new harvest of Dark Bloods would
emerge from her labs. No matter how many Corpses
Roland turned Immortal, he could not train them quickly
enough to outman her unending supply of warriors. His
fighters might seem nearly supernatural, but sheer numbers would win this war.

Still, he fascinated her as much for his aggression as
for the rumors of his brood's eerie ways. She would shed a
tear, perhaps, on the day his head adorned the great Citadel gate, if only because there would be no more foe of
interest. No foe at all.

She lifted the fork from the plate, toyed with the edge
of meat so tender it required no knife. She'd once taken
great pleasure in the rite of every meal. Life itself had fas-

cinated her by its very process. Her craving for food, for the sun that fell through the window onto her skin, for water falling over her thighs in the bath and dripping from her hair—it had all intoxicated her once, just as the fealty of nations and the stripping of their power had intoxicated her the day she'd dismantled the senate.

But only for a while.

She bit into the meat, a portion larger than what might be considered couth, and then tossed the plate onto the table, watching the fork scatter across its surface.

She heard a knock at the side door.

She took her time chewing and swallowing the venison, neatly wiping the juice from her chin. Then she rose from the chair and paced toward the window, where the dull light of day shone through her dressing gown like a scrim.

"What is it?" she said.

Corban's voice sounded through the door. "My liege, we have a prisoner of interest."

"Come."

The door opened and the master alchemist entered, dropping to his knee. His hair hung past his shoulders toward the floor, nearly touching it. His strange and silent Corpse acolyte, Ammon, knelt two paces behind.

"What kind of interest?" She folded her arms, studying the master alchemist. It strained him to kneel. She could see it in the tension on his forehead.

"A live Sovereign, my liege." He lifted his head slightly, his gaze crawling out to the rug just beneath her bare feet. "Rom Sebastian, leader of the infidels."

She went very still. Was it possible? Rom, who had tricked her into consuming the Keeper's ancient blood, though there had not been enough for her to know its effects for long. And if there had been? So much might have been different. She herself might be living in hiding, serving a dead boy's memory, and Saric might be standing here now.

"How and where was he taken?"

"My liege," Corban said with a raised brow, "he came to us."

Came here? Willingly?

He was a trickster still. A fanatic whose zeal knew no end. And now his foolishness had delivered him to her once again.

She walked to the settee and retrieved her heavy velvet robe, fastening the hooks up the front with slender fingers. She stepped into the low-heeled brocade shoes waiting nearby and said only, "Come," as she brushed by the kneeling alchemist.

Rowan, Sovereign regent during her stasis when the usurper Jonathan had laid claim to the throne, had long sealed the old door to the subterranean chambers of the Citadel. Corban, at her command, had unsealed it. As they passed through the abandoned senate chamber to the ancient door, a strange sensation prickled her nape.

In the first two decades of her life she'd only visited these chambers a handful of times, having found them morbid for their history of captivity, murder, and secrecy. Now, she didn't need to wait for Corban to fumble with a switch to light the way; she knew the passageway well.

But as they arrived at the heavy steel door of the ancient dungeons, she slowed. The last time she'd seen Rom, he'd been a headstrong lover who could plead passionately and persuasively. A fighter after the Nomad way. A protector—the leader of a cause and a people. And yet he was a slave to his convictions; leader only to an impotent and dying group of vagabonds.

Corban caught up to her, breathing slightly more heavily than before, Ammon's step light behind him. Her master alchemist was aging quickly. The day would come when he could no longer kneel before her. On such a day, she would force Corban to turn Ammon Dark Blood to her service. For now, she allowed him his illusion of mastery over another.

He pulled the heavy steel door open, and she stepped inside. At first she didn't smell the sterile odors of the vast laboratory that had taken up residence in this space, nor see the heavy glass sarcophagi of her newest prototypes lining the far wall. For a moment, she was back in the dungeons of fifteen years ago, where she had stolen in secret to meet a different prisoner: the old Keeper.

But that moment quickly passed.

She strode down the aisle of stainless laboratory tables, hardly noting the startled expressions of the alchemists who abruptly dropped to their knees. One of them fumbled with a glass vial that shattered on the ancient stone floor. Overhead, electrical fixtures gave off cold, brilliant light. For the first time in years, she did not drift toward the sarcophagi to admire the Dark Bloods within them.

Instead, she walked directly to the back, where the smooth walls of the great lab gave way to the old hewn corridor. Here, the ancient cells remained untouched by time or history. Only the locks on the iron bars were new—as were the living samples kept behind them.

"The one on the end, my liege," Corban said, waving Ammon away.

She slowed her step as she came to the last cell and then stopped.

The man inside stood in the shadows at the back wall, arms folded at his waist. By the faint glow of the lone corridor light she could see enough to know it was him.

Rom.

But how he had changed. His hair was shot through with gray. He was thinner, his shoulders not as broad. He'd aged, far more than she. Even through the stubble on his face she could see evidence of scars, of the deepening furrows of time, of worry and hardship. The leader might remain, but the impetuous poet of their first meeting was gone.

The last time she'd seen him, he had been sun-dark. The man before her was pale, pallid. So it was true, then, that they had hidden themselves belowground.

"Still unpredictable, after so many years," she said.

He stood still, his eyes fixed unwaveringly on hers. "You feel it still, don't you? Faintly, perhaps, but it's there, running in your veins."

She arched an eyebrow. "Perhaps not so unpredictable." He had been beating this drum for fifteen years.

"Why have you come here?"

He was quiet.

"His eyes, my liege," Corban said, speaking of the brilliant green of Rom's irises. "This is the first one we have taken alive—the dead ones don't have such eyes. My alchemists would study his blood and his flesh to better know our enemy."

A strange scent wafted through the cell. The telltale stink of Rom's kind. Where was it coming from, his clothing or his skin? Did the Sovereigns occupy themselves with the burning of incense at all hours, or was he slathered in it for some purpose?

Rom lifted a hand and coughed into it. The scent became more acute. He was not wearing the scent, it came *from* him.

She tilted her head. What strangeness was this?

"Indeed you must. Study him."

"We would like to take one of his eyes."

"Of course you would."

"With this sample in custody, we may not only better understand the changes in his blood but glean information about the Nomads."

"They call themselves the Immortals," Rom said quietly.

Corban didn't seem to have heard him. He was brimming with more life than he had in months at the excitement of this find. She stepped closer to the iron bars, cutting him off.

"It was foolish of you to come here," she said.

"Only as foolish as saving your life."

She gave a crystalline laugh. "*My* life?"

Silence.

"I see." She sighed, laced her fingers together. "We've played at these conversations too many times through the years. What is it you can possibly hope to accomplish in coming here? I have no interest in sparing those who subvert my Sovereignty by daring to call themselves by that same name. I will mercifully allow them to keep their delusions to the death. But death is inevitable—by my hand or by Roland's. He seems to bear you no more love than I for whatever divided you. My alchemist is all but biting through his leash to dissect you. And I can assure you that my Dark Bloods will only benefit from anything we learn and find useful. So you see, you've come here in vain."

"In fact, my lady, I have accomplished half of my objective in coming here already."

She had not been called "my lady" in years—the words made her bristle. "And what objective is that? Ah, I forgot. To save my life."

"Yes."

"Indeed?"

"And the sanctity of Jonathan's legacy. But there's another reason."

"There always is. And what might that reason be?"

"The truth."

"And which truth is this?"

"That I've come to make you Sovereign."

She gazed at him for a long moment. Beside her, even Corban's breath had stilled to silence.

"I *am* Sovereign."

"Are you?"

She pursed her lips. Perhaps the strain of mere survival these last years had been too much. Was it possible his mind had broken at last? The thought disappointed her.

"How many of your kind are left, Rom? We retrieved Triphon's head. A pity for you, that loss."

"Few."

"And now you have foolishly left your remaining number leaderless."

"Jonathan is their leader."

"Then a dead man leads them. Tell me, is this the 'salvation' you sought? Having ranged so far and wide, only to end up here?"

"I am not alone."

She flicked a glance at Corban.

"No one else was found, my liege."

She looked at Rom. "Of course not. I forgot. You come with Jonathan. The man my brother killed."

"He didn't die."

She'd left the scene of the battle before it had happened. Now, for the first time, doubt crept into her mind. But these were only words from a crafty man. There had been too many witnesses to Jonathan's death, all of them loyal. No Dark Blood would—or could—lie to her. The boy had been cut in two. And she didn't mourn him. She'd been put into stasis for the boy once, and that death had put a bitter taste in her mouth.

"You've gone mad, Rom. I daresay I'm disappointed."

He pushed away from the wall and moved toward the bars and into the light. Now she could see the story of scars along his cheek and temple. The hair, tied back, strands hanging against his face. He did indeed look haggard. But his eyes—a brilliant emerald she had never seen—were not those of one unhinged.

"Take my blood into your veins." His was the first direct gaze to meet hers in years.

"Will you ever tire of this game?"

"Your very life depends on it."

"Have you forgotten? Your blood kills our kind."

"But not you."

"No? Because I am special?" she said with a sardonic smile. "Because I took some of your ancient blood once? Clearly, you've come to such an impasse that your only hope is to convince me that there's something more than what I already possess. That you can offer me more, even, than the world."

"I can't. But Jonathan does."

That name again.

She shook her head and turned to Corban. "Do what you will. Learn what you can from him. Keep him alive, if not comfortable." She stepped past him but turned at the end of the corridor. "And leave at least one of his eyes."

CHAPTER SIX

THIS JORDIN KNEW: Immortals only came out in darkness. With their vastly expanded sight, they could see at night like a preying hawk by day. In that same darkness, she would be blind by comparison. Venturing into the wastelands at night would be a death sentence.

This Jordin also knew: Dark Bloods roamed the streets of Byzantium like packs of rabid dogs both day and night, ready to cut them down. Like the city's two million Corpses, they could smell the rich scent of Jordin's kind and moved to immediately eradicate it, oblivious that the very scent they reviled was life itself.

Still, between the threat of Immortals or Dark Bloods, she would choose the Bloods.

She made quick preparations for the task before her in the dimly lit privacy of her chamber. No one could know what she was about to do. She would go alone and immediately; seven days was far too short a time to attempt what she was unsure could be accomplished.

It was also far too long a time to attempt survival in the wastelands.

Ignoring waves of doubt and fear, she stuffed her most rugged wear—heavy trousers, a beige tunic, a head scarf—into a canvas backpack, along with five good throwing blades, enough bread and nuts to sustain her for two days, and a canteen of water. She had already appropriated a short shovel from one of the back caverns as well as several other supplies she would need if she succeeded.

Mattius had been right on one thing: what she meant to do was virtually impossible.

The Book once speculated that Roland and his Immortals had evolved these last years in a way similar to the Dark Bloods; that Jonathan's first Mortal blood had changed in them in ways his postmortem blood had not. The thought that Jonathan's truest followers should decline while his enemies strengthened was just one more bitter pill to swallow.

Of course, the continued evolution of Immortals was an unproven theory. No one had actually seen an uncloaked Immortal. But the speed and efficiency with which they attacked was undeniable. Had she ever been so deadly in her Mortal days?

No. And so this, too, she knew: if anything, the rumors surrounding Immortals did not do them justice.

Jordin slipped into tan pants and a long-sleeved shirt, over which she fastened a snug vest. There, she hid four additional blades, easily accessed by either hand. Her bow and quiver slid easily down her back, inside her shirt, the tip just barely hidden by her hair, which she left down to better cover its presence between her shoulder blades. She would not have ready access to it—the knives would have to suffice until she got clear of the city.

Except for her scent, which couldn't be covered up without the use of other strong odors that would only attract their own attention, she might pass for any common Corpse.

She slung the pack over her shoulders, grabbed a pair

of dark glasses, and headed for the tunnel to the surface. There, she would have to contend with the first-watch guard, after which word of her departure would spread like fire. First Rom and now Jordin, gone to the wolves.

They wouldn't be wrong on either account.

She pushed back the sudden onset of doubt and ran toward the exit, already sweating beneath her tunic. The tunnels were rougher here, unevenly cut, less care taken in the excavation of the caverns so many years ago than in the painstaking labor put into their original carving millennia before.

A form stood up from behind an outcrop of rock, startling her. Kaya. She'd forgotten the girl's habit of reading alone. Now she saw the faint glow of lamplight, barely visible in the flicker of the nearest torch.

"Jordin?" The seventeen-year-old girl eyed her with suspicion. "What's wrong?"

"Everything." A beat. "Nothing."

"Where are you going? To the surface?"

"Yes."

"To find Rom?"

"No. No questions, Kaya."

"It's day above."

"I know. That's why I'm dressed like a Corpse. And that's why you won't spread alarm—it's the last thing we need now."

Kaya watched her with round eyes, the faint glow of light catching her high cheekbones. Jordin couldn't help but notice the beauty the girl had grown into. Six years ago Jonathan had found her, dirty and locked in a cart bound for the Authority of Passing. He had snatched her from death then, and she'd followed him with a devotion that rivaled Jordin's own.

Of them all, it was perhaps Kaya who maintained the most childlike love for Jonathan.

But clearly, Kaya was no longer a child. She might not be able to fight with the same skill Jordin did, but she loved as well. There were no more eligible men her age among the remaining Sovereigns—Jordin had always thought to help her find and seroconvert a handsome Corpse from Byzantium.

None of that mattered now.

"You're going to find Jonathan," Kaya said.

Jordin ignored the comment and made to pass, her mind on the wastelands already. Getting to them would be no easy task; she would only have one shot before the alarm went out or she found herself in real trouble.

"Rom went to find Feyn, and now you're going to find Jonathan! That's it, isn't it?"

She rounded on Kaya, eager to shut her down. "Don't be absurd! And don't spread any rumors or get anyone's hope out of balance."

Kaya frowned, unconvinced. "No need to snap at me. If you're not going to find Jonathan or go after Rom, then where are you going?"

"Kaya . . . look, I wish I could tell you more, I just can't. You've put your faith in Jonathan; keep it there, in him, not in me. I'm doing what I must, that's all."

"You're leaving us," Kaya said. "You're going to find Jonathan, and you're not coming back unless you do." Her voice was thick with emotion.

On one count, Kaya was right. Jordin might not see her again—or any of them, for that matter. Jordin swallowed past the lump in her throat and clasped Kaya by her shoulders, drawing her close and embracing her.

"I have to go, Kaya. Don't lose faith. Beg the Maker on my behalf."

"Let me come with you."

"You can't go where I'm going."

Before Kaya could push the matter, Jordin snatched the torch from the wall, dipped into a side tunnel, and took the rising stone steps in pairs. Then she extinguished the flame, drew a deep breath, and pushed aside the heavy, filthy canvas that obscured the entrance. She stepped into shadow; a thick screen of brush blocked most of the clouded sky beyond.

The Sanctuary existed beneath the massive footings of a ruin that had never been reconstituted or demolished. Stunted shrubs had taken up residence in the most recent decades, nearly obscuring the crumbling stone.

Jordin slipped out the opening, glancing back once to make sure the canvas had fallen over the breach in the old wall. Satisfied, she placed the glasses on her face and eased through the brush to check for passersby.

Only fifty-eight Sovereigns had come to the Sanctuary a year ago. Fifty-eight of the hundreds that had once been so sure, so fervent in their ways, survivors of an Immortal raid on their caves south of Byzantium. They had come to the city for refuge and to escape Roland's horde...only to throw themselves in the way of eighty thousand Dark Bloods and two million fearful Corpses.

The narrow path that snaked past the south side of the ruins was clear. Jordin ducked out and headed toward it, along the ruin wall. Rusted oil drums and heaps of rubble littered the vacant yard. The ancient ruin was located in a sparsely occupied section of the city far south of the Citadel. But she was about to enter the Dark Blood perimeter that monitored all activity to and from the city.

Keeping her head down, she walked naturally, as any Corpse out for a stroll in the morning might, hands stuffed in her pockets. She was just that, she kept telling herself. An ordinary Corpse out for a walk and lost in thought.

The first man she saw looked to be no more than in his twenties, squatting on a half wall on the far side of the compound fifty meters distant. His arms were wrapped around his knees, and he was watching her. She diverted her gaze. Had he sensed the spicy scent of her skin and breath? Which way was the wind blowing? Her pulse quickened.

Just a Corpse like him, Jordin told herself. Nod and walk on. It's nothing.

So she did, without changing her pace. It had been at least a month since she'd seen a Corpse in daylight. They looked the same as any Sovereign except for the dullness of their eyes.

She came to the edge of the abandoned complex and eased sideways through a gap in the fence that circled the rubble and ruins. She angled for an alleyway across the adjacent street, eager to cross before an oncoming bicyclist could scent her. There were far fewer people here than to the north, which lessened her likelihood of exposure. It also made her more noticeable to each Corpse she encountered.

Only when she reached the relative safety of the alley did her anxiety subside. So far, so good.

For an hour Jordin made her way south, cutting east and west to access alleyways, keeping as much distance as she could between herself and any Corpse by exiting those narrow ways only when the street was clear of carts, intermittent crowds of pedestrians exiting the underground, and the occasional car or truck, though they were few. The sun had climbed a third of the way into the sky by the time she reached the massive culvert that ran into the waterways beneath Byzantium's southern neighborhoods. Dark Bloods often took up post at the end of the open drain, but likely more so as evening approached, guarding against any Immortal who might use the passage for easy entrance into the city.

She made it halfway through the culvert and pulled up hard. The circle of light at the far end was broken by the clear silhouette of a Dark Blood facing away from her. She glanced over her shoulder. Dark. They wouldn't be able to see her approach.

The sound of her footfall was another matter. Dark Bloods often patrolled in groups of four, which meant three more might be loitering nearby. The wasteland's barren hills waited beyond. She would have to reach them without raising an alarm—Dark Bloods had no qualms about giving chase during the day.

Jordin slung the pack off her back and pulled out the beige tunic and head wrap. Shrugging out of her vest, she changed into the lighter colors that would help her better blend into the wasteland. And then she gathered her pack and her bow and moved to within thirty paces of the unsuspecting guard. She set four arrows on the curved concrete, notched a fifth on her bowstring, and knelt to steady her aim. At this distance the steel-tipped arrow would pack the power of a pickaxe.

She drew breath, held it, and sent the arrow directly at the Dark Blood's head. She didn't see it hit, but the sound of metal into bone was unmistakable. The Blood grunted once and pitched forward, dead before planting facedown on the ground. A cry of alarm sounded.

She strung a second arrow and waited, her sighting eye trained on the culvert's left edge, ready to switch to the other side if they came from the right. Two Bloods stepped into view fifty paces beyond the culvert, far enough to avoid any projectile. They obviously had no intention of suffering the same fate as their comrade.

But staring into the dark culvert, they couldn't see her. She eased to her belly and waited, eyes fixed on the Bloods, who waited to see if their attacker had taken a quick shot and ran or intended to engage them again. Bonded as they were to their Maker, Feyn, Bloods had little concern for their lives, which made them utterly fearless warriors. Brutal. Luckily, that same disregard for their own lives often put them in unnecessary danger. They rarely retreated or called for assistance, at least when Sovereigns were concerned. Immortals were a different matter, but Immortals did not attack during the day.

She watched them discuss the matter for a full ten minutes, during which time they were joined by a third Blood. Finally one of them strode forward, sword drawn. They'd evidently concluded that a Sovereign had made the kill and ran. After all, Sovereigns were cowards in their eyes, preferring to hide rather than fight.

Jordin waited patiently until the Blood was at the opening peering in, and then longer until he turned and waved the others forward.

She rose to a knee while the Blood was turned and sent an arrow at his head. Without waiting for the impact, she grabbed her remaining arrows and launched forward into a sprint. The Blood lurched, an arrow through his temple.

The other two seemed unaware that their comrade had been attacked until he hit the ground, and by then Jordin had closed the distance by another ten paces. Twenty before they realized that they were caught in the open.

Jordin exited the culvert at a full run, leaped over the two fallen bodies, and slid to her knees thirty paces from the fast-approaching Bloods. In rapid succession, she shot her remaining three arrows into their bodies.

Two struck the one on the left, one in his gut, the other in his chest. He dropped his sword and let out a roar, clutching at the projectile in his breast, then fell to his knees.

Her third arrow took the last Dark Blood in his side as he turned to evade, hand on his hilt.

Without hesitation, Jordin sprinted to the one who'd fallen, keeping low. She grabbed his sword by the handle and rushed the upright Blood.

He spun to face her, face red with rage. Swung his steel with a grunt.

Nomadic instinct did not abandon her now. She ducked, committed, and sliced her newly acquired sword up and into the Blood's jaw while the warrior was still ending his swing.

Her blade nearly took his face off. Roland had taught her how to compensate for her size with quickness. She'd successfully beaten many a larger opponent at the Nomadic games—on occasion, all of them. It was one reason she'd been chosen as personal guard for Jonathan.

Had the Dark Blood a jaw and mouth, he might have screamed. As it was, he flung his hands to what had been a face, lurched forward three steps, and toppled to the earth where he twitched for a few seconds and then lay still.

Dead by Jordin. Four with five arrows and one borrowed blade. The arrows' steel tips would alert Feyn that these hadn't been killed by Immortals, who preferred bone heads on their arrows, but by a Sovereign. It was the first such attack in several months, and she had all but inscribed her name in blood.

For the first time in days, Jordin felt alive.

She straightened and scanned the city edge. No sign of any more Bloods. Or Corpses. But she wasn't alone.

Jordin stared back at the culvert, horrified by the sight of a lone Sovereign standing in plain sight, watching her through dark glasses, dressed in taupe leggings and a brown tunic.

Kaya.

"Kaya?"

The seventeen-year-old ran out to meet her, wearing an expression of relief, ignoring the dead Dark Bloods. Death wasn't a stranger to Sovereigns.

"What are you doing?" Jordin cried. "You followed me?"

Kaya pulled up, yanking off her glasses to reveal wide, emerald eyes. "Yes!"

"No!"

The girl's expression faltered.

"But I can fight too. You'll need someone to watch your back—"

"No! You don't even have a weapon. You're a child!"

Kaya glared at her for a moment, strode to the blade abandoned by the faceless Blood, and snatched it up. "I may not be trained to do what you do, but that doesn't mean I'm useless. Jonathan thought enough of me to save me, didn't he?"

"Not for this!"

"Yes for this," Kaya snapped. "I'm not going to stay in that hole and wait for the Dark Bloods to finish us off while you find Jonathan. I'm coming with you."

"This isn't about finding Jonathan, you fool."

"Then tell me why you're heading to the wasteland."

Jordin dismissed her with a curt wave of her hand. "Get back before they know you're gone."

"They already know. Adah tried to stop me. But life isn't worth living without Jonathan. I will go to him for love."

Jordin ignored the pang Kaya's words brought. The pain, still just beneath the surface. The empathy. The strange and irrational jealousy. But of course the girl loved him. They all did. And then she realized it wasn't Kaya's love that roused her envy, but her unbending faith.

"How did you follow me? I left no trail."

"Adah said you'd come here, to the culvert."

"She did, did she? And did she also tell you that I probably wouldn't return alive?"

"Yes."

"And yet you came."

"I'm here, aren't I?"

"Yes, here you are, a child in a harsh world of warriors." Jordin paced, furious. No one had noticed them, but she had to get moving before anyone did. She jabbed her finger at the culvert. "Go back. You can't go where I'm going. Out of the question."

"And where is that?" When Jordin refused to answer, Kaya set her jaw. "I'm not going back. You just killed four Dark Bloods here. They'll be discovered, and the streets will be crawling with them. If you make me go back, you might as well kill me here. I'd never make it."

She was right. Sending her back would just as likely get her killed as taking her into the wasteland.

"Please, Kaya..."

"Jonathan—"

"Didn't die so you could get yourself killed!"

"Then what are you doing?" the girl said more quietly.

Jordin stared at her for a long moment. *What am I doing?*

Jonathan, where are you?

"Go back or stay with me, you'll end up dead. I'm in no position to protect a child."

"I'm not a child," Kaya said. "Haven't you noticed?"

Jordin looked away, shook her head.

"Are you jealous?" Kaya asked.

Jordin strode toward her and yanked the sword from her hand. "Don't be ridiculous."

Kaya stared at her for a long moment, frowning deeply. "Fine," she said. "Then send me to my death. When you find him, tell Jonathan that you abandoned me. Tell him I died trying to come to him."

"I'm not going to find Jonathan. Are you deaf?" She tossed the sword away.

Kaya spun on her heel and headed back toward the culvert, arms spread wide as if to offer herself up. She would never make it. Dark Bloods seemed to have a sixth sense that alerted them when harm had found their comrades. Others were likely already on their way.

"Kaya."

The girl marched resolutely on. She was incorrigible—the very recipe for certain disaster.

"Kaya."

The girl stopped but did not turn.

"If you come, you follow my lead to the letter."

Kaya turned around.

"I don't have food for two," Jordin said.

"I won't eat."

At least the girl had the sense to bring the canteen at her waist. She wore dark-brown boots that rose mid-calf. She wasn't properly dressed for a journey out of the city, but street shoes and black pants would have been far worse for daylight travel through rough terrain.

Too frustrated to speak, Jordin turned her back on the city and headed out into the wasteland, well aware of Kaya behind her, hurrying to catch up.

She closed her eyes. Death was now ensured.

Jonathan might have done better to leave the girl to the Authority of Passing. At least there she might have lost her life in peace.

CHAPTER SEVEN

THE WASTELAND south of Byzantium held several advantages for Jordin. She knew the terrain intimately— Sovereigns had lived in caves to the southwest for several years before their discovery by the Immortals a year ago. The Blood War between Feyn and the Immortals had been two months old at the time, and with so many engagements focused to the north, the Sovereigns had remained largely unmolested—until that day. Though Roland penetrated the city from all sides today, Immortal attacks remained concentrated on northern Byzantium, where the Citadel and the bulk of Feyn's Dark Blood army stood heavy guard.

For the moment, the likelihood of a daylight encounter with Immortals this far south was thin, but come nightfall plenty of patrols would sniff them out. She was counting on it.

She glanced up at the sun, just shy of its zenith. They had been walking nearly two hours at a healthy pace and were already running out of water. With any luck, the small seasonal creek that snaked through the Basil canyon an hour ahead would still be running.

By her reckoning, they had almost eight hours to reach the canyon she had in mind and prepare.

"Jordin?"

Kaya walked to her right, half a step behind, keeping mostly to herself. For as many complications as the girl's presence had introduced to the situation, Jordin couldn't deny that her companionship offered some relief. If they died tonight, they would at least die together.

"Keep your voice down."

Kaya cleared her throat and spoke just above a whisper. "Jordin?"

"What is it?"

"Do you have a plan?"

"A plan for what?"

The girl hesitated. "I mean, if we aren't going to find Jonathan, what do you plan to do?"

Keeping the truth from Kaya would serve no purpose.

"I'm going to kill an Immortal."

They walked in silence for a few minutes. The deep canyons here had been carved by rivers, most of which were dry, the rough, scrubby terrain having yielded years ago to desert with as much sand as rock. They climbed a sandy slope, leaning forward to gain better purchase, and topped a rise that overlooked a small canyon to the south. A gentle, forgiving breeze cooled the sweat beneath Jordin's tunic.

She scanned the horizon for any sign of movement. None, as expected.

"Does Rom know?" Kaya asked.

She eyed the girl, knowing the objection she voiced in the question.

"He knows it may be necessary."

"Why necessary?"

Jordin headed north along the ridge. "Because we need Immortal blood."

"For what?"

"It's the only way to become Immortal," Jordin said.

Kaya stopped in her tracks. Jordin walked on.

"What do you mean?"

"I mean the only way to become Immortal is through seroconversion. That means I have to inject Immortal blood into my veins."

"What?" Kaya hurried to catch up. "You're going to *become an Immortal?*"

"Not so loud. We don't need to go out of our way to be discovered. Not yet."

"Is it even possible?"

"Would I do it if I didn't think so?" she said.

"But you'd no longer be Sovereign."

She and Rom had discussed the notion on several occasions, an option for desperate straits. He'd gone to Feyn, knowing he faced possible conversion to Dark Blood, and her mind all but told her she must do the same with the Immortals. In becoming their enemies, they might defeat them.

"That's true," Jordin said.

She dropped off the ridge and angled down into the wash. She could only imagine the thoughts careening through Kaya's mind. To become Immortal was tantamount to turning one's back on Jonathan. To leaping off a cliff into the abyss of Hades itself. And that was assuming that seroconversion from Sovereign to Immortal could work. Even though they'd all once been Mortal before taking Jonathan's blood, no one knew if it could be reversed. For all she knew, Immortal blood would kill her.

"It's mad!" Kaya said. "You'll become Immortal and set out to kill Sovereigns!"

"Maybe."

Kaya grabbed her arm. "You can't do it! Jonathan would never approve!"

Jordin spun, wrenching free of the girl's grasp. "Jonathan isn't speaking!" She felt her frustration boil over but made no attempt to calm herself. "He's left me to lead, and this is the only thing I know to do."

Kaya looked as if she'd been slapped.

"If you think I'm in love with the idea of becoming the enemy, you're wrong," Jordin continued. "I'd rather slit Roland's throat than eat with him—let alone become like him. And make no mistake, I will slit his throat. But the only way to get close enough for that to happen is to become like him. If you have a problem with that, you'd better hurry back and take your chances with the Dark Bloods. Otherwise, keep your doubts in your own head."

They remained locked in that stare, Jordin's face red . . . Kaya's white. But the girl's eyes were flashing with offense.

"If you had no doubts you wouldn't be so cross," she said. "I'm only asking what any reasonable Sovereign would ask."

"We're past the time to be reasonable."

"But not the time to be kind," Kaya retorted. "I don't think Jonathan would like the way you're speaking to me."

Jordin looked at her, at a loss for words. There was nothing quite as annoying as a self-righteous priss, particularly when she spoke smatterings of the truth.

She looked away, mocked once again by her own shame, which only aggravated her more. They were on a fool's mission. One that Kaya had no business being on.

But that no longer mattered. Her own bitterness might be more of a threat to their safety than Kaya's naïveté. Between the two of them, Kaya was more in line with Jonathan's spirit. And yet her frustration refused to yield.

"How many Dark Bloods have you killed in Jonathan's defense?" Jordin asked, eyes fixed on the rise.

"I haven't killed anyone," the girl responded after a moment.

Jordin looked at her. "Do you think I enjoy killing? That when I fought in Jonathan's defense I relished each swing of my blade?"

"No."

"Do you think I don't have his heart?" She felt tears pooling in the corner of her eyes and quickly blinked them away. "That the man whose arms held me, whose lips kissed me, would disapprove of my heart?"

A tear broke from the corner of her eye. She swiped it with her wrist.

"No, Jordin. No, I didn't mean to suggest—"

"Have you ever even loved a man? Loved him, and kissed his lips?"

"I . . . no, not yet, but—"

"Then don't assume you know anything about love, much less my love for Jonathan. I have gone and will go to the ends of the earth in his service. If he calls, I won't just answer. I'll run to him."

"I know you would," Kaya said softly. "Jonathan was so fortunate to have you. I meant no disrespect. You saved me as much as he did."

The tables had somehow been flipped. She, not Kaya, should be the reassuring one.

"Has he called to you?" Kaya asked. "In your dreams?"

The question stopped her cold.

"Has he called to you?" Jordin asked.

"I dream of him calling to me in the desert."

Maybe there was something to it after all. Her heart quickened—both with the possibility of it and with something like envy. Why hadn't he called to her, if not alone, then uniquely?

She took a deep breath and let it out slowly. "Forgive me, Kaya. I don't know what's become of me. I...it all seems so hopeless right now."

"Don't be sorry," the girl said. "We're all facing this. But we can trust Jonathan, can't we? You always taught me to trust him, didn't you?"

Jordin nodded absently. "Yes, I did. And you're right. I'm just struggling a bit right now. I'm sorry for letting you down."

"You haven't!" Kaya grabbed her hand and pressed a fervent kiss against her knuckles. "You lost more than I did when Jonathan was killed. But you've seen him, right? In your dreams."

Jordin nodded. "Yes, in my dreams. And Rom has as well."

"He's calling to us, Jordin. That's how I know he's still alive. I'm just not sure he would like us killing Immortals."

Jordin considered the girl. Perhaps having Kaya by her side was meant to be. She took in the sight of her, eyes brilliant as a green sea in the sun. Her hair billowed with the breeze like a dark sail, a stray tendril teasing at her cheek and catching against her lips. The Nomads would have prized her for her sheer beauty alone. A stunning creature, she could have taken any lover. But what would the Immortals make of her? Roland, she thought, might eat her for dinner. The strong and sudden instinct to protect the girl surprised her.

"But," Kaya added, "that said, I will follow you."

Such simple faith—faith in her—nearly broke Jordin's heart.

"Unless you have another idea?" Jordin asked, for the first time genuinely open to any suggestion.

Kaya shrugged. "We could just walk into their camp."

"We don't know where it is. And even if we found it, they would never allow us to approach it alive."

Kaya diverted her eyes, lost in thought. "Maybe we could take one captive and force him to take us."

"We have the wrong smell. They're much more highly skilled than we are. Mortal perception has evolved in them. There's no way we'd stand a chance."

Finally, Kaya nodded. "Then I suppose you're right." She sighed. "We have to kill. Or at least wound one? Couldn't we just cut off a hand and take the blood from it?"

Jordin smiled. "Unlikely. But you're not far off."

"You're sure about becoming Immortal?"

"This is my path. I'm not sure, but it's what I'll do. Or at least try." She almost said "die trying," but she stopped herself in time.

"Then I won't try to discourage you."

For all her artlessness in some matters, Kaya was surprisingly astute in others.

"What about you?" Jordin asked.

"Me?"

"If we manage to acquire Immortal blood, will you take it?"

"I don't know. I'd have to think about it."

Jordin turned and resumed her march north, adjacent to the canyon over the rise. "Then you'd better think quickly," she said over her shoulder. "Time is running out."

THE PLACE Jordin had chosen lay near the mouth of a small canyon. She'd once holed up in the narrow passage at the end of the ravine to escape a band of Dark Bloods. That was before the Blood War that pushed Feyn's warriors back into the city. To call it a passage overstated its dimensions. It was more of a crack in the canyon wall, which jutted skyward on either side. Only two paces wide, it ran deep, a hundred meters at least.

Unaided by the Immortals' acute sense of smell and oblivious to Jordin's hiding deep within, the Dark Bloods had passed by the fissure, waiting at the mouth of the canyon until nightfall, when they'd given up and headed back to the city.

During the long hours of waiting them out, Jordin had noticed the precarious balance of the boulders perched along the western rim of the fissure. The narrow passage was practically a death trap.

It was to that place she took Kaya. There, they worked with the small shovel for several hours, loosening enough boulders to make for a crushing landslide along a twenty-meter section of the cliff wall above.

They stopped an hour before sunset. They were running out of time, and setting a trap would prove useless without baiting it. Even if they managed to bait and spring the trap, they would have to survive—no easy task in the proximity of any approaching Immortal. And no Immortal traveled alone; others would be nearby to come to his aid.

"I don't see why any Immortal would be stupid enough to enter," Kaya said, peering over the cliff. "They travel on horseback. Can they even turn a horse around down there?"

"There's room if you know how to handle a horse, and trust me, they do. I could."

Jordin stood and scanned the horizon again. Her nerves were tingling. The greatest advantage was their own scent, which Immortals would hopefully pick up and follow into the canyon, if all went according to plan.

They would have to make sure the Sovereign blood she'd brought in her pack did its work.

"How can you be sure they will come?" Kaya asked.

Jordin reached for her pack and pulled out the thick glass vessel filled with Sovereign blood, red and rich in the late sun. "What Immortal can resist the scent of Sovereign blood?" she said. She looked at Kaya who stared, wide-eyed, at the blood. "Do you know why they hate it so much?"

"Because they can smell the scent of the one they betrayed."

"That's right. And now Jonathan, in his own way, will lead them to us."

"To us?"

Jordin lowered the jar. "That's where it gets a bit dicey. We'll need some luck. We have to be here to send the boulders down, so we'll be exposed, but the scent of the blood is much stronger than our skin. With any luck, they won't be able to isolate us."

"We have to depend on luck?"

"Or Jonathan's providence. Take your pick. I can tell you this: if they start to come up this hill, I've got seven arrows and nine knives that will put up a decent argument. We won't go down without a fight."

"Wouldn't it be safer to hide?"

"Hide where?"

Kaya looked around and shrugged. "I don't know, maybe we could bury ourselves in the sand."

"You don't think they would see the disturbed earth? Besides, we'd suffocate."

"It was an idea, at least."

Jordin grinned. "Yes, it was." She stroked the girl's hair. "You're thinking. That's good."

Kaya returned her smile.

Through the day she'd become increasingly thankful to have Kaya with her. Kaya had rekindled an ember of her own faith. Death had yet to smother the idealism of Kaya's youth. The girl reminded her of herself once. She'd been a Nomad orphan, taken in and protected by Roland, to whom she'd vowed her lifelong service. Then Jonathan had come and given all Nomads blood from his veins, and their world had forever changed.

She had always been the quiet one who watched from the edge of the campfire, unnoticed by the others. But Jonathan had noticed. She'd fallen in love with his gentle and quiet ways, and he'd returned that love in a way only he could, as much with his eyes as with his words or his blood, which he gave willingly to any who wanted life.

She would have gone to Hades itself to save Jonathan, as Kaya would now. The girl's spirit was infectious. Her simple love refused to be denied.

"Tonight this blood, not a hole in the ground, will keep us hidden."

"Hopefully," Kaya said.

"Hopefully." She stood and headed south, along the rim of the canyon. "Let's go."

It took them half an hour to dribble tiny drops of blood every fifty paces beginning directly beneath the section of loose rock above, out of the canyon, and up the rise west of the ravine where they splashed it on the ground.

The wind drove north as it always did this time of year, carrying the scent deep into the wastelands. Any Immortal within miles would know a Sovereign had passed this way and would follow the trail into the canyon thinking a wounded Sovereign had sought refuge for the night.

The sun was below the western horizon, and dusk was upon them before they settled into a hollow between two large boulders that offered cover and a clear view of the canyon below. Jordin's bow and her seven arrows rested against the stone to her right; four knives waited in their sheaths, two on each leg. Three more at her waist, two on the ground.

"Now we wait?" Kaya said.

"Whisper," Jordin said in a hushed tone. "They can hear as well as they can smell."

For fifteen minutes they sat in silence, both lost in thought. Jordin rehearsed the play in her mind a dozen times. How many would come? Two, if it was a scouting party based on the Nomadic way, which she assumed Roland still practiced. Four or more, if it was a patrol. A dozen, if they were headed into the city, where they might split into two groups, penetrate with ruthless precision, leave dead Dark Bloods in their wake, and be gone before Feyn's commanders knew they'd been breached.

Roland undoubtedly relished his lethal reputation, but he had so far failed to cut through the layers of Dark Bloods to the Citadel where Feyn ruled untouched. Knowing him as she had, it was a failure that no doubt ate at the Immortal Prince. She was counting on it.

But none of that mattered if she couldn't reach him alive, however detestable the thought of being in his company might be.

"When will it happen?" Kaya asked.

"Hopefully tonight. I just don't know how often they range this far south. If not, we try again tomorrow night."

"That long? Then why are we whispering?"

"Because for all we know, they're coming already."

Kaya slumped back against the boulder, clearly disheartened. She hadn't grown up hunting with the Nomads, who learned early in life that patience was the better part of catching or killing any prey.

"It's all right, Kaya. We'll manage. Better here than under the city, right?"

"But two days?"

"Let's hope not." Mattius had given her a week, but she'd said nothing of Reaper to Kaya. There was no telling what would happen to their loyalties if they reached Roland. The man would tear the world to shreds if he knew the Sovereigns held a virus that would kill all Immortals. No one could know.

She touched Kaya's knee. "Maybe you're right. Maybe this will all lead to Jonathan. If so, he'll be proud of you. Think about that, rather than two sleepless nights."

They waited deep into the night with nothing but darkness before them. Eventually, even whispering became too dangerous. They had to listen carefully for the slightest disturbance. Twice, Kaya tried to start conversation. Twice, Jordin cut her short.

"What was it like?" Kaya asked suddenly. "Kissing Jonathan."

The question caught Jordin off guard. Thoughts of silence slipped from her mind, replaced by the memory of Jonathan's embrace that day of his death. Of the tender, innocent, beautiful man who could wield a sword with the best warriors when he gave himself over to it. Of how effortlessly he'd cut down the Dark Bloods before surrendering himself to Saric's sword.

The memory swallowed her, leaving anguish in its wake.

"Jordin?"

"It was beautiful," she whispered. "I held Bliss in my arms."

"Do you think a man will ever hold me like that?"

Jordin looked at her in the soft starlight. What young woman would not want what she'd had, if only for a short time?

"Of course. I can't imagine a man in his right mind who wouldn't want to hold you like that."

"I'll never have that if I die."

"You won't die, Kaya. I won't let you." She said it for the girl's sake. She said it for her own. She hoped it was true.

"Isn't becoming Immortal like death?"

"Maybe. But we aren't Immortal, are we? So right now we can rest in Jonathan's love. Both of us."

Kaya sat cross-legged, staring beyond the cliff at the darkness. Silence stretched between them for a minute. Nearby, a lizard scurried over a pile of loose pebbles.

"Do you feel his love now?" Kaya asked.

That was the question, wasn't it? The one that had taken up permanent residence in all of their minds.

"Sometimes," she said. "Not enough."

"Then why be Sovereign?"

Jordin knew the answer, but it didn't warm her heart. She remained quiet, thinking that in her simple way, Kaya voiced the impossible irony of Sovereignty itself.

"If we have Jonathan's blood and are like him, shouldn't we feel his love at all times? And if love is so beautiful, why does everyone seem to live in misery?"

"I don't know."

"I think they're pretending. I think they'd rather be Immortal to feel the love and peace they once felt." She paused. "Is that why you're going to become Immortal?"

Jordin blinked in the darkness. *Was it? Maker, no.* Then why did the question bother her?

"No," she said.

"But you're still sad, even though you have Jonathan's love in you."

"Because I'm only human, Kaya. I lost the love of my life."

"He's not gone."

But he's not here. "Don't you miss him?"

"Yes. But I'm not miserable." *Like you*, Jordin heard without Kaya saying it. "He saved us from death and gave us love—so why is everyone so miserable? He saved us."

"Yes, of course. And one day we'll all relish that love. But today we survive."

"What good is 'one day' when that day doesn't come until you die? Then why survive at all?"

Jordin wanted to tell her that she was thinking in too-simple terms. But there was also strange magic in the simplicity of her logic.

"You still feel him, don't you?"

She should. And in some ways she often did. But not the way Kaya meant, like breath itself, every moment, made possible by the very blood in their veins. It struck her then, as clear to her as a blue sky. Something was wrong with their understanding of Sovereignty. Somehow they'd missed the whole point.

"Yes," she said. "Of course."

Why she felt such annoyance at Kaya's obvious questions was beyond her. Weren't these the same questions she'd asked herself a hundred times? But it was there, niggling beneath the surface: somehow, they were getting it wrong.

"We have to be quiet now, Kaya. Ask Jonathan in your dreams. Maybe he can answer."

"I've decided," Kaya said, ignoring the urge for silence.

"Decided what?"

"I'm going to do whatever you do...if we get the blood."

The faint sound of a jingling tack drifted to Jordin's ear. Or was it? She held up her hand for silence and listened.

There, again, the sound of a horse's hoof on rock.

The Immortals had come.

CHAPTER EIGHT

FOUR. All mounted on black horses, shadows swathed in pitch black from head to foot.

Jordin lay on her belly, peering through the scrub at the cliff's edge. The Immortals came slowly into the wide section of the canyon to her far right, guided by scent. The scent of Sovereign. They appeared not to have a care in the world—what was this to them but a wounded animal whose misery they would end with a single blow?

But they weren't stupid. Their apparent ease was as much caution, finely tuned to the night terrain around them. The scent had brought them, but acute sight and hearing would serve them now...as well as that sixth sense known only to those who lived to prey or be preyed upon.

Jordin held her bow in her right hand, heart pounding against the rock face beneath her chest. She could not deny her envy at the sight of them. While Sovereigns cloistered hungry and hunted beneath the City of the Dead, these Immortals burned with vibrant life that screamed superiority even in perfect silence.

Neither could she deny her hatred. Hadn't they spit on Jonathan's grave in choosing that very life? And yet, if she succeeded, she would save the very lives of those she hated.

For Jonathan and the sake of his legacy.

The lead rider stopped halfway into the canyon, the other three two horse lengths behind. She knew they did not study their surroundings as much as *know* them. Perhaps she was giving them too much credit. They would bleed as easily as she.

Kaya crept up beside her. Jordin pressed a hand to her arm, demanding absolute silence. Kaya laid her cheek on the ground but then eased her head up to see.

The riders started forward again at a slow walk. One of the horses snorted softly. They heard a gentle clucking sound as its rider calmed his mount and then the muted plodding of horse hooves along the canyon floor.

The Immortals would assume they had nothing to fear. They were in pursuit of a Sovereign who possessed none of their expanded senses, and a wounded one at that, caught in the wastelands where all Sovereigns feared to tread. Any conflict here would be welcomed by the Immortals as sport.

They didn't stop until they'd reached the entrance to the fissure. For a long stretch they sat mounted in silence. When they spoke it was with few words, which Jordin couldn't make out. She kept her head down and begged the Maker to push just one Immortal inside the trap.

Finally the one to the right of the leader nudged his horse, guiding it into the fissure. He silently slipped his sword from its scabbard and rode deeper into the narrow passage.

From where she lay, Jordin could take him with a single arrow, but doing so would only defeat her purpose. If she took one out, the others would come after her and then return for the body of their fallen comrade. They never left their dead, and she needed the body.

Only when the rider was directly below them did Jordin ease back, roll to her left, and place her palms on the rock they'd set to trigger the landslide. With a final glance at Kaya, whose eyes were wide in the dark, she gave the boulder a shove.

It tipped, hung in precarious balance for a moment, and then lazily rolled over the edge. The sound of tumbling rock broke the stillness as the boulders careened down the wall, taking others with them. With a rocky clatter punctuated by loud *thumps*, they crashed down into the passage and landed in a thundering crescendo that echoed through the canyon.

Behind the sound, a cry of alarm—a whinnying horse cut short as rocks crushed rider and mount.

The trap had been sprung, but it was only the beginning. In an instant, the three remaining Immortals would realize that they'd been led into a trap.

"Hurry!" Jordin whispered.

She rolled away from the edge, came up in a crouch, grabbed her pack, and ran north along the cliff top, keeping away from the Immortals' line of sight below. They had to execute the escape with precision—one misstep and they would be caught.

Jordin had sprinkled the blood leading directly east, away from the canyon and toward the city for a good two miles, knowing that pursuing Immortals would follow the heady scent. She just didn't know if they'd turn back when the scent weakened or conclude that their prey's wound had dried and continue the hunt.

Jordin led Kaya north, a hundred meters to the end of the passage, slinging her bow and the knapsack over her back. She dropped onto a small ledge, then she reached back to help Kaya down. For the moment they were safe, out of sight.

Hooves pounded in the distance. They were in pursuit, making their way out of the canyon to the top of the cliffs for a quick kill before returning to their fallen comrade. It's what she would do.

It took them only two minutes to scale down the steep slope they had descended twice in rehearsal, dropping onto the sand at the bottom from a ledge seven feet high.

Jordin rolled to one knee and listened as Kaya dropped down beside her. A thin cry sounded ahead, from the direction of the rubble. It was possible one of the others had stayed to try to help. It no longer mattered; they were committed.

"You good?" she whispered to Kaya.

"Good."

"Stay behind me. Here." She shoved one of the knives into the girl's hand. "Just in case."

Kaya stared at the blade as if holding one for the first time. The girl could shoot a bow relatively well, but knives were not her forte by any means. For that matter, the bow wasn't either.

Jordin unslung her bow and notched an arrow, ready in the event that they were not alone. The first order of business was to find the body, alive or dead. If alive, they would have to kill the rider and harvest the blood. If dead, their task would be much easier.

She ran forward in a low crouch. The sand softened their footfall.

The first sign of rock came at fifty meters—smaller boulders that had rolled the farthest from the pile, just visible to her in the darkness ahead. She pulled up at the sound of a call from an Immortal, apparently searching for the fallen warrior.

No reply. The first was dead or unconscious. Considering the rubble, she guessed the former. Not even an Immortal could survive such a pounding.

So they'd left one for the rescue, which could pose a problem. Now she had to make a choice—either try to kill the living one or wait, hoping he would leave to meet the others on the cliff top when they returned.

Each minute they waited was one less they could use to put distance between themselves and the canyon, and the Immortals would be back to retrieve their comrade soon enough. She had no intention of being anywhere near the canyon when they returned.

She held her space, crouched low, breathing steadily through her nostrils. Only a minute, and then she would go in to test fate.

She needed only thirty seconds. She heard the creak of horse tack and then the sound of a retreating gallop—the Immortal had gone to join the others in the hunt.

"Hurry!"

Jordin ran forward to the pile and quickly searched for any sign of the body. The boulders had fallen in greater number than even she had hoped for, burying both horse and man beneath a small hill of stone.

"Move the rock—look for a limb. We don't have to get him out, we just need enough access to drain some blood."

"He's dead?" Kaya asked, her voice high.

"He won't feel any more pain, if that's what you're worried about. Dig!"

They began to push and roll stones off the pile. The clatter would be heard easily from above, but with hope the Immortals were too far to the east to hear it. It was a chance she had to take.

Kaya grunted and jerked back, nearly falling off the boulder she'd mounted for better access to the boulders on top. She covered her mouth, staring into a gap between two boulders.

"I think I found something."

Jordin scrambled to her position, doing her best not to twist or break an ankle—that was the last thing they needed—and saw the broken bone jutting from torn flesh down in the opening. An Immortal arm, torn through a black sleeve. Next to it, the leg and hoof of the rider's mount, battered and lifeless. She felt more for the animal than the rider.

"That'll do."

She shrugged out of her pack and pulled out an empty collection jar and the large syringe she'd brought. They used the same device for the seroconversion of Corpses.

There was no need to puncture the skin with the thick needle; the wound was seeping plenty of blood already.

"Keep your eye on the cliffs," she said.

"How much do you need?"

"As much as will fill two small jars—it's all I have. Hopefully he hasn't bled out completely."

Jordin quickly inserted the needle into the bloody mess that had once been an elbow, filling the syringe three times before switching jars and repeating the operation. The Immortals would never be able to tell that blood had been drawn from the wound.

She secured the lid on the second jar, shoved it back in her pack, and waved Kaya forward, over the pile and down the far side.

"Run, Kaya. Run."

They ran, side by side, out of the narrow passage and through the canyon. They slowed to a jog as they headed southeast along the same trail where they'd left the traces of Sovereign blood earlier. It would now mask their retreat.

They had the blood. All that was left was to put it into their veins.

And pray they lived to tell.

"YOU'RE SURE about this?" Kaya asked. "What will happen if our blood rejects it?"

They'd jogged and walked off and on for nearly an hour eastward, deeper into the wasteland beyond the point where they'd first sprinkled the ground with Sovereign blood. She knew that the Immortals would eventually circle around, searching for any scent of the Sovereign who'd killed their own.

"Then we'll know it didn't work."

"Assuming we live."

"There is that."

"You've never heard of it being done?"

"No."

Jordin stood on the rise and studied the horizon for movement against the night. It was as still and lifeless as it had been half an hour earlier. Satisfied, she dropped to one knee beside the girl.

"I'm not sure this is wise," Kaya said.

"Neither am I. But I know that if we're still Sovereign in a few hours, they'll eventually pick up our scent and track us down. Trust me, they won't give up."

"So if we don't try the blood, they'll find us and kill us."

"Yes."

"And what if we take the blood and live, but find ourselves dead, like we once were?"

"We've already been over this."

But Kaya was brimming with questions.

"Immortals hate Sovereigns. Will we hate Sovereigns too? Will we hate Rom?"

Jordin didn't want to entertain that question. *No! Impossible*, she wanted to say. But was it?

She had less than a week. She couldn't let herself become crippled by questions like those. She dare not.

"I don't want to discourage your questions, Kaya, but none of them will change the fact that becoming Immortal is our only hope for survival right now. And if I fail . . ."

She stopped short of completing the thought. But she'd already said too much.

"Fail to do what? Find Jonathan?"

This time Jordin didn't try to shut her down. They were about to leap off a cliff—a few moments of transparency were understandable. Perhaps even called for.

She let her shoulders relax, elbow on one knee as she squatted on the rise, peering into the night. "You're right about one thing, Kaya: Jonathan is in us, if only in his blood. I've always known that. But I don't feel it anymore, and at times I wonder if I ever did."

She took a deep breath and studied the girl who knelt back on her heels, watching her.

"Something's broken in me. I can't find the love I once had. My mind's full of darkness. You said it yourself. Misery follows me like a cloud. I'm Sovereign, but I feel completely lost. It's not Jonathan I need to find but *myself*."

A calm seemed to settle over the girl. She finally nodded, her expression placid.

"Then we'll help each other find ourselves. Sometimes my mind's as dark as yours."

"I hope not."

"I don't have all the terrible memories you have, but I wonder all the time why we seem to be getting weaker. I think it's getting worse by the month."

Astute words for such a young woman.

"I think the only way we can find ourselves is to find Jonathan," Kaya said.

"Then let's hope he comes out of hiding."

To this, Kaya said nothing.

"Promise me one thing," Jordin said. "If the blood changes us, remind me often that we want to be Sovereign."

"And if I forget?"

"Then I'll remind you."

Kaya might have pointed out the obvious challenges they faced if they both forgot their purpose. Instead, she stood up, pulled off her amulet, and stuffed it inside the waistline of her pants. "I don't want to lose it," she said.

Jordin gave a slight smile. Being caught with the Sovereign amulet around their necks could be hard to explain. And yet keeping them near would prove a constant reminder.

She stood and did the same.

"What about our clothes?" Kaya wanted to know. "This isn't what they wear."

"You're right. I'll handle it."

Kaya nodded. "Well then, I guess that's that."

"Yes."

Jordin rolled up her sleeve to expose the crook of her elbow and quickly applied a rubber tourniquet to her upper arm. A large vein swelled below it. She took a small pouch from her pack. It contained one sanitized needle attached to a short tube with a rubber inline pump. She unscrewed the lid on one of the blood-filled jars and lowered the end of the tube into it, primed the pump, then she set the jar carefully on the sand.

"I'll inject you if it succeeds with me. If things go badly, find a place to hide for the night and head back to the city at first light."

"We both know I wouldn't survive the night."

"Then this had better work."

With a last glance at Kaya, Jordin pressed the tip of the needle against her vein. It pierced the skin then slipped in. Releasing the needle, she took the pump in her right hand and squeezed. Holding her breath, she watched the blood fill the translucent tube and flow, sluggishly at first, into her vein.

The jar emptied in less than thirty seconds. She pulled the needle out and handed it to Kaya. Then released her tourniquet.

"What's happening?" Kaya asked.

"Give it time."

She tried to observe any change in herself, but a full minute passed with no sign of transformation. What if it didn't work, as the old Keeper had once suggested? She had seven arrows left—she could kill one or two perhaps, but Kaya was right. They would never...

All at once, heat bloomed in Jordin's head. It spread down her spine as if it were filled with gasoline and lit with a match.

She gasped.

"What is it? Is it working?"

The night exploded with color. A flash of white light turned the night to day, blinding her to all but the silver horizon.

Panicked, she leaped to her feet, arms spread wide for balance.

And then the night returned, and with it her focus. The heat had spread to her extremities, leaving her fingers and toes prickling to the point of pain. The top of her skull felt as if it were crawling with a thousand ants.

She closed her eyes. Opened them. This time, when she peered into the night, she knew she had been changed.

She'd been seroconverted three times: from Corpse to Mortal with Jonathan's blood before his death, from Mortal to Sovereign with Jonathan's blood after his death, and now from Sovereign to Immortal. Her two previous conversions had left her in a cloud of overwhelming peace and love.

Not this one.

She felt the terrible urge to run, so great was her fear. She didn't know what frightened her, only that she was terrified.

A green phosphorescence laid the night landscape bare before her. Nearby, a snake slithered across the sand to her right, she could hear it. The breeze had suddenly shifted farther to the west, she could feel it. The air tickled the fine hair at her nape, hot as breath.

For the first time, she could smell the Sovereign scent, strong as spice, like jasmine but more pungent. So acidic it stung her nostrils.

Her pulse raced and for a moment she thought her heart might rupture.

"What's happening?" Kaya cried.

The girl was on her feet, hands on her head, eyes wide.

Jordin pulled deeply at the night air, first through her nostrils, then through her mouth when Kaya's scent proved too much. The air tasted of death and life at once; water and earth, blood and sweat.

It also tasted of hope. With each breath, ease began to settle in her mind.

And then it was over. She was an Immortal—or a Mortal, as they had once called themselves—and filled with awe at the tactile expression of the physical world, her senses fired.

Could she still slow time with her eyes?

"Move," she said to Kaya.

"Move? Are you all right?"

"Pretend you're swinging your fist to hit me."

"What?"

"Just do it."

Kaya did, in a far too unskilled manner. It came in slow motion. The vibrancy of living with heightened senses flooded her memory, drowning out the fear that had engulfed her earlier.

"Why are you looking at me like that?" Kaya asked. "Did it work?"

"Yes."

"You're Immortal?"

She lifted her hand, moved her fingers, the skin paling before her eyes. Living underground, she'd lost the color of those who ranged beneath the sun, but now she could practically see the veins beneath her skin. This was different, more like the skin of the Brahmin royals than the Mortal she had once been. So then, the Immortals *had* evolved these past six years. And she was changing into what they were now, rather than what they had been.

Were her senses sharper as well? It had been so long but yes, she thought so. She couldn't remember ever tasting the air so strongly. Or feeling the pleasure of the breeze—the tiny grains of sand carried in it, the dryness of the air itself—crossing her skin with such intensity.

Her whole body hummed with sensory perception. A tuning fork, set on edge. But it brought her no peace. Instead she found it unsettling.

"Will you kill me?" Kaya said.

"Why would I do that?"

"I'm a Sovereign. Immortals hate Sovereigns."

At the sound of that word, "Sovereign," Jordin felt slight revulsion. Or perhaps it was just the stink from Kaya's skin and breath.

"No, I don't hate you. I'm a Sovereign at heart and always will be."

Are you so certain? You missed this life...

She dismissed the thought, knelt to her pack, and pulled out the second jar of blood.

"Roll up your sleeve."

CHAPTER NINE

THE RANGE of emotions that swept through Jordin in the wake of becoming Immortal came in like an unrelenting storm that only began to ebb near dawn. The feelings weren't alien in the way emotion was to a Corpse coming to life for the first time, but they were devastatingly visceral and only intensified when she tried to resist them. And then again as she realized she didn't really want to resist them.

She'd watched Kaya's seroconversion with morbid fascination—particularly the paling of her skin. The girl might have passed for Brahmin royalty, her flesh had turned so white. She looked like a ghost in street clothes, her steps silent on the barren earth as they headed north in search of their new kind.

The first shock waves of visceral emotion and of the color fleeing Jordin's skin were subservient to the greatest change of all—the change in her senses. The entire volume of life had crescendoed in her ears. What she had barely heard or not heard at all just hours before came full fledged to her now: a cricket under a rock a hundred yards away, the wind sighing over the low hills, the trickle of a tiny stream a quarter mile east. The wasteland, lifeless to her before, crooned her secrets in majestic symphony.

She could see perfectly for a mile and make out the veins on an insect's wings as it careened overhead. She could smell the scat of a rodent on a far hill and taste the tang of a juniper's berries brought to her on a breeze so faint she could feel it lift the tiny hairs on her neck.

Alive. So very much so that it terrified her, tempted her. But she wasn't truly alive, was she? Not as a Sovereign was. Not as one who'd died with Jonathan in the communion of his blood. But with her senses blooming to almost unbearable highs, she couldn't help but wonder why he had ever wanted them to leave such an exquisite existence.

Or had he?

These were the thoughts that plagued her now. Sovereigns taught that emotions other than love and peace were merely bodily reactions to thoughts—reactions that alerted them when something required resetting if those thoughts were negative, much in the same way that physical pain alerted a person that something might be wrong with his body. Change a thought, change the emotion. A practice that had become increasingly difficult as of late.

Now her emotions seemed to be running amuck, requiring far too much effort to control. She assumed Kaya felt the same as they walked side by side in introspective silence. The girl's talkative nature had taken leave.

For a panicked moment, she wondered if she was losing her mind to the change.

No. She clung tenaciously to her truest identity as Sovereign. A weaker will might easily forget the value of Sovereignty in the headiness of becoming Immortal. No wonder Roland had only grown bolder as his kind had evolved, sure that they would live a thousand years barring death in battle or from disease. No wonder the

Immortals had only increased in number while the Sovereign population had dwindled. Who could resist such an existence?

At Jordin's insistence, they'd walked through the night. With any luck, they'd put themselves in the way of an Immortal patrol or raiding party, a task made easier in the darkness with their expanded sight.

But they found no one that night.

They'd stopped by a tiny watering hole to refill their canteens as the first gray of dawn tinged the eastern horizon.

"Jordin?" Kaya's voice cut the silence for the first time in hours. It sounded different to Jordin's ear since her conversion—sinuous, somehow, as the woman herself.

Jordin reached for her canteen.

"Are my eyes black?"

She glanced up at Kaya and immediately saw the change in her eyes. *Maker.* They'd gone black in the night, ringed by a golden burst as though they glowed from behind. Disturbing and strangely beautiful.

And far too similar to the eyes of the Dark Bloods.

That wasn't the only change. Her lips were darker—they had deepened in color to a rich burgundy, as if stained by wine. Against the pallid skin of her face, they seemed to pout passion. Gone the flush of innocent pink on her cheek, the coral of her lips. She was stunningly seductive. Her tongue was darker as well, colored by the same rich wine as her lips.

Kaya lifted her hand and touched her fingers to her lips. "What's wrong?"

Jordin's gaze fell to the girl's fingertips. Her nails had turned several shades darker than her lips, so they appeared nearly black.

She lifted her hands and saw that her own nails were the same. Marked. Altered in body, mind, and soul. Her heart was racing but not with fear or even with disgust. So this was what it was to be Immortal. A part of her eagerly embraced the transformation.

The more reasonable part of her felt defiled.

Kaya dropped to her knees and stared into the small pool's glassy surface. "We have the eyes of Dark Bloods!"

"So it would appear."

She might have expected a stronger reaction from the girl, but Kaya only stared at her dim reflection with strange wonderment.

"You don't sound terribly disappointed," Jordin said.

Kaya looked up at her. "It's ghastly!"

But her tone wasn't as sharp with disgust as it could have been. Or was Jordin only projecting her own hollow guilt onto the girl?

"Will we forget? What it means to be Sovereign—will we forget?"

"Never," Jordin said. "I'll die before I forget." But she had heard her own hesitation before the answer.

They filled their canteens and bathed, doing their best to wash away any lingering Sovereign scent from their skin and hair. And then they slept for two hours against a large boulder near the watering hole before resuming their trek northeast, into the canyon lands.

She would have insisted they sleep longer, but they now had only five days to accomplish the impossible.

"THEY'VE SEEN US."

"Yes," Jordin said, gazing down the long valley from a rise overlooking a system of shallow gulches.

Danger had come to them at dusk.

They'd spent all day heading toward the northern road into Byzantium, knowing that Immortals routinely patrolled the supply routes into the city, intent on cutting them off.

The moment she'd picked up their scent, she'd climbed the tallest nearby rise and issued three long, high-pitched whistles in the direction of the faint odor. The call for help had been used by Nomads for decades—it was one she knew well. If the signal had failed, she would've tracked them on foot.

It never came to that. They'd been heard, and four of the black-clad warriors were riding toward them, shimmering specters on the horizon.

"How do we know they won't hurt us?"

"We don't. But there's no reason to think they would. Unless you begin acting strange." She cast Kaya a firm stare. "I am the only one to speak, do you understand?"

"Of course."

"No, not of course. One wrong word and you could get us killed. So you won't speak at all. Just imagine that you're a mute."

"A mute Immortal."

"Something like that. Follow me."

Jordin started down the hill to cut the distance between them. Within five minutes the Immortals were fully formed riders on dark horses, their posture that of those who owned the world, warriors protecting their realm. In the wasteland, at least, it was true. Roland had carved out his world and ruled here free and supreme.

While Sovereigns cowered beneath Byzantium.

Jordin halted when they were a hundred meters off and let them come. She quickly reviewed their state. The markings on her bow and the steel of her arrowheads were of Sovereign design, so she'd buried them in the sand along with her pack. That left them with only the clothes they wore and their canteens. She'd hidden a single vial of blood in her canteen—with any luck it would go unnoticed.

Her mission had come to this moment. She had no idea how Roland organized his Immortals or what kind of persuasion might get her to him. She'd killed an Immortal— a feat she would have celebrated just last week. But today, with the hours growing short, it was only one step in an impossible journey. Now she would see her first Immortals face to face. Then she would know.

The leader of the patrol nudged his horse into a trot and approached at ease. He broke to his left and circled them once, ten paces distant, far enough to avoid attack, close enough to study them with every sense. Jordin couldn't help but admire the surety with which he rode—it wasn't caution but simple reason. His eyes peered at her through the slits in his head covering. An Immortal Ripper. A wraith disguised as a man.

Did she know him from her days as a Mortal? If so, he would recognize her as well, and she'd have to talk fast— and perhaps act faster. She reminded herself that she'd once been able to best the most skilled Mortal in combat. Whatever advances they enjoyed due to the change in them she also possessed.

The other three Immortals stopped five paces off, horses abreast. No one spoke until the leader completed his circuit and angled in closer.

"I can see that you have Immortal flesh," the man said. "But I see nothing else Immortal about you."

Jordin dipped her head in respect. "Then you serve our prince well." She lifted her eyes and met his stare. "As do I."

"As a lost vagabond in the wasteland?" one of the others said. "And what of the pretty one beside you?" His eyes shifted to Kaya. "You might serve him better by offering us your comforts."

Heat flared up Jordin's neck. But she would put the man's simple lust to good use.

"I doubt he would allow it."

"Then you don't know our prince."

"And you don't know what we have to offer him in exchange for whatever service he desires. Unfortunately for you, what we have is for Roland alone, not for young studs in training."

The air went still. She could actually hear the man's heart beating, like the rhythmic throb of a moth's wings in the air. Its rate did not fluctuate. The rider on her far left finally chuckled.

"You obviously don't know who you're speaking to. Sephan isn't exactly young. He does, however, train the best of the prince's coven. You should watch your tongue if you hope to keep it, pretty."

"And here I thought Kaya was the pretty one," Jordin said.

The leader nudged his horse a step forward. "Kaya, is it?" he said, looking down at the girl. "And what do you have to say for yourself, Kaya? What kind of service do you and your speaking friend here have to offer our prince?"

Kaya shot Jordin a quick glance, but the leader stepped in.

"Look at me, not her," he said. "Your life's in my hands now. What's your friend's name?"

Kaya stared at the tall rider as though he were the prince himself, seemingly captivated by those deeply drawing eyes, the sultry voice.

"I'm not free to tell you that," Kaya said.

"Then neither will you be free to live."

"She travels with me," Jordin said. "I speak for us."

"You are in my jurisdiction, and you will both answer my questions."

"I mean no disrespect. I only say that I command Kaya as you command your men."

"You command nothing but my attention, and even that's wearing thin. Keep me interested, and you might do well."

The man regarded Kaya again, dismissing Jordin.

"What's your name?" Jordin asked before he could speak. "Roland will want to know who it was that so quickly dismissed the one he himself once trained to be champion. The one who now brings him news that will win him a war."

Slowly the leader's head swiveled back, his eyes betraying true interest for the first time. He glanced back at his men before casually pulling a knife from his belt. He tossed it into the sand at her feet.

"Show me," he said.

"Which one would you have me kill?"

"Any you think you can."

Stillness settled between them, broken only by the buzz of a fly and the swish of a horse's tail. Jordin was suddenly overwhelmed by the urge to kill them all. How many Sovereigns had these very Immortals massacred a year earlier?

But attempting to kill any one—much less all—of them would only end tragically. They were battle hardened and keenly alert. And they were her way to Roland.

"Pick one," she said.

"I give you that choice."

"Without a direct order, I can't kill any who serve my

prince. But I can assure you that I've killed many Dark Bloods. They, not you, are my enemy."

The commander sat in silence for an extended moment, then withdrew something from under his black cloak. An apple.

"Pick up the knife."

Jordin bent for the blade, eyes never leaving his. She had straightened only halfway when he nonchalantly flipped the apple into the air.

Jordin let the world about her slow. Time slowed with it. The apple hung lazily in the shimmering air, a suspended thing, impossibly large. She felt one knee drop to the sand as she reacted without thought. She snapped her wrist to send the blade into the fruit, knowing already that her aim was true.

But even as the knife left her hand, she saw that the apple was only a distraction meant to test her true skills. The Immortal who'd commented on Kaya's beauty was already flipping his gloved hand in a throw. A circular blade cut through the air with blazing speed.

She threw her weight back, arching her back. The Immortal's blade hummed past her face, narrowly missing her nose, and thudded harmlessly into the sand behind her. Then she was over on her back in a roll and immediately on her feet again.

The apple lay on the ground ten feet away, cut in two.

The Immortals did not move.

Jordin calmly pulled the circular blade from the sand and tossed it to the one who'd thrown it.

"I think you misplaced this," she said.

He deftly plucked the steel orb from the air.

"So you have some skill," the leader said. "My name is Rislon. I need yours."

"Mine is known only to Roland. As you can see, we're still in street clothes from our mission in the city. We made it out on a transport but don't have horses. Either give us one of yours or take us back to the coven with you now. We've wasted too much time already."

Rislon stared, but she knew she'd won him over already.

"You'll be rewarded, Rislon. I can promise you that the news I bring Roland will be celebrated by all Immortals."

He dipped his head. "You're with me."

Kaya glanced at the others, tentative.

"You, pretty Kaya..." He jutted his chin toward the first one to call her that. "Ride with Sephan."

CHAPTER TEN

FEYN STOOD before the one-way window of the observation room, a misleading name for a chamber that was not truly a room at all, but a cell set apart from the ancient dungeon deep beneath the Citadel. Neither was it often used for observation. Few had the stomach to peer at Corban's most intimate investigations. Ammon, she noted, was conspicuously absent.

A lone electrical fixture hung dormant from the dungeon's pocked stone ceiling. Torches were far more effective in moments like these. Two of them illuminated opposite ends of the ten-foot cell, hissing at the occasional drop of sweat from the ceiling. The iron bars of the cell had been replaced by a wall with the single one-way window. The heavy door, adjacent to the window, served as the chamber's sole entry. One entry. One exit. Usually by means of a wheeled cart for the one seated in the chair.

The chair was high-backed and heavy, with sturdy ironwood arms and legs. Its hard seat and broad arms were accustomed to struggle and indifferent to it. But the figure seated on its unforgiving seat had not yet struggled once.

Rom.

Inside the cell, Corban stepped away from a short, steel table situated just below the torch on the right, long syringe in hand. He paused thoughtfully before the chair, momentarily blocking her view.

"How many of your kind still live?" the alchemist asked.

"Enough."

"Enough to what? Make more?"

To this Rom said nothing.

"Where are they hiding?"

Silence from the chair.

"We have the means to make you tell us everything, you know. You must realize that."

If Rom did, he gave no indication.

"Did your old alchemist, the one you called 'the Keeper,' track the changes in your blood from week to week, or once a month?" he said. His voice through the concealed speaker sounded thin to her ear, nasal and unappealing.

Silence from the chair.

"It would help me a great deal to know what changes he found in your blood and at what specific intervals he studied it. I assume he accumulated quite a body of research with as many conversions as you claim to have undergone." He turned, syringe in hand, and paused, unbothered by Rom's silence.

He stepped closer, leaned over the arm strapped to the chair, and inserted the needle into Rom's vein. The leather restraints around the arms and legs of its occupant had long been reinforced with heavy steel bands. Even Seth had been unable to break free of them when he'd been brought down to have his loyalty tested.

For the first time since she had come to stand before

the window fifteen minutes ago, Rom lifted his head, his gaze drifting just to the bottom of the wall below the window.

His face was smudged, as much by the grimness in the cell they'd kept him in as by the sport the guards had made of him. His hair had come loose from its binding to hang in his face; several peppered strands plastered against his neck. A recent cut had dried above his eye. A darkening bruise swelled his right cheek.

"I admit to my own puzzlement," Corban said as the syringe in his hand filled with blood. "I haven't seen any astounding differences in your blood to explain the color of your eyes. Perhaps a draw taken from a living specimen will reveal something more. In the meantime, I'm curious. If you will indulge me—why do you call yourselves 'Sovereign'?"

Another moment of silence passed before Rom spoke for the first time. "Because ours is a new kingdom." His voice rasped with thirst but was void of defiance and strangely calm.

The alchemist lifted his head from his task and considered him. "But there is only one kingdom."

"How would you, a dead man, know this?"

"There is only one world and one world government. One Maker of my life, one new Order under that Maker."

"Only one that you can see."

"Do you live in a different kingdom then?" the master alchemist asked. He said it lightly, in the way one indulges the slightly unhinged. "Have your followers seceded from the government of this one?"

Corban had glanced down at the syringe and didn't see the quirk of Rom's mouth. But Feyn did. "In a manner of speaking."

"And you consider your leader, the dead boy Jonathan, your true Sovereign?"

"He was, and is."

"It doesn't seem so, given that he's dead and that our liege lady is Sovereign."

"My Sovereign lives."

Corban's right brow arched. "Does he?"

"You think him dead. But then you also think you're alive."

"I am very alive, as you can see. Your so-called Sovereign, on the other hand, is quite dead. And yet you say you live and I do not, and that a dead boy is Sovereign and our liege lady is not. Clearly you see the madness of your twisted logic."

"Jonathan came to bring a new kingdom. Not of political power—I know that now—but a kingdom of life. I'm a part of that kingdom. In truth, I'm more Sovereign than your 'liege lady.' "

"Black is white with you, and white is black."

"How do you know what black is, what white is?"

"Because I see truly."

"Do you?"

"The evidence certainly points in my favor. There's nothing to suggest superior life in your blood at all." Corban withdrew the needle and paused. "And yet you believe yourself superior, don't you?"

"I consider myself alive," Rom said, eyes on the alchemist, the green of them vivid even in the chamber's shadows. "Alive in a way that you can never be. Feyn, on the other hand, can and will taste true life."

Corban moved toward the table, not once showing any sign he was bothered by Rom's claims. "What evidence do you have of this so-called life?" he asked. "There's the color of your eyes, certainly, though alchemists have engineered such variations for centuries. There's your stench. There's a slight variation in your blood, but nothing else. Do you have any abilities I'm unaware of?"

Rom sat still for a few beats, then spoke quietly.

"Only life itself."

The alchemist went on as though he hadn't heard him, and Feyn wondered if indeed he had not. "The Immortals have a highly evolved sense of perception, we've observed. You, I recall, have experienced that. But we haven't noted any such attributes in those of your so-called Sovereigns."

No answer.

"You don't have the strength or speed of a Dark Blood, nor the supergenetics of one. I would even say that you've aged significantly since I saw you last." He withdrew the vial from the body of the syringe and lifted a pen to label it. "Do you have the long life expectancy of the rogue Immortals?"

"No."

He set the vial in a wire rack. "Then what does this... 'life'... offer you, exactly?"

"Hope."

"Hope. In the next life?"

Rom hesitated. "Bliss is a mystery, understood by none."

"I see. So then hope for this life." He lifted a small pair of scissors and returned to the chair. "And yet in the midst of this life you've gone underground to escape the systematic extermination of your cult." He bent to one of Rom's fingers and cut off a portion of a fingernail. "You've all but been wiped out, I understand. Your life doesn't seem like much of a life at all."

There was unmistakable satisfaction in the alchemist's

voice as he straightened. He turned. "You've given up so much, and for what? What have you gained?"

"All that you have lost."

"And yet I've lost nothing." He returned to the table and dropped the clipping into a small vial in the rack. He retrieved another syringe—a smaller one—and stuck the needle through the rubber stopper of a vial. Filled it. He returned to Rom and slid the needle into his shoulder through his shirt without preamble.

Rom showed no sign that he felt the pain, though it had to be excruciating.

"I can find no marked advantage over a common Corpse other than simple emotions." He tossed the syringe quietly into a bin and then withdrew a silver instrument from the pocket of his lab coat. "You have no evidence to show me that you have this new life you claim to possess?"

Silence. But Rom's eyes were clear, his expression unflinching...even as Corban leaned over with the instrument, which resembled a cigar cutter, and cut off his smallest finger with a hard *snick*.

Now Rom's face trembled and his breathing thickened.

"One piece of evidence only," Corban said. "It's all I ask."

"I can't," Rom said through a tight jaw. Blood drizzled from the stump of the finger to the floor. Visible beads of sweat appeared on his forehead. "I simply know."

"And what is knowledge but belief that it is knowledge?" the alchemist said, carrying Rom's finger to the table. "No one who's deceived ever believes he is wrong."

Again no response. Perhaps Corban's words were getting through.

The alchemist retrieved a small plastic bag and placed

the finger inside it. "I've injected you with a clotting agent. It should help with the bleeding, if not with the pain."

Feyn had thought it an anesthetic of some sort. And yet in all this time he had not screamed or cried out. The drizzle of blood slowed to a trickle, the stump of the finger angry and red despite the clean cut.

Rom's gaze traveled to the glass through which Feyn looked. A vein had started to throb in his temple.

"Can you defy your master?" he said quietly.

"To what end?" Corban said, his back still turned.

"If only to know that you can."

"I will never."

"Because you can't. You, better than anyone, know it. You have no choice. It was bred into you with the blood that made you."

"A mercy by my Sovereign maker. I will never have the opportunity to defy her new Order."

"Only the dead make no choice."

The alchemist paused.

"Have you loved her by choice? But no, you can't, can you? The dead cannot love. Your master commands obedience but goes without love. You wonder why we would do as we have. The answer is love. You tell yourself in your mind that I am mad. But do you see a madman before you?"

"The deceived are always mad." Corban was looking curiously at him.

"And yet even your master knows I'm not mad. She knows that I have never proven wrong. Rash? Yes. Fanatical? Perhaps. But mad . . . never."

He paused, taking several breaths through his nostrils. When he spoke again, his eyes were fixed on the window.

"From the day I brought you out of your chamber and

took you outside the city, you knew I carried the truth. The day I came for you after you awoke from stasis, you said you needed no saving, but the day you met Jonathan, you knew it was true. All of it. And what I say is true now."

A cold shiver raced along Feyn's arms. Could he see her? But no, he only hoped she was watching.

"And now I've come because the truth remains. You will die. I've come one last time to save you. For the truth. For love."

Something about him...He was fervent. Magnificent, even in his haggard state. He had won her with his conviction before. With fevered and persuasive arguments. She knew then that he would weather any experiment, any pain visited upon him by an entire team of alchemists. One thing was true: he believed. A conviction without evidence—without even a living leader. It amazed her. It disconcerted her.

The dark vein itched beneath the surface of her hand, and she scratched it, one of her nails drawing blood.

He'd been right about many things, that was true. But how many lives had he spent in the chasing of this thing—of this faith in something to give his life a purpose greater than the dream even of Bliss or the fear of Hades? It would be a mercy to kill him now.

"Love, you say," Corban was saying. "And does love give you less pain? Less anger? More peace? I would think your kind must be a bundle of nerves living as you do now. Filled with misery."

Rom didn't respond. There could be no doubt that his kind knew misery.

Corban pushed Rom's head up by the chin, and fixed it to the back of the chair with a leather strap across his forehead. Another, beneath his chin.

His faith would kill him, and he would let it.

The alchemist retrieved a small metal spreader from the table and returned to the chair. He pulled open Rom's left eye and fixed the edges of the device to his upper and lower lid until the green of his eyeball fairly bulged from his skull.

Rom might die in a pool of his own faith. For what? To prove something? To supposedly save her? No. Because he believed, however misguided that belief was.

As such, he was many times the threat they had thought him. The Sovereigns had laid down their lives to the Immortals. To her Dark Bloods. Not because they'd been overpowered, but because they were willing to die for belief. Pain or threat of death would prove insufficient to bring them into submission. Reason could not dissuade them.

And that made them deadly foes. Even if Rom and his band of holdouts didn't present an immediate challenge to her rule, they would make more of their kind, all who possessed the capacity for rebellion. She could not tolerate any such threat to her Sovereignty.

Rom was the key to his kind.

If he would respond to neither pain nor reason, she would earn his trust. Hadn't he done the same to her once?

Corban had returned to the chair with a uniquely crafted instrument that resembled a rounded claw with a long handle. Its edges glinted in the torchlight as he carefully guided the blade toward Rom's left eye.

Feyn stepped forward and flicked a switch. The electrical fixture overhead stuttered to industrial life and flooded the chamber with light.

The alchemist paused as she pushed a button next to the switch.

"Leave the eye," she said. "He's already blind."

CHAPTER ELEVEN

THE IMMORTALS led Jordin and Kaya northeast into the canyon lands once known only to the earliest Nomads centuries before they'd escaped north to greater Europa, there to live free of Order's statutes. Jordin had heard the campfire tales of deep, twisting gorges and towering cliffs. It was said that unless one knew the maze of the canyon lands like the lines of one's own palm, one could get lost within them, never to be found.

The air cooled as darkness settled around the four horses and their riders. The Immortals had kept the counsel of their own thoughts, characterized by silence as much as the Mortals had been by frivolity. Perhaps it was only because they were dressed for engagement and wary of exposure, but Jordin sensed that it was something more. They didn't waste words or movement. Even their breathing seemed exceptionally controlled, as though it were not an unconscious act at all.

This, she understood. Her own breath had lengthened, each long pull into her lungs laden with sensory meaning.

Riding behind Rislon, she found herself at first put off by the impossibly close proximity to the powerful Immortal and the pallid skin she imagined beneath the black shroud covering his face and head. She wondered how many Sovereigns he had killed—if his was the sword that had cut down any one of those she'd called friend. But as they wound their way through the canyons, their faces, once so clear to her, were shadows before her mind's eye; their memories distant against the texture of the canyon stone and the powerful muscles of the stallion beneath her. Even as a second rider, she felt one with the powerful animal and the deafening pound of its massive heart. Even with Rislon himself.

Kaya rode with her arms wrapped around Sephan, cheek pressed against his back, watching Jordin with round eyes. She appeared neither frightened nor uncomfortable, but lost in wonder.

It occurred to Jordin that she wouldn't recognize any of their host captors among a throng of other Immortals—their clothing was darkly uniform, their faces wrapped in black muslin. One of the unnamed other two might be Roland himself and she would never know it.

No, that she would know.

Still, their proclivity to remain covered even so far from civilization was a mystery.

They'd traveled three hours and entered a deep canyon by the time Rislon slowed his mount to a walk, angling it toward a fissure no more than five paces wide in the cliff face. She followed the line of the sheer rock up—there, where the cliff met the sky. Sentries, seven to a side, silhouetted against the pulsing stars. As imperceptible as shadows, she would never have seen them without keen Immortal sense.

As they drew closer to the breach, a dozen mounted Immortals joined the sentries on either side. Then a hundred more. They looked down in perfect silence. Surely they wouldn't express such interest in the approach of any random Immortal delivered from the wastelands. Word must have traveled from posts unseen by her.

For the last hour, Jordin had all but forgotten her mission. Now memory of it filled her with morbid dread. She'd come in a bid to collect the heads of her two greatest enemies: Feyn. Roland. But now, at the sight of the Immortals lining the cliff, she knew that any attempt to collect Roland's head would result in nothing short of certain death—hers. Kaya's. Even if she managed to convince the prince to join forces in her mission to kill Feyn, thousands of loyal Immortals stood between her and Roland himself.

One of the stallions snorted. The sound reverberated in the narrow passage. Above, a dozen riders had matched their plodding pace along each rim of the cliff. One errant move, one suspicious motion, and she knew she would find her heart pinned to her spine by a dozen arrows. She would hear the *twang* of the bowstring, see each arrow's lazy approach, shift in the saddle to avoid the projectile. But she couldn't avoid them all.

The sheer rock walls on either side widened, yielding to a massive natural bowl carved into the cliffs. A hundred meters across, it was lit by a ring of evenly spaced torches. From the sky, the narrow fissure leading into the large bowl might look like a key. What secrets lay locked in the high cliffs of this Immortal lair?

Only one that mattered: the Immortal Prince himself, the heart of the blood that now pumped through her own veins.

To her left, stairs like the ringed seats of an amphitheater hewn in the rock stepped down to a low pool fed by a small nearby fall. Water, in the middle of the wastelands! Three deciduous trees rose from the sand near the water's edge. Above, one grew directly out of the rock itself.

Toward the right: two gaping entrances in the rock face. Torchlight glimmered from within, giving the appearance of two glowing eyes. A long, open stable was situated in between.

By her count, there were only a few dozen horses. Surely there were more nearby. The Sovereigns had estimated Roland's local force to be in the thousands—and who knew how many Immortals might live beyond the reach of Byzantium, spread out like dark fingers to grasp at the rest of Europa. Could the caves in these cliffs house so many? Surely not.

So here, then, were his most deadly guerilla warriors and any others deemed necessary to their mission. And yet, the sight before her was not that of a standard war camp.

Smoke escaped in gray tendrils from two pits on the canyon floor. The smell of roasting meat wafted across the enclave, reminding her she'd gone two days without a proper meal.

A shade of a figure appeared on the edge of the amphitheater, having emerged from a darkened entrance in the rock near the top of the stair. White fingers clasped the front of a cloak that trailed like an inky spill down the carved stone. A woman, by her movements—confirmed the moment she slid back the hood of the cloak and then dropped the cloak to the stair altogether. Moonlight struck her full in the face, and Jordin barely resisted the urge to gasp; it was the first time she had seen an Immortal's face, much less a body without its covering. The woman was strikingly beautiful. Even from here she could see the dark stain of her lips, the colorless cheeks that reflected the very stars more than the warm glow of the nearest torch. The long raven's wing of hair that fell nearly to her waist.

Beside her, she felt rather than saw Kaya's rapt attention. The Immortal woman paused and glanced up toward the line of sentries along the cliff, as one takes note of a new scent in the air, before giving a barely perceptible nod. And now Jordin saw that these were not the lithe legs of most women, but they were carved lean. Her shoulders were corded with muscle that comes only from swinging steel.

She descended down the steps into the pool and then into the water itself until only her shoulders remained above its surface, her hair a black oil spill on the water. The surface rippled, reflecting the firelight of the torches, and Jordin almost shuddered: for a moment, the water seemed as red as blood.

The woman made no sound but slipped, eyes open, beneath the water for an impossibly long moment before emerging on the other side. She did this twice more, and it occurred to Jordin that she was not bathing for the sake of hygiene, but as though for ritual purity.

Beyond the pool, the thin waterfall cascaded down a cleft in the rock, freefalling twenty feet to a stone platform, there to slip into the rock before no doubt feeding the pool. A man might stand beneath that fall as the water sluiced over him. For an odd moment Jordin had the image of Roland doing just that, naked, chest thrown out and arms wide, as the Immortals descended to the pool in communion below.

Was it a vestige of the Sovereign cognition or her mind running away with her?

"Hold your tongue unless spoken to," Rislon said, leading them toward the stables where the nameless other two were already dismounting.

"You need not tell me how to conduct myself among my own," Jordin replied as they entered the row.

"The Rippers are not your own, or I would know you. I don't know what mission you claim to have been sent on by the prince without my knowledge. Until told otherwise, consider yourself a prisoner. Dismount."

She slipped off the stallion's back and landed lightly on the sand. Her thighs were sore from the ride, but she welcomed the discomfort. She'd been born to ride, a Nomad to the bone. It had been too long.

Kaya, on the other hand, had been born Corpse and only spent days among the Nomad Mortals before Rom and Roland had split ways. Sephan seemed only too willing to help her down before deftly shedding his black head wrap to reveal a black shock of long hair and a goatee against pale flesh. He winked when Kaya stared at him.

"That goes for you as well, pretty," Rislon said to Kaya. It was then, with both men's attention on Kaya and as the stallion shook its head with a jingle of tack, that Jordin dropped her canteen into a nearby pile of hay. She gave it a soft, rubber-soled kick. It slid at an angle inside the nearest stall, behind the front wall. It was the best she could do for now; she dare not take it with her into any closed space filled with keen Immortal noses. Here, at least, the smell of manure might camouflage the canteen's contents.

Rislon turned toward the cave entrance farthest to the right. "Follow."

The hewn cave walls formed a short tunnel that ended at a large wooden door with three heavy bolts that could be opened from either side but only locked from one: within. Rislon slid the bolts, top to bottom, and then pulled the heavy door open with the handle of the last. It opened outward toward approaching visitors rather than inward on one who might be manning the other side, Jordin noted, a testament to its history as an ancient holdout.

She had to will her heart to a steady beat as she followed Rislon into the widening inner passage. She knew that *he* was here somewhere.

But there was something else. As they passed into the broadening corridor—no more roughly hewn rock but a series of carved arches worthy of any ancient basilica— she had the strange sense that she had come to a place where she belonged.

Although she'd never been to this place, the blood within her had come home. The jolt within her was exhilaration and panic both. Again, she willed her pulse to calm, to quiet beyond the hearing of Immortal ears.

Torchlight ahead. And then the arches fell away as the corridor opened into a soaring cavern three stories tall.

Kaya, beside her, sucked in her breath.

The space was lit by a massive iron chandelier. At least ten feet in diameter, it was laden with dozens of candles, burned low onto their wicks at the late hour. A broad staircase curled up along the far wall and became a landing large enough for fifty people before descending down the other side, the last step ending just before another small corridor. On the landing, which was supported by giant wooden struts, two Immortals lounged against the balustrade, lazily tracking the small party's entrance. The candlelight of the chandelier, practically on a level with them, cast its glow in their pale faces. Now Jordin saw that the rail was composed not of iron balusters but a staggering collection of swords, tip down, some with jewel-encrusted hilts.

Below the landing the floor was covered with thick and exotic rugs and set about with velvet settees, love seats, and wingback chairs, several of which were occupied by men and women in various stages of romantic pursuit or languid intoxication. A man lay sideways over the arms of a heavy chair, eyes following the sinuous movements of a woman dancing to music heard only by her.

In the middle of the most spacious part of the chamber sprawled an impossibly large wooden table laden with three great candelabras, their tapers burned low, several jugs of wine—she could smell the tannins—and seven Immortals. They lounged against the carved chairs, some of them dangling heavy goblets off wooden armrests.

Beyond the table, which was surrounded by at least thirty chairs, heavy silk curtains partially obscured the entrance to at least three more corridors on the lower level and one on the upper landing. More silks and tapestries spanned the walls no longer roughly hewn but carved high up with reliefs of serpents amid a star-filled night and, closer to the floor, into windowless seats adorned with cushions below the stone-cold moon.

The entire chamber was occupied by nearly thirty Immortals, most of their gazes turned to the new arrivals.

Beside her, Kaya stared as one mesmerized.

Jordin's pulse spiked as she took a quick, sweeping inventory of those present. But no, she didn't recognize any of these faces as those she'd known before, Mortals from the Nomad camp where she'd been raised since a child. Was it possible that Roland had expanded his coven so much? Or had those she'd known before—warriors all—been killed and replaced?

Jordin became aware of her thickening breath, made worse by her realization that any Immortal familiar with Roland's new ways would never react with as much apparent wonder as she and Kaya were. She glanced at Rislon, who seemed as aware of her visceral response as she.

He didn't need to speak; his deadpan stare said enough.

"Wait here," he said, turning to Sephan and adding, "Don't let the others hurt them." He strode for the stairs on their right. The eyes of the others were fixed upon them.

She told herself it didn't matter what any of them thought of her presence. Roland would know her the moment he saw her and either summarily cut her down or hear her out, if only out of curiosity. If she could get him to listen, she stood a chance.

This much was now obvious: the Roland she'd known as the Nomadic Prince was not the same man who commanded these Rippers. His new world was dark yet breathtaking; offensive but alluring. She felt oddly as one and alienated at once.

One of the men seated at the long table slipped out of his chair and approached, his stride as sinuous as a cat's. His eyes remained fixed on her, unblinking dark orbs rimmed in light.

His black silk shirt was open in the front, draped over a lean, well-muscled chest and stomach. In his hand dangled a goblet of wine. At first glance one might think the man feminine, but Jordin knew she was looking at a vicious warrior.

A thin, wry smile pulled at the man's face as he came close. His gaze dripped like hot wax over Jordin before lingering on Kaya...and then returned to Jordin, as though tasked with a choice. He finally settled on Kaya, who stared back at him with painfully obvious innocence.

"Well, well, dear Sephan. What tender morsel have you brought me today?" He reached for Kaya's hand and then glanced at Sephan. "I hope I'm correct in assuming she's a gift."

"That is for the prince to say," Sephan said. "They came for him." To Kaya: "Don't mind Cain, pretty. He's harmless. It's the women you should stay clear of. Cain's lover has been known to rip out the throat of her rivals."

Kaya didn't seem to hear Sephan. She lifted her hand and let Cain take it with deceptively thin fingers.

Had she lost her mind?

"We're not here to play," Jordin said, to Kaya as much as to the predator who had ensnared her with nothing more than oiled words and a gesture. "Only for Roland."

"Only Roland," Cain said. "Of course. But until Roland calls, I'm sure he would wish his prizes properly entertained. Isn't that right, Sephan?"

"As I said, she's for Roland. As for entertainment, I trust your judgment." Clearly, Cain was higher on the pecking order than the Immortal who'd brought them— likely a celebrated fighter accustomed to his pick of the spoils.

Cain lifted Kaya's hand and touched her knuckles with lips so dark they appeared nearly black in the dimly lit chamber. "What is the name of your friend, my little princess?"

"I'm Kaya," she said, sounding lost.

"So you are. But I asked for the name of your friend. The fierce one who thinks I'm a viper." His gaze slid to Jordin. "Perhaps she would like to see my fangs? It might make a night worth living for."

Jordin was so caught off guard by his unabashed appraisal that she lost track of her thoughts for a moment.

The allure of his undeniable attraction to her came like the strain of a song remembered, an urge fanned to flame once more. She'd thought the Mortal passion Sovereigns had surrendered in the name of wisdom dead in her. And so it had been. But it burned in Immortal blood. In her blood—searing the insides of her veins, enflaming and terrifying her both.

"You wrongly assume I have any interest in whether you live," she said. "Let go of her hand."

Cain paid no mind to her challenge.

"Now."

Every eye in the room was on them.

"A prisoner commands the Rippers?" He made a deliberate show of releasing Kaya's hand, of stepping past her toward Jordin. "You tempt my appetite for strong women. Now I must know you more." He dipped his head and bowed. "Consider me at your service, madam."

In that moment Jordin became aware that she could either take further offense or play the hand before her. She was Immortal, was she not? So she would only be served by *being* Immortal, if for no other reason than the sake of her mission, no matter how distant it now felt.

She glanced over his shoulder at the table where the others lingered with expressionless interest. And then it struck her: every surface in Roland's sanctuary dripped sensual life, but the black eyes that stared back at her appeared as hard as the carved stone walls.

Only Cain, still waiting for her response, seemed to feed on any delight, and only because his lust was engaged.

"Then serve me," she said. "We've had a long journey and need food. Feed us."

His brow cocked, and he offered an approving smile. "And what is the name of the one who commands me?"

"That of a fighter who was killing Dark Bloods while you were still a Corpse."

"She grows ever more mysterious." He stepped to one side and swept one arm toward the long table. "Your food awaits."

Jordin walked with him toward the table, ignoring the eyes of those seated there, aware of her plain clothing cached in dust and dirt.

"And I want to get out of these city clothes as soon as possible. I assume you can accommodate both of us?"

"It would be my pleasure. I will see to dressing you myself. Preferably alone."

She took two more steps before stopping, suddenly aware that all eyes at the table had diverted to her left. She followed the direction of their gazes to one of the far corridors. There, a woman had entered the room.

She was dressed not in black but in deepest red, her gown trailing the stone floor behind her like a bloody spill. Her shoulders were not those of a fighter, but slender and bare, the long sleeves cut away to reveal white arms. She didn't acknowledge the others in the room—in fact, she seemed not to even notice them.

Beside her strolled a young, golden lion, looking about the room with casual interest, never once straying from her side.

As singular as the sight of the animal was, every eye in the chamber was fixed on the woman. Awareness of her had robbed the room of sound. Where an Immortal had been lounging, he straightened; where eating, jaws had stopped moving. The dancer stopped and backed into the shadows. The group that was congregated around the settee near the bottom of the stairs stood and parted before her.

She didn't acknowledge them as she passed. It was as though they didn't even exist.

She rose up the stairs on bare and silent feet, the gown trailing crimson behind her. The Immortals below didn't move.

The woman had risen halfway up the stairs when she stopped. As did the lion by her side.

Slowly, she turned her head to stare directly at Jordin. For several long seconds she fixed her with an unfathomable gaze, as if trying to remember why the sight of Jordin interested her.

Then she turned back, resumed her silent ascent of the stairs, and passed through one of the ways on the landing. Deeper into the Rippers' sanctuary.

For three beats, silence. And then the room returned to its former state. Cain pulled out one of the chairs at the table.

"Who was that?" Jordin said. Kaya was still staring up at the passage on the landing.

"Talia," Cain said. "Roland's queen." He gestured to the chairs.

A hundred questions ran through Jordin's mind. She'd known Roland's wife. This woman was not her.

Jordin slid into the chair, distantly aware of the intense focus the seated Immortals gave them both. Of Cain's eyes on her as he seated Kaya, stroking her arm. Of the cutlery placed before her and the plate overflowing with meat and crusty bread...the goblet reeking its sweetness beside it.

A woman came up to Cain, now seated across from them, and draped herself over his shoulders. He pulled her down into his lap, his goblet in one hand, the other on the woman...his eyes never once leaving Jordin.

Kaya ate in silence, too much, too ravenously, drinking too deeply, but Jordin hardly had the presence of mind to stop her.

She was struck with the certainty that she'd made a terrible mistake in coming. To what end? To save Rom. To kill Roland. To kill Feyn. To save Sovereigns from deadened emotions. To save Immortals if only for the sake of Jonathan's legacy, even if everything in her before had cried to kill them all.

Perhaps Mattius was right. Let his virus take them. But could she willingly let the Immortals all die? Wasn't Roland her Maker now?

What was wrong with her?

The image of the queen, Talia, drifted through her mind. The way she'd turned to stare. So silent, so otherworldly absorbed...so deceptively aware. She glanced up at a drip of wax from a dying taper in the great chandelier. It hissed on the wood of the great table. The entire lair dripped with seduction. Haunting beauty.

And danger.

She desperately wanted space to think, but the curling tendrils of a thickening fog had begun to obscure her mind. By the look of wonder on Kaya's face, she had begun to get lost in it too.

Her anxiety grew with the passing silence and she found herself deadening it with wine and praying that she be taken to Roland. She felt as if she might be falling into an abyss. As if those watching her had worked a spell to lure her into their grasp. But she was already in their grasp, if only by virtue of the very blood in her veins.

So lost was she in her own introspection that she didn't hear Rislon's approach. He touched her shoulder, and she jerked back, startled.

He glanced at her, then the others. Finally he nodded once.

"Roland will see you," he said. "In the morning." Then to Sephan, who lounged in a chair off to the side of Cain. "I'll be back in an hour. Keep them out of trouble."

CHAPTER TWELVE

THE TABLE had been set in the old hexagonal chamber. Tucked two stories beneath the Senate Hall, the chamber had once been a repository of sorts—of ancient artifacts like the weapons forgotten for a time by the world. Books, written for their sordid emotional journeys, goblets even, from a time when the ancient basilicas of Byzantium called the Maker by a far more arcane name: God.

They had been Saric's playthings. Feyn's brother had come here in the first days of his dark reawakening, drawn to the artifacts of Chaos after finding emotion through alchemy.

Feyn had stripped the room of its relics and moldy tapestries. But though the walls had been scrubbed and covered with fine Abyssinian linen, nothing could staunch the sweat of the stones, as though they harbored secrets too terrible for even the earth to bear.

Here, Order had been conceived. Here, its founder had been martyred by the first world Sovereign.

The table was set in the middle of the room, attended by two chairs. Two settings lay perfectly placed on its top; fruit, nuts, and thin slices of cold meats arranged on each of them.

She stepped to the large candelabra, leaned close enough to feel the heat of the nearest flame practically on her cheek, and inhaled deeply. Jasmine. A tribute of Asiana.

The heavy wooden door opened. A clank of iron chains. The shuffle of feet—one pair booted, the other near silent.

"Remove his chains," she said, leaning in toward the candelabra again as one does a fragrant bush. She could smell the offensive odor. Him.

"My liege—"

"Now."

The clink of a metal key, of the chains collected. She glanced over her shoulder and slowly turned.

Seth knelt beside Rom on the thick Abyssinian carpet she'd ordered brought down earlier. The head of the handsome Dark Blood was lowered. She was accustomed to the play of shadows along his chiseled cheek at that angle, among others. Beside him knelt Rom, head erect, eyes on her.

But of course. He'd never observed her station from the first night he'd broken into her chamber to recruit her for his desperate mission so many years ago. And in her waking years since, he'd never failed to push her toward his own purpose.

The time for that had come to an end. She was no longer the naïve young woman she had once been; she too could play at these games.

She slipped out of her brocade shoes and walked on silent feet past the table to stand before Rom.

His eyes were remarkable, not only for their vibrant color, but also for their lack of fear. She saw no gratitude in them for the saving of his eye, nor anger for his severed finger, now bandaged. He appeared sure. But there was something new. Was it arrogance? No. Something else.

"Please. Get up. We're past the time for that. We were a long time ago."

He leaned forward, hand on one knee, and rose without a sound, albeit stiffly. Seth, beside him, did not move. Did not so much as twitch a muscle. He would stay there all day if she let him. What a contrast, these two men!

"Seth, wait outside."

The Dark Blood did not glance upward so much as forward, along the carpet. She was both touched and irritated by his hesitation. She knew he didn't want to leave her alone with the Sovereign. Out of protectiveness, certainly. Out of jealousy, perhaps. But after a beat he rose, fixed his gaze meaningfully on Rom, and then stepped out, quietly closing the door.

Feyn had no doubt he would be standing there in that very posture, listening intently, ready to seize Rom by the throat if she but lifted her voice.

"Come, sit with me. You must be famished," she said, moving to the table and pulling out a chair. When was the last time she'd ever done that?

"Feyn—"

"Please."

Every other man she knew would have quickly sat.

"I didn't come to you for food."

"Then indulge me. I'm hungry."

He acquiesced with a slight dip of his head and gestured her to the seat instead.

She slipped into it. "That's better," she said with a smile, as he took the chair adjacent to her. But rather than eat, he turned toward her, elbows on his knees. Now she could see the signs of fatigue across his shoulders. In the straggle of his hair...the shadows beneath his eyes. She'd ordered them not to allow him sleep.

"I'll arrange a bath for you. Clean clothing. But for now, you must eat something. And as we do, you can tell me plainly what you've come for." She crossed one leg over the other, the long slit in her gown opening to her thigh.

His gaze dropped toward her lap.

She plucked a rare fresh strawberry from her plate, held it out toward him.

"I already told you what I've come for," he said. After a moment's hesitation, he took the strawberry.

"Ah, that's right. To make me Sovereign."

He bit into the strawberry, and she tilted her head, watching him. His chewing slowed and his eyes closed—few were accustomed to fresh fare of this quality. His gaunt frame spoke the truth: the Sovereigns were barely surviving. She wondered when he had last had anything fresh to eat.

She gave a soft chuckle. "Here," she said, moving the bowl toward him. "If you're going to make me Sovereign, you'll need your energy."

"I am not the one who makes Sovereigns. Jonathan is."

"His blood, you mean."

"Yes. But him as well."

"I wonder what possessed you to take the blood of a dead man into your veins. I've heard the stories, and my sources are reliable." She sat back and regarded him. Strawberries were her favorite normally, but her appetite was ruined by Rom's heavy odor.

He set the fruit down. "A vision," he said. "A dream. Jordin's, the girl who loved him."

"And now he's dead."

"Jonathan isn't dead."

"Is his body not in the grave?"

"Yes. But he lives."

"What a paradox. Explain it to me."

"I can't. I just know it to be true."

There was something in his eyes...

"You truly want me to be as you are, don't you?" she said with some wonder.

"Not as I am. As Jonathan meant you to be."

"A Sovereign, which I am. Not your dead blood kind of Sovereign...ruler. I was born to it. And yet here you are, once again asking me to embrace another life. Will you never tire of this game?"

"No." There it was, the fervor of a zealot in his eyes.

"What *did* Jonathan come to bring you, exactly?"

"Life."

"You say this over and over, and yet you live like a rat in hiding. You're half starved. You're hunted, not just by my own Dark Bloods, but by Roland's Immortals. Didn't he have the same blood as you once? And now you're at each other's throats? This is what you hoped for?"

The zeal left his eyes. "No."

"And so I ask you again: What has the blood brought you? Ease? Meaning?"

"I don't know the answers. I only know that this is what I am meant to be. And that this is where I'm meant to be now. Here, with you."

"And if I follow your way...what will I gain? Has this life even brought you peace?"

He stared at her, silent.

"No peace, then."

"Not yet."

"Not yet. Clearly. Look at you."

"Has yours? You own the world. Has it brought you peace?"

She gave a brittle laugh. "There's little peace for me. The humblest artisan sleeps better than I do." She tilted her head, studied her own hands. "You must remember something of that. You were a humble artisan once."

He gave a nod. "Yes. Once."

"No longer?"

He shifted his eyes and stared at a tapestry on the wall. "I have little time now."

"No. You're too busy trying to stay alive. Please, eat more. You're not hungry?"

He returned his eyes to her. "I can eat later."

Rom, the ever-focused one.

She picked up a strawberry, considered eating it, then set it on her plate. "Do you ever wonder if we might have been together, had things been different?"

He blinked, and again she was startled by the color of his eyes. She had to work to reconcile the grizzled man before her with the boy of fifteen years ago, but there— she saw him in flashes, in the turn of his lip.

His gaze slid to her hand.

"Perhaps."

"I demanded a poem from you once. Do you remember? That day, in the meadow. You were a poet then, so young. But clever already. You had tricked me, giving me the blood. And I'd come to life. You were the first thing I saw, and I was in love. Do you remember?"

"Yes," he whispered.

"'We rode together through the night, chasing love, chasing light...,'" she said softly, reciting his words.

He glanced up, eyes startled.

"'All has changed for you and I...'"

His lips parted, he had begun to voice the words before the sound even came out of his mouth. Now, his eyes locked on hers, he said quietly, "'You're a queen, and what am I? Let us live before we die.'"

The air seemed to still between them; the table, the food, forgotten.

"If only we could have had that moment forever," she said. "If we could have held it and forgotten the world."

He broke her gaze, his own falling to her simple silk gown. Amber and black threads woven together, so it shimmered both dark and light.

"I'm sorry," he said.

His words surprised her.

He glanced up. "I should have given you that life. I wanted to. I couldn't, I didn't have enough blood." As he said it, the man he was today fell away, and there he was, the impetuous twenty-four-year-old she'd met so many years ago.

"If I could, I'd have kept you from death—from returning to it. You'd have come with us. You'd never have had to give up your life. If I could have saved you then, I would have. But I didn't have enough blood."

It wasn't often that she was surprised. But now with his admission, and his apparent anguish over it, she found herself staring at him.

"I was preparing to come for you while you slept in stasis," he continued. "My face would have been the first thing you saw when you awakened. And Maker, how I prayed that you would love me again!"

She looked away.

"But then Saric found you first and converted you to Dark Blood. You don't know how many times I regretted it. What he did to you . . . it ate me alive."

"And yet," she said with forced lightness, "here you are again."

"Yes," he said, more evenly. "History's brought us here, to the place where I can bring you life, finally. Not my own, and not through trickery. You aren't lost to the Dark Blood. The ancient blood is still in your veins."

"And so you've come to save me at last."

"Jonathan's blood will."

Jonathan! Jonathan! Always Jonathan!

She drew in a slow breath through her nostrils. Willed it to remain even.

"Then...if what you say is true, give me a show of faith. Surely you owe me that."

"What do you want? I'm here of my own volition, knowing you could easily have me killed. Your alchemist would dismember me, given the opportunity, and I would let him. What more proof do you need?"

"Perhaps if you told me where the rest of your people are, I would see your kind as less than rebels in hiding."

He went still. "They don't know you as I do. They know you as the one who betrayed Jonathan."

"I gave my life for Jonathan."

"That was a different you."

"Yes. It was a different me," she said. "I'm Sovereign now. I gave my life for your cause once. Don't assume I am so different."

"I'm here, at your mercy. Isn't that enough to earn your trust?"

She nodded. "Perhaps. But don't you see, Rom? All is as Jonathan would have had it. He believed he was fulfilling something. He believed that he needed to die. If he didn't want me to rule as a Dark Blood, he wouldn't have made the way for me. But here I am. Perhaps this is the way it was always meant to be, and the way your Jonathan always wanted it. Ask yourself who has honored him better. You, who wished him on this throne, or me, whom he wished on it?"

He stared, at a loss.

"He made me Sovereign of this world. Now you subvert my authority by refusing my rule?"

He still made no reply.

She had accomplished enough for now—seen him soften and shift as far as he might in such a short time. Her argument had been carefully calculated, and his response was what she had hoped. But in the end, his heart, not her arguments, would be his downfall.

Rom still loved her.

She pitied him. Perhaps more, another reason to leave him now. She had no interest in being swayed by him.

"Help me and I will help you, Rom. I'm Sovereign, you see? I must know where my subjects live. I promise to think on what you've said; I trust you'll do the same. We will see each other again soon."

She rose and left the room, leaving him alone with his thoughts.

And his heart.

CHAPTER THIRTEEN

THE VOICE was a mere whisper, spoken from beyond, calling to Jordin in her dream like a distant memory that she couldn't quite recall. Like something on the wind, unseen and not quite heard. But more than the wind. Someone... it was someone...

The whisper died. A dense black fog settled into her mind.

No one.

Jordin opened her eyes, aware only that she was lost. Her heart was hollow, but she couldn't remember what might fill it. Deep might call to deep, but in that moment the deep felt only like absence.

She could feel the straw mat beneath her, surprisingly soft. Where was she? In a dark womb, carved from the rock. Not in Byzantium...

Roland's Lair.

Jordin's pulse surged, and she blinked as the events of the night filed into memory, pressing form and identity into her being. Capture by the four Immortals. Entering the lair. Cain's inviting eyes. The feast, too heavy with wine...

Cain's lover had abruptly taken him away, which had

come as a relief to Jordin, not only because she had no desire to be with him, but also because she could see the possessiveness in his lover's eyes.

Shortly after, Rislon had collected her from the table. He'd led her up the stairs, through a labyrinth of passages, to this room, where she'd closed her eyes and let the world fall away.

Jordin sat up and stared into the darkness around her. Was she alone? She could hear no breathing in the small space. Yes, she was alone. Strangely lost. And yet home.

She was Immortal, reborn into a state of belonging she had not felt in years. She couldn't at first remember why she'd been reborn, only that the conversion had taken her body quickly. Her mind had soon followed. Now would it consume her heart? In becoming Immortal she'd been grafted into a brood that felt like her own.

But more pricked her mind—a thorn of realization that made her cringe. She had become Immortal to save Rom.

Mattius. The virus.

Her deep sleep had momentarily stolen her memory, but now it came back with alarm.

She only had four days.

But she suddenly wasn't clear about how she would save Rom and kill Feyn. She was going to lead Roland where? Into the Citadel through a virtual maze of underground tunnels that she and Rom had once drawn out with the Keeper. Yes. But she couldn't quite recall the way through the labyrinth. Her mind was in a fugue state, clouded by her seroconversion.

Jordin rolled from the mat and pushed herself to her feet. She had to think! If she couldn't remember the passage, all would be lost.

How long had she slept?

Across the room she saw the faint outline of a heavy door in the darkness, set into the stone.

The handle refused to yield. They had locked her in.

She turned back, took in the shallow cave without need for light. Nothing but the single mat on the floor. The place was a prison cell.

Where was Kaya? Had Cain taken her after all?

The idea was at once natural and deeply offensive. Unpracticed in warding off the advances of men and blossoming with Immortal sensory passions, she would be easily wooed. But Kaya was Sovereign at her core.

With a simple faith even to surpass Jordin's.

The thought settled over her like a dead weight. She too was loyal to Jonathan. He had loved her, and she him, in ways that few would ever know. But that love had felt more foreign with each passing day. And today...

She was cut loose of her moorings, adrift in a sea of darkness. Sovereign. Immortal. And now she was forgetting why life as a Sovereign held any appeal.

Jonathan...

The sound of a key in the lock jerked her back into the present and she spun around. A moment later, amber light filled the frame as the door swung wide to the tunnel beyond. Rislon stood in the doorway.

He tossed her a bundle of clothing. "Get dressed."

"What time is it?"

"Midday."

So late! "Where's Kaya?"

"Hurry." Any friendliness or amusement he'd shown in the wasteland had evaporated. Here in the lair, unseen tension held them in thrall. "It's not wise to keep him waiting."

Him. Roland.

She stepped to one side and quickly stripped bare of her clothes, mindful of Rislon's watchful eye. The clothing consisted of nothing more than a short black gown that hung to mid-thigh and a golden tie—to hold it closed around the waist. No shoes.

But of course Roland would be more interested in inspecting a new slave than the absurd tale of how he might win a war—from a stranger who refused to give her name, no less.

That would change the moment he recognized her.

"This way." Rislon stepped aside so she'd have to walk ahead of him. The long tunnel was lit by a single torch. Water dripped somewhere behind them. The musky scent of wet earth filled her nostrils. No scent of Immortals. Did they live at night and sleep during the day?

"How many live here?" she asked

No response.

The tunnel intersected another.

"To the right," he said.

At the end of the passage was a door, which Rislon ushered her through.

She stopped, struck by the change. The larger hallway they'd entered was lit by six torches, three to each side. Unlike the arcane tunnel behind them, the stone here was covered ceiling to floor with tapestries and velvet hangings. Carpet runners, five feet wide, ran the entire length of the tunnel, ending at a majestic arched door lit by two candelabras, each holding a dozen white candles.

Jordin didn't need to be told that the prince was beyond that door.

Her predicament suddenly struck her as impossibly surreal. How many times in the last twenty-four hours had she left one world and entered another?

Jordin took a calming breath, pulse heavy as Rislon grasped the large iron handle and pushed the door wide. And then she stepped inside the large chamber and immediately felt the air still.

Lit by a dozen candelabras, the room was filled with haunting amber, revealing every detail to her expanded sight as clearly as in the light of day. Thick purple velvet draped the walls, accented by tapestries bearing images of wolves and hawks. Old chests bound with brass bands were stacked along the back wall. Silk carpets obscured every inch of the floor, laying two and even three thick in some places, their gilt tassels flung out like the ringed fingers of trampled hands. On a side table stood a jug of wine and a plate of rare fresh fruit.

She took all of this in at first glance in a way that only an Immortal could, with unrestrained sensory awareness. But it was Roland, the prince, who captivated her attention.

Four stone steps covered in burgundy carpet rose to a platform on which sat a great iron chair draped in a silver pelt. Wolf. He lounged more than sat in the chair, his right elbow propped on the arm, chin cupped in his palm. His legs were encased in black leather, booted to the knee. He wore no shirt. Dark tribal tattoos of the Nomads sprawled across his thick shoulders and halfway down his arms, made stark by the paleness of his skin.

His black hair hung devoid of braid or beads to pale shoulders strapped with the corded muscle of a warrior. Thick leather bands edged in gold wound around both wrists; three heavy chains joined at his sternum to carry a single large silver pendant embossed with a crescent moon that shone in the candlelight.

To a Corpse he would have been fearfully magnificent. But to Immortal eyes, he was nothing less than supreme. Maker and ruler. The giver and taker of Immortality.

He returned her rapt interest with mild boredom.

The woman who'd passed through the main chamber lounged on a low sofa nearby, her legs folded back to one side. With one hand she stroked the lion Jordin had seen last night, laying on the carpet just below her. Rings glinted on her hand, pale quartz the color of the sky. She was adorned all in white, the only one in Roland's Lair who seemed to wear anything other than black.

The lion lifted its head the moment Jordin stepped in, watching her with far keener interest than either Roland or his queen. Its dull gold collar glinted in the candlelight.

The only other person in the room was a servant, standing at the end of the side table, hands folded, her pale arms in sharp contrast to the simple black silk of her gown, so like Jordin's own. Behind her, a thick wooden door led ostensibly deeper into the lair.

"This is the one?" Roland said, chin in hand, dark nails as stark as his burgundy lips against that pale flesh.

Rislon bowed his head. "Yes, my prince."

"The woman with no name who claims I sent her on a mission I know nothing about?"

Jordin felt herself inexplicably drawn to the voice. To the man who'd once rescued her from destitution and trained her as a champion. Who'd chosen Immortality and by all appearances had come into his full power.

But there was also an air of discontent about him. He had the look of a man no longer interested in his own world, driven to conquer a more significant one.

The one Feyn controlled.

Access to Feyn was the only advantage Jordin held, and that advantage was a slivered hope at best.

"Do you not recognize the girl you once brought to your tribe?" she said. "I served alongside your best warriors once."

The words brought a wave of memory with them. Roland, her prince, as a newly made Mortal a decade ago, riding into camp, color high in his cheeks, the sky in his eyes. Dancing around the late-night fire, his braids wild down his back, a stallion of a prince among the other warriors. He had been the desire of every young Nomad girl. Roland, who happened upon her outside of camp one day in her late girlhood and asked if she was happy among his people. She had been flustered and flattered that he'd even remembered her name—what was she but an orphan girl he'd taken in as a castoff from a neighboring tribe? But then he'd noticed the sling in her hand, the pile of nearby stones, the tracks of frustrated tears on her face. He'd taught her how to fling them properly that day—no one else had thought an orphan worth the time. A year later, he set her first sword in her hand.

She'd adored him once. But staring at him now, she could not reconcile this brooding leader with that man. The prince she'd known was gone . . . and soon the Immortal he'd become would be as well.

He stared at her. Recognition came slowly, but when it did, his entire demeanor shifted.

He slowly lowered his arm and stood. For several beats he stared, face drawn, cautious.

"I remember a girl I once made one of my own—only to lay down her loyalty and become Sovereign," he said, eyes as hard as onyx set in gold.

"Now Immortal," she said. And then, before he could

voice judgment, she added, "It was either Immortality or death. My allegiance to the one we once both served runs deep, but I see no purpose in dying for him."

"And yet you come to me. The one who brings death to all Sovereigns."

"Do I look like a Sovereign to you? I'm surprised you would use that name to describe anyone but yourself. Or Feyn, who now holds that office."

He ran an appraising gaze down her body. Again, she felt like little more than a slave to be inspected for worthiness. But didn't he have the right? Roland wasn't only prince, but her prince now.

The thought should have repelled her. It did not.

A finger of fear traced her spine. He was Roland, the one she'd come to kill. Yet standing before him now, the very notion felt treasonous. Insane. She could no more kill him than kill herself.

And then it struck her: all of the Rippers had surely come to life through Roland's blood, not directly through Jonathan's blood as Roland himself had. And by extension, so had she now.

"Come closer," he said.

She took a stiff step toward the center of the room.

"Closer."

She hesitated and then took three more steps, forced now to look up at his face.

Roland descended the steps with muscular fluidity. She'd known Roland in his former state as an exceedingly ruthless warrior, able to best ten men in hand-to-hand battle, perfect in his use of Mortal sense. She harbored no illusions that he was now any less ruthless or skilled. On the contrary, those arms and hands that moved with such deceptive ease would be more deadly than ever. If he drew his sword now, she might not even realize that he'd struck her until his blade was halfway through her neck.

The thought sent her blood racing, but not out of fear.

"If I didn't know your kind was so opposed to killing, I might think you were here in a vain attempt to assassinate me," he said.

"As you see for yourself, I am Immortal. I have no compunction against killing Dark Bloods or Sovereigns, who have no hope for redemption. But I do not kill my own kind."

He crossed his arms and paced a step to his right. Whatever boredom had possessed him earlier was gone. The queen, Talia, watched Jordin through the veil of her elsewhere gaze, idly stroking the fur of her young lion.

"Why have you come, beautiful girl?" she said in a soft tone that sounded more like a purr than a voice. "If not to make an attempt on the life of my prince?"

"To give him the keys to the kingdom he desires," Jordin said.

"And what are these keys?"

Jordin looked Roland squarely in the eye. "I can show him a way into the Citadel where he can take Feyn's head from her shoulders and the ring from her hand."

He smiled slightly. It was not warm. "Such a bold claim."

"And yet you know that I, the one you yourself trained, have never lied to her prince."

"If you knew a way to approach Feyn, you would have used it already."

"Sovereigns do not possess the same skills as Immortals. Nor do they have the numbers. They are three dozen elderly and young, hiding, hungry, and hunted by both

Feyn and your Rippers. Sovereign blood will soon be extinct."

"And Rom"—he said it as one voices a name not spoken in years—"does he know of your plot to infiltrate my lair?"

"He's being held captive in Feyn's dungeons. But yes, he knows it's the only way."

Roland lifted a brow.

He studied her for a moment and then circled around her, his gaze traveling over her again. The hardness was gone from his face, replaced by curiosity. She'd offered him direct access to his only true enemy, but he had no reason to take her seriously.

"So my enemy comes to give me Feyn's head on a platter," he said. "Knowing full well that if I take the throne there will be nothing to stop me from exterminating the Sovereigns. I can't imagine Rom would like that." His fingers touched her hair as he crossed behind her. "My queen is right. You're more beautiful than I remember."

"You don't know Rom," she said, her throat suddenly dry. "He speaks only well of you."

"Of course he does. He's at my mercy." He rounded her, dark eyes glittering with the hardness of one who knows no fear. "As are you."

"As am I," she said softly.

"I have your unquestioned loyalty, is that it? We aren't Dark Bloods, you know. Immortals are fully capable of treachery."

"I've seen nothing but loyalty here," she said.

"I've earned their loyalty. And they've earned mine. But you have not."

Her heart was hammering against her ribs. Surely he could hear it. "How would you have me prove it?"

"You will tell me the way to Feyn now."

Jordin hesitated, knowing that the truth could end her life. Now. This moment.

"I can't," she said at last.

"No? Why not."

"Because I can't remember."

"You can't remember." He gave a wry smirk. "Did you hear that, my queen? She says she can't remember what she came to tell us."

His face darkened, the smirk gone.

"Don't toy with me."

Jordin blinked, surprised by the hardness of his tone. The absolute bitterness in it. And she saw that beneath his veneer of power and passion, Roland lived in misery. He was surrounded in luxury, by beauty, and for as much as he possessed, he could not enjoy the Immortality he clung to with iron claws. For all the apparent loyalty of his Rippers, could he believe the love of a single one?

In that moment she knew that he held no advantage. The man before her had no more found abundant life since Jonathan's passing than she.

"It bothers you, doesn't it?" Jordin said. "Having so much life and still feeling so powerless to grasp what you seek."

The muscles along his jaw bunched. "I have more life than you can possibly imagine."

"What is life if you can't find peace in it?"

His eyes narrowed. "Only Corpses rest in peace."

"So we once said. It must be a terrible thing to live a thousand years in misery. Maybe Immortality is better called Hades."

Roland held her in a dark stare, and she considered the possibility that he might fly into a rage and rip her to shreds.

"You have everything this world has to offer," she said. "Everything except the throne. And when you have that, you'll still be as miserable because in reality you seek true life and peace. Power won't give you either."

"The kind of peace you've known?" he demanded. "Cowering in hiding while those of your kind are picked off one by one? Is this Jonathan's rule of love in your hearts?"

Jordin didn't know what to say. His words rang as true as her own. So she said the only thing she knew: the truth.

"Sovereigns are as miserable as you seem to be."

Her confession seemed to cut him off at the knees. She continued quickly. "Which is why I'm here. We once shared food at the same fire and fought a common enemy to save the life Jonathan brought to us. I've done everything I believed was right, and what has it brought me? A wretched existence, surrounded by death. I have nothing more to lose. So now I come to the same prince who once saved me from the wasteland."

"To ask for something in exchange for a promise you can't deliver."

"But I can deliver."

"How?"

"By becoming Sovereign again."

Maker, she hoped it was true.

Just then the door behind her opened and she heard the footfall of two entering the chamber. She didn't turn. Her eyes remained fixed on Roland.

His eyes flicked over her shoulder. He turned toward the side table, calmly took the goblet from the servant, who had apparently already made sure it was full, and took a long drink with his back still turned to them. The two arrivals walked toward him at the table with only an offhanded glance her way.

"No sign," one of them said—a woman. Jordin knew that voice, tried to place it...

"Whoever they were, they must have escaped into the city," the woman continued. A warrior in the customary black of the Ripper, there was something about the posture of her stance, the ease with which she carried herself that was both more regal and casual around Roland than the others.

The man beside her was older, with long gray hair and a beard as white as his skin, dressed in a black robe rather than battle dress. Someone with authority. When he spoke, Jordin recognized his gravelly voice immediately.

"If the heretics have taken to open attacks on us, we must eliminate them. We don't need this thorn in our side. We should have cut them all down a year ago when we had them in our grasp."

This was Seriph, the council member Jordin had once served under when they had all been Mortal.

"Seriph has a point, my prince," the woman said. "I would send Cain and his twenty to hunt them down. One by one if we must."

"That won't be necessary, sister," Roland said. "The Sovereigns are no longer a problem."

Jordin started. Michael. Roland's sister.

"As you said when you demanded we spare some last time," Michael said. "And now they've killed Jalarod. His sister is furious with grief."

Jalarod. The name of the Immortal Jordin had killed. A moment's horror passed through her—perhaps because she now shared Jalarod's blood. The faceless Immortal had a name and family. They mourned their dead as Dark Bloods could not.

They'd always wondered why the Immortals had pulled back before killing them all. Now Jordin knew: Roland had ordered they spare some. He wanted them crippled and immobilized, not vanquished.

Roland turned and offered Jordin a halfhearted gaze. "I already have Jalarod's killer. She's one of us." There was no mistaking the irony in his words.

Michael and Seriph turned as one to stare at her. Michael went very still as recognition filled her face.

"Jordin."

"What's the meaning of this?" Seriph demanded.

"Jordin has defected," Roland said. "And, being the warrior I taught her to be, she did what was necessary to acquire our blood. Unfortunate, but rather ingenious. More important, she can lead us to the others. Her loyalty now rests with me. Isn't that right?"

She'd always known that Roland might test her in this way. And so she would play her only trump now and let fate take its course.

"It's good to see you, Michael. I can't say the same for you, Seriph. You were always the most mistrusting of us. I'm amazed Roland hasn't put you down by now."

A hint of a smile crossed Roland's mouth. It was all she cared to see.

Jordin spoke quickly, taking advantage of the moment. "You know Sovereigns don't take the lives of Immortals, so you have to ask yourself why I felt obligated to kill one of you. Simply to become Immortal?" She lifted a hand and watched her fingers move. "I admit, I like the skin. Feeling and seeing the way you do shows me how much I've missed." She lowered her hand.

"But what none of you know is that unless I succeed in my mission, you'll all be dead in four days. The survival of every Immortal is entirely in my hands. Bow to your petty pride, Seriph. Kill me now and take the life of every living Immortal with it."

She let the statement stand.

"You believe you can deceive us with this ridiculous threat?" Seriph hissed, his face now closer to the color of his lips than his beard.

Roland lifted a hand to silence him. He studied her for several long moments. For perhaps the first time he found truth in her face. And how could he not? She was speaking it without reservation.

"Go on."

"One of our alchemists has created an airborne virus that will swiftly infect the entire world population. He will release it unless I kill Feyn and return Rom to him in four days' time." She paced, feeling at last the liberty to move, to breathe. She, not Roland, was now in command of the room.

"It will bypass all Corpses and kill both Dark Bloods and Immortals within days. So you see... I had good reason to do whatever was necessary to place myself here. If you weren't so eager to cut down every Sovereign that crosses your path, I could've come in peace. Jalarod's death is the result of your hatred, not my own."

"And Sovereigns?" Roland said.

"They will survive," Jordin said. "After all, it was one of our alchemists who created the virus. It may mute Sovereign emotion. But they will survive."

"Which is why you would become Sovereign again," he said darkly. "Better to exist in peace, stripped of the emotion that drives us all to our insanity than to be fully alive. Isn't that what Megas once said before he turned the world into a graveyard filled with walking Corpses? And so history comes full circle."

Seriph pointed a crooked, accusing finger at her. "Heresy! This is what drinking Jonathan's dead blood has brought to our door. Heresy and death."

For an instant, his words struck her as nothing but true. The very notion of muting any aspect of life seemed profane. Giving up Immortality itself seemed like madness. Who would forsake the gift of expanded life as she felt it now?

And yet, Immortals were no less miserable than Sovereigns. So then where was Jonathan's abundant life?

"Why would you return to Sovereign blood?" Michael asked. "You've only just regained full life."

"Because it's the only way I can lead you to Feyn."

"What is this?"

"She claims that she can't remember what she came to tell us," Roland said, disbelief etched on his face once more. "Evidently, if she becomes Sovereign, she'll remember."

"More lies," Seriph scoffed.

Was she lying—even to herself? Her mind was being pulled back into an abyss of forgetfulness, hardly remembering why she *should* become Sovereign again. But that was the whole point, wasn't it? She had to become Sovereign again, and soon, before she was hopelessly lost.

And she had to give them more or she'd never have the chance of finding her way back.

"You have to ask yourself why I'm here to warn you. What else would I have to gain by coming to you? I needed you to hear me, so I became Immortal. Now I need to lead you, and for that, I have to become Sovereign." She was groping in the darkness now.

"Sovereignty might not gift me with the expanded senses you know so well, but there's more than simple memory at stake. As Sovereigns, we know more. Which is probably why I can't remember the way into the Citadel now. These heightened senses seem to rob the mind of other capacities."

"You think us stupid?" Michael said with an incredulous laugh.

"No. But Sovereigns have a different kind of sight. We can sometimes see glimpses of the future. It could be of great value on a mission to kill Feyn."

The gift had never been predictable, and claiming it might only set up an expectation that would later damage her credibility—or get them all killed—but she needed every means to persuade them now.

She had to become Sovereign again, or all would be lost. The Immortals would all die, and she along with them.

"More insanity," Seriph said with a deep frown. "If such a gift were remotely valuable, they would have used it to stay alive. She's leading us into foul play."

"Everything I've told you is true," Jordin said.

Roland was watching her carefully.

"Then I'll give you the opportunity to show me how true it is," he said, crossing to the steps that rose to his throne. He ascended, calmly took his seat, and leaned forward, elbows on the arms of the chair.

"Tell me where the rest of the Sovereigns are hiding. Prove your loyalty, and I'll allow you to become Sovereign. Refuse and you will die with us, assuming there's any truth to your claim."

She hadn't anticipated the ultimatum. Hearing it now, Jordin felt her blood run cold. Revealing the location of the Sanctuary to Roland's Immortals was as good as sentencing the Sovereigns to death.

"Or have you forgotten that as well?"

"I'm loyal, my prince. But—but my final loyalty rests with Jonathan."

"Jonathan is dead."

"He lives in the blood of Sovereigns!"

"Who are miserable and demonstrate far lesser life than Jonathan ever did. If you refuse and this virus of yours actually exists, then we all die, including you. Feyn will be dead. If Feyn turns Rom to Dark Blood, which she undoubtedly will, he too will die. And then what is left? A handful of heretics who call themselves Sovereign, perpetuating their own kind of misery."

Jordin felt herself spiraling toward a full-fledged panic.

"If I tell you, you'll only kill me and slaughter them all! Mattius has taken the necessary precautions—he'll release the virus before you can stop him."

"I won't slaughter them all. Not now."

"And me?"

His lips twisted into a menacing grin. "Your fate will be tied to mine. It's the only choice I'm giving you."

Jordin stood still, appearing calm, she hoped, but her mind screamed treachery and despondency, pushed to such a terrible choice.

The only choice, and yet hardly a choice at all.

"I need some time," she said.

"Of which you claim we have none." He paused, studying her. "You have until the sun goes down."

"I may not need that much time."

"Are you the keeper of time in my world?" He waited

only a moment. "No, I thought not." His eyes lifted to Rislon. "Take her back to her cell. Leave her in darkness."

"Yes, my prince."

His eyes were back on Jordin.

"And bring me the other one."

CHAPTER FOURTEEN

STRINGED MUSIC filled the Sovereign office. Tense with poignant longing, the concerto was a study in Chaos and genius, as ancient as the old human emotions that had once ruined the world. Her father, once-Sovereign, would have condemned any who possessed or listened to such music. Her half brother had brought it to his fortress for his personal enjoyment. She now listened to nothing else—the staid music of Corpse composers felt rote and dead by comparison.

Because they *were* dead.

She'd donned the amber-and-onyx earrings. Fifteen faceted stones hung from each ear, set in gold, shimmering like dark fire nearly to her shoulders, framed by the dark fall of her hair. The velvet gown was her customary black, the sleeves glovelike past her wrists, ending in a tapered point over her fingers. It pooled on the floor behind her, an inky spill shot through with gold beading, the hem edged in gilt thread from the ancient Indus Valley.

For the first time in years, she stood before the great window, not looking out but at her own reflection.

Am I beautiful?

She'd never cared because it had never mattered. Beauty could not win her more than she already had: the loyalty of the world, the tribute of the continental treasuries, the unending devotion of the population to the Maker's hand on earth.

It no longer mattered to them that she'd disbanded the senate and abandoned the Book of Orders along with her weekly visits to the basilica. The Book, basilica…they were the undergirding of lives that required structure—an unbending roadmap to Bliss, or at least the hope of it.

Feyn knew better than to hope for the next life. No one knew what would become of one's soul after this existence. There were no guarantees even for the most devout. They lived in fear until their dying breath, and what had it ever gained them but the misery of uncertainty?

She'd seen things she couldn't explain—most recently six years ago, at the hand of Jonathan himself when he'd darkened her eyes and revealed her soul. But what had come of his little lesson?

Nothing.

It saddened her a little. She'd found herself wishing, almost, that there was something more to him than the strangeness of his blood and the mutation it brought. The death in his blood had only returned Rom and his kind to a lesser experience of life, and still they claimed to be superior. A delusion as dangerous as it was fascinating.

She tilted her head. Her former maid, Nuala, had never adapted to the heavier cosmetics Feyn preferred of late. Unfortunately, the maid had experienced an accident during her seroconversion, an error that resulted in an infection grievous enough to send her to the Authority of Passing. Feyn had held a quiet private dinner alone in her chamber in her honor. Caviar, if she remembered correctly.

She smoothed the edge of the dark liner around her eyes with the tip of a finger. She attended to these matters herself now. Far preferable to allowing the direct gaze of another, which she only found offensive. In any case, beauty had become far less interesting to her.

Until now.

How strange, to not feel like a caricature of oneself. To actually feel *seen*.

She studied the splay of dark veins up her neck and onto her cheek. The smudge of her lashes, the dark stain of her lips.

Am I beautiful?

Beautiful enough to win the heart and trust of a man with the will to deny her? A man and a heretic at odds with all that she was?

For the first time in years, she had an opponent worthy of interest in close enough range to engage. The first personal challenge she'd faced in years. She would relish the day that she played a similar game with Roland, but that would be a far deadlier game with much higher stakes.

A knock at the door.

"Enter."

The servant came in with a cart, knelt beside it as the aromas of roasted meat, onions, and exotic mushrooms filled the chamber.

"My liege. Where would you like—?"

"On the table."

Feyn allowed her gaze to travel down her neck to the broad neckline of her dress. Was one beautiful if she was called so by those afraid of her? Did they come, eventually, to believe it, if they hadn't before?

The servant was still finishing when another knock sounded at the chamber door.

She turned away from the dark window. "Get the door," she said to the servant, who hurried to the door and slowly drew its great bulk wide.

Feyn folded her hands.

Kneeling on the threshold were two familiar forms. Seth, with his godlike stature, and the figure of the man she'd known far, far longer.

She strode forward past the servant and stopped before Rom.

He was dressed in a simple gray tunic and trousers, wearing a pair of fine boots that were no doubt more expensive than any he'd ever worn. His hair was still damp, neatly tied at his nape. And as always, he was looking directly at her.

Why the stirring within her?

She smiled and reached out a hand.

"Come."

He rose, and Feyn drew him toward the table. "Thank you, Seth."

From the corner of her eye, she saw his brief hesitation before he rose and pulled the door shut. For an instant, she felt as much distaste for Seth, the creature of her own making, as she felt renewed intrigue for the man beside her. The servant finished, and Feyn waved her away, then turned to Rom, who'd lifted his head, listening in wonder.

"Ah, the music," she said. "Do you like it?"

"It's..." For a moment he looked like the impulsive young man she'd once known, eyes wandering as if to see the music in physical form. "It's beautiful."

She smiled. "Still the artist at heart."

"Even as a Corpse, I sensed that the music I wrote was the palest shadow of something more." The last word fell to a whisper.

"The dead, as you call them, cannot produce such fruit."

"No." His attention returned to her.

"Will you join me?" She stepped toward the table, the chaise situated near it. "I've requested venison. You probably haven't had much of it these last years."

He looked at the low table on which the servant had set the food. Feyn walked around the end of the chaise before it and sat down, then slid a little farther to make room for him.

"In another life, you might have come to the Citadel with me that day. We would have dined like this for the rest of our lives."

"I never took you for the sentimental kind," he said, taking a seat beside her.

"Of these last fifteen years, we've spent only a handful of days together. How strange you think that. And yet it's true."

"Perhaps because, in my mind's eye, I've spent many days with you," he said.

"Oh? How many?"

He hesitated and said only, "Many."

She was quiet for a moment.

"You loved me once, I think," she said. She lifted the heavy knife and a three-pronged fork and began to carve the venison. It fell away from the knife, tender to the bone. "I think that's the reason for this mission of yours."

He said nothing as she laid a large portion of meat on his plate, to which she added steaming roasted vegetables and mushrooms dripping with butter and their own juices. She tore off a piece of bread from the loaf swaddled in the middle of the table and laid it along the edge of his plate, and then glanced at him sidelong.

"Surely, it's not *all* about Jonathan."

"No," he said quietly, as she laid a napkin in his lap.

"I've thought about what you said," she said, serving herself. "And I want to know something."

"Of course."

"You came to me to save me. Why now?"

He was silent a moment. "Because soon it may be too late."

"Wasn't it too late the day Saric resurrected me with his blood?"

"No, I don't believe so. And I don't believe it is now."

"Your blood kills Dark Bloods. But you believe that, because I took the ancient blood fifteen years ago, I would live."

"I'm staking my life on it, coming here."

She lifted her fork and glanced at him. "Why does it matter so much to you?"

He took a bite of venison, and though she knew it had to be the best meat he'd had in a very long time, he seemed too distracted to notice its flavor.

He swallowed the first bite. "Because I've never believed you were meant to be what you are."

"Jonathan clearly did."

"Sovereign, perhaps. But not this. Not a Dark Blood."

"A bit self-righteous, isn't that? Are you the Maker, to decide?"

"No. But I know what my heart's always told me."

"Why? We are so similar in so many ways. We feel. We have desire. We live a life fuller than that of any common citizen. But you don't think we're similar at all, do you? And because you believe one thing, so should everyone else."

"I know it must seem that way to you. If I were in your position now, I might think the same. I just know, Feyn."

"And so in turning me, you hope to turn the world."

"I only know that right now, I'm here for you. After that…" He gave a faint shake of his head and looked at her. "I don't know."

"Not the best laid plan, if you mean to bring the world to Jonathan's knees," she said with a quiet smile.

"My plans have amounted to nothing. All that I thought I knew…I was wrong. But in this moment, I know this: I came here to save you. And with the hope, too, of saving my people and yes, Jonathan's legacy."

She'd left him in the hexagonal chamber in a more pliable state than this. He seemed to have recovered some of his former resolve. She shouldn't have waited the day.

"I'm nothing if not a woman of logic. You know I can't afford to allow your people to undermine the loyalty of my subjects."

"I know."

They ate in silence for a minute.

"You're handsome still," she said quietly. And he was, in his rugged way. More so for the hardship etched on his face and in the gray streaking back from his temples. Something about it spoke devotion. It was zealotry, of course, but what was zeal if not fanatic devotion? Seth and any one of her Dark Bloods would die for her, lose an arm, allow their skin to be flayed from their bodies for her. Because they had no choice.

But here was a man who had chosen his way and not wavered from it, no matter how misguided and seditious that way was. That, at least, she could admire.

She set down her fork and leaned into the back of the chaise.

"I'm still waiting, Rom."

"For what?"

"For your grand persuasion. For your clever trick. For your angle on how you will convince me, seduce me, guilt or argue me into your way of thinking. It's what you've always done, isn't it?"

He quietly laid down his fork and knife and turned to her.

"I know only that I love you." He said it gently, and though she waited a beat, he added nothing else.

"And so this is love," she said. "That you want me to be as you are?"

"No. This is love: that my life means nothing to me beside yours."

"And you would choose my life over that of your people."

"No. Because my life is also nothing to me beside theirs."

"Ah. And so you won't tell me where they are, even for their own sakes."

He glanced down and, after a moment, slid the fingers of his good hand through hers. "For their sakes, I can't."

She tilted her head against the back of the chaise. The odor of him was thick in her nostrils, threatening to stifle her every breath. Was he as conscious of her lotus perfume, wafting from the warm pulse of her throat?

"Let me put them under my protection, Rom. They'll live in better conditions and I'll know they mean no threat. Containing them is all I care about. They can live out their days, and I won't care whose blood is in their veins as long as they convert no others. And you will live here, with me, if you choose."

"As much as I wish I could, I can't."

"Which? Let me protect your people or live with me?"

"Jonathan's blood is far more important than you or I. I can't allow it to die out."

She felt her eyes narrow slightly. "I could make you."

"You could only try."

She toyed with his fingers, so rough between hers. "I could turn you Dark Blood. As one of my kind, made by me, you would desire only what I wished. Would it be so very bad to prefer my wishes over your own if you truly love me?"

"When I said I came knowing you could kill me, I knew that included chasing the life from my veins by turning me."

Talking in such calm tones, his hand in hers...the moment was more surreal than any she could remember. But her frustration was building. If he saw it, the game would be over.

"I'd hoped you would tell me of your own choosing."

"I can't. I'm sorry."

Was he so thickheaded? She let go of his hand, afraid he would sense her agitation.

"You would rather I turn you than offer what I ask for in exchange for preference? I have power over whether your people live or die—make no mistake, it will come to that. Don't let it. I have wealth. Comfort. Emotion! I'm not dead. I am no Corpse."

He studied her eyes for a long moment, then spoke in a gentle tone. "No, you're not. But you aren't Dark Blood either. Not entirely. It's your only hope of surviving. The rest of your Dark Bloods have no hope. Please, Feyn, I beg you. You trusted me once. The only way you can live is by becoming who Jonathan wants you to be."

She gave a soft, incredulous laugh.

"Jonathan. Everything is about Jonathan. Does he serve you in his living death as attentively as you have served him all these years? He left you, Rom. He's gone! You say he isn't, but where is he? You've given your life already—not to me, but to him. And what do you have for it? Life, you say. Are you certain? So you're not a Corpse. But neither are you much more. You gave up Immortality. Your people are dwindling to nothing. You'll have wasted your life...for what?"

Feyn could no longer mask the frustration in her voice. She got up off the sofa, stepped away from the table, and turned back.

"You're being obtuse. The fact is, you need *saving* just as much as you believe I do. You've lost yourself, Rom. You might have spared yourself all of this and stayed in your rat hole. At least then your people might have lived longer. But now you force my hand. You have as good as killed your own people."

He leveled his gaze at her, but it was concern, not fear, that filled his eyes.

"You're wrong, Feyn. It's Dark Bloods, not Sovereigns, who will die."

"Yes, yes, of course. Even though you claim we are dead already. I've heard it a thousand times."

"Not this, you haven't. I'm here to save you, as I've said. There's an alchemist among us who's made a desperate bid to save all Sovereigns."

"Please, spare me the melodrama."

Rom came off the sofa and stood before her, eye to eye. "He's successfully created a virus that will kill every Dark Blood who breathes in a matter of days. Your lover, the Dark Blood Seth, is as good as dead. As are you. I hoped to persuade you without threat, but we're running out of time."

She felt the heat leave her fingertips and then drain from her face.

"I don't believe you. It's a trick. Another of your manipulations."

"What reason do I have to lie to you? Why would I risk leaving my people leaderless?"

"And if there is a virus, will it not also kill the Corpses? The Immortals? You?"

"It will kill the Immortals. It may affect some Corpses, but few of them. It may affect our emotions as well, but no, it won't kill us."

She felt laughter welling up in her throat. It bubbled up and spilled out in a melodic laugh. But she felt only fear, not humor.

"You think I would believe such a desperate lie? What irony. The world would be returned to the rule of Corpses, and Sovereigns without full emotion would be no better than them. Everything you've given your life for would come to nothing!"

"Yes. I realize it." He was speaking with urgency now, and she knew that he believed every word he was speaking. "My people will assume you've already turned me Dark Blood, as subject to death as you if they release the virus. It was my best move in keeping them at bay. I'm fully committed to keeping Jonathan's blood pure."

She paced away, her mind raging like a storm. Rom had bested her. And this time without mercy, if what he said was true.

And it was, wasn't it? Rom didn't know how to lie.

Feyn spun back. "You do realize that Dark Blood might kill you. It's never been done with a Sovereign. Corban's undecided on the outcome. And yet if I do and you survive . . . you say this virus will kill you anyway. So you're dead either way. This was your great play?"

"If you took my blood, we would both be safe and Mattius wouldn't release the virus."

"Are you such a fool? I would never take your dead

blood and live in misery as you do! The only way to rid
the world of this threat is to crush this virus. Now! Before
it's released. Don't you see?"

"If you attack, he'll release the virus."

"That's a chance I will have to take. You have to
help me."

"I'm trying!" he thundered.

"Tell me where he is!"

He stared at her, jaw set. "I can't."

She stared at him for a long moment.

"Then you force my hand."

Her hands were trembling, but she no longer cared.
With quick strides, she crossed to the great doors of the
office and pulled them open. Seth stood before her, hands
folded, and lifted his head.

"Take him to the laboratory. Tell Corban. We turn him
tonight."

CHAPTER FIFTEEN

RISLON HAD taken Jordin back to her cell and, despite her plea to be heard the moment she'd reached a decision, had unceremoniously shut and locked the door, leaving her in near darkness.

"We don't have time for this!" she cried through the door.

His receding footfall was his only response.

Roland's play strung through her mind. She'd asked for time and he'd granted it, but only on his terms, knowing that forcing her to stew while the hours ticked away would keep her firmly in a position of lesser power.

Meanwhile, he would ply Kaya with the hopes of learning the Sanctuary's location. He would fail—surely Kaya didn't know the city well enough to give up the precise location. And even if she was able to give Roland enough detail, he would wait until dark to utilize the advantage of Immortal sight.

Kaya had only been out of the Sanctuary once, following Jordin down unfamiliar streets. There were many ruins similar to the one under which the remaining Sovereigns were cloistered. With so little time before the release of the virus, Roland would want to be sure of his destination, assuming he believed Jordin's warning. Strangely, he hadn't seemed too concerned one way or the other.

He would be soon enough.

According to Rislon, she'd wakened at midday. Nightfall must be at least six hours away, perhaps as many as eight. Four days was about to become three. She was running out of time!

She'd paced in the dark cell for what felt like an eternity, rehashing her predicament, pulled apart by the impossible dichotomy warring in her mind. She had two masters now: Roland, her prince—and by extension her maker—seated in unquestioned power, brimming with the same life that flowed through her veins.

And who was the other master? She could no longer easily identify her bond with Jonathan. A distant memory… a voice calling to her in dreams from the beyond. Or was her master Rom, to whom she'd pledged her loyalty? Or perhaps her own consciousness, whispering in the deepest caverns of her mind?

She was losing herself, but somewhere beyond her Immortal thoughts and emotions she had to believe that she was still Sovereign.

But what was Sovereignty except misery? What power or wholeness had she found after the initial euphoria of rebirth had faded?

And so here was the truth: the ways of both masters were bound up in misery and suffering. At this rate, it might be better to find death and take her chances on whatever waited beyond. But Jonathan insisted that his kingdom was of this earth, here and now among them all. Then where was it?

Her thoughts swirled in a gray fog. This much she

knew: the fate of the world rested with her choices now, and not one of them seemed to lend itself to an outcome short of doom.

If she refused to tell the prince where the Sovereigns were hiding, she would remain Immortal, and any hope of rescuing Rom would be lost. Assuming her dead, Mattius would release the virus. She would die along with all Dark Bloods and Immortals, leaving every surviving Sovereign stripped of their full existence and under the thumb of Mattius.

If she gave Roland misinformation to buy herself time, he would quickly learn of her betrayal and never trust her again. Without his trust, she would fail on all fronts.

If she told him the Sanctuary's location, he would send Cain with his Rippers and kill or take captive every living Sovereign left. Even if she successfully led Roland on a mission to rescue Rom and kill Feyn, the prince would still be in a position to kill them all and leave no trace of Sovereign blood to survive the virus. If she tried to move the Sovereigns to a new hideout, he would track her movements and find them—not that there was anywhere to take them; the Sovereigns had long run out of places to hide in the city.

The hopelessness pressing on her mind felt no more movable than the tons of rock above her tiny, hollow cave. She could see no way out, no light, no choice that seemed capable of delivering them all from certain death. History was bound to repeat itself, and she was powerless to stop it.

The cave's cool air dried the sweat from her brow as quickly as it broke onto her skin, offering no relief from the furnace in her mind. Her hands were trembling as she paced. And then her thoughts began to fail her utterly.

She would have to tell Roland whatever she knew, as soon as she knew it. Tell him and trust him. There was no other choice.

She sank to the mat and settled on her back, arms clasped over her chest, staring up into the darkness. Tears filled her eyes and streaked down her temples, wetting her hair.

"Jonathan..."

Her whisper sounded impossibly hollow and distant here, deep beneath the surface of the canyon lands.

"Jonathan, why have you left me? I beg you. Please... you left me once. Find me. Save me."

It was her last willful thought.

She fell loose from her thoughts as though she had fallen through a fissure in the floor of the cave. Silence quieted her, leaving only darkness... and peace.

She lay severed from time. Breathing. At rest. There was nothing more than darkness and the sound of her breath.

She didn't know when she became aware of the faint sound, only that it was there just beyond her mind: a faint hum that sounded as if it had been there all along, suppressed and silenced by her incessant mind until now.

No words, only a long, soft tone. The voice of a child, perhaps, that gradually changed from a hum to a tone, a word sung through parted lips. The voice of a boy calling in the wilderness. Beckoning her. A perfect strain of haunting notes from a single throat that flowed directly into her nerves.

The darkness began to part. Or was it her mind itself giving way to the soft gray of light? She could actually see it, as though a way had quietly opened—a way that had been clouded until now.

Or was it a dream?

The boy's voice was joined by a chorus of strings, so faint at first she wasn't sure she heard them. They were there and not there—had been there, perhaps, all along.

Beautiful. So beautiful. Here, there was no choice to be made. No anxiety, no world to save. Here there was salvation already, fully realized and riding the strains of music that seemed to have existed since the beginning of the world.

Just when she thought she might be swept away by the sound, the child stopped singing, as if suddenly aware he'd been discovered. The strings went silent. But the peace remained, suspended somewhere beyond thought.

Lead him, Jordin.

She caught her breath. Jonathan's voice. As a man or a child, she wasn't sure, but it was his voice; she would have known it anywhere.

Death is not the end.

And then the presence of that voice was gone, and she knew that she was once again alone.

Her eyes snapped wide. She was awake, lying on her back, hands still clasped over her chest.

And breathing hard.

"Jonathan?"

Her voice echoed softly in the cave. She sat up and stared into the darkness.

"Jonathan?"

The door suddenly swung open, flooding the room with light. For the second time that same day, Rislon stood in the door frame.

"The prince asks for your decision," he said.

She blinked. "It's night?"

"If it wasn't, he wouldn't be asking."

Jordin's mind spun, searching for an answer to the questions that had flogged her. But there was no real choice to be made now. She already knew what to do.

"Tell my prince that if he allows me to become Sovereign, I will lead him to our Sanctuary myself. My life and the lives of all Sovereigns will be in his hands. Tell him I will lead him tonight."

THE IMMORTAL warriors under Roland's command numbered two thousand, only three hundred of whom were called Ripper, his elite force occupying the great cave known simply as Roland's Lair. Of those, two hundred now filled the main chamber, all adorned in black battle dress and boots. One might be tempted to think Roland had called them to witness greatness.

But Jordin knew he only wanted them all to see what happened when Sovereign blood entered an Immortal's veins and turned them into something less.

Rislon had delivered her answer to Roland and returned to collect her within the hour. They were ready, he said. Where had she hidden the Sovereign blood? In her canteen, which she'd shoved into the hay of the open stall upon arriving. He'd given her a hard stare, then told her he'd be back.

Now she stood beside an ancient wooden table they'd set at the center of the great room, directly under one of the massive chandeliers. No fewer than a hundred candles lit the chamber, casting a wan amber glow over the ghostly Immortal faces that seemed to float above black-clad shoulders, each of them watching with those black eyes illuminated by their own golden fire. They stood in eerie stillness, some leaning on the railing along the upper level, others arrayed along both stairs, more on the main level.

Rislon and Sephan were two among many now, their faces cold. Cain stood somberly in the presence of his prince, as the queen, Talia, watched without expression from a high-backed, red-velvet chair. Kaya stood just behind and to Roland's right—Jordin would know her wide eyes anywhere—dressed in a simple black gown that bared her pale legs to mid-thigh. If she'd given up anything to Roland, it must not have included information on the location of the Sanctuary; evidently he still needed that knowledge.

What else she might have given Roland, Jordin didn't care to guess. A pang of jealousy spiked her heart. How had she come to feel such affection for Roland? And if she felt such a draw toward him, how much more had Kaya? The girl was unspoiled fruit, eager to love with new sensory passion. If the young woman felt any longing to recover her Sovereignty, her face showed no hint of it. She appeared fully and unabashedly Immortal, and all too aware she had been chosen to stand at Roland's side.

In any other group so large, Jordin would expect signs of individuality—a cough here and a whisper there as curiosity got the better of onlookers. Varied dress, color, different lengths and color of hair.

But Roland's Rippers all looked strangely similar. The cadre of their faces was white, their long hair mostly braided and unadorned. Clad in the same black as their leader with only the occasional piece of jewelry—a necklace around a warrior's neck or a ring on a pale finger—she could find no hint of the Nomad within them, of the anarchy of color and riot of individualism that had celebrated life beneath the stars of the wilderness.

Except, of course, for Talia, who stood out in teal, a single drop of ocean in a sea of black.

Only four others stood out in the gathering, all dressed in long cloaks with red bands around their long sleeves. Two men, a woman, and Michael. Gold-hilted swords hung from their belts; crescent moons from chains around their necks. Rislon had made mention of his War Lord, Lydia, during the long trip to the lair. These were the War Lords then?

Roland had donned a loose-fitting, dark-blue shirt tucked in at the waist beneath a similar longer black cloak that hung to his calves. His hair was pulled into a ponytail. His dark nails were perfectly manicured and his sleeves sharply buttoned. His burgundy lips offered no smile, only quiet resolve.

But Maker, he is handsome, that brooding prince. The very image of deadly perfection.

He lifted a hand and motioned to the side, his gaze never releasing Jordin. Seriph emerged from the outer circle of onlookers, carrying a black bag.

The instruments of seroconversion.

He set the bag on the table and withdrew a single translucent tube affixed to a thin, stainless steel needle and then set them on a white cloth beside the vial of blood they found in her canteen.

Fear snaked down Jordin's spine. The realization that she was about to forfeit the Immortal life suddenly filled her with dread and strange insult. Her breathing thickened.

Roland had stepped to her side, hands clasped behind his back, a hint of a smile now pulling at his lips.

"You will get your wish, my dear. But make no mistake, you will do as you say. And if you fail me in even the smallest way, I will return you to your current state and learn what I must one way or another. I have a way of getting what I want. If you have any doubts, you may ask Kaya. Bringing her to me was thoughtful. I suppose I owe you my gratitude."

He was baiting her, calling on her desire to be with her Maker as one of his brood. The fact that his play upon her jealousy had such a cloying effect on her mind terrified her, even now before all these faces.

She set her jaw. "As you said...my fate is now tied to yours. Let's get this over with."

He nodded at two Immortals behind her. They stepped up and put hands on her silk dress, as if to remove it. Jordin shrugged them off.

"You wish to humiliate me as well?"

"Humiliate you?" And then she realized that Immortals harbored no fear of nakedness.

But Sovereigns did. Didn't they?

"Forgive me, but when I turn Sovereign I might feel strange. Leave me dressed."

The faces floating in the gathered assembly looked at one another in shock; Immortals didn't speak this way to their prince. Her own ear was offended by her tone.

"Please," she followed. "I mean no offense. But Sovereigns aren't so free."

"Perhaps that too is part of your misery," he said. "Didn't Jonathan set us free from all such rubbish?"

Had he? She couldn't quite remember.

"Leave her dressed," he said to Seriph. "But get on with it, we don't have all night."

Seriph frowned at her without any intimation of approval. "On the table."

Jordin rolled onto the wood surface and lay on her back, staring up at the great chandelier. The faint hiss and sputtering of a hundred candles joined the steady breathing of the Immortals. She couldn't shake the feeling that they'd gathered around their table for a feast.

Seriph's cool hand gripped her wrist, and she closed her eyes.

Lead him, Jordin. Death is not the end.

Had he meant she was to die?

The memory of the music swept over her and momentarily quieted her mind, but the peace left as the Immortal tied a tourniquet above her left elbow and slapped the vein on her arm to turgid life.

Please, don't let me die.

The needle stung her skin. She held her breath, expecting more pain or heat—something to indicate the shift in blood type entering her veins.

She felt nothing. No surge of power, no swell of emotion, no pain, no wonder, not even the slightest tingle beyond the prick of the needle itself.

Nothing.

But she'd been here before, as a Mortal changing to Sovereign, and then, as now, the conversion had taken some time. Why would changing now be any different?

And then it came. Sorrow settled over her like a suffocating blanket. What if she was wrong and reconversion only killed? What if Jonathan had meant that she would indeed die now?

The Immortals made no sound—if they did, her heightened senses were failing her already, leaving her deaf to their whispers. Where was the music from her dream now? She strained to hear, but there was only the silence, complete and smothering.

Tiny dots of light floated through the darkness, falling to a black horizon like shooting stars, winking out. It wasn't too late! She could still stop them! Panic swept through her, pushed sweat from her pores. In her mind's eye she was reaching across her chest, clawing at the needle, tearing it out with a cry.

Her body began to tremble.

The last prick of light faded. Darkness, deeper than any she'd known, edged into her psyche like a heavy black fog. She felt her breathing thicken, her pulse slow, her body cool.

She was dying.

When the realization hit her, it was already too late. She tried to open her mouth and cry out for help—they would help her, wouldn't they?—but her muscles didn't respond. Her arms remained at her side, quivering with the last vestiges of life.

She felt the needle slip out. And then she felt nothing. Only perfect peace.

Darkness.

Silence.

Death.

And then, without warning, light came out of the darkness that was her nonexistence. It did not seep into her consciousness or grow from a mote spark; it exploded with a white-hot flash. It didn't change her dead world, it created a new one. Let there be life. There was nothing, and there was everything.

She was only vaguely aware she had a body that was reacting to the sudden eruption of life, distorted beyond what occurred naturally, because in the moment nothing was natural. All was new.

A hum filled her ears, soft and haunting. Formed tone and long notes, carried by a single voice—the same one she'd heard in her dream earlier! Music. The light was music, calling to her from the desert.

Come to me, my beloved. Awaken from your slumber and know that you are one with me.

The very air was his music, and she breathed it like a drug that strained her synapses to the breaking point. A sensation so exhilarating and beautiful that she felt powerless to resist its unrelenting power.

Do you feel my life, Jordin?

Jonathan's whisper echoed through her new world, soft but laden with as much power as the light and music both.

Why do you resist what is real? Why do you forget who you are?

And with those whispered words she heard a distant scream. Hers.

Find me, Jordin. Find yourself. Come to me.

She was shaking violently, weeping unrestrained, her mouth spread wide. She wanted to say *I will. I will find you*, but all that came out were screams.

Jordin didn't know how long that first explosion of life lasted—it felt timeless. She was life. She was home. And then the light and the music faded, leaving her in silence once again.

She felt her body go slack on the wooden table, spent. Undone. Redone.

Alive.

The sound of her own breathing like billows in her ears, Jordin opened her eyes. Her first thought was: what happened to the music?

It was gone.

Her heart surged, skipped a beat, then rediscovered its rhythmic gait. Music was for dreams of awakening, not for life. In real life, she was here in Roland's Lair, surrounded by his Rippers with their drawn faces. She'd screamed as one dying—if any of them had ever had the slightest curiosity about becoming Sovereign, they had surely lost interest now.

She lifted her hand and stared at her fingers. The skin had darkened already.

Jordin sat up and stared at Roland, who stood with arms crossed, his gaze wary. For a few moments no one spoke. Kaya looked on with black eclipses for eyes, obviously frightened.

"So this is what it looks like to die," Roland said. "Terrifying. I always wondered why you would do such a thing." He stepped up to her and took her hand with a curious frown. Turned it over, rubbed her skin with his thumb. Then sniffed at the air.

"What's that scent?"

"Life," she said.

"I know it—acacia."

Her mind was still preoccupied with the power of life carried to her on the strains of that music. Sorrow pulled at her heart. Was this to always be Jonathan's way—to whisper life and then vanish, leaving her alone?

"Corpses and Dark Bloods hate it," she said, referring to the scent.

Roland studied her with obvious fascination. His hand took her chin and gently turned her head, as if inspecting the change in her face and eyes. Their eyes met. His lingered.

"So," he said, releasing her face. "We have a Sovereign in our company. Please tell me that you remember what you came to tell me."

She couldn't recall what he was talking about. Her mind was still caught in the spidery web of death, life, the fading echo of Jonathan's voice. She was here for a reason, she knew that much, but the details had escaped her.

"Tell you what?"

"You play me?"

"No. I'm just not sure what you're talking about."

"You're Sovereign. Tell me where the others are hiding."

Now she remembered that she'd become Sovereign to lead him to the others, but she couldn't recall any of the details linking her to their hiding place.

"Byzantium," she said.

"Where in Byzantium?"

She blinked. It was all she knew.

She glanced around the room. To a soul, their eyes were fixed on her, sitting on the table, disoriented and at a loss.

"I..." She faced him. "I'm not sure. But I'm sure I'll remember."

Roland's jaw flexed with displeasure. "So you've said." He turned to his right and headed toward the stairs. The Immortals fell away like rain swayed by a strong wind.

"Bring her to my chambers immediately. Michael, assemble a raiding party."

And then he was gone.

CHAPTER SIXTEEN

JORDIN STOOD in Roland's chamber, pulse thumping. Rislon and Sephan had dragged as much as led her up the stairs, down the long hall, through the throne room where she'd first encountered Roland, and into his inner bedchamber. If their treatment of her had been forbearing before, it was now intolerant. Bowing, they'd shut the door behind her.

Summarily left alone with him, Jordin took in her surroundings. The prince had reserved his most luxurious appointments for this, his private enclave, where he apparently ruled with as much passion as on any battlefield. Warmth seemed to beckon from the heavy sheepskins that covered the floor, the dark velvet drapes that blanketed the walls and enclosed the far side of the great canopied bed at the center of the room.

No less than six pillows in dark burgundy and gold silks sprawled against the black wood headboard. The headboard itself was carved with gothic arches the likes of which Jordin had only seen in the ancient basilicas of the city. Equally ancient crosses topped the bed's four posters, their middles inset with amber. Beside the bed, a stack of books stood sentry on a low table, the faded gold of their titles obscured in the dim light, the candles in the iron holder beside them burned down to nubs.

Across the room a sofa sprawled low to the floor, another stack of books near the foot of it rising halfway up the height of a candelabra housing no less than a dozen candles. She had never thought Roland the scholarly type, but there on the chaise, one of the books was upturned, open, as though it had been put down in haste, like a lover left in the middle of the night.

He'd removed his cloak, rolled up his sleeves, and was pouring wine into one of two pewter goblets that sat on an ornate wooden table. He lifted the cup, drank half of its contents in one long gulp, then set it down and topped it off before filling the second. Without turning to face her, he pulled the tie out of his ponytail. His hair cascaded to his shoulders. She had never seen it without the braids, beading, and feathers of the Nomadic warrior. But now, plain as it was, it might have been the envy of any woman.

He took another drink before he rested one muscular hand on his hip and drew a breath in through his nostrils. She couldn't see the expression on his face, but she guessed it well enough by his impulsive movement. In her offer to be of service, she'd managed to awaken the beast in him.

Lead him, Jordin.

Lead him where? Jonathan felt as distant as her Immortal senses and left her feeling just as hampered. She couldn't understand why her memory was so fragile. Why she could hardly remember what it meant to be Sovereign, much less the details of where she'd lived or what specifically she was to do. Those details flitted through her mind, as elusive as specters.

Other memories, however, echoed with unmistakable clarity.

Why do you resist what is real?

What was she resisting? Was this chamber real? Was the distinction between Sovereign and Immortal real? How could she accept what was real if she couldn't remember?

Why do you forget who you are?

Who was she? A Sovereign, yes, but who was a Sovereign? Was her memory so tied to her blood as to remind her only what was important to the nature of that blood?

She'd died and then come back to life, she knew that much. The ordeal had been explosive, filling her with barely containable joy. But as the ecstasy of it had faded, her memory had with it, and now, without a clear context, she felt bereft of identity.

How she wanted back in the womb of that rebirth, to know who she was with as much clarity as she'd known it then. She couldn't remember feeling this way the first time she'd taken Sovereign blood, six years earlier. Why this time?

Why do you forget who you are?

She wanted to scream: *I don't want to forget. I want to know who I am!* Instead she stood at a loss, breathing deliberately through her nostrils, as if she could force memory into her mind like breath into her lungs.

Roland set the cup down and turned to face her, both hands on his hips. For a long time he only stared at her, eyes black. She was supposed to hate him, wasn't she? Yes, she had hated him.

She'd come to kill him. That was right—she'd come to use him for something and then kill him. She could remember that much as well now.

Did she really hate him?

"Why am I here?" she asked.

He watched her as if undecided.

Jordin glanced around the room, struck again by the richness of it. It was filled with objects of comfort, peace, light. Every token of abundant life. And yet she knew somehow that Roland had forgotten who he was as well. For as much as the room had been designed to exude warmth, it could not suppress the chill of its cold stone walls, or chase the darkness from its corners. Just as the wine on the table could not guarantee rest.

"I don't know what's happened to me," she said, facing him. "I'm sorry...I know you aren't pleased, but I just can't seem to remember things."

"This is what it means to be Sovereign?" he said. "It's no wonder you've become so miserable."

"Miserable?"

"Perhaps more now than before you took the dead blood."

Misery. Now she remembered that as well.

"No more playing," he said. "You came to me with wild claims that a virus threatening all Immortals will be released unless we deliver Feyn's head to your alchemist. My council seems to think your intentions are less than noble. That you don't have the strength to survive so you're resorting to deception with our demise in mind. That this nonsense regarding your memory is nothing but a charade."

Slowly the pieces of her puzzle, her mind, began to fall into place.

"Your council's wrong," she said. "I swear on my life, my death and resurrection have swept my mind clean."

"Is that so?"

"I think it is."

A slight, wry smile softened his face. His gaze slipped down her body to her toes. He appeared genuinely curious, but she suspected his show of interest was only his way of manipulating her. He stepped to the table and took both goblets in his hands.

"If only I could read your mind and know, Jordin," he said, turning. "Honestly, I don't know whether to take you seriously. Sovereigns are nothing like I imagined."

"And what did you expect?"

He came to her and offered her one of the goblets.

"I don't know. Something less interesting. They say you're conniving. But I see only a lost girl here in my room."

He was attempting to soften her. To win her trust. Perhaps more... She felt her pulse quicken, but she wasn't sure why. She knew that she hated him, but her heart hadn't yet fully caught up with her mind on the matter, which in and of itself served as a warning.

She *did* hate him. Feyn's wasn't the only head she'd promised to deliver.

"No need to be frightened," Roland said. He lifted the pewter cup to his stained lips and took a sip. "Truth be told, I have more faith in you than my council. I expect you'll prove me right."

"Of course I will."

"Drink. We took this wine from a transport bound for the Citadel. Wine stolen from the Sovereign's table, may she die in misery."

Jordin took a token sip if only to appease him before he took the goblet from her hand and placed both on the stack of books on the table beside the bed.

"You might prove your loss of memory to me."

"You already know I'm telling the truth," she said. "If

I knew what it is you wanted to know, I would tell you. Sovereigns are nothing if not truthful."

"Oh, I'm sure." He took her hand and lifted it, turning it over slowly. "Tell me, is it also true that Sovereigns love Immortals despite our differences? Wasn't that Jonathan's way?"

She wasn't sure what to say. Love, yes, she supposed. But *love?*

His eyes met hers. "No?"

"Yes," she said.

He traced her hair with his fingers. "I find myself strangely taken with you."

"You have the queen."

"She doesn't share my bed."

The confession surprised Jordin. Even in her state of disorientation she couldn't mistake his intentions. He was testing her to see if she recalled her hatred of him.

"My mind may not be as clear as it should be," she said, "but I know I'm not here for love."

"And here I thought love was all that Sovereigns cared about, being so saturated with it. You must know pleasure as few can."

She knew he could hear her heart racing like a spooked horse. Feel the rising heat off her skin. Smell her perspiration. He might even mistake it for desire.

Was it?

He couldn't possibly be sincere. And if he was, she dare not fall prey.

And if it was sincere?

She could not return his affection.

Another thought on the heels of the last: rejecting him would only undermine his trust. Winning his affection, on the other hand, might gain it.

Roland stroked her cheek with the back of his fore-finger. "I never would have guessed that I would find the sight of the skin I left behind so appealing."

She hesitated. "We were the same once."

"We were the same an hour ago." His voice was sooth-ing. "You are the one who changed, as you did six years ago. So. Show me what it means to be Sovereign."

"How can I when I don't remember?"

"You've forgotten how to love?" Roland's lips brushed against her hair, his breath hot in her ear. "Then let me show you."

She felt like a trapped animal. Worse, a part of her did not want to push him away. And that frightened her.

His raw power called to her like a drug, terrifying and alluring at once. Her salvation came in a simple thought: whether he was truly drawn to her or toying with her, Roland obviously liked his women strong.

She withdrew her hand from his, stepped away, and turned to face him, her jaw set. "The fate of your kind is in the balance, and all you can think about is your bed? Am I just a flower to be plucked?"

He looked genuinely stunned. "Is that what you think?"

"How could I not?"

His face, so pale, had actually gone a shade of pink.

"What you need is locked in here, and not below my waist. Help me, don't seduce me!"

"I *am* helping you!" he shot back. She was surprised by how easily she'd set him back on his heels.

"How?"

"I'm trying to free your mind."

"Along with my dress?"

"Perhaps some liberation of your body would also lib-erate your mind."

"And that's all you were thinking."

Roland gave a soft laugh as he relented. "Not entirely, no."

She glanced at him sidelong.

"You find me attractive."

"If I were pressed to," he said. Then, as if in a forced confession, "Yes."

"Only if you were pressed? Like one forced to consider the crumbs on the floor?"

"I said I find your skin appealing, didn't I?"

"My skin."

He hesitated. "More."

"Then it's a little more too much. I'm Sovereign, one you would kill, not bed. Or have you lost your memory as well?"

His face went flat.

What was she doing? She'd gone too far. This was Roland, the prince of the Immortals. Her enemy.

Whom Jonathan had loved.

Lead him, Jordin.

She needed him as much as he needed her. She couldn't afford to leave him feeling dejected—too much was at stake. Already he was turning away as though he might call for Rislon or dismiss her.

She took a quick, deep breath and reached a hand to his shoulder.

"Roland. Please. I'm here because the stakes are as high as I've said. From the day you left, I despised your choice. I would never come to you unless it was my last option. You want the truth? That is it. There's more, I'm certain, but I need your help to remember it."

He stepped away, and her hand slid off his shoulder. But then it came.

"The keys to the Sovereign lair! The Citadel!" she blurted out.

He threw back the rest of his wine, set the glass down, and, casting her a dark glance, began to pace, hands on his hips. He looked more like a sulking lion than an Immortal prince. But then, his predicament was as uncertain as hers, wasn't it? For a moment, she wanted to comfort him.

Comfort him? This man who'd seen to the massacre of so many Sovereigns only a year ago! What would stop him from taking the lives of those who remained in short order?

Nothing.

And here he was, shrouded in comfort. But for as magnificent as he appeared, he exuded misery.

As did she.

Why do you forget?

A heavy weight settled into her heart. She was filled with Jonathan's blood but without peace, a hollow vessel, a vacant thing.

Jonathan had abandoned them all.

The air itself felt too thick to breathe. Despair edged into her mind. Her only cogent thought was that she must not allow Roland to sense it.

But it was already too late. She couldn't hold back the tears that filled her eyes. She stood frozen, hating herself, as one slipped down her cheek.

And then they flowed silently, unrestrained. No amount of will could stop them.

Roland had stopped his pacing and was watching her, but her vision was too blurred to see his reaction.

"I'm sorry...," she managed, turning half away. "I don't know what's happening to me."

"It's all right."

His voice was low and soothing, and it pulled a sob from the deepest part of her heart. She had to gain control.

Her show of emotion was unbecoming, if not for an Immortal, then without question for a newly made Sovereign. What would any Immortal—let alone the world— think of such a reaction from one claiming to have the love, joy, and peace of Jonathan's blood in her?

Roland crossed to her, put a hand on her arm, looked down into her face. She stared up and saw the face of a gentle man, not the powerful warrior who'd hunted Sovereigns and conquered women. He brushed her tears away with his thumb.

"I didn't mean to hurt you."

She finally found a semblance of control.

"I'm lost," she whispered.

He stared at her for several moments, touched her cheek, and then drew her to his chest. They stood still, her breath too hot in the air between them, her tears too mortifying on the black silk of his shirt.

His arms too willing to be strong around her.

He released her, and she hauled in a heavy breath as he strode for the door, where he turned, hand on the lever.

"You will sleep here tonight, alone and undisturbed. Find yourself, Jordin. If what you say about this virus is true, the lives of my people will depend on it."

CHAPTER SEVENTEEN

"Y OU SHOULD be honored," Feyn said, gliding along the length of the heavy stone table on the dais. "It was on this very spot that I came to new life."

The man on the table did not speak. Corban had fastened a gag around his head and trussed him like a sacrifice—binding his hands and feet, cutting away his shirt, securing his head with thick bands to the surface of the table. But she had a feeling he wouldn't have responded. He was given to quiet in this last stage of his zealotry. Soon the delusions that propped up all his naïve beliefs would collapse.

She would show him suffering. And she would also show him perfect peace.

Feyn turned away. "You realize that it's a kindness I do you," she said, her voice carrying perfectly throughout the tiered chamber.

The electrical lights in the old Senate Hall had been turned on, dimly illuminating the paintings of another millennium on the ceiling. Just above the dais, a large dark blot above the place where the senate torch once burned day and night obscured what might have otherwise been a priceless work. She'd often thought she could just see an image resembling a hand, forefinger extended, emerging from the edge of the black mar that had only darkened over the years. It was meant to burn forever, that torch.

Until the day she extinguished it.

She turned back as Corban finished his preparations, propping Rom's eyes wide open with metal instruments that looked wickedly like clamps but had the opposite effect. Rom lay faceup, eyes wide in the stainless steel frames. The scissorlike handles gleamed above his temples. Corban had asked to study the change in Rom's eyes during his conversion, and Feyn had granted the request.

His breathing was labored, if steady. Controlled, though audible enough to betray what had to be an accelerating heartbeat. He thought he knew what was coming.

He had no idea.

She hadn't touched the table since entering the chamber, standing back as Seth and another of her Dark Bloods lifted Rom onto it. Though she wouldn't trade who she was today—for which she ultimately owed Saric gratitude—she'd never been able to repress revulsion at the sight of the stone table since the day of her making. She would've had it destroyed had it not been the symbol of the Sovereign's presence in the theater of world government. It was as much a tangible reminder of the Sovereign's headship over Order as the Sovereign was the visible hand of the Maker on earth.

No one had known that the table was the main reason she'd stopped attending senate hearings. After that, it hadn't been such a leap to disband the senate entirely.

"Soon, the burden of loyalty for your people—indeed, of any knowledge that troubles you—will be gone," she said. "You won't live in misery, hiding from the sun as you have. You'll eat from my table. You may even sleep in my bed, if I grant it. And you'll know peace absent of struggle, loyal to one will alone: mine. Think on that in the hours to come. You'll need something to cling to."

Corban folded his hands behind the table, waiting. When she nodded, he lifted a simple stainless steel stent attached to a clear rubber tube with a second stent on the opposite end. She suppressed a shudder with sheer will-power, conflicted by the urge to kiss the instrument of her own conversion.

"My liege," Corban said, gesturing to the space beside him.

"You realize this is an honor I didn't give even Corban," she said, coming round the side of the table. "But Corban won't begrudge you, will you, Corban?"

"Your will is perfect, my liege," the alchemist said.

But of course the man was jealous. Which one of them wouldn't have bitten off his own arm for the opportunity to receive what Rom was about to receive: a full dose of their Maker's blood drawn directly from her.

She lifted the hem of her heavy sleeve. Blood red, hemmed in gold, black onyx glittering along its edge. Folded it back, baring the dark vein just below the surface of her skin.

The mitigating factor of Corban's envy—aside from his inherent desire to please her—was his own curiosity. He seemed aware of nothing but his precise movements as he wrapped a tourniquet around Feyn's upper arm and applied astringent to the vein. She felt the cold bite of steel as he slipped the stent into her arm.

"I can't guarantee he'll survive it," Corban said, reminding her yet again.

"We'll know soon enough," she said.

Watching Corban, she wondered if she was ready for Rom to die. So much history...But looking at him, eyes pried open, she knew he was dead to her already.

She said nothing as Corban carefully slid the other end directly into Rom's jugular without any indication of pain from Rom but a flick of his eyes.

She gave a curt nod, and the alchemist glanced at her. Lowering his eyes, he twisted the small valve. The dark blood in the primed tube began to flow.

Her blood. Maker's blood.

She felt nothing but a slight drawing against her vein as she opened her hand, eyes locked on Rom. He breathed heavily, fists clenched, a thick vein twitching along his neck.

She glanced at Corban, who seemed to be monitoring the flow through the tubing, glancing every few seconds at the great clock at the back of the senate. Time seemed to slow.

"Is it working?" she said.

At first she thought Corban hadn't heard her.

She glanced at Rom. The vein along his neck had started to twitch.

"Yes," Corban said.

The twitching became a visible spasm. His eyes stared at the ceiling, pried open by the steel devices, but she knew they would be as wide with horror without them.

What did he see? she wondered. For her, it had been the tearing of her soul. Her conversion had wrenched her from the womb of stasis, of a beautiful nothingness that was neither Bliss nor fear, that held no dreams or memory. A place where she was aware of the very molecules in her skin. There she'd felt more than heard the silence of a world unseen by natural eyes, as though she had one finger in this world and another in its mirror image.

Saric had ripped her away from it all. From the only wholeness she had ever truly known.

Now, staring at Rom, she remembered the blackness and the creeping tar of fear that had pulled her from that place. Of pain. Of the realization of dark life. She'd entered it as one squeezes oneself flat to enter a flat world, as though through the crack of a door. Impossible and excruciating at once.

Sweat beaded and dripped down the sides of Rom's chest, over his ribs, along his brow. He jerked and grunted fiercely into his gag. His arms were rigid against his sides, his wrists straining against the rope.

Feyn glanced at Corban, who was leaning over Rom's head, looking at his eyes.

Rom arched up off the table, heels dug into the stone, his back impossibly bent. He arched up higher, muscles locked, arms corded tight and rigid. Hips so high, arching up at such a sharp angle that Feyn wondered if it was possible that he could break his own back. Were it not for the band holding his head down, she was certain he would have twisted so far that she might hear the snapping of his vertebrae.

The gag muffled a ghastly scream.

"What's happening?" she demanded.

"The change, my liege. You reacted similarly."

Rom screamed again, panted against the gag, at the exertion of his muscles, at the obvious pain. The sound devolved into one long string of screams.

She'd never heard Rom like this, so beyond himself. Gone was the self-possessed man. A demoniac lay in his place; monsters warred in his veins.

"It's killing him." The sound of her own words chilled her.

"Give it time, my liege. Come, come see!" He gestured,

moving aside. For the first time since her own conversion she gripped the edge of the table, slid closer against it to lean over his head.

"His eyes. You see? His eyes!"

The green, once so vibrant, had begun to dull to a milky hazel. She watched enraptured as they paled until they were white, surrounded by bloodshot eyeballs. For several seconds they remained pallid. An inky swirl spooled into the iris of his left eye, like black ink poured into water. It flooded through the iris, along the inside ring, and then appeared in the right, as though a black serpent had slithered through his head. His eyes clouded over—the churning of the Byzantium sky before a storm—and then blackened to obsidian. They seemed to harden before her gaze.

Rom's clenched teeth had bitten off his screams, replaced with desperate pulls of air through his nostrils. Dark marks appeared on his chest. No, not marks, but the creeping black of his veins under his skin. Up from his neck, over his jaw and toward his cheek, like cracks in glass before it breaks.

He fell back to the table and began to shudder. The shaking started from his feet through his legs and to his torso. He quaked with it, more and more violently until the table shook with him.

"It's killing him!"

Corban glanced up at her with a blank look. In his view, the loss of Rom might be a pity if only for intellectual and scientific reasons, but Feyn realized that she'd cared, for a moment, whether Rom lived or died.

But of course she did. If he died, he wouldn't survive to tell her the location of the Sovereign hideout.

Blood stained the gag. He had bitten his tongue. A drop slid down his cheek toward the table. Not red blood.

Nearly black.

Her eyes darted to his irises, searching for any glimmer...

A faint light behind the dark orbs mushroomed. Her pulse quickened at the familiar sight of new life. It brightened and blazed for an instant, causing those eyes to seem to glow, before receding, leaving only a ring of gold around his irises.

The quaking stopped. His body went slack. His breathing stopped. Rom's eyeballs twitched and then went still, fixed on the ceiling.

For a moment she and Corban stared, the alchemist with tilted head.

"Is he dead?" she demanded.

"Maybe he wasn't strong enough."

Feyn turned away from the table with a last, doleful look at Corban. "Now he's no good to me at all."

"My liege, forgive me."

She turned back, was about to tell Corban to take him away, that he might as well conduct all the experiments he wished while the body was still fresh, when the form on the table sucked in a breath through the bloody gag.

She whirled back.

He was still, as though lying in repose. Corban bent over him, peered into his eyes.

"Take his gag off!" she said, coming closer.

The eyes within the grips roved toward her as Corban removed the gag and then the instruments holding his eyes wide.

Rom blinked. Stared at her strangely. It was the look of one on the brink of a question, or of recognizing a face.

"Get him off that table."

"My liege, I'm not certain whether—"

"Seth. Radus." She snapped her fingers. "Get him off."

The Dark Bloods strode down the central aisle and up the side stair of the dais. They untied him and lifted him up.

"In the chair," she said, pointing to the seat behind the table once occupied by the Sovereign.

Rom was unsteady on his feet as the pair hauled him to the chair and dropped him into it.

Once more, he looked from them to Corban and back to her, where his gaze lingered.

"Lower your eyes," she said.

He hesitated and then looked at the floor.

For a long while she studied his drooping form, his arms draped like empty sleeves over the chair arms.

"So...," she said, rounding the table to stand before him. "Now you've experienced what I once did. Do you know where you are?"

He remained silent. Surely he wasn't able to resist her.

"Answer me!"

"Yes," he said quietly. His voice was low and raw.

"And who I am?"

His answer came late, hardly more than a whisper. "Feyn."

"And what are you now?"

"I..." She saw his eyes blink again, still fixed on the floor.

"Let me be more specific. *Whose* are you?"

He glanced up.

"Lower your eyes," she snapped.

He dropped them again.

"Who do you belong to?"

"To you," he said.

"Which makes me what to you?"

Slow again. Too slow. She felt her pulse quicken. Perhaps his making wasn't complete.

"My maker," he finally said in a quiet, rasping voice.

"Your maker. And as such you are bound to my word without compromise."

She glanced at Corban, who was taking the scene in with interest. Seth and Radus stood off to the side.

"Now tell me." She paced three steps before him and stopped. "Where are the rest of the Sovereigns?"

She could see his gaze turning this way and that, as though watching a rodent scurrying across the floor. A slight tremble shook his hands.

"I ask it again. Where are the rest of your people?"

The tremor ran up into his arms to his shoulders, as though he were straining against a great weight, muscles fatigued.

She tilted her head.

"Speak!"

He remained mute.

She shot a harsh glance at Corban, who quickly dropped his gaze.

"Was this not successful?"

"By all accounts, it was. But we've never turned a Sovereign. His body has converted, but his mind may take some time to complete, my liege."

"How long?"

"Perhaps an hour. Perhaps longer."

"Longer? We don't have longer!"

"He claims the virus will be released—"

She cut him off with a half-raised hand and turned her attention back to Rom. The virus would be released in three days if he'd been telling the truth. The thought of it brought a chill to the back of her neck.

"So. You resist me. You resist the very blood in your veins."

No answer.

Feyn stepped up to Rom, seized his neck with one hand, and jerked him to his feet. Then higher, until his feet dangled inches from the ground. She stared up into his face, her own arm shaking with rage more than exertion. She rarely displayed her own strength so openly.

Saric had created far more than he'd anticipated the day he'd made her.

"You will understand one thing, Rom Sebastian. I am your maker now. Your loyalty is to me. You will obey me without thought or hesitation. It would behoove you to understand this, and quickly. It will be far less painful for you."

She released his neck with a slight shove. He slid off the edge of the chair and crashed to the floor, too weak to break his fall.

She swooped down, seized him by the cheeks, and turned him toward the two warriors standing nearby.

"Do you see them? Those two?"

"Yes," he managed through heavy breath.

"Radus, hand your sword to Seth."

The man drew his short sword with a hiss of steel and held it out to Seth, who took it.

"Seth, kill Radus."

Radus's eyes widened slightly—and then completely as Seth shoved the blade up under his rib cage, to the hilt.

Radus fell to his knees, hands on the sword sunk deep in his chest.

"Beautiful, isn't it?" she whispered against Rom's ear. "Do you not understand that my power is absolute?"

She heard him swallow. Felt him tremble.

"Seth."

"Yes, my liege." His voice was like a purr. He was ready, she knew, to do anything to please her. That he, in fact, relished it.

"Take out your sword."

He slipped his blade free of its sheath, eyes steadied on Rom, narrowed to catlike slits in anticipation.

"Cut your throat."

His head snapped up. For the first time in her service, he stared at her wide, with a hint of question. But his loyalty could not be compromised.

He lifted his sword and slowly, eyes fixed on his maker, dragged the blade across his throat. For a moment, he stood there, shock and devotion warring on his face. Blood gushed from the wound and spilled onto the dais between them.

Ah, but he was magnificent! She'd been right in thinking he was the pinnacle of her creation.

He staggered only one step before collapsing on the floor, draining of the dark blood that gave him life.

"I will give you some time to collect yourself," she said, shoving Rom's face away. "The next time I speak, you will obey."

She stood, brushed herself off, and looked at the collapsed form of Seth with a slight moue of regret.

"Corban." The alchemist was visibly trembling.

"My liege?"

"Take him below. Send word when his transformation is complete—body, mind, and soul."

CHAPTER EIGHTEEN

JORDIN AWOKE with a start, eyes wide, heart pounding in her chest. The events of the previous night cascaded into her mind with the thunder of a waterfall.

She sat up, gasping. The drapes of the large bed were closed around her, the faint glow of a candle throwing shadows across the ceiling, reminding her that she was not dead or suffocating.

Roland had left her alone to sleep. And to remember.

She'd taken Sovereign blood and died a hollow death before being reborn in an explosion of love. But the beauty of that moment had fled as quickly as it had come.

She pushed aside the curtain and stared at the candle on the nearby table as Jonathan's words filled her mind. *Why do you forget?*

She didn't know why. But with that forgetting, she'd lost her sense of identity. Fear had pushed her to a break-ing point, and she'd wept, acutely aware of her own misery in the wake of having felt so much beauty in her rebirth.

Why had the beauty left her so quickly?

She'd forgotten not only what it meant to be Sovereign, but the particulars of her existence.

Jordin blinked.

But she knew now, didn't she? Precise details of the Sovereign Sanctuary returned to memory. The passage through the ruins. The canvas flap. The large chamber with the circular seats...her own small room with the worn curtain over the doorway. What had been hidden by the fog of Immortality was clear for the first time since her arrival at Roland's Lair. As were the details of the underground labyrinth that led to the Citadel. Other specific memories strung through her mind: places, people, dates...each of them falling into place, one after the other.

But Jonathan hadn't been referring to that forgetting. His words had questioned her very soul. The *being* of Sovereign. The abundance of life he had promised.

That had not come back to her.

How could she remember what she'd never known? Or had she known it once in those first days as a Sovereign?

Her chest felt hollow. Her eyes misted as the truth settled around her, thick as the darkness, heavy as the pelt on the bed. Whatever peace Jonathan had promised was as absent now as it had been before becoming Immortal.

Perhaps more so. Next to the memory of her recent rebirth, her emptiness only seemed to run deeper, a gorge cut by the river of her reconversion.

She'd rediscovered her memory only to find herself... lost.

But she knew the way to Feyn. That was all that must matter now. Time enough to discover the source of her misery later, assuming she still had the emotion left to feel it.

Jordin threw the covers off and slid out of bed, dressed still in the short black dress. She stumbled to the door, flung it open, and ran down the corridor, her mind suddenly consumed with only one thought.

She had three days to return both Feyn's and Roland's heads to Mattius or the virus would be released. And somehow, after knowing the Immortals as they were now, she understood that their extermination would deeply offend Jonathan. Dark Bloods were one thing, but she'd seen the humanity in Roland's eyes last night and...

She meant to kill him.

Jordin pulled up sharply, halfway down the vacant hall. Kill him? The prince who only loved with passion and hated in misery like herself? He'd treated her with tenderness last night. He'd given up his bed for her, left her alone.

She hurried on, shoving the dilemma aside. Nothing would matter if they didn't first kill Feyn. Time was too short.

She burst through the door at the end of the corridor, veered toward the right flight of stairs, and flew down them, hand on the rail, watching her bare feet to be sure of her footing. Only when she'd descended halfway did she glance up and see that perhaps a dozen Immortals were seated at the long dining table on the main level, that their heads had turned, all of them staring at her.

At the head of the table sat Roland, leaning against the carved high back of the chair.

She flushed at the sight of him, felt a slight smile tug at the corner of her mouth.

And then she noticed Kaya. Sitting to his right.

The sudden heat that flashed up Jordin's back surprised her. The girl had no business being near him!

Jordin had told Roland precisely how much Sovereign blood she would need, no more. The rest was for Kaya. But only now did the urgency for Kaya's seroconversion fill her.

She gathered herself and continued her descent, more slowly now, aware that her hair and dress were tossed and wrinkled from a night in Roland's bed.

Jordin crossed to the table and stopped three paces from Roland. He made no effort to rise or pull a chair out for her, choosing instead to stare expectantly. Gone was the tender man who'd held her briefly last evening.

Here was the prince, making a show of command before all of his Rippers and the girl sitting at his side who obviously worshiped the very air he breathed.

"I need to talk to you."

"Talk," he said.

"In private."

"You have no secrets here."

"No?"

"No."

Her irritation swelled.

"If we have any hopes of stopping the virus, we have to leave now," she said, assuming the revelation would be new to all except Michael, who leaned back in a chair three down from the prince, arms crossed.

Her glance at him confirmed Jordin's suspicion. But Roland didn't break focus.

"So you remember everything."

"Yes."

His gaze was heavy on her for several long seconds; silence was thick in the great chamber. His right arm rested on the table, and he lifted a single finger—a dismissive gesture. Immediately all the Immortals except Michael and Kaya rose. Then, with a glance at the others, Kaya did as well.

"She stays," Jordin said, staring at the girl.

Roland's brow arched. The others paused, the room bathed in sudden tension at the unspoken standoff.

"I need her," Jordin said.

Roland hesitated and then gave a curt nod. Kaya eased back down, hands in her lap. The others resumed their departure in silence, some to doorways along the wall, others up the stairs, like dark phantoms vanishing into the walls, leaving only Roland, Michael, and Kaya at the table. The prince waited until the last door was closed before speaking.

"Quite the entrance. You would do well to remember where you are."

She was looking at Kaya, who returned her stare with indifference. "How could I possibly forget?"

"Indeed," Roland said. "And yet you've forgotten so much lately."

"It's apparently easy to lose your mind in this place."

"And yet you seem to have found yours in my bed," he said.

She gave him a sharp look. But his tone had not been mocking, and she saw that his face had softened.

"Yes," she said. "I slept well. I trust you did also."

He gave a slight smile. "Very." He motioned to a chair with an open hand. "Please..."

He was dressed in black, his sleeveless shirt half buttoned up the front. Black armbands hugged each arm where his biceps met his elbows. Taut muscle pressed his veins to the surface of his forearms; his fingers, curled and at ease, looked strong enough to crush a man's neck as an afterthought. She was surprised by her reaction to him even now, even as a Sovereign and fully rested.

And yet this was the man she must kill. The thought terrified her.

"We don't have time to sit here," she said. "I may know the way into the Citadel, but getting to Feyn and Rom could take some time."

"Yes, of course. We kill Feyn today. I'd nearly forgotten."

"You don't believe me?"

"You haven't told me what it is you remember. Tell me now so I know what to believe."

She stared at him, trying to judge his sincerity, aware of Michael studying them. He was playing with her, knowing she had no option but to play along. She needed him as much as he needed her.

"I will. As soon as Kaya becomes Sovereign."

His placid expression remained in place. "That is her choice, not mine."

Kaya glanced between them, silent.

"Go on, my little darling. Tell us if you would take the dead blood and lose your Immortality."

"Why would I do that?" Kaya asked.

"Because you were a lover of Jonathan before you crawled into this man's bed!" Jordin snapped. "Get ahold of yourself, Kaya!"

"Isn't this what Jonathan wanted?" she said, far too innocently.

"He died for this?" Jordin demanded. "Are you mad?"

Kaya blinked, with shock or simple realization, Jordin couldn't tell. Roland seemed content to leave them to their exchange. Relished it, perhaps.

Jordin walked behind the prince's chair and squatted on one foot next to Kaya. She took the girl's hand and looked into her black eyes.

"Please, Kaya…think about the Sovereignty that Jonathan died to bring us. How many have given their lives to protect his blood? You, maybe more than any of us, know what it means to come to life. He saved you from the Authority of Passing! You have to take his blood again and find that life again."

"I've never felt so alive," she said. A hint of fear crossed the girl's face. "I can't take dead blood! Not now. I've just found life."

Jordin felt her ire rise to the breaking point, pushed higher by the acute knowledge that she had felt the same...and the fear that she might be wrong. Was the right thing supposed to be so difficult? Was the wrong supposed to feel so very natural, and so right?

"Don't be a fool!" she said, standing abruptly, not knowing if she was speaking to Kaya or herself. "You took his blood and found a new life, just as I did!"

"A life of misery," Roland said, echoing her own words of the night before.

Jordin shoved a finger at him, her eyes boring into Kaya's. "He sweeps you off your feet and lifts your skirt, and you forget who you are? Don't mistake pleasure for truth."

Kaya's face darkened. "What makes you think I've lifted my skirt for anyone? You think I'm a tramp? That I've lost my mind just because I still have the life you gave up?"

Jordin suddenly felt foolish—and ashamed for doubting the girl, at least when it came to Roland. She felt her face flush.

Kaya stood up, face now firmly set. "I have no intention of taking your blood! I'm Immortal now, and I've never been happier. With your permission, my prince..." She faced Roland. "I would like to leave."

"Of course," he said gently. "And stay clear of eager hands, yes?" He glanced at Jordin as he said it.

Kaya bowed her head. "I will." She turned and hurried toward the stairs without a glance at Jordin.

"The virus will kill every Immortal, Kaya!"

The girl didn't acknowledge her warning.

"You'll only find misery!" Jordin cried after her.

Kaya spun at the first step. "You're the only miserable one, Jordin." Then she flew up the stairs and was gone.

Roland said with dry amusement, "I guess she told us, didn't she?"

Her words burrowed into Jordin's mind like a tick. She could no longer pretend that she wasn't miserable.

"You're dragging her to the grave with you," she said, sitting heavily in the chair Kaya had vacated.

"And yet you may be in the grave well before her. Immortals are, after all, immortal."

Jordin faced the short life of a Sovereign. Perhaps very short. Roland might kill her yet. She could die on this mission. She likely would. The fact that she'd survived seroconversion twice meant nothing.

"Now . . . as you said, we're running out of time. Tell me where I can find this alchemist who wishes us all dead."

"The only way to stop him is to kill Feyn."

"I'll put my faith in my own intuition, if you don't mind."

His smile vanished, replaced by a look of absolute command.

"I assume you know the way back home. Take me yourself or tell me where it is. Either way, we will be at death's doorstep by nightfall to make our own fate."

His brow arched. "Or would you rather allow this virus to run its course?"

CHAPTER NINETEEN

FEYN FOLDED her hands inside the observation room. Beyond the glass, Rom sat slumped in the ironwood chair. There was no need for restraints, though by the look of him he might have benefited from them, if only to keep him sitting erect.

An hour, Corban had said.

Too many had passed.

She stepped to the door and entered the inner room. Rom made no move, his head hung over his chest. She wondered if he was sleeping. She glanced over at Corban, who offered a single nod, then walked around the chair and stood before Rom.

"Good morning. I hear you had a rough night."

Still quiet.

"I'm sorry you had to endure such a slow turning—only full surrender can give you peace. Do you, Rom? Feel peace?"

He looked up, the circles of fatigue beneath one eye as dark as the blackened bruise beneath the other. His skin had paled to a ghastly pallor since she'd seen him in the Senate Hall. The dark tree of veins along his neck, creeping up toward his jaw and over the back of his hands seemed less like the inky elegance of her own veins and more like dark fissures in something about to crack.

He lifted his head, struggled to keep it from bobbing back down. His eyes never made it higher than her knees.

"Somewhat," he said.

She flashed Corban a glance, and he gave another reassuring nod. Standing near his table, the alchemist looked worn, though he was certainly in far better condition than Rom. He had changed his tunic, she noticed.

She returned her attention to Rom. One of his hands occasionally trembled, as one who has palsy. Was that a product of the conversion or the lack of sleep?

"Good. Full peace will come as you fully submit. Tell me, are you pleased about this new change in you?"

"I..." He swallowed deeply, looked around, a strange bewilderment in his gaze. She gave him time.

"I'm having trouble remembering the change." His eyes rested on her.

"What about your change are you unclear about?"

"I...I don't know. What it was like before."

She gave him a slight smile. "Do you realize, Rom Sebastian, that this is the first time that we are of like kind?"

"I don't know what you mean..."

"This is the first time you and I are both of the same blood. I your maker, you my slave. You said yesterday that you loved me, an appropriate sentiment for a slave. That you wanted me to be as you are. Now I have granted that wish."

She paused. "You do recall that you love me, don't you?"

"I don't...I don't remember the conversation."

What else might he not remember? Clearly, he'd surrendered his state of resistance following the conversion, but if he couldn't remember the details of his former life, all would be lost.

She looked at Corban, brow raised in question.

"Is it a ruse?"

"I don't believe so. His conversion is complete—body and will. If not his mind or emotion. Those will follow, I'm quite sure."

"I do love you," Rom said. His gaze lifted to her face. "Yes . . . yes, I do love you."

"As you should. Then you would do all that I ask of you." He was quiet.

"Am I wrong?" she asked more sharply.

"No," he said, his tone strange, as though he didn't understand the word—or that it had come out of him.

But in that moment Feyn knew she had Rom Sebastian, leader of the so-called Sovereigns. Truly had him, despite his failure to find full peace. What was peace anyway? She felt little of it herself, and her Dark Bloods knew even less. She needed only their unquestioned loyalty and service, not their joy or peace. Their love, not their pleasure.

"Then show me your devotion and address me properly."

He glanced at Corban, then turned his eyes back to Feyn.

"Lower your eyes," she said gently.

He did as she directed.

"Who am I?"

"My liege," he said quietly.

"And?"

"My maker."

"And?"

"The one that I love."

"Good. Now tell me where the rest of the Sovereigns are hiding."

His brows drew together.

"Now."

"I can't…"

"Now!"

His struggle to recall appeared genuine. She could not fault him for that.

"In ruins," he said.

"Ruins? Where?"

"In the city…"

"The city is full of ruins. You will tell me which. Now."

"Ruins—south. The south part of the city. I can't—" His eyes lifted, face drawn.

"Lower your eyes!"

He did at once. "Forgive me, my liege."

"Which ruins? Think!"

Sweat had beaded on his forehead. "I can't remember…"

"Focus!"

He went silent, his eyes searching the floor between his feet. The memory was beyond him.

Feyn turned toward Corban. "Send a thousand men. Sweep the southern sector of the city. Comb every ruin you find."

"My liege, that could take days. And the virus, if what he has said is true, will release in three."

"Then send ten thousand! Now!"

She turned with a rustle of black silk. "And keep working on our new friend. The information is hidden somewhere in that thick skull of his."

Chapter Twenty

BYZANTIUM LAY beneath a charcoal night sky, a sprawling city unaware that the fate of the world hung in unforgiving balance, final judgment to be rendered in a mere matter of hours.

Jordin sat atop her stallion between Roland and Michael, staring down at the capital from the rise. Forty of Roland's most skilled Rippers were mounted abreast, silent and unmoving, hooded and clad in black. Anyone peering out from the city might have thought them a cadre of reapers come to drag the unwitting to Hades.

And they might be right.

Behind the closed doors of a hundred thousand houses and as many apartments, Corpses prepared an evening meal consisting mostly of simple starches, canned meats, and aged vegetables. They would not venture out, far too aware of the bloodshed that visited their streets after dark. And so they remained imprisoned by fear as much as by the city's evening curfew, praying over their supper for the Maker to grant Feyn favor against the plague of white-faced Immortals whom they feared more even than her Dark Bloods.

Eighty thousand of Feyn's guards patrolled the city in

an ever-broadening perimeter around the Citadel, roaming the vacant streets in packs, eager for a kill. Bringing the head of an Immortal to Feyn would catapult even the lowest-ranking Dark Blood to a high position within the ranks.

At least, that was the assumption. The feat had yet to be accomplished.

Roland's Rippers had never come into the city in such numbers as they would tonight. Theirs was a guerilla campaign, dependent on the stealth and sharpened perceptions that made them prized targets for the stronger and faster Bloods.

Jordin had agreed to lead Roland in; she needed him, end of story. He was unyielding in his conditions, knowing she had no choice but to agree. He'd even made a reasonable case for his ability to stop Mattius from releasing the virus. They still had two full days, did they not? With his Immortal skills, he might stop the older Sovereign before he could trigger the release. Wasn't it better to cut the alchemist off at the knees before going after Feyn and confronting her formidable Dark Bloods?

They'd ridden hard and arrived an hour before dusk. But now that the time had come, Jordin couldn't settle her nerves. She'd run through all possible approaches to the Sanctuary a hundred times. With his far superior eyes and sense of smell, Roland might be the better choice for initial penetration, but she had the advantage of delivering Roland if he agreed to go in as a captive. She would be fulfilling part of her bargain, which might at least cause Mattius to pause and buy her more time.

She hadn't suggested the approach to Roland yet.

Roland flipped his hood from his head. His hair fell down over his shoulders. "Tell us the way now," he said, not bothering to turn to Jordin. His attention was fixed on the distant barriers along the entrance she'd led them to on the city's eastern border. She stared, barely seeing them in the dark, feeling practically blind compared to the creature she had been mere hours before, unable to keep from wondering if she might have been better served in this mission as an Immortal herself.

The call of those intoxicating senses, so rich and full of the sensual life all but renounced by the Sovereigns, was hard to ignore. She could hardly blame Kaya for refusing to give them up in exchange for an uncertain and less vibrant future spent toiling under the wretchedness of Sovereignty.

Wretched? Less? She shoved the insane thoughts aside and set her mind on the task at hand.

"What guarantee do I have that you won't kill me the moment I tell you?"

He turned toward her, his expression set. "The virus is our common enemy. Return my belief in your warning with trust in me."

"Mattius is no fool. If he manages to release the virus, it'll go airborne. Once that happens, we have no reason to believe it can be stopped. I have a better way."

"Tell me."

"I take you in as my hostage. Bound and gagged."

The prince arched a brow. One of the horses gave a quiet snort.

"I can understand how you might prefer me bound and gagged. And if I were anyone else I might agree," he said dryly. "Tell me, have you ever heard of an Immortal being killed in battle over this past year?"

"No."

"No." His affirmation was low and utterly sure.

"There's a reason for that. And you will be better served trusting my abilities over any crafty plan. Believe me when I say I will be in and out of your Sanctuary before this Mattius realizes he's not dreaming."

Perhaps she was underestimating him. Jonathan had simply said, *Lead him.*

"Have it your way. But I lead."

He gave a curt nod.

Turning to Michael, he said, "Ride hard down the streets. Pound Hades from the cobblestones. I want every Dark Blood within ten miles to hear. To rush to the fight. Don't engage them, just draw their attention away from us."

To Jordin: "I need to know the direction."

"Southeast," she said.

He studied the dark city then spoke to Michael again. "Send them northeast with Marten leading. No more than an hour in the city. Then exit north, into the western waste. We will rejoin in the Bethelim Valley."

Jordin knew of the valley by hearsay only, so named by the old Nomads who had their own names for any landmark on the map. It was the barest valley in the land, once lush but now unmade because in truth there was no Maker, as the saying went by those who had defied Order. There, godlike weapons had turned the earth to dust during the Zealot War five centuries ago. No life had returned. Not a soul traveled there. Ever.

None but Immortals, evidently.

Roland looked to his left. "Cain."

"My prince," the Ripper answered. The man who'd approached her with such wanton affection only two nights earlier was now fixed on nothing but dealing death. Of the four War Lords among Roland's wraiths, only

Michael had come, but Cain would surely one day be one himself—if he lived long enough.

"Your men with me and Michael."

He dipped his head. "As you say."

"Now, Michael."

She nudged her stallion with her heels and trotted toward the far right where Marten waited.

"Lead us," Roland said to Jordin, "but I will take point. I won't allow anyone to put us in danger for lack of sight. Direct me from behind."

"Fair enough."

Without a word, twenty horses to her right broke from the line and plunged down the steep slope, riders leaned back in the saddle, singularly focused on their mission. Hooves pounded, but the black-cloaked Rippers seemed to float like phantoms down the hill.

Jordin felt her pulse surge as the warriors blended into the night. How many times had the Immortals entered the city in this way? How often had they cursed Feyn's new Order of death by dealing their own? She was witnessing a wonder—nothing short of magic, however dark.

Could a race so deathly beautiful—birthed to life by Jonathan himself—be so wrong?

The sound of thundering hooves grew distant, leaving the night to silence once again. Not another word was spoken as they awaited Roland's command. A hundred thoughts began to race through Jordin's mind.

None of them good.

Roland's command came by silent action. He stepped his stallion forward five paces and stopped. He turned, locked gazes with Jordin, and then he was off, spurring his mount down the slope at a full run.

As one, Michael, Cain, and the Rippers under his

command broke on his heels, leaving Jordin alone for a moment. And then she dug her heels into her mount and gave the horse its head.

The stallion knew its place among the others well and took her after them at a full gallop. The still night came to life—dust in her nostrils, wind in her face—carrying away thoughts of what awaited.

Roland didn't seem to care that she'd fallen behind, his mission was set and his focus was clear. Sovereign or not, she would catch him—hadn't she always? And so she did, thundering through the pack to ride just behind and to his right.

She expected him to slow before reaching the barriers, but he didn't. He leaned low in the saddle and sped—directly toward the concrete wall the height of a horse's shoulders.

His stallion left the ground gracefully, as if to mock its crushing weight. Needing no guidance from her, Jordin's mount followed, lifting her to the sky in a powerful leap that took her breath away.

They landed with a bone-crushing jar and galloped on without breaking stride.

Only when Roland reached the middle of the empty street did he slow to a trot, head forward, attention fixed.

They were in Dark Blood territory. She pulled up beside him, comforted by his strong presence on such dangerous ground. There was no breeze—if any Dark Blood came within half a mile, he would know by their scent alone.

"Direction is yours," he said as the others fell in directly behind.

"Left at the next intersection," she said.

"And then?"

She hesitated. "And then I will tell you."

Roland glanced at her. He alone was hoodless, as if to make plain that his place as leader was meant to be seen by all.

"Then you'd better keep up, my little Sovereign. We take to these streets like the wind."

"We'll be heard."

He didn't bother responding but kicked his mount to a full gallop, leaning into the night.

Jordin followed hard, twenty Rippers behind her. The thunder of hooves echoed off the buildings, announced the coming storm.

She pushed her horse to catch him. Taking the turn, the prince made no move to slow for direction but took them straight down the middle of the road.

Lead him, Jordin.

"Left at the end!" she cried.

Instead he veered into an alleyway and cut behind the street she'd indicated. Naturally, the Immortals knew their hunting grounds as well as the ones who'd built the city. Likely better than Feyn herself.

He followed the alley the length of two blocks before cutting right and rejoining the street Jordin had first indicated. She assumed he'd simply avoided possible contact, alerted by his senses. Tonight he wasn't hunting Feyn's minions.

Though countless Corpses had surely heard the approaching ruckus and peered out of their windows to see dark Rippers flying by, they encountered only one Corpse in the half hour it took them to reach the edge of the ruins. They'd left the older man gawking beneath a streetlamp. On they rushed, loudly enough to summon the dead.

And then they were only a hundred meters from the edge of the ruins.

Roland knew before she told him—how, she had no idea. He suddenly jerked back on his reins and lifted a hand. Her horse pulled up hard, nearly pitching her off its back.

"What is it?"

He stared down the vacant street. The fence surrounding the abandoned ruins was in sight...she'd told him nothing of the place. Could he smell the Sovereign scent beneath the ruins?

His face was drawn tight; eyes wide with unmistakable concern.

"What is it?"

He gestured, and half of the Immortals swept to his right flank as he urged his horse into a swift trot. Jordin kept pace, her mind spinning with questions. Dark Bloods?

They reached the edge of the compound, and Roland studied the ruins, riding parallel to the fence. No sign of movement or Dark Bloods. A quick glance—every Immortal was keenly fixed on the compound.

Only when she saw that a ten-foot section of the perimeter fence had been cut away did Jordin know something was wrong. She rode on, heart lodged in her throat, hoping that her fears were misguided. There could be many reasons for the breach in the fence. It meant nothing.

But Roland seemed to know more.

He guided his mount through the opening, followed by the others who fanned out wide once past it, angling for the hedge that hid the Sanctuary entrance.

But there too was a problem, one far more telling: the hedge before the entrance had been torn away.

Jordin kicked her horse into a run, bounding over heaps of rubble and large stone blocks.

The entrance was gone. Stone had been piled up in its stead. Perhaps Mattius had ordered the opening closed for protection. But that didn't explain the trampled hedge.

She slid from her horse and ran ten paces to the stone pile, frantic. Most of them were the size of a human head, none larger than a horse's, and they came away easily in her panic.

"Help me!"

Roland sat upright in his saddle, scanning the perimeter warily. "Do it," he ordered.

Three of Cain's men dropped to the ground and quickly cleared enough of the rocks to reveal the darkness beyond. Jordin stood back, panting, fear lodged in her throat.

Roland dropped to the ground and walked to her, eyes on the gap in the wall. "Michael and Cain, with me." He stepped past her. "The rest stay here. You know what to do."

"No, you can't go in," Jordin whispered harshly. "If Mattius—"

"We're beyond that, my dear."

He ducked into the tunnel, followed by Michael and Cain, neither of whom gave her more than a passing glance.

She looked over her shoulder and saw that the others were forming into a wide arc, horses facing away from the entrance, sentries of the prince.

Jordin edged into the unlit opening, aware of the deep darkness beyond. Roland had already vanished below with Michael and Cain. She took the flight of stone steps by memory.

She reached the bottom landing and was about to call out in the darkness when dim light flooded the cavern.

Roland stood at a wall-torch he'd apparently lit for her benefit, and was looking back to see that she'd made it.

"Where's the virus?" he asked.

Unable to form words, she rushed to the torch, snatched it from him, and ran past Roland, her mind lost. Down the tunnel that fed into the main chamber.

The moment she spun into the massive cavern where they normally congregated, she saw that they were gone. They would have put up a fight here. Both Dark Bloods and Sovereigns would have fallen here. But there was no one and no sign of blood that she could see.

Taken captive then?

She hurried through, searching the corners for any missed sign in the dim light.

"Check every door!" Roland's order echoed through the cavern.

Jordin pushed herself into a run again, thinking now only of one room: the council chamber. She reached the large door, twisted the handle, and shoved the door open.

Coils of smoke wafted past her, flooding her nostrils with an odor as offensive and putrid as any she could remember. Two oil lamps were burning, one on each wall. But the smoke didn't come from them...

But from the charred bodies on the floor.

She staggered back. Her heart refused to pump blood; her lungs ceased drawing breath.

More than ten bodies. More than twenty.

All of them!

"Here, Roland!" Michael called. "The laboratory!"

She blinked at the sight, fighting to understand, knowing that there was nothing to comprehend beyond what her eyes told her already. She didn't know what to do—her mind was no longer processing thought properly.

"Jordin!"

Roland. His voice urgent.

She reeled back out of the chamber, staggered. Roland was standing in the doorway to the laboratory thirty paces down the hall.

"Come."

Her feet refused to move.

"Come!" he thundered.

Jordin stumbled over something on the floor, caught herself with one hand, and lurched toward him, hardly aware of her feet.

And then he was there, grabbing her arm to steady her, pulling her down and into the lab.

A thin veil of smoke partially obscured the instruments and broken vials of alchemy strewn across the work benches. But Jordin's eyes were immediately drawn to what she saw on the ground.

She could not mistake Mattius's partially burned body, dead eyes staring wide at the ceiling, his blistered mouth twisted in its final cry of horror.

His bloody fingers clung to a single vial sealed by a cork and resin.

The virus, surely. Mattius would go for no other vial in such dire straits. The thing for which they had gone to such desperate measures. For which all the others had lost their lives.

Roland strode past her, crouched by the burned body, and pried the stiff fingers from the vial stuck against the palm. The Immortals had what they'd come for. If Rom was Dark Blood, she was now the only living Sovereign. And then Roland would make her Immortal, leaving no trace of Sovereign blood on the earth.

Jonathan's legacy had met a gruesome end.

He slowly stood and stepped back, eyes fixed on the vial stuck in Mattius's hand. Bloodied. The alchemist's palm was cut. Not by a Dark Blood's sword, but by glass.

The vial lay in two pieces, snapped at its center. He'd broken it in his own hand. There was an "R" marked on the upper half of the broken vial. *Reaper.*

Jordin looked up at Roland. His eyes bore a hole through her very soul. He knew as well as she: the Prince of Immortals, glowing with life now as he stood tall, was already a dead man. Along with all of those under his rule who boasted Immortality.

Mattius had released the virus.

CHAPTER TWENTY-ONE

F EYN STOOD before the great desk of the Sovereign office, staring at the lone object sitting on its surface but not really seeing it. Her mind was in a coil, the events of the last twenty-four hours spinning like a tempest around her.

The ten thousand Dark Bloods had split among three sectors of the city. South, Rom had said. They had gone southwest, south central, and southeast and combed every block, storming apartments, homes, and commercial buildings, offices and basilicas. Left fleeing Corpses and screams in their wake as they searched back rooms, closets, stairwells, attics, rooftops. Even the old crypt of one of the basilicas. At least eight deaths had been reported, many more beatings. None of this was uncommon where Dark Bloods were concerned, and was of no concern to her.

All that had mattered was finding the Sovereigns.

It had taken seven hours for word to return that the Sovereigns had been found and summarily slain.

Her minions had come back with no bodies, under orders to kill and burn. But they'd brought racks of vials... three of them marked with an ominous "R." *Reaper.*

Corban had immediately sequestered himself in his

laboratory, feverishly working to unlock the secrets of the viral code. An hour ago, Ammon had come to report: It was indeed a virus. It appeared lethal.

Feyn stepped around the side of the desk, sagged for a moment against its edge before slowly sitting down in the great chair behind it. She clasped the chair by the arms until her knuckles went white.

The Sovereigns were dead, their heretical coven purified by fire. She would have been deeply satisfied except for one thing: the unsettling report that they had struck down a Sovereign alchemist in the underground lab.

The look on Corban's face as they received the news had echoed her own dread—her own rage that even the Sovereign of the world could not know what events had transpired in the moments before they'd found him.

Had he released the virus at first alarm? Or had her Dark Bloods killed him before he could consign them all to a death sentence?

She remained utterly still, as one does in the eye of a storm. But that storm was nothing compared to the squall within her heart—one made worse by the knowledge that she, the most powerful being on earth, could do nothing but wait as Corban tried to unravel the virus and create an antivirus before it was too late. Every passing minute was one fewer that she might have left in this life. One fewer that Corban might have to create an antidote. One fewer before she learned the truth, for herself, of Bliss or Hades.

Strange...she hadn't believed in either when she'd emerged from stasis. Hadn't contemplated death even once since the moment before she'd been cut down fifteen years ago. But now she wondered for the first time in years about those who had gone on to the next life, assuming there was one.

Her gaze lifted to the heart in the glass jar standing on her desk again. It had belonged to the living once. Where was its owner now?

A knock sounded on the side door. Adrenaline spiked in her veins, disconcerting her cultivated stillness. She bowed her head, touched her fingertips together, elbows on the arms of her chair, and drew a slow breath through her nostrils. She might have prayed in that posture, but the only Maker she recognized was herself.

When she felt the steadying of her pulse, she lifted her head and said at last, "Come."

She pushed up from the desk as the man entered and walked toward his kneeling form. A Dark Blood, young, his hair like a dark waterfall about his shoulders.

So Corban was still working.

"Yes?"

"My liege," the man said, lifting his head only enough to stare at the toes of her leather boots.

"Well?"

"A citizen unknown to us has come with an urgent message. He waits for you in the Senate Hall."

Annoyance flared up her neck. "What do you mean he waits for me in the Senate Hall? A Corpse?"

"Yes, my liege."

"And does this Corpse have a name?"

"No, my liege."

"Nameless Corpses don't just walk into the Citadel, let alone the Senate Hall."

"No, my liege."

She stared at him.

"My Dark Bloods return from routing the south of the city, and you come to say a stranger expects me to meet with him?" She reached down, seized him by his beautiful hair, and lifted him up onto—and then off of—his knees. "Whom do you obey? Me or him?"

"You, my liege! He said to tell you that he's come to see the white dove."

The meaning of the phrase fell into her mind. White dove?

She set the man down and stepped back, stunned by the implications of those two words.

For a moment, she stood unmoving. The room seemed to rotate around her of its own accord, as if rewinding time. She couldn't put thought to the words.

A Corpse.

It couldn't be.

"Fetch Seth," she said at last, barely hearing the words over the thunder of her heart.

"My liege?"

"Seth!" she cried. "Get him immediately!"

"Seth . . . but Seth is dead, my liege."

Dead. At her hand.

"Come."

She stepped past the man and willed herself down the passageway, followed quickly by the Blood. They went out through a side door before it descended toward the laboratories and ancient subterranean chambers—into the public corridor.

White dove. How long had it been since she'd heard the words?

She gestured to one of the guards lining the corridor, one of perhaps thirty spaced at even stations. Officials and their assistants, administrators and visiting royals, stopped at the sight of her, instinctively drew back beneath the arched and gilded ceiling, dropping to their knees, eyes averted. She strode past them, her pace picking up speed, not bothering with the pretense of decorum. The guard fell in behind her.

She pulled open the great door of the senate antechamber and crossed the room in quick strides as the younger Dark Blood rushed ahead to haul open the great door of the chamber itself.

It was lit within. The electric lights of the unseen panel had been switched on.

She entered, walking slowly along the back row of the political theater, her pulse a drum against her temples.

Then she saw him—a lone figure sitting behind the stone table on the dais. In the Sovereign's seat.

His head was bowed beneath a cowl, face obscured in shadow.

She forced her step to an even stride as she walked down the great aisle, remembering the stride of the Sovereign—the true Sovereign—ruler of the world. She could all but feel the gold beading of her bodice glinting beneath the artificial light, the heavy gold of the ring hurting her fingers, which were clenched into a fist.

She made her way up the stairs, stepped onto the edge of the dais, her eyes not once leaving the figure. She crossed to the stone table and stopped, facing him squarely.

The man's hands were folded before him. Dry, cracked, and rugged. The robe he wore was coarse and threadbare in places along the sleeve. A grizzled, dirty-gray beard fell just to the neckline of the robe. The man's mouth was parched, lips peeling.

"There's only one man alive who knows what my father used to call me," she said with dangerous quiet. Her Bloods had ascended the dais, ready to strike the man down at a word. To halt him forever if he moved too quickly.

"The white dove," he said, his voice graveled but gentle. "Though now her feathers appear to be black."

"Reveal yourself," she said, very softly.

For a moment the man didn't move. And then one of the hands slowly lifted to his head and pushed back the hood of the cowl to reveal a head of long, tangled gray hair. A face darkened to leather by the sun. A face she knew all too well.

"Hello, sister."

Saric.

She stared, her ribs straining for breath against the bodice of her gown.

The last time she'd seen him, his skin had been alabaster. His veins as dark as hers, his eyes so black as to have no pupils. But now...here sat a Corpse.

How was it possible? But there—the tan of his skin, once so pale, peeling in places from the sun. His eyes, the pale blue of Brahmin royalty—as pale, almost, as her own had been once. No trace at all of the dark veins anywhere—not even the blue shadow of them that the royals so prized beneath their pallid skin.

He was utterly himself as he had been long ago. And utterly unremarkable.

"How did you survive?" she demanded.

He offered no answer.

"You're a fool if you think you can claim that throne."

"I have no interest in thrones."

She laughed, the sound brittle as shards, echoing up to the domed ceiling.

"Then you're an imposter. The brother I knew cares for nothing but power."

"The man you knew is dead."

"And yet far too alive." She was shaking with the rage

of the past. Of his blood within her. The dominance he had exercised over her. The ways he had both ruined and made her.

"But perhaps you are right. I don't see a dead man—I see something far more pathetic." She planted her hands on the table and leaned over it toward him. *"I see a Corpse."*

His eyes met hers.

"Do you?" His expression was devoid of emotion.

"I don't know by what alchemy you renounced the Dark Blood, but it suits you. You always were a fool."

He offered no explanation. All these years, she had assumed him dead. And yet here he sat.

"How did you get in here?"

"You forget, I know the Citadel as well as I know you."

"You know nothing of me!" She felt nonplussed. "What do you want this time? Your years of seducing and bending me to your will are behind you. Did you come to beg? Have you seen my army?" She swept her arm out. "Have you seen the glory of them flooding the city streets? I am ten times the Sovereign you ever would have been."

He remained unmoving, showing no emotion, pale blue eyes steady on her. She could understand his lack of ambition as a Corpse, but there was no fear in his eyes either. Perhaps the wasteland had baked his brain.

"You can't help but play the role of the pathetic fool, can you? Always wanting what was mine."

She started to turn away but then wheeled back and spat in his face.

He blinked once but otherwise showed no reaction, even as saliva ran down his cheek.

"Take him away to the dungeons he so loved," she said to the younger Dark Blood.

"Sister."

The Dark Blood started forward.

"I have news that will save your life," Saric said.

"Seize him!"

The guard hesitated. Blinked once, as though confused.

"Sister," Saric said.

She might have flown into a rage at the guard's hesitation but for Saric's use of the word a second time: *sister*. Hatred swelled in her veins.

She snatched up her hand to stop the Blood.

"No. The dungeon is too good for you. If you would be a Corpse, I should do you the mercy of killing you here."

"If you refuse to hear me, you will soon be dead."

Ice flooded her. He knew about the virus? How could he?

"They're coming for you now. You'll be dead before dawn. How can you be Sovereign if you're dead?"

"Don't be absurd."

"They're coming for you now."

He stared at her, unyielding.

"Who?" she demanded. "Tens of thousands stand in guard."

"They've found a way. If you would live through the night, you must stop them before they breach the Citadel."

Them. The Sovereigns were annihilated. He could only mean the Immortals.

Roland.

"You're mad." She gave a brittle laugh. "You speak the impossible. How would anyone make it past my defenses?"

"The same way I did."

His claim stalled her. Indeed, the Dark Blood had said he'd simply shown up. No one knew the subterranean tunnels of the Citadel like Saric.

"Where? How?"

"Through the ancient maze."

"I know of no maze."

Saric slowly pushed back. The Dark Blood beside him stepped back, clearly at a loss for protocol in the presence of a former Sovereign, her father's successor. "You will find it in the Book of Sovereigns locked in the back vault of the archive."

"What Book of Sovereigns?"

"Had you succeeded our father as decreed, he would have given it to you, in secret, on the evening of your inauguration."

"No one has ever spoken of such a book!"

"When I murdered Father and became Sovereign, I took his key." He slid a simple, ancient-looking key out of a pocket in his cloak and set it on the table. "My gift to you, so you may indeed be Sovereign. Consider my debt paid."

But of course. When he resurrected her to dark life, he had never meant for her to rule. He had retained the secrets of the office for himself.

She reached across the table and took it as he pushed up from the Sovereign seat.

"Hurry. They will come."

Saric quietly walked toward the door behind the dais. And then he was gone.

It took her a moment to recover her wits. It occurred to her then that Saric had found a way to become Corpse through some kind of alchemy. As such his blood might hold another key, one that could offer an antidote to the virus.

"After him! Bring him to me alive!"

*   *   *

SWIFTLY, TO the dungeons. She had found the book. Within, a map of the ancient maze. She'd dispatched a thousand Dark Bloods to the assembly grounds within the hour. Death would not claim her so easily a second time.

Now as she descended, the glass object curled in the crook of her arm, she found the storm of her anxiety gone, replaced by cold rage for Saric's undeterred appearance.

And disappearance.

The first two Bloods had given chase down to the archive, all the way to the laboratory and ancient dungeons, but had come up empty-handed. She'd sent others to hunt him down.

How had he known Roland was coming?

Why had her guard hesitated?

She told herself it was shock. That the Dark Blood standing beside him hadn't known who to defer to—the seated Sovereign or the former one.

Her own hesitance bothered her even more. That even now Saric had that effect on her, though his blood—now in her veins—no longer flowed through his own. That by the smallest token of a key, she had learned that her Sovereignty had not been complete.

Once more, Saric had disappeared without consequence.

Why had he warned her? To worm his way into her confidence again, no doubt. He would have further surprises in store for her—he always did. This time she would be ready.

Assuming, of course, that she lived.

No word from Corban in all this time. Ammon reported only that he worked feverishly by the hour, thus far without success. He'd taken up work on samples of Rom's blood taken before his seroconversion, but she was afraid it was too old already. A living Sovereign's blood might offer a key to an antidote. But there were none.

She passed the guard to the ancient laboratory and was tempted to step inside Corban's private chamber, but her presence would only prove a distraction. He needed no further goading; his own life was on the line.

Instead, she strode to the back of the cavernous chamber, toward the ancient cells, directly to Rom's chamber.

He was sitting along the back of the wall, a shadow beyond reach of the torchlight.

"I have a gift for you."

Rom raised his head.

She lifted the glass jar that had sat on her desk for hours, morbid and repugnant at once. She saw the whites of his eyes go wide as she threw it to the ground. It shattered with a resounding crash of splintering glass, the heart tumbling to the dirty floor.

Avra's heart.

Rom leaped to his feet. She kicked it through the bars into the cell. He stared, his face white, knowing very well the implication.

"We found your Sanctuary. The Sovereigns are no more."

He slowly raised his gaze to her.

"Tell me I'm right," she demanded. "That there are no more living Sovereigns."

His eyes twittered, fighting back emotion.

"Speak."

"Not all of them," he said.

She paused, felt her veins chill. Was he lying? No, not possible.

"What do you mean?" she said, her tone dangerously quiet.

"There is one more."

"Ah yes, of course," she said. "Your precious Jonathan, whom you refuse to call dead."

"No. Another."

She stepped toward the bars, grasped them with white hands. Peered directly into the darkness at him.

"Who?"

"The one coming for you."

"Who is coming for me?"

"Jordin."

CHAPTER TWENTY-TWO

M AKE THIS plain to me!" Roland paced before Jordin in the Sanctuary's great chamber like a lion in a cage. "Tell me everything!"

Michael stood to one side, glaring at Jordin as if she, not the virus, were the scourge that hung over her own life.

Cain leaned against a carved pillar to her left, the seduction gone from his eyes.

The change in them was profound. The realization of Immortality cut short wasn't sitting well with them.

"I have," Jordin said. "Maybe you should have listened more closely the first time."

Michael was on her like a cat, hand around her throat. "You will remember your place, Sovereign!" she hissed.

"I . . . do."

"Release her!" Roland snapped.

That Jordin was the only one in the room who might survive the virus could not be lost on them. If this didn't give her an advantage, it at least emboldened her. The only thing was, she hardly cared if she lived or died at the moment.

Michael slowly released her grip. "Then watch your tongue or I'll cut it out," she said, shoving her.

"Enough!" Roland said, gathering himself. "And yes, I was listening. I want to hear it again. You're sure the virus was in that vessel?"

"I have no doubt. Releasing it was his great obsession. The vial is marked with an 'R' and the virus is called Reaper. Do you need more?"

"And your claim is that this Reaper is carried on the air."

"It's no claim. Every Dark Blood who set foot in this place is infected and has taken the virus into the city."

"Infected. As are we," Roland said with a glower.

She hesitated.

"Yes. As are your Rippers outside. The virus has a three-day latency, after which every Dark Blood and Immortal breathing today will become deathly ill and die. By coming here, you have executed your own death sentence. I tried to warn you."

"Does it matter?" he said, sweeping his arm wide. "The damage was done before we came."

"By Rom," Michael said. "If everything you say is true, he betrayed all of us."

"Betrayed you? He *fought* for you!" She shoved a finger toward the exit tunnel. "He could have destroyed all of our enemies without raising a single blade! Instead he went to Feyn, knowing the danger, to save you. If you would have listened to me when I first arrived, we might have reached Rom before Feyn wrung it out of him. This falls on *your* head, not Rom's."

"Reached Rom how?" she shot back. "Your memory failed you, remember?"

Jordin drilled Roland with a glare. "I was *delayed*. One day might have made all the difference."

"By your own stubbornness!" Michael said.

Roland lifted his hand to silence them.

"What happened no longer matters. Only the preservation of our kind."

"Who are no longer Immortal," Jordin said.

"Enough!"

The room echoed with his roar.

"Tell me what else you know."

She turned her exchanges with Rom and Mattius over in her head.

"We have to assume that Rom is Dark Blood and will soon be infected as well."

"And? How do we stop this virus?"

She gave a faint shake of her head. "There is no way. It will infect the world. All Dark Bloods and Immortals will die. Corpses will come down with a common cold and Sovereigns will probably lose their emotions. The damage is done."

He stared at her.

She drew a slow breath, not knowing if what she said next might get her killed for the mere suggestion. "There is one way to live. Convert using my blood. Only Jonathan's blood can save you. It seems that we've come full circle."

"Never!" His response could not have been put more forcefully.

"Not even if it means *living*?"

"Under the tyranny of fear once again? Never!" He took two strides to his left before spinning back, his face dark. "You forget that we were Nomad before we became Immortal. For five hundred years we rebelled against the Order of fear on principle. I am a prince bound by my own history as much as my blood. Your Sovereignty is nothing but humanity stripped of life. The virus returns us all to Corpse. I will *die* before I put even a single drop of death-tainted blood into my body and so betray the true life Jonathan brought us!"

His words sank into her mind and heart like lead, pressing hope from her bones. There was far more truth in them than she would have admitted even a week ago.

Mattius, in his shortsightedness, had sentenced the world to a future not of peace...but of misery.

"I'm the only living Sovereign," she said. "It's not certain that I will lose my emotions. But what *is* certain is that if you refuse to take my blood, you and all your people..."

"Did I not make myself clear? Never!"

Had she expected any other response? Roland would far prefer to die in battle than give an inch to fear or Sovereignty, which he saw as a living death in and of itself. And the example of her own wretched existence had done nothing to convince him otherwise.

Nothing to show him the abundant life Jonathan had promised...

Because she hadn't found it herself.

She turned away, rubbed her temples with her fingers as if to force cohesive thought through her mind. The door to the council chamber rested closed, as did the door to Mattius's laboratory. With the world pressing in on her, she couldn't begin to think of how to properly honor the dead. So many children and elderly...the thought sickened her. If there was any grace in the situation, it was that they'd died as Sovereigns. And that they had died by sword before fire.

She could only hope that Rom might yet be converted from Dark Blood. And Kaya.

"The virus isn't *proven* to kill Immortals," Cain said. "How could this alchemist know if he hasn't tested it?"

"Because Immortal blood is the same as Mortal blood," Jordin said. "He was sure, trust me. Do you truly want to take a chance on him being wrong?"

"I am known to take many risks," he said calmly. "The only one I refuse to consider is changing my nature."

Cain squatted on one heel and looked up at Roland. "Rom may know what she doesn't."

Roland glanced at Michael, but she offered no opinion. He'd come to heads with Rom six years ago when the Mortals had split, but any difference between them was now moot.

Jordin seized the moment. "He has a point. If Rom's a Dark Blood, he may be able to return to Sovereign. His blood might be resistant to the virus in ways mine isn't, having contracted it." It was a long shot, and she knew it. "If not, in the very least he may know more than I do."

Roland's jaw tightened as he considered her words.

"It was his suggestion, months ago, that one of us might become Immortal to reach you, Roland. He might well become Immortal himself if he thinks it will save you. He's never abandoned his beliefs."

Roland gave her a distinctly wry look.

"Don't you understand? He doesn't want you to die!"

He hesitated only a moment longer.

"Then there's only one course of action," he said at last. "We go to the Citadel. I can only hope you know as much as you claim."

"I know the way. That's all."

"Then take us," he said, moving toward the exit already. "We will rip Feyn's head from her shoulders."

She strode after him. "And Rom?"

His words came over his shoulder. "Let's pray he can save us all."

CHAPTER TWENTY-THREE

JORDIN LED the twenty Rippers through the city, flanked by Roland on her right, Michael on her left.

It should have been a time to savor. She, the lone Sovereign, leading Roland and his most accomplished warriors to a destiny of her choosing. Indeed, even now she might lead them astray and leave them to die, forever ridding the world of Jonathan's scourge.

She could lead them into a pitched battle with Dark Bloods, stand back and watch as they slaughtered each other, soaking the ground with their defiled blood. Or she could use them to kill Feyn and rescue Rom as she had intended. What did it matter?

She was the only one among them who would survive. Jonathan's legacy, tainted by the effects of Reaper on her emotions, would live only in her. A crippled salvation.

But she felt no salvation. Not a hint of glory or peace in the thought. The circumstances of life had long ago slashed her heart. Somehow, inexplicably, it had not stopped, each pump of her Sovereign blood the living reminder of abject failure. Of Jonathan's illusive love, long lost. Of the brutal slaying and burning of so many whom she'd loved. Of every Corpse oblivious to the salvation that had once lived among them.

That Feyn had found the Sanctuary meant Rom had given up its location. She had known the moment she smelled the fire within the cavernous chambers that he had been turned and forced to reveal the Sovereign remnant. If he could betray them, what was she herself capable of? She touched the seroconversion kit in her jacket and prayed she would not fail him.

And then there was Roland. She could not deny the pull of the prince on her heart, even now. The memory of his gentle embrace just last night refused to leave her mind. The prince in him had commanded her once. The heart in the Immortal called to her still.

Kaya was waiting for him, she knew—a young Immortal yearning for her master. She ignored the strange jealousy she felt and pitied the girl her naïve oblivion; death waited for her.

They'd ridden quickly, their thunder of death faded to a silent whisper—toward the west perimeter of the Citadel, Jordin at the lead, detouring past Dark Blood posts at Roland's signal. With each passing mile, Feyn's defenses became thicker. They made no attempt to avoid those few Corpses they encountered, knowing they would only run into hiding, perhaps make a frantic call to alert forces—too late.

Their objective: the ancient maze known only to sitting Sovereigns and ancient keepers of secrets—a labyrinth of passages reserved for royal escape. For hundreds of years the knowledge was regarded mostly as myth passed from Sovereign to Sovereign.

Which is why, Jordin had explained to Roland, it was unlikely Feyn would know of the maze. Saric had taken his father's life—there was no time for Vorrin to pass the secret to him. And Saric had seated Feyn as his successor before Jonathan had come of age.

"How did you come by knowledge of this maze?" Roland had demanded.

"When we took refuge in the Sanctuary under the ruins, the Keeper found ancient papers containing, among other secrets, the existence of the maze by those who first worked on it. He showed only Rom and me."

"And why haven't you used the maze to take the head from this snake?"

Jordin gave a wry look. "If it's Feyn you mean, Rom refused to touch her. Any Dark Blood but her. You know how he has protected Feyn since the beginning. More practically, the maze comes up to the assembly grounds behind the palace. The palace is highly protected by more Dark Bloods than we could have taken on head to head."

He frowned. She made the case even more plain.

"The Dark Bloods swarming the grounds would have *smelled* us coming. We've only ever had a few warriors amongst us. Without our former Mortal sense..." She shook her head. "It would have been suicide."

"But with an elite force of Immortal Rippers...," he said.

She leveled her gaze at him. "Yes."

He gave a faint nod.

"I will get you past the walls of the Citadel," Jordin said. "You will fight your way to the palace."

The entrance to the maze was in the cellar of an old basilica north of the Citadel—too close to the Citadel itself, too much in the thick of the Dark Bloods surrounding the capital. They had to come in from the east.

Riding through the abandoned streets, the kit tight against her in her jacket, Jordin couldn't help but wonder if she would live to get to Rom at all.

An instant later, Roland stopped, hand raised.

Michael and Cain's Rippers halted as one, leaving Jordin's horse to trot on several paces before she reined it in.

Roland walked his horse abreast, eyes narrowed down the street. For several seconds he listened closely to the night. She heard only the silence of the city, but that meant nothing; Roland himself might hear a cat land on padded feet a block away . . . or the scrape of a Dark Blood boot along the pavement a block beyond that.

"How much farther?"

"Half a mile."

"They're too thick ahead. It's Feyn's way, these bands of her minions around the Citadel. We could fight our way through, but we'd take too many losses."

"You are unaccustomed to losses," she said, unable to keep the tinge of acid from her voice. "Some of us aren't so fortunate."

He turned in his saddle and studied the side of her face.

"I'm sorry for your loss."

"You'll have your own soon enough."

The moment the words entered the night, she regretted them.

"Forgive me."

He faced the street. "We have to veer east," he said, and then tugged his mount round without waiting for direction. Still the Prince of Immortals till his dying breath.

Roland took them east and then north, ignoring Jordin as they circled out of range of the Dark Bloods ringing the Citadel like a swarm of black hornets protecting their queen.

Only when they were much farther north did he turn to her with a nod and allow her to take the lead once again.

She took them in several blocks to the Basilica of the Gates—the one reportedly used by Megas five hundred years earlier. Megas, the first Sovereign, who had canonized the Book of Orders, murdered the Order's founder and unleashed the virus that rendered every living human in the world dead. Megas, who was so paranoid in his new fear-filled world that he had the ancient maze built as a means of escape from the Citadel.

Jordin pulled her horse to a stop before the gate and nodded at the large arched door. "This is it."

Roland scanned the grounds. The basilica was no longer in use, maintained only as a historical site in tribute to Megas.

True to its name, a large black gate in the basilica's wrought-iron fence separated the grounds from the street. Patchy weeds had taken over what had once been a wide concrete yard within. It was broken into crumbled pieces, their edges peering through dirt where they were not obscured by the trash that had managed to blow inside during any one of Byzantium's characteristic storms.

Two columns stood sentry at the door, joined by another iron gate. The great door behind it, arched and ominous, was chained and padlocked shut. Overhead, stained-glass windows ran intact along the walls. Jordin couldn't make out the scenes but they were always the same: the horrors of the Zealot Wars...the philosopher Sirin cradling a dove of peace...and always, just above the altar, Megas holding the bound Book of Orders, canonized under his rule.

Jordin considered the wrought-iron fence. Five feet tall, it ran fifty yards in either direction from the outermost gate and apparently around the whole complex.

"The grounds behind are our best bet. There's a rear entrance."

"Where is the entrance?"

"In the cellar."

"And from there?"

"We follow the tunnel that leads to the Citadel." That was putting it simply; the maze itself might trap the unwitting pursuer for hours—even days. Longer, if they never found their way out.

"You remember the way?"

"I hope so."

He cast her a glance. Her memory was clearly a sore spot with him.

Roland turned his mount to face the fence and took it straight toward the iron gate. With a powerful leap, the stallion cleared the rail and landed deftly beyond.

Before Jordin could turn her horse, the others were following, horses' hooves clearing the pointed iron balustrades without so much as a nick. With the muted thunder of a drum, they landed in the darkness of the yard and disappeared after their leader. Jordin held her breath and spurred her mount into the short takeoff. For the second time that night she sailed high and landed with the grace of a superbly trained horse and rider.

She might not be Immortal, but as a Nomad she'd ridden with the best.

When she rounded the corner, half the Rippers were already dismounting, slinging reins around the overgrown hedge along the back wall. Roland watched from horseback as Michael examined the industrial door.

She turned with her report. "The windows."

Roland dropped from his horse, and jabbed his forefingers at two mid-height windows on either side of the door. Cain put his boot through one, another Ripper slammed his elbow through the other. Glass shattered and crashed into the building.

All of this happened before Jordin thought to dismount. Watching the precision and speed with which Roland's Immortals worked, the way they executed commands seamlessly and without question, garnered respect—regardless of the circumstances.

"Jordin."

She glanced at Roland and dropped from her horse. Quickly tied it off.

With a nod, she strode to the window cleared by Cain and slung first one, then two legs in, and ducked into the darkened basilica.

Before Jordin had time to collect herself, Michael entered through the other window, gracefully pivoting on one palm with both knees bent to clear the windowsill, like a dancer sailing through the air.

Others flew in in rapid succession behind her.

"Move."

The order came from one of the Rippers behind her. She stepped to one side and glanced down the hall, attempting to gain her bearings as the rest of the Rippers entered, filling the dark space.

"Follow me," Roland said in a low voice, taking her arm.

Despite her years of training under Roland, her former status as a champion, Jordin felt like a child among them as Roland pulled her forward.

For a moment, blinded by darkness and at Roland's mercy, she despised her Sovereign state. A part of her wondered if it would be better to die as an Immortal if only to feel—really *feel*—full life once again before entering whatever fate awaited her beyond the grave. To go down fighting but vibrantly alive to the last.

She could see only dim outlines, lit by the streetlamps

beyond the pale windows. Down one hall. A soft report from the far side of the basilica: one of them had already found the way down. It would have taken her many minutes, groping in darkness.

All the while Roland's hand was curled around her bicep.

"Where in the cellar?" he asked.

"In the back, there should be a storage room," she said.

Roland passed the information on, led her into a stairwell. Here, darkness faded to pitch black, and while she managed to navigate the first three steps, she stumbled on the fourth, remaining upright only by Roland's steadying hand.

"Cain, find a torch," he ordered. Then to her: "Forgive me, I forget how limited your sight is. If we can't find a torch, I'll have to carry you. It would be better for you to tell me the way and remain behind."

"No." The thought of being left alone terrified her. "No, I have to guide you."

The way through the tunnels was dependent on precise turns at only three of nine intersections—the second, the seventh, and the ninth—but she wasn't about to give Roland this knowledge. She didn't trust Roland to bring Rom back alive.

"Just find a torch."

He hesitated, then guided her quickly down the stairs. Gravel slid underfoot. Flame flared before Cain's face—a small lighter in his right hand three paces away. His eyes were on her as he touched the fire to a makeshift torch. Orange light flooded a large cellar lined with racks of barrels. Incense? Lantern oil?

Half of the Rippers stood ready, watching Roland for command—the others spilled down the stairs behind Jordin. Roland released her arm and strode toward wooden barrels stacked neatly on their sides against the far wall.

He kicked a wood block wedged at the base of the barrel on one end, placed the heel of his boot on the barrel, and shoved it hard. The container rolled away and the small mountain of kegs collapsed with a pounding roll.

Jordin's pulse surged as the telltale outline of old grayed slats appeared on the wall. An entrance, hastily sealed long ago.

"Take it down," Roland said.

Cain handed the torch to one of his men, stepped up to the wall, and slammed his boot into one of the slats. It cracked. Another hard kick and the ancient wood shattered. Five more hard thrusts of his boot and the entrance was cleared of all but one slat on the right, two paces wide and just high enough for a tall man to pass under without restriction.

Cain stepped in and peered down the dark passage. He turned to Roland.

"Clear."

"Take the lead with the flame. At your back. Michael, rear." Roland eyed Jordin. "We stay close to Cain's torch. Be certain of your turns. When we get to the final passage, I lead."

His words were direct and calm, but she knew he was seething behind his dark stare. What was it like for a man so possessed by Immortality to learn he was infected with a lethal virus for which there was no cure—no cure short of becoming what he'd lived to annihilate?

The silent ride through the city had apparently only strengthened his resolve. There was no search for salvation in those glittering eyes. This was a mission of vengeance.

She followed Cain, who'd taken the torch and headed into the passage ahead of her.

Roland kept stride without a word. The sound of the others' boots on the stone floor echoed softly around her—a company of guards, ushering her to her execution, she thought.

No. It was *they* who were sentenced to death.

It occurred to her then that in the face of his own demise, Roland would not only be hard pressed to take Sovereign blood but to allow any Sovereign blood to survive him.

That he would not afford her mercy.

By killing her, he would effectively end the day of Keepers, Nomads, Mortals, Immortals, and Sovereigns alike. Only the Corpses would survive them, dead as they had been for nearly five hundred years.

The ancient tunnel smelled like earth, must, and mold. The limestone walls overhead were rough-hewn; the passage had been hastily cut, purely utilitarian. It ran straight without so much as a single alcove or marking. A mile, at least, she imagined. They were likely passing directly beneath the fortifications of Dark Bloods immediately outside the Citadel wall itself.

It took them ten minutes to reach the first intersection, smaller tunnels branching to the right and left.

"Farther," Jordin said.

They continued, still without speaking.

Only twenty paces later they found a second junction.

"To the right," she said.

Roland exchanged a glance with her and nodded at his man.

They turned into the passage, which took them a hundred paces before intersecting a third and then a fourth, fifth, and sixth. At the seventh, she directed them to the left.

Another long, straight tunnel, past an eighth intersection. Only at the ninth did she indicate a right turn, which led them into a passage that ran at an angle rather than perpendicular to the way they had come.

"How many more turns?" Roland asked softly.

There was no reason to lie.

"None."

He pulled up, as did Cain and those behind.

"To the rear."

"No."

"Do as I say." His tone, though quiet, could not have been more demanding. "They'll smell you coming."

"I'll go to the rear at the exit, not before."

"You'll do as I say." It was a dangerous growl.

"What are you going to do? Hog-tie me and drag me behind?"

"If necessary. You're a liability."

"I won't be able to see."

"To the rear!"

She tried to think of another reason why she should hold her ground but failed. Her hesitation took the matter out of her hands. Roland glanced at the men behind her, and strong fingers wrapped around her arm. She tried to pull away, but the effort was completely wasted.

"Take your hands off me!"

"Bring her, Michael." Without a backward look, Roland and Cain headed deeper into the passage, their pace quickening with the length of their strides.

"Rom's blood may contain the only antidote for the virus!" Her voice echoed down the tunnel. "His death could seal your own!"

The Rippers filed past her as if she were nothing more than a stone in a riverbed. And then they were moving at a jog, picking up speed like a pack of hounds that had scented prey, until they were rushing down the tunnel at a full-out run.

"Stay close!" Michael snapped, taking her arm firmly and pulling her along with her. "Keep your feet!"

"Our blood may offer a deterrent to the virus, Michael," she panted. "At least Rom's might. You can't kill him."

"Keep silent or I will silence you!"

Jordin had no reason to doubt the warrior. The woman she once called a friend had hardened in the years since they had fought and ridden together, and she had been hard then. Jordin let her mind settle, keeping close the thought that Michael had nothing to gain by her stumbling or running into a wall. Roland had ordered her to bring Jordin, and so she would, despite the fact that they no longer needed her to breach the Citadel.

It took another few minutes to reach the end of the passage. The file bunched close at what at first appeared to be a dead end. By the light of the torch, burned nearly to a nub, Jordin could see the outline of brick limestone blocking the way.

"Dark Bloods," Michael muttered.

Michael kept her gaze ahead, focus intense.

"Too many."

How many? Turning back would not be an option for Roland. He was committed, consumed with one mission: killing Feyn.

Darkness suddenly swallowed the passage, the flame extinguished. She heard grating and crashing stone blocks. Michael tugged on her arm, dragging her forward. They were moving. And quickly.

After no more than twenty strides, Jordin was at the jagged outline of an opening framing a dull yellow glow beyond.

Michael released her, leaping over toppled blocks, knives in hand already. She rushed after the Rippers, suddenly eager for protection regardless of what awaited them. She barely sidestepped a two-foot boulder and spilled out of the passage.

The assembly grounds lay at the center of an open-air arena carved from the limestone, with thirty or forty rows of tiered bench seating around the circumference. But it was the scene that greeted her, lit by a hundred torches, that pushed her heart into her throat.

No fewer than five hundred Dark Bloods lined the tiers, their black-and-gold eyes fixed on the Rippers spread out to Jordin's left, ready for their prince's order, hands poised to snatch at weapons.

Jordin's lungs were devoid of breath. How had they known?

The grounds lay in perfect silence. She scanned the tiers. She was wrong—the Bloods numbered closer to a thousand. They were utterly still, waiting for some command, showing not a hint of concern for the elusive Rippers trapped before them at last.

They had to turn back!

The thought screamed through Jordin's mind and then was gone, replaced by the certainty that Roland would never show such weakness. And neither would she. A Nomad would have run once, but they were no longer Nomads; they were Mortal, however divided by blood type now. Defiance lived in their blood. In the face of death, it sprang to fiery life.

Five Dark Bloods stood abreast on a platform that

served as a stage, hands folded and at ease. She couldn't see their faces—only by the red markings on their breastplates did she note that they were commanders. On either side of the stage, dark banners—the ancient compass of Sirin without its markings, a single golden circle on a black background—lifted silently with the gusting air.

No sign of Feyn.

Roland stood, feet planted at the ready and arms loosely at his sides, hood thrown back from his face. His warriors appeared no more concerned than their prince, though their minds were surely sifting through options unapparent to Jordin. Angles of attack, splitting the enemy, a means through the sea of Bloods.

One last, deadly stand.

Deadly, because they had nothing to lose.

"Too many," Michael muttered in a hushed tone. Roland's keen hearing would have easily picked up the words.

"Hold." Roland responded, barely above a whisper, his voice calm.

"There's a better way," Michael said.

Roland ignored her and began to walk forward, hand on the sword at his waist, eyes on the five commanders on the stage. He walked thirty paces before stopping and turning to slowly scan the horde.

His voice thundered through the arena with uncompromised power. "I am Roland, Prince of the Immortals, slayer of thousands. My enemy is Dark Blood. You, who have yet to strike down even one of my Rippers."

He paced, scanning the Bloods with defiant eyes. Without fear... Jordin knew he felt none. As though in answer, her own heart swelled with the kind of boldness familiar only to those who have faced insurmountable odds and surrendered to fate.

Then she remembered that she was the only living Sovereign.

Boldness melted away.

"You see only twenty before you," Roland said, sweeping his arm toward his warriors. "Send down fifty, and I alone will show you how a single Immortal earns his rank."

"Careful!" Michael whispered.

He was stalling. Jordin knew it, Michael knew it. Even now, in the face of a thousand, the mind of the prince was searching out any strategy that might see them past these Bloods and into the palace. But there was no way for twenty Rippers to prevail against a storm of Dark Bloods. No number of arrows and knives could fend off such a swarm, the moment they chose to attack.

But why hadn't they?

The answer presented itself in that moment. It wasn't the Immortals they were after.

It was her. They wanted her blood. If they knew Sovereign blood wouldn't succumb to Reaper, any hope of an antidote would come from her veins.

Would they take her alive?

"And so you stand there considering your fate," Roland called out, "knowing that you must obey your maker when she calls you to die."

The commanders made no move.

"There's a better way," Michael said again, defying Roland's command for her to hold her tongue. Silence ensued, but for all Jordin knew they were communicating in tones too low for her to hear.

But the fact that Michael expressed as much concern as she did, sister to Roland or not, was deeply disconcerting. This was all a bluff. There was no way through the horde before them. So then why stall?

The commander at center stage suddenly stepped forward and faced them under the light of two tall torches on either side, arms strangely limp at his side. His voice was strong but strained.

"Give us the Sovereign, and we will spare the rest." She knew the voice, despite its throaty depth. "Give us Jordin."

Something about him...his face was slightly heavier and his skin pale, etched with dark veins. But it was the way he held himself, as though his limbs were animated not by his own will, but that of another. The set of that jaw, the absolute war within those eyes...

Rom. Rom turned Dark Blood.

Rom, standing with Feyn's minions, under her authority.

Jordin moved before she knew what she hoped to accomplish, walking toward Roland with quick steps.

"Back!" Michael snapped.

She had no intention of going back.

Roland hadn't turned despite being aware of her approach.

She stopped three paces to the prince's right and stared at Rom, whose dark eyes looked at her, black as ravens trapped in a cage.

"You play a dangerous game," Roland said in a low voice.

"So do you," she replied, eyes fixed forward.

To Rom she said, so all could hear, "The virus has been released. Mattius released it before they killed him. Every Dark Blood and Immortal on earth will be dead in days. Hours, perhaps. Roland will never allow the Dark Bloods to take me alive. You and I will be his first kills. Surely you can see that."

His response came slow, heavy with emotion and conviction at once. "I am my Maker's, and I have my orders. If you come willingly you will live—"

"No, Rom. Feyn will use me and kill me, the same way she will kill you." She'd meant her words about Roland's intent to kill her as a bluff, but knew she'd spoken the truth. Allowing Feyn to take her hostage so he could run and hide would only add insult to injury. And Roland would never allow that.

She had to offer them whatever misinformation she could conjure up to buy more time.

"I spoke to Mattius before finding Roland. Sovereign blood must be of the purest kind if any hope of an anti-virus would come from it. I am the world's only living Sovereign. If I die, so does Feyn. Allow us to pass, if only to save Feyn!"

He stood in silence.

"He's lost, Jordin," Roland murmured. "He can't save you."

"And you can?" she said, her lips barely moving.

"Give us Jordin and the rest of you can leave this arena alive," Rom said. "These are the only orders that matter."

She felt both outrage and empathy for Rom, so gripped by a power beyond his will. And grief; there was no way she could reach him before the virus ravaged his body.

"There's only one way out," Roland said under his breath. "Only one."

"Which way?"

"Through the darkness."

The only way out was through her blood and that was no true way out either, she thought. Had Jonathan meant for her to die surrounded by Dark Bloods, as he had? Was death life's legacy? Was *this* the salvation his blood offered the living? Better to not have been born at all than suffer as they had since his death!

Roland was walking toward her.

"Your maker wants Sovereign blood to create an anti-virus?" He reached Jordin and ran his fingers across her back as he crossed behind her. "This one soul for the lives of my Rippers, allowing me the freedom to return with my army and crush you all or die in battle?" He stopped and faced Rom, his hand on Jordin's shoulder. "This is what you require, Rom?"

He didn't answer.

"Then you will have your Sovereign. On my terms."

He gripped her arm and pulled her around, walking back toward Michael. The twenty Rippers stood poised.

"The moment the first one moves, Michael," he said under his breath, "come to me quickly. Alive."

For the space of six full strides nothing happened behind them. What Roland had in mind, she couldn't know. But neither could the Bloods.

Dull thumps sounded behind her and she twisted to see that not one but dozens of Bloods were dropping to the ground, like black stones falling on hard earth.

But these stones had powerful legs and were already sprinting, faster than any Immortal could move. They emptied the tiers and flooded the assembly grounds, a swarm of minions intent on their prey.

"They—"

Before Jordin could finish her warning, Roland swept her into his arms and was walking with sure steps, ignoring the commotion behind him, following the other Rippers as they began streaming back into the tunnel like a line of bats flying into a cave.

All except Michael and Cain, who streaked toward the

rush of Dark Bloods, a swiftly formed rear guard, ready
to thwart the enemy long enough to ensure safe exit of
their comrades.

The Bloods were coming too quickly! Hundreds were
now on the ground, swarming.

Roland threw her over his shoulder as he might a mere
gunnysack. She twisted in time to catch a clear view of
the dervish that was Michael and Cain, tearing into the
leading edge of Dark Bloods as they flooded the sand
around them.

She heard the swift sing of steel—distinct, even to Jordin's ear—against the heavy crash of Dark Blood armor.
A head went sailing into the sky, the pale face agape in
shock. Michael dropped her sword in a deadly arc, and
three more went crashing to the ground without the benefit of legs. Cain's hands flashed from his hip. The impact
of his knives sent two Bloods sprawling back into those
behind them. He swung, relieving one of sword and arm,
and sliced through the armor and ribs of another.

As the darkness of the passage narrowed like an iris
behind them, Jordin saw the Bloods descend by the hundreds. A battle cry she knew to be Michael's pierced the
air. They backpedaled in a flurry of steel and blood, slowing the leading edge of Bloods. A sea of black folded
around the two Rippers.

Michael and Cain had been overtaken.

Roland stopped short. He spun around and gazed down
the tunnel as Dark Bloods surged past the point where
Michael and Cain had fallen.

His body trembled beneath her. A ferocious grunt
made his rage clear.

Without another moment to mourn his sister's death,
he rushed deeper into the darkness and turned down the

first tunnel, sprinting behind the others. Complete darkness enveloped Jordin as the clash of melee faded in the distance.

Roland remained silent, his breath a deep and deadly rhythm. Michael and Cain had bought precious seconds with their lives. The maze and its darkness would buy them more. Enough.

But Jordin knew that a new darkness had entered Roland's mind.

A darkness that would be the death of them all.

CHAPTER TWENTY-FOUR

FEYN STALKED the length of the Sovereign office. Stopped once to stare out the great window at the changeling night. Paced again. Gone were the long velvets, replaced by leather leggings and boots latched over the knee. Gone, the amber earrings, only the gilt of her cuff reflecting the gold blazing behind her eyes. A short sword with jeweled hilt rode her hip. Deadly, almost, as its owner.

Roland and his Rippers had escaped. Not only with their lives, but the Sovereign girl in tow.

She stopped at the window and stared out. The clouds over Byzantium shifted high against elusive stars.

A thousand Dark Bloods. Twenty Immortals.

Escaped. Even grossly outnumbered, they had eluded the sheer force of numbers.

The two Immortal bodies had proven useless—fascinating, perhaps, to her team of alchemists on another day, but as prone to Reaper as the Dark Bloods.

As she was herself.

Fury swept through her at the ineptness of her army, the geriatric speed of her so-called master alchemist, the fate dealt her by an unnamed Sovereign. Fury at the very blood of Jonathan himself.

But there was something far worse within her, spreading up through her heart and into her mind like acid: fear. As base as any creature, as common as the Corpse. She hadn't felt its fingers—not like this—for more than a decade.

In all of this, her thoughts had turned to one unlikely target. Saric.

He had come to her as a Corpse. The realization had only hit her after his departure that when Reaper claimed its last victims, Saric would be left standing.

And that was the bitterest pill of all.

She had wracked her brain, pushed Corban to his limits. But the alchemist who had perfected the dark serum claimed he knew of no way to reverse it. And yet there *was* a way. Saric. And even he had left unchallenged, taking the secret in his blood with him.

Hades knew where he might be now. But he was out there somewhere. And though she'd sent trackers in search of him, somehow she knew he would not be found. Saric always found a way to live.

Hate twisted in her mind like a corkscrew.

She heard a soft shuffle behind her. She glanced up through a break in the clouds at the cold brilliance of the moon, drew a slow breath, willed her heart to slow.

And then pivoted on her heel.

Five Dark Blood commanders stood before her—those who'd stood on the platform of the assembly arena only an hour earlier. No, four commanders and Rom. And though he was dressed the same as the commanders beside him, he stood as though he were bound, still resisting what could not be defied.

Near her desk stood Corban, the stent and tubing that had become the trademark of his work in his hands, the bags under his eyes so dark they looked like bruises against his white skin.

She appraised the line of Dark Bloods before her—the great girth of their shoulders, the cast of their eyes toward the floor, the broad knuckles and thickly muscled thighs. Each of them hers. Hers to walk the streets and cut down her enemies, each of them driven by one will—hers—like fingers of her own hand.

Saric. Roland. Jordin. All had slipped through a thousand of her fingers. Not only that, but each of them had spirited away keys to her own salvation.

"We have one day to prepare!" she said, her voice ringing out as she walked slowly down the line of commanders. "Roland is on a suicide mission. He knows he cannot live. He will not limp off into the waste to die on the sand, but he will return to take as many with him as he can. Rom has identified one of the bodies left behind as that of Roland's sister." Her lips curled. "How poetic."

She paused before the last of the commanders and lifted his chin with a finger. His gaze remained fixed to the floor past her.

She dropped her hand.

"We will give him the battle he wants. A battle the likes of which he has never seen! Here, in Byzantium. Our birthright. Our land. Our terms."

She strode to the other end of the line, past Rom, to stand a hand's breadth in front of the first commander. "You will clear a mile swath around the Citadel."

"My liege—the Rippers will avoid the battlefield for darker streets," the man before her said. "There are a thousand homes in the sectors south and east of here."

In an instant, her hand was on her hilt. With a hiss, steel slid free of the scabbard as she shoved the blade up under the edge of the man's breastplate. The man's face registered silent shock as a thin rivulet of blood trickled from the corner of his open mouth.

"Roland sees only blood, you fool! He will throw himself against our army."

She yanked the sword free and turned away as the Dark Blood thudded to his knees behind her.

"We will give Roland as many Dark Bloods as he can imagine on a battlefield he cannot resist. The people in those homes will have one hour to evacuate or they will die. I want every structure leveled by morning!" She turned and shot Corban a pointed glare. Even harried and sleepless, he nodded, having gone even paler than before.

"You will bring me the master engineer at once. All the power on the city grid will be redirected to the Citadel for our defenses. We will light the battlefield like the sun." She hefted the sword in her hand, rolled the hilt along her palm. "I want two thousand pitch torches illuminating every shadow within a mile. Shut down the rest of the city. Call in the guards from the posts beyond the perimeter. All eighty thousand will be here, placed as directed."

She strode to the commander who lay toppled, unmoving within an inky pool of blood, and walked to the second commander in line. Looked him directly in the face. He made the mistake of looking back.

"You dare look in my eyes after such a failure?"

"No, my liege. I—"

His eyes went wide as she sheathed her sword in his middle.

The next one did not make the same mistake.

"Arcane," she said. His breath was serrated. She could *smell* the sweat rolling down his neck.

"My liege?" he whispered.

"Carry out these orders without compromise."

"I will, my liege."

She lowered the sword, tip to the floor. Twirled it once. Blood splattered the marble, speckled the black of her boots. She lifted it, walked another two steps to the next man, set the tip down lightly again. A twirl of metal. His throat visibly worked as he swallowed. The cords in his neck stood out; he was clearly prepared for the swing of her blade. She lifted her fingers from the hilt, let the weapon clatter to the ground.

She turned on her heel. "Kill him, Arcane," she whispered.

By the time she had crossed to Corban, the man's grunt had filled the chamber behind her. She turned back in time to see the two men remaining: Arcane, his short sword dark and naked in his hand, and Rom, stiff yet, an arm's reach away.

She stopped before the alchemist. His hair, normally so neatly groomed, was held back from his face in a tangled mess. His rumpled robe hung on thin and aging shoulders; he had lost weight in the last two days. But most telling of all was the shadow of resignation lurking about his eyes.

"What news?"

The alchemist shook his head. "The Immortals are useless. The sample we took from Rom before his conversion is no better. Our efforts to unravel the virus and create an antidote...useless."

"There must be something," Feyn said through gritted teeth.

The alchemist was silent.

She spun back, fixed Rom with a glare.

"What more can be done?"

He turned his head, looked her in the eye, and spoke as though the air were forced from his lungs to form the words. "There is no cure, my lady."

"I will not accept it!"

Beside her, Corban said, "We are grasping at slivers. We've tried everything. The only thing left is Sovereign blood."

"You had that with him," she said, jerking her head in Rom's direction.

"The sample we retained from before his conversion proved...inconclusive. Perhaps if it were living, taken from the vein...but even then." Again, he shook his head.

For a moment, the room spun.

Two days. Two days before the world slipped from her fingers along with her life.

She dropped her gaze to the stent and tubing in his hands.

"You tapped him today?"

"Yes. We will try again." But his voice told her plainly that he already knew it would yield nothing.

She grabbed the stent and tubing from his thin fingers and strode closer to the candelabra burning on her desk. Jerking up her sleeve by the embroidered cuff, she shoved it back. Without preamble, she stabbed the stent directly into the dark vein running along the crook of her elbow, gestured to Corban, already rushing to her side to quickly connect the vial to the other end of the tube.

"My liege—"

"He claimed for years my blood knew life once. Well, we shall see if he's right." Fifteen years ago, it had been enough to send her to her knees on the platform of her own inauguration. To spread her arms to the Keeper's sword, and to die. The barest hint of remembrance even after the Corpse-death had claimed her senses again. Just enough.

Enough to cheat death and rise again.

She glanced toward Rom as she turned the knob on the tube.

But as she watched the black ichor of her own blood fill the tubing, she knew that it remembered that life no more.

The vial filled. She yanked the stent out. Shoved Corban away when he tried to staunch the wound.

"Take it and make me an antivirus! Your life depends on it. And take him." She shoved her finger in Rom's direction. "Drain him dry if you have to. As for you…" she turned, strode to Arcane, leveled him with a stare. "Make ready. Roland wants battle? We will slaughter him and his Rippers in the streets. Do you hear me? We will kill them all!"

CHAPTER TWENTY-FIVE

THE BETHELIM VALLEY lay in silence, its forbidding slopes and hard-baked earth stark beneath an unforgiving sky. The sun rested on the eastern hill—a lone orange eye tracking the thirty-eight black-clad Rippers and the sole Sovereign who'd ventured into the desolate place.

Roland stood on the rise to the south, facing away from Jordin and the rest, hands on hips, staring out at the long rolling stretch of barren desert that ran all the way to the distant sea.

He hadn't spoken a word since the arena, seemingly oblivious to the load on his shoulder as they raced through the tunnels, despite Jordin's insistence that he set her down. Only upon reaching the cellar had he unceremoniously dumped her to the ground before ascending to the main floor.

He was mounted and already spurring his horse into a gallop by the time she'd stumbled out of the basilica. It had taken her a full minute to catch the others speeding north through Byzantium after their leader. Roland had ridden like a man possessed. Even when they'd put the city safely behind them, he hadn't slowed his stallion to a trot for several more miles.

Michael, dead. She could barely comprehend it. Even the unflappable Cain. The first Immortals slain in battle.

Her fault.

They'd ridden through the night without words, Roland refusing to even glance at her. And so she'd let him alone, the cadence of their horses pounding the ground beneath her.

Roland's grief was obvious. But tonight she knew he had been dealt an additional blow: Roland, the invincible Prince of the Immortals, had been proven fallible.

Jordin had fought growing despair as the night passed, searching in vain for any thread of hope—of absolution. They had no hope of recovering or saving Rom. Feyn was alive. The Immortals were soon to die. And where would that leave her? Jonathan, Triphon, the Keeper, every Sovereign she had lived and fought with, the Immortals she had known as a Nomad...And soon Rom, Kaya, and Roland—all of those she had known in this life—would be dead within a day. Two at most.

The one mercy in all of it was that soon she would be void of emotion.

Jordin glanced at Rislon and the other Rippers. They rode tall in their saddles, pointedly ignoring her, eyes on their leader. None of them seemed to notice that she was even present until she nudged her horse up the hill toward Roland.

"Back!" Rislon snapped.

Ignoring him, Jordin dug her heels into her mount's flanks and took it to a gallop up the rise.

Roland didn't move as she pulled up behind him. She stopped a pace off to his right and stared at him for a moment. His brow was beaded with sweat, his hair damp and tangled, matted against his neck. He'd shed his cloak and outer shirt, leaving him in only a sleeveless black undershirt that covered little of his brawn. The tattoos on his arms looked darker than she remembered in the daylight.

Tears had dried on his face, leaving trails of grief on his cheeks and chin. She realized she had been wrong to think he knew nothing of anguish—including the sharpness of her own loss at Jonathan's death and the guilt she bore now, over Michael's and Cain's.

She followed his line of sight to the sun rising above the horizon.

Jonathan was supposed to have risen to power like that sun—light to a world lost in darkness. But here in the Bethelim Valley, the indifferent orb seemed only a reminder that it would outlast them all.

"You blame me," she said. "I swear to you, I don't know how they knew we were coming."

He stared into the sun, as if daring it to burn away his sight.

"Are you going to shun me forever?"

"Who can a dead man shun?" he asked bitterly.

"I'm so sorry about Michael."

"Don't speak her name."

She fell silent.

"She and Cain weren't the only ones to die—they're only the first. Isn't that your argument? That all Immortals die at the hand of a virus created *by Sovereigns*?"

"By a rogue alchemist! One who saw Immortals butcher those he loved! Rather than stand here burning your eyes to a crisp, why not help me think of a way out of this?"

"Dismount."

She hesitated for a moment, then swung down from her

saddle, only vaguely aware of the sore muscles along her back and thighs.

He said, too quietly for human ears, "Call him, Rislon." And at that moment she remembered that every word she had uttered could be heard by them all.

A whistle from the valley floor. The horse turned and ambled down the hill.

"You want to know my thoughts," he said, facing her. "Fine. Listen carefully."

She nodded, miserable. She should be more courageous than any of them. She was going to live, after all. They all faced imminent death. And yet here she was, mired in self-pity, unable to see any advantage.

"Of course I'll listen," she said.

"Carefully," he reiterated. "A person facing the undoing of all he's lived for isn't necessarily reasonable, so you'll forgive me, but it turns out that I am that man. The fact that Feyn wanted you alive only means she believes the virus poses the threat you claim. She would take you and drain your blood in hope of finding an antivirus in short order—clearly she's as unreasonable as me."

He took a deep breath and went on, otherwise unchecked.

"If I'd listened to you when you first came, perhaps I would've been able to save my people, a fact that only makes my reason seem less stable. Even so, stable or not, the past is done."

Plain words from a prince. She could not fault his honesty.

"Yes. It is done."

"And yet, I must say this: it was one of your kind who released this virus. If you feel it was wrong of him to do so, you should have found a way to stop him."

"What do you think I was trying to do? I came to you!"

"I didn't say find someone else to stop him. You should have killed him yourself, long ago."

"He claimed that doing so would only ensure the release of Reaper."

"Then you should have ensured the loyalty of your subjects long before they could turn on you. I hold you personally responsible for your failure to foresee and stop this event."

"And I hold you personally responsible for pushing him to the point of creating the virus," she said. "You should have thought of that before butchering my people!"

"I am life!" His face shook as he pushed the words out, betraying the full rage seething behind his eyes. "And now I will die for that life, as did Jonathan."

"Jonathan?" She was instantly shaking. "You *dare* speak his name? You rejected his blood!"

"I took his blood while he still lived! I can no more accept your arguments for the life you claim in his *dead* blood than I could accept a rumor that this parched desert"—he jabbed a finger at the valley floor—"is a lake surrounded by trees. Your life is no more vibrant than this ruined earth!"

"And yours is?"

He lowered his arm. "Ask Kaya. No. Ask yourself. You were Immortal just two days ago."

Even seething, righteously irate, she couldn't argue. She was unable to point out his own deep-seated unhappiness for the blaring accusation of her own. How many times had she envied the Immortals their semblance of life—real life?

"In your very being, you fail to live," he said.

She set her jaw, willed back the tears. If they came now, they would not ever stop.

He gave a slight nod, sighed. "If there's anything you haven't told me, say it now. Short of that, I have only one course left before me."

"There's always more than one course. You taught me that."

"Then speak it now. Quickly...time is no longer my friend."

She swallowed, trying to imagine the right words delivered with the appropriate conviction. What came out surprised even her.

"I love you," she said.

He blinked. Stalled.

She glanced away before the tears could threaten again. "I mean, you terrify me, but I've also seen who you really are, and it's not this. I need you."

Saying it, she knew she was overreacting in a moment of terrible desperation, but she also knew there was more truth behind the words than she cared to admit.

"Maybe I'm only saying that because I know that soon I'll be alone in the world. I'll be...alone." Her lips were quivering and refused to stop no matter how hard she tried. "But at least I'll be *alive*."

She reached out, took his arms. "I need you. To *live*. Live for me, Roland. Please. And we will have time to figure this all out."

His eyes darkened. "By becoming Sovereign?"

"It's the only way. I—"

"Never! In another time I might have made you my queen. Now I can offer you only my death" He looked as though he might spit at her. She knew she was a fool for voicing what she knew would be soundly rejected. But she was without options. Utterly desperate.

"We could still go back for Rom."

"*Go back?* Even now Feyn is gathering her army. She knows full well what I will do. She's a leader with a leader's mind, and no fool! There is no trick to play now; no tunnel that isn't already collapsed. No. I will go for Feyn on my terms."

"And die on hers."

His gaze bore into hers. When he spoke again, his voice was even.

"On mine. I have twelve hundred warriors waiting. We will carve out death in Byzantium to honor Michael. We will not leave a soul alive in our wake. It's no longer *who* we kill, but *how many*."

In another life, she would have been galvanized by his words. But hearing them now, his life so fleeting before her, they only terrified. "You won't reach the Citadel!"

"You're wrong. I was never willing to risk the life of my own. Now there's nothing to lose. I will spend them all to the last soul. We are dead already. No one has yet seen the full fury of Immortals unleashed." He leaned in, his lips curled back from his teeth. "But I tell you, it will be a fine, fine day to die."

"They don't need to be dead already! As the last Sovereign, I can offer you life."

He spit to one side in disgust.

"Please, Roland, I beg you! Your way won't gain you anything."

"It will gain me honor, one of the many worthy traits you have sacrificed by drinking the blood of a dead man. Without it, there is no life. It is I who live, Jordin, not you."

He strode past her, toward the way she had come. She turned and called after him, "You know I can't come with you."

"You'll remain here," he said. "On foot."

Jordin hurried after him, panicked. "You can't just leave me here to die!"

He ignored her, plunging down the side of the hill in an easy gait that made his intentions clear. She pulled up halfway down, realizing he would never back down after making such a statement in front of his Rippers, who had heard every word.

He swung into his saddle, reins in hand. Uttering a command she couldn't make out, he kneed his mount and headed east at a quick trot before breaking into a gallop.

Rislon dropped two canteens on the ground, cast her one last look, and took the company after Roland. In less than a minute the sound of pounding hooves faded, leaving her staring after them in a silence so complete it seemed to ring through her ears.

For a long time, she didn't move. Her mind didn't seem capable of finishing fully formed thoughts.

And then one thought rose, clear and devastating at once. Jonathan had abandoned her. As had Rom. And now Roland as well. She was alone.

She scanned the horizon slowly, looking for any sign of life. Heat was rising off the white hills as though portending the hell to come. Jordin slowly fell back onto the ground.

The end had finally come.

CHAPTER TWENTY-SIX

THE MIDDAY sun stared stark-eyed at the shallow rises of the desert northeast of Byzantium. Cut by the occasional canyon, the Bethelim Valley existed on no map of the Order, having been so named by the Nomads. A mile long, the stretch of inhospitable ground ran north to a wide, rocky canyon hemmed in by a short cliff on either side.

Three alien objects lay on the bleached ground at the valley's mouth. Small and insignificant from atop the cliff face, even the vultures took little interest in what appeared to be two dull-brown rocks. The third object, larger, lay as unmoving as a boulder.

A human eye might have recognized the forms of two canteens...and the third as a woman lying on her side curled tightly into a ball, forehead nearly touching knees.

The faint markings of a trail stretching from the unmoving human to the east suggested that others had left the scene, leaving one of their own to be parched by the sun and scattered to the elements.

But there was no human eye peering down from the sky. Even in her near-catatonic state, Jordin knew this. Nor from the hills. Or from the valley. She was alone, utterly and completely, as was the heart expanding and contracting within her as it mocked her true state of being.

She was, after all, already dead. If not in body, then in spirit and mind. Her flesh would soon catch up to the realization. Her breath would join the air for the last time; her heart would offer up one last pathetic throb; her blood would cease flowing through emaciated veins; and one day her carcass would dry to dust and blow away with the wind.

She'd sat on the slope for an hour after Roland's departure, sinking slowly into despair that hollowed her chest and left her mind numb—she could remember that much.

Or had that been a dream?

She'd finally risen, plodded toward the canteens, and stood there, staring at them, before settling down to her side, wrapping her arms around her knees, and coiling inward. As if by hugging her body she might offer her heart some comfort.

But her suffering had only deepened.

Her memory of why she suffered abandoned her, replaced by an unrelenting awareness of torment. By the inexhaustible *need* to suffer, if only for the comfort of penance. She deserved nothing less.

She was just alive enough to wish for death.

The sun was high, glaring down with enough heat to inflame her exposed skin. She looked at the canteens. It occurred to her that she should drink some water.

But she didn't. She should move, but the thought dissipated before reaching her arms and legs along with any memory of why living might be important.

Did Bliss await? Then why live? To extend suffering?

The thoughts slogged through her mind like new Rippers to keep her company—twice as stealthy and three times as dark.

An hour later, she was staring at the dark fold of her

tunic sleeve. A tangled mop of hair covered her face, a dark net filtering the sun. A strand caught in her lashes moved slightly with a gentle, hot breeze.

And then she remembered. Rom was Dark Blood and would soon be dead. The Sovereigns...all dead. Roland, on a mission of death.

Jonathan...

Dead.

And here she lay on hell's barren ground, clinging to a life she had no right to possess. A life she would renounce because it had shown her no power, no grace, no peace, no love—nothing but suffering and shame. Lying on the valley floor, she cursed the day she took Jonathan's blood into her veins.

For how many years since had she played the fool, speaking of a power that failed to prove itself no matter how persistently she confessed it?

Too many.

She closed her eyes. Felt tears swell behind her lids and snake down her temple. Her mouth curled into a silent cry of self-pity. A single sob choked her throat. Then another, and another, until her body jerked like a sputtering motor, void of thought, fueled only by shame.

"Jonathan...Please, I beg you..."

They were her first words in hours, a whimper carried away with the breeze.

"Please..." But she'd called to him so many times, only to be rewarded with silence. "Please. Come to me." *Save me.* And then the mantra faded from whisper to memory and was gone.

There was no Jonathan to save her.

The heat of the valley floor rose up at her back, a gentle dervish lifting the hair not matted to her face. Memory of faded dreams murmured through her mind. A time not so long ago when she'd dreamt of raw energy coursing through her body, borne on the pure tones of a child's song, calling to her.

Absurd, that memory. Distant, vacant. Mocking.

She blinked, drew a slow breath through her nose, and arthritically pushed herself up to her elbow. A wave of warm nausea washed over her as she pushed up farther so her palms pressed into the hard earth.

She peered at the valley's wide mouth, open to the south like a funnel, the ground sloping up on both sides of an expansive floor. The air shimmered with rising heat, distorting her view.

She reached toward one of the canteens, her hand hovering just above its brown-cloth covering. A single leather tie had been strung through the top and tied off on the neck to keep the cork from falling to the ground when unplugged. The end of the leather tie stuck an inch into the air beyond the hole in the cork.

At first she thought its movement was another distortion of fatigue, dehydration. Her mind wasn't working properly. It seemed to quiver.

As did the ground beneath her palm.

So this was what it was to die.

But then a slight vibration rose up her arm. The kind one might feel at the approach of an army, pounding earth underfoot in the distance. Had the Rippers returned? She turned her face toward the sun, still mid-climb into the sky. No.

She glanced at the horizon again and, seeing nothing, lowered her ear to the ground. The hum she heard was faint enough to be mistaken for the rattle of her own breath. But it was there, beyond her held breath, the cumbersome pulse of her heart.

Jordin sat up and twisted around and looked north, deeper into the valley.

But she did not see the valley. Her sight was arrested by a vision not twenty paces from where she sat. A hooded man, arms at his sides in a tattered garment. She blinked, squinted again to find him staring at her with pale blue eyes from a deeply tanned face.

She tried to scramble to her feet but fell back. She pushed slowly up again, hands held to the unsteady earth. Her head was pounding.

"Hello, Jordin," the man said.

He reached for his hood and lowered it to reveal long, tousled gray hair. He was walking toward her.

Her mind scrambled for recognition. She saw only a ghost from another life before her but something in her knew him.

"Don't be afraid, child. I'm not here to harm but to help you."

He stopped three paces away. His smile was gentle.

"It hurts, doesn't it?" he said.

She wanted to ask him who he was. What he meant. But her tongue, too dry, refused to form the words.

"My own journey was as painful, I can assure you."

"Who are you?" she croaked. She cleared her throat. "What journey?"

"The journey from Dark Blood to true Sovereign."

"Dark Blood?"

He walked toward her, and she instinctively backed away. Hands lifted to assure her, palm out as he stepped around her. And then he bent for one of the canteens, plucked out the cork, and took a long drink. Satisfied, he sighed and offered her the flask.

"You look like you could use this."

She took the canteen with an unsteady hand but didn't lift it to her lips.

"Who are you?"

"I realize I don't look the same. You never knew me before I turned dark."

Only then did his name come to her like a whisper through the canyon.

Saric.

Her lungs tightened, and she backed up a step.

Saric, who had slain Jonathan, severing him nearly in two with flashing blade. Saric, the one man she despised more than any other. The epitome of evil materialized like a mirage in the desert.

"So you see me now," he said. "Not as who I once was, but the one to whom Jonathan granted a life not even you yet know."

She was hallucinating. She had to be. His eyes weren't green but light blue. He was no Sovereign but a Corpse once more.

She opened her mouth to laugh at him. The sound was dry and filled with scorn.

"You lie," she said. "Dark Bloods cannot be brought to life!"

"And yet here I stand. In the flesh." He held out his hands, baring his forearms. His fingers were worn, his nails filled with dirt. His veins, blue beneath sun-darkened flesh without the telltale ink of the poison within them.

"I spent years in the desert, living among outcasts, mind lost to my misery, knowing that the blood in my veins bound me to death. Then he came to me and opened my eyes in a way I had never thought possible. You see?" He took a step closer. "He made a way for me before his death and for you in his death."

Her eyes darted to his face. "You have the eyes of a Corpse."

"They were green like yours when I first became Sovereign. Then I was transformed."

"You could never become Sovereign."

"For a year after killing Jonathan I wandered the wilderness, fleeing Feyn's Dark Bloods, destitute, scraping survival from whatever I could find. I lost all hope; even ambition abandoned me. And then the will to live. I climbed to the top of a cliff, and it was there that Jonathan came to me. Soon after, I entered the Sovereign Realm. There, I was transformed. I've been living among Corpses, refugees from the city, ever since, waiting for this day and the final task before me. So you see, it is I, not you, who have found salvation."

"You lie! There is no salvation for one like you!"

"No? Were you saved a moment ago, as you wept on the ground? Show me your love, your joy. Your peace. These are the fruits of Jonathan's kingdom." His smile was gentle. "Not green eyes."

There was a deeply settling tone in his voice, one she couldn't comprehend. But she knew Saric as a man who knew no end of trickery and manipulation.

"He calls for you," he said, holding his hand out to her. "Have you heard him?"

Memory of her dreams flooded her mind.

She narrowed her eyes.

"It was I who warned Feyn," he said.

She stood perfectly still, drawing breath evenly now, managing to swallow though her throat was dry and her mind rejected the notion that Saric might stand before her now, like this. She'd sworn to kill this man if she ever laid eyes on him again.

And yet here she was, weak and at his mercy, devoid of the peace that seemed to flow from him with his very breath.

His last words belatedly bloomed in her mind. *He'd betrayed them to Feyn?*

"What?"

"You had to be turned back for your own sake," he said. "For you to come here and meet me in this hour. Even the deaths of Michael and the other have worked for your good. You will see, as Jonathan helped me see. I have waited and prepared for this time."

For a moment she held the familiar grip of her anger, her hatred, but the weight of her suffering was too great to hold for long, and she felt herself slipping even as she stared into his eyes.

The instant she let go, the air seemed to spark. The ground beneath her feet felt alive with unseen power. She grappled for understanding, to comprehend. This was Saric—the killer of Jonathan, speaking of life to her, Jonathan's lover! What divine joke, what great injustice was this?

And yet he stood here more drastically changed than any Sovereign she had ever seen. Not in his eyes or his skin, but in something that radiated from him that she had never seen in any one of the Sovereigns before.

He smiled and tilted his head down, spread his arms in invitation. "Do you want to see, Jordin?"

See?

Her mind began to fall away, unable any longer to sustain even her desire for understanding. *Yes.*

Let me see. She tried to speak it. Tears brimmed in her eyes.

"Do you want to see the kingdom within you where true peace and love call to be joined?"

"Yes," she whispered.

"Say it and mean it, dear Jordin. Many are called, few choose."

"Yes!" she cried as her own wretchedness erupted within her. All the pain, the disappointment and sorrow, the anger, rushing into her mind at once. "Yes," she sobbed. "I want...to see."

"Then you must open your eyes," he said. "The ones closed in slumber."

"Help me," she said. Then, very quietly because her breath was gone and her throat constricted, she added, "I beg you."

Saric lowered his arms as he moved toward her. His hand lifted, and as it neared her face, she let her final resistance slip away and surrendered to whatever might come, offering up all the suffering and confusion that had lived with her for so many years. Too many.

"I'll wait for you on the other side, my dear."

His hand covered her eyes a moment, and then he slapped her on the cheek, as if to wake her with a firm hand.

"See," he said.

Her world blinked to black, and she felt herself falling. Then she felt nothing.

CHAPTER TWENTY-SEVEN

JORDIN REGAINED awareness before she opened her eyes. She didn't know how long she'd been unconscious—only that a new consciousness had awakened her. A certainty that *what was*, was meant to be.

When she opened her eyes, it was still light. Lighter even than it had been before. The ground was bleached nearly white as before but somehow it seemed purer. Not brighter, but *more* than what it had been.

She jerked up and looked around, searching for Saric. The hills still rose up around her, the valley still spread wide to the south where a dark storm gathered on the horizon.

Over Byzantium.

But here in the desert, the sun still shone above, having barely moved. The canteens still lay on the ground, one where it had been dropped, the other near the place where Saric had offered a drink she'd not taken.

Nothing had changed.

And yet, somehow it was different.

She became aware of the faint hum again, more definite now, tingling her flesh; speaking to her bones.

Pushing up onto her right arm, she twisted around

and looked up the valley—and then caught her breath, gripped by the sight before her.

A translucent veneer seemed to rise from the ground just fifty paces away. A shimmering wall that bisected the valley and distorted her view of what lay beyond. The hum was coming from something beyond it, or from the wall itself.

Jordin lifted her eyes and saw that it went as high as she could see, that it ran in either direction past the hills, from east to west. It seemed to ripple, to reflect the sun like water.

She scrambled to her feet, breathing hard, eyes wide, knowing somehow that beyond the veil lay the world of dreams. The world of Saric...

The world of Jonathan.

Wake up from your dream, Jordin.

The words whispered through her mind, as if carried in the hum.

She was dreaming?

Come to me. Wake from your dream of flesh and blood.

"I'm dreaming?" Her voice sounded like that of a younger woman, innocent and curious.

Faint laughter beckoned her. And then a voice she could not mistake. *"Come, Jordin. Run! Wake up!"*

Jonathan!

Reason lost to the four corners, desire flooding her in its place, Jordin tore toward the veil.

"Jordin!"

She pulled up hard at the unmistakable cry of Roland's voice behind her.

Roland...he'd returned for her? There was no way he could be back so soon.

Slowly, she turned in time to see Roland plunging down

the slope on his stallion, dressed for battle in the same shirt and boots he'd been wearing earlier. The breeze lifted his hair as he rode. His eyes were intent on her.

He reined in beside her and dropped from his mount. "Jordin…" He searched her face, appearing conciliatory, almost regretful. Dropped to one knee.

"Forgive me." A tear broke from his eye and edged down his cheek. "I had no right to leave you. Forgive me."

She didn't know what to think. Only that here knelt her prince, begging her forgiveness.

"I sent the rest on to gather the army while I came back. I won't die denying the truth."

"What truth?"

"That there would be no queen among the Immortals but you. You've taken the throne of my heart."

She stared into his eyes, knowing in that moment that she loved the prince before her far more than she ever could have had Saric not opened her eyes to receive him.

Tears swelled in her eyes.

At that, Roland rose and closed the distance between them in two strides and gathered her into his arms. He buried his face in her neck.

"Forgive me, my love. Accept my confession and absolve me." He lifted his head, ran his hand over her hair, then drew back and gently kissed her.

"Make me Sovereign," he whispered.

She looked up and saw past the eclipse in his eyes to the love kneeling before her heart.

"You would become Sovereign?"

"Yes."

"Now?"

"Now," he said, and lightly touched his lips to hers again.

Come to me. Wake up from your dream of flesh and blood.

Jonathan was calling...

"Come with me," Roland said. "Ride by my side. Make me Sovereign and let us live out our days as one."

She twisted her head and saw that the glimmering fissure still cut the valley in two. It had brought her Roland. Somehow, the world had righted itself. Jonathan had delivered her...

Roland took her chin and turned her face to him. "Jordin. We must hurry. My Rippers are riding for the city with revenge and death on their minds. We have to stop them!"

"I don't have a stent," she said.

"Seriph has a stent. Ride with me."

Roland seemed oblivious to the anomaly behind her. She glanced once more over her shoulder.

Wake up, Jordin. Hurry!

"Do you see it?" She looked back at him. "Do you hear it?"

His eyes lifted to look beyond her and settled back on her face.

"I see only my savior, standing before me in the flesh. Flowing with life-giving blood." He began to turn, pulling her arm with him. "There's no time. We have to ride!"

"Wait!"

Confusion spun through her mind. She'd come to find Jonathan, not to save Roland. How could she ignore the call of Jonathan's voice?

"Jonathan's here!" she said.

He glanced about. "Jonathan? What do you mean? In your blood, you mean? Come with me before your blood fails you and Jonathan is no more. Hurry!"

He started again, pulling her toward his mount. She followed him four steps before pulling back. She couldn't leave now—not when Jonathan was calling to her!

"Roland, wait." His hand slipped off her arm.

"There's no time!"

"Jonathan!"

"There *is* no Jonathan!"

Come to me, Jordin.

With those words humming through her mind, she knew that she could never leave with Roland—not until she grasped the truth of what lay beyond the veil.

Without another moment's hesitation, Jordin twisted around and began to run toward the distortion.

"Jordin!"

No. Roland must be an apparition.

She'd taken only three long strides before awareness of the changing landscape struck her. The earth darkened under her feet, sprouting lethal blades. They snaked up like shrill tongues, filling the air with screams of protest and accusation, even as her boots crushed them underfoot.

She ran faster, glancing to her right.

The hill, the same slope Roland had descended, was rising up like an angry black wave. She pulled up hard, suddenly terrified. The world had become a nightmare. She was dreaming!

And yet, this felt like no dream.

Above, storm clouds gathered with frightening speed. As she watched, they spawned four and then ten and then a dozen twisting tendrils, each of them descending toward her, pointing like accusing fingers.

"Look at me, Sovereign!"

She whirled toward the guttural voice behind her. Roland had vanished. Saric strode toward her, not twenty paces distant, dressed in a long black robe. He was Dark Blood again, and death was in his eyes.

"Your life is that of a pathetic rat digging in the sewer for rotting refuse."

Earsplitting thunder crashed overhead. Saric came on, marching with long strides. Panicked, she tried to turn back for the veil, but found the blades from the earth had coiled up around her ankles.

"You deserve only what you choose, and you have chosen only misery," Saric snarled.

One of the fingers from the sky shot down at her, a narrow funnel of hot air that slammed into her chest, jarring her very heart.

But it wasn't just air. Visceral guilt and condemnation slammed through her gut. She screamed—until horror cut off her breath.

You're waking, Jordin! Now run to me. Leave your fears and see what is real. Come to my arms.

Jordin screamed again, this time with a fury she didn't know she possessed. She jerked around with enough force to free her legs from the black vines. They sliced through her legs like razors. Gasping for air, she ran pell-mell toward the rift that divided the valley and threw herself into it.

As if she'd plunged into a lake, the sounds behind abruptly faded, replaced by a gentle thrum and ebb. Her skin, thrashed and cut and bleeding, forgot pain, came alive with the sensation that every cell of her body was humming to life.

She gasped, sucking in the galvanized air. When it hit her lungs, rapture flooded her chest. Exploded into her mind like ecstasy.

Come to me, Jordin…

As she fell headlong past the veil, Jordin knew that she had entered Bliss.

She sprawled on the white desert ground and lay panting, facedown, surrounded only by the sound of her own breath.

Perfect silence.

Her skin tingled as if submerged in a living sea. She was filled with peace. It was in her cells, filling her lungs, in her very veins.

She slowly lifted her head and gazed at the hill to her left. It was the same slope as before, but now it seemed to move, as though each grain of sand were alive. She blinked, thinking her vision would correct itself, but it positively shimmered.

As did the earth beneath her palms and arms.

She looked around, saw no sign of Jonathan, but she *knew* that he was here, with her. In her. Surrounding her.

She rose to her feet, stared about her as though she'd stepped into a foreign world, staggered by the splendor of what had been only a barren desert valley before. It was the same valley, but now it shone with beauty.

How had she not seen it before? Known it?

She knew other things now as well. She knew that she wasn't dreaming. That she'd somehow woken from a dream—one of her own making, which she'd mistaken for her true life. That she was one with Jonathan and had been all along, but had only now become aware of it.

The Sovereign Realm. Jonathan's realm. It was inside her, as he was inside her—while all the while she'd been searching for him.

The awareness shook Jordin to her bones. Jonathan had called her to wake, and she had woken. To love. To the heart of the Maker himself.

Love. She was filled with it. It rushed inside her, rolled down her spine, coaxing from her every nerve a pleasure so exquisite she wondered for a moment whether she might die—a thought that brought not a single fear of death with it.

She spread her arms and stared at her fingers, moving them through the air. Space swam with visible power, barely seen but palpable as a stream of water curling around her fingers.

No. She was the stream. She was flooded with love, from the crown of her head to the heels of her feet. She felt it mushroom, gather in her chest, and pass out of her body.

She saw the silent shock wave of it entering the air before her. Watched the ripples of it spread through the space around her.

She stood in awe, aware that the power of it had in no way been depleted by its departure. It seemed to occupy two places at once. Both inside and outside of her. In infinite supply.

"Hello, Jordin."

She whirled around and saw the thing she had craved all her life. Even in her life before she had known what it meant to live.

Jonathan.

He was standing not ten feet away, dressed in the same kind of tunic she'd seen him in dozens of times before. His hair was long, tangled, and free, and his eyes glimmered with mischief above a broad smile.

A scar just visible in his neckline angled down, disappearing beneath his tunic, a vestige left from his execution at Saric's hand.

Tears slipped down her cheeks. They were not born of sorrow but of joy.

Jonathan's eyes pooled with tears above his smile. He

laughed and ran forward, unable to contain his own joy.
Throwing his arms around her, he swung her off her feet
in a hug so exuberant that she couldn't help but wrap her
arms and legs around him to keep from falling backward.

He chuckled with delight, twirling around with her
arms clamped around his shoulders as she buried her face
in his neck and wept her gratitude.

"Here you are!" he cried. "You've finally come home!
I missed you so much, Jordin. I love you so much."

She was lost in him. In love. His love.

They were one.

One!

Jonathan set her down, twirled away, and bowed at his
waist, one arm extended in invitation.

"Welcome to my dance," he said, flashing a daring
grin. "I call it the Sovereign Realm. It doesn't get any better, I can assure you."

She laughed, smiled, as she stepped up to him. She
took his hand in hers. "Well then, my prince. Show me
this realm where you've been hiding, waiting to rescue
me in my hour of need."

He straightened and cocked his head. "Hiding?"

She immediately knew his meaning.

"No, you haven't been hiding, have you? I am the one
who has been hiding."

He dipped his head once. *Go on…*

"Hiding behind a dream from which I've finally awakened," she said. She considered her own statement, then
asked, "It was a dream, right?"

"In a manner of speaking, yes. The dream you call
your life."

"All of my life? Not just the images I saw before passing the veil?"

"All of it. Like a dream. Is it more real than what you see now?"

She looked deeply into his eyes, imagined diving into them.

"No," she breathed. "Not even close."

"When you put a stick in the water, does it look straight or does the water distort it?"

"It distorts it."

"In the same way, your mind distorts your life. Your mind doesn't know it, but it's looking through dirty water most of the time. Soon, I'll show you a new kind of water."

"You will?"

He flashed another smile. "I will. Look around you. What do you see?"

Jordin lifted her gaze from him for the first time since he'd set her down and looked around at the desert. At the hills, the valley floor, the two canteens, the trail left by Roland's horses. All as they had been, now shimmering with energy.

"I see the Bethelim desert," she said. "I see it new. I see it truly."

"And you see me," he said.

"Yes," she whispered. And then, in her heart: *Yes!*

He walked up to her. Lifted his hand. Pressed his palm against her chest. Love pressed into her lungs and wrapped itself around her heart, her spine, rode through her nerves to every fiber of her being.

"I am here, Jordin. I am the *I am* in you. And you are in me. Do you feel it?"

"Yes." Tears spilled from her eyes again. "Yes."

"The moment you took my blood you became Sovereign. I offered you salvation, and yet you found none from fear and anger. You found no true love, no true peace, no true joy. They're the fruits of my realm, not the anxiety spawned by a diseased mind. Now you may be set free of your mind."

"I was possessed by a mad mind," she said, lost in thought.

"There's no need to become perfect, Jordin. Only to *be* perfect, not in what you do, but in how you are being. Beneath the layers and lies of the mind, you are perfect already. So *be*, even as I am."

It all made sense. Jonathan had repeatedly spoken of the fact that his kingdom was within. Not one of earthly thrones or political futures.

"You've called yourself Sovereign. As have Rom and the others. But you haven't lived Sovereign. How can you be saved from hatred and yet imprisoned by it at once? You've spoken of love, but now you know—love and fear cannot remain in the same heart at the same moment. Your mind has become your master, imprisoning you in a dungeon that's bound by flesh and thought. You aren't your mind or thoughts, Jordin. You never were. Now you know a new realm, one with me. And in this Sovereign Realm, my love, there is more power than you can possibly imagine."

"How is it possible to be one with you? We're the same?"

He removed his hand from her chest. The warmth remained.

He winked. "Let me show you."

Stepping back, he lifted his hand and snapped his fingers. Immediately, a green plant sprouted from the desert floor ten feet away. Jordin watched, stunned, as the plant grew before her eyes, first into a sapling, and then larger, and larger still, until its branches spread out, full of rich green leaves that threw shade over them both.

"You see? The tree of life. The same veins run through trunk and branch to offer life to the world. Are branch and trunk not one?"

Of course!

"I see," she whispered. And then: "I see!"

He laughed, grabbing her hand and spinning her around. "You see!"

"I see! I really see!"

Why this simple revelation was so profound, she wasn't sure. But at that moment it felt like the gateway to an entire universe.

He took both of her hands in his and drilled her with a mischievous grin. "Would you like to see more?"

"I *have* to see more!"

"Would you like to see me move mountains?"

"I would like to see you build a new earth!"

"Would you like to dive into a lake and breathe the water?"

"Yes! Yes!"

"A lake within you. An eternal spring of life-giving water as vast as an endless ocean."

She threw back her head, eyes closed, and cried for the heavens to hear her every word. "I want to dive into a lake and breathe your love!"

Mirth peeled through the air, her own, carried by the unbridled enthusiasm of the child she'd become in Jonathan's Sovereign Realm.

"I want to dance and sing!" she cried. "I want to fly and laugh and sing and dance and swim in an ocean of love! I want to…"

She stopped short, unsure what else she could possibly want. Only then did she become distantly aware that the very faint hum in the air had shifted. It sounded more like music—a perfect strain of haunting, harmonic tones that flowed directly into her nerves as though they were highways of light, taking her back to the dream she'd had in Roland's Lair.

Come to me, Jordin...

Her eyes snapped wide. The blue sky swam with long, ethereal, wavering swaths of red and purple against a deep, golden background.

She lowered her chin. Jonathan was no longer holding her hands. Was not before her. The hill directly in front of her was no longer hardened, pale desert. It had been transformed into a lush landscape, alive with green grass, blossoming with white and yellow flowers. She turned her head.

Jonathan stood on the sandy shore of a lake fifty paces to her right, stripped of his shirt. The water before him stretched north, as far as she could see, brilliant aqua shimmering under the colorful sky. Trees lined the hills—the same acacias Jonathan had called the "tree of life."

Jonathan's eyes flashed with daring. He held out his hand, palm up, inviting her.

"Do you want to dive deep, Jordin?"

She spun to face him and tore toward the lake, breathless with desire.

Chapter Twenty-eight

THE INTERIOR of the tower was dark, the windows an eye into the night. Below, two thousand torches glowed against a mile-deep swath of newly cleared land surrounding the perimeter of the Citadel wall. The rubble had been pushed into giant berms high enough to obscure many of the shorter buildings beyond it, a great barricade that opened in only one direction: south. Within the cleared battlefield, no less than fifteen rings of Dark Bloods, staring outward like one great black iris around the Citadel, fifteen thousand mounted, sixty-five thousand on foot, eighty thousand in all.

Clouds had gathered, thick and black, over the city. Restless, low, and volatile.

Feyn turned from the view that had been her preoccupation for the last several hours. She'd berated the servant when he'd brought food and sent him to wait outside the door. On a nearby table, a goblet of wine stood untouched. In the center of the room, Rom stood silent and still as a pillar, clad in silent misery.

"What keeps them?"

When he didn't respond, she crossed to him, took his chin in her hand, and turned his gaze directly to her.

"Roland knows no fear. He has every reason to come at me with everything he has." She shoved his face away. "And so here I wait," she muttered.

She stalked to the other side of the tower, scratching at the inside of her forearm, just above the wrist. The vein beneath would give her no peace. It had always prickled, like nettles in her blood, but in the last day it positively burned.

It's the virus. It's killing you now.

"How long was the incubation period on this virus?"

"Three days," he said quietly. "It was an estimate."

She lowered her arms and faced the window again. Roland would come from the south. Through the city. It was the way of greatest resistance. The least logical, and therefore the most expected. His bravado would demand he be seen.

She laughed, the sound brittle as shards in the tower room. "What a pair we might have made, he and I. Now there, I tell you, is a man worthy of Dark Blood."

Outside, the torches burned like so many amber beads on a deadly gown of velvet.

"This is the way it always should have been. You see? Nothing has changed."

Except the final outcome.

They would all die. Zealot Wars would reshape the world again. But where were they? Was it possible she'd misjudged him? That he'd led his people into the wasteland to die?

No. They might move like ghosts, but Roland would leave his indelible mark before becoming one. He would have his Immortality one way or another. Nor would she be deprived.

She'd given the command for her guards to throw open

the great southern gate, for her Dark Bloods to thicken their formation before that gate. The glut of them before that entrance would be irresistible to his ego.

Then where was he? If she looked carefully enough, she could just perceive the subtle movements of her warriors, shifting where they stood, glancing up every so often at the sky roiling overhead. Twice she thought she'd heard one of the commanders bark an order to hold. Their movements had quieted for a time after she'd given the command to open the gate, only to become restless again.

They were spoiling for a fight. Three hours ago she'd stood on the rampart of the wall and delivered news of the virus. That the Immortals would come against them in one last, desperate stand. That to outlive her would be treason... but to outlive any Immortal, victory.

She willed the anxiety that had crept up her spine back to submission. Told herself that it mattered for something, this last theater of blood—if only to prove to Roland that he was vanquished, utterly, before he died.

And then what?

Born once into life, we are blessed. Let us please the Maker through a life of diligent Order.

The words of the old liturgy sprang to mind unbidden. Words without meaning, meant to control the fearful.

She knew now that Bliss did not await her.

So there is only this.

She crossed back to the southward window.

"I'm glad he hasn't come yet," she said, eyes fixed toward the city. She didn't finish the thought aloud: that when it was over and the Immortals lay slain alongside any number of her Dark Bloods... she would have accomplished nothing.

Rom shifted behind her. "My liege."

"What?"

"Surely you know that none of this will save you. Only Jordin can save you now."

She whirled around. "Well, there's no chance of that now, is there! You've failed in your useless attempts to save anyone. What has your life gained you but the death of everyone you have ever loved? Avra. Jonathan. Now me."

A tear spilled over the rim of his eye. The sight of it enraged her.

"Spare me your pathetic sadness! Isn't this what you wanted?" She strode toward him, grabbed him by his tunic, and heaved him toward the window so hard that he had to put up his hands to keep from crashing through it. "Look out there! Order and the Corpses who cling to it are all that will survive us. The aftermath of your efforts, your manipulations, your schemes! All in the name of what?"

"Love," he rasped.

"The Maker, if there is one, *spits* at the curse of your love. There"—she grabbed him by the hair, shoved his cheek against the glass, and pointed—"there is love, the only kind that there is! Loyalty—blind and deadly…"

Her rancor fell away; something had caught her eye. There, to the south. She let him go, laid her hands against the sill, and leaned forward. A spark of light. It vanished, and as she stared down the length of the darkened street, she wondered for a moment if she had imagined it, if it were an effect of the virus, burning the back of her retina. But no—there, emerging past the distant silhouette of that basilica. And there, another, traveling even with it—and two more, speeding through the black city toward the Citadel.

Her arms prickled.

The Immortals had come.

Two more, and then two more. She pushed Rom aside, seized a long looking glass from the table, knocking over the goblet of wine in the process. She raised the glass to her eye. Now she could see that they held torches, traveling as fast as a horse could run. Evenly spaced—every third or fourth rider. Every fifth. A glowing worm of light rushing down the wide street.

An order, shouted from below, sounded muted through the window glass. They'd been sighted. The distant street was by now ablaze with light, the flames of the torches trailing behind their riders. She sucked in a breath as the first of them came within blocks of the barricade.

The black of their hoods and cloaks was gone. Flames shone on bare skin, off the hard panes of chest and corded muscle of shoulder. Roland was showing his gall.

She focused on the front of the line, the rider to the left seemingly carved of white marble, quiver and bow slung over his back, sword belted around his waist. His arms were veined with tattoos that shot out like the barbs of an arrow toward his shoulder.

To his right, a rider as white, with his chest smeared in red, as though having killed already. His hair was unbound, glinting in the light of his torch. A long red sash trailed from his bicep and no less than fifteen knives were belted around his waist. He rode hard, seemingly without effort except for the deadly intent on his face.

Roland.

She lowered the glass and leaned as far forward as the window would allow. Horns from the field. Two flags rose from the southeast and west quadrants. Her Dark Bloods had begun to shift, amassing at the southern edge of the battlefield like black water running into a broad basin.

The Immortals came. Three blocks away from the barricade.

Two.

The riders behind rode low in the saddle, racing to close the gap between themselves and the horses before them so their mounts rode nose to tail.

Just before reaching the barricade, they closed rank. Feyn's body went rigid as she watched a spearhead form with blazing speed—two and then four and then six, ten, twelve riders abreast. Crashing through the opening in the barricade, those on the farthest edges of it leaping the rubble. Straight toward the bulk of massing Dark Bloods waiting to engulf them still fifteen lengths away.

Torches went flying as the leading Immortals tossed them aside and reached not for swords but for knives, hands flashing, steel glinting in firelight. One of the Dark Bloods on the front line buckled, grabbing at his face—and then another, as blood gushed from a gash in his side.

They dropped back against their comrades as the Immortals rushed toward them. The second line of Dark Bloods struggled to push past the first.

And then the Immortals were in their midst, Roland getting as deep as the fifth line. She waited for the crash, the clash of steel and armor as the Dark Bloods fell on them.

But before they could press in and crush Roland's force, the spearhead split into two. The commander angled east; Roland veered west. They curled off, churning in opposite directions, each leading hundreds of Immortals, like twin snakes striking for opposing ends of the battlefield.

She pushed back from the window with a slight gasp, unable to take her eyes away. Roland was dividing her forces.

Both columns of Immortals suddenly coiled around,

their white chests pale against the milling black. They took the fight into the edge of her pursuing Bloods, like deadly vipers that slashed into her men, cutting them down along the flanks before curling back out into open ground, never once slowing, never allowing themselves to be pressed by sheer numbers, captured in melee.

Maker. He was brilliant.

Her warriors in the thick of formation couldn't get close enough to fight. They shoved forward, hungry for battle, as the Immortals kept coming, curling off in either direction, chewing through her army as they did. She watched her Dark Bloods begin to fall as the Immortals sawed their way through the once-orderly lines. Fifty. Seventy. A hundred. Only a dozen Immortals had fallen.

And still the Immortals came, streaming through the barricade, driving down the middle, curling off and away.

A gap opened in her force directly in front of the gate.

Feyn clawed at her hair. Roland was taking the battle to opposite sides of the field, one east and one west.

Throw the lights!

Banks of bulbs mounted on the walls beamed to life, turned outward, flooding the massive clearing in stark white light. The Immortals would not be allowed the advantage of darkness.

And yet the Immortals fought on, never stopping, always in motion. On the northwestern side riders were visibly stumbling over the fallen, the carpet of bodies heavily one-sided: Dark. Within minutes they had cut down at least a thousand of her men to their—what? Twenty losses?

And still the Immortals kept coming. They raced through the barricade, down the broadening corridor of the field, fanning out in either direction. Roland had

already completed one wide arc and was coiling in and
through his own line. They were herding her army like
sheep!

Horns somewhere from the far side of the Citadel.
More Dark Bloods flooded to the south from the east
and west sides, rushing in like black waves. Feyn pressed
against the window, searching for the red chest and sash
of Roland. There! He was up in his stirrups, sword arcing downward even as the Immortal nearest him cut down
the Dark Blood slashing at his mount. Roland swung
wide. Not one but two heads of those Dark Bloods closest
flopped back on their necks as though on hinges, necks
opened to the light. His mount reared up, hooves churning at the air—only to come down on the closest Blood
before him.

A dozen Immortals blazed past the edge of the rubble, leaning low, sweeping the torches near the ground.
Feyn grabbed the looking glass, raised it again. Now she
could see the saddlebags hanging on either side of their
horses, limp and nearly depleted, an obvious gash in each
of them.

The street ignited in a highway of fire.

Something went flying. A saddlebag? And then there
was another, thrown up like a bladder into the massive
army of black. One of the Dark Bloods reached up and
caught it—just as a torch came flying at him.

It exploded in a burst of flame.

Another explosion—and then another, lobbed into the
mass of Dark Bloods.

Feyn pressed against the window, eyes tracking Roland,
already veering out in a new and broadening arc. Her
army was now evenly split in two sides. Their lines were
disrupted, horses penned in, those on foot falling beneath

sword and hoof—some of them trampled by their own men.

Something niggled. She knew the Immortals to be at least a thousand, and yet not all were accounted for here. And even these were making meat of her minions, sawing into their flanks like a chainsaw before curling back into the open ground at the center, now nearly a quarter-mile wide.

Still, her Dark Bloods would prove too many. It would be her victory. It had to be.

Just then a horn blared from the other side of the melee. Feyn turned, almost stumbled against Rom, and then stared at him.

Tears slipped down his cheeks.

She glanced past him, through the southern window. Something was shifting in the darkness beyond the rubble. Something...

And then she saw them in the distance. More Immortals. Flying toward the Citadel, streaming up and over the barricade like ravens.

Right into the backside of her army. She spun to the east and saw it was the same. She lowered the glass and glared at Rom, who was silently weeping.

She lifted her hand and slapped his face, suddenly enraged by such a show of weakness. "You sicken me."

Below, the muted clash of swords had increased in volume. Rom took one last look toward the battle, tears streaming down his face, and then retreated to the far side of the room.

For long minutes the battle raged. The Immortals' infuriating tactic—hitting and running, hitting and running—showed no sign of weakening. Like long serpents with teeth on all sides, they continued to cut into her army's flanks on both sides of the battlefield before circling back to safety, only to curl back in for another swipe.

She cursed and paced before the window, clawing at her hair. In the space of twenty minutes his Immortals had cut down nearly thirty thousand of her own.

But not even Roland would outlast her superior numbers.

She traced his movement again as he fearlessly led his Rippers, sword flashing, his mount barely slowing as he leaned low to slash directly into the middle of one Blood, to slice clean the head of another.

By the Maker, the man was magnificent. And she despised him for it.

To the east, Roland's commander was nowhere to be seen. She watched as her Bloods hauled two Immortals from their mounts after cutting the equine legs out from beneath them.

Both sides were making the horses a primary target.

The Immortals pressed in with deadly speed, slicing at the necks of Dark Blood stallions. But her Dark Bloods were in endless supply. For every one that fell, three more seemed to take his place.

Across to the west, Roland's deadly coil had finally broken; only a small band fought behind him. Dark Bloods had gotten between him and the rest of his company. As she watched, his arm flew out as though for balance even as his other slashed down. Too late—his mount buckled beneath him.

Feyn paced, biting at her nails, disgusted by the sweat staining her gown. Within the space of half an hour her company was cut in half. Their bodies blanketed the ground, tripping up their infantry comrades as others rode over them. But the Immortals were down to a few hundred.

The perimeter lights suddenly blacked out. The Immortals had found the power banks and cut them.

She pressed against the window, stared out, waiting for her eyes to adjust. The torches along the barricade were still burning, but the battlefield was a nightmare of reflected flame and shadow. She could still make out the white chests of the Immortals against the blackened sea, churning them down, more bodies in their wake.

She searched, tried to make out Roland in the darkness. The lights had been meant to neutralize the advantage of their uncanny sight. But it didn't matter now.

He had lasted over half an hour. He might yet cut down another thousand. Another ten thousand. He might survive a half hour more.

But he was too outnumbered.

Within an hour at most, it would be finished.

Beyond the field, a part of the city was aglow. But that wasn't possible—electricity had been cut in every sector, redirected to the Citadel. But as she watched, she realized it glowed only orange. A moment later, a building burst into flame. Beyond it, she could just discern another muted light, and there, another.

Byzantium was on fire.

Feyn let her breath out slowly and stared at her burning city. Billows of smoke rose to seed a churning sky.

She would win. But her reign would go out with those fires.

"My liege..."

She jerked her head and saw that Rom stood to her right, staring out at the night. She followed the line of his pointed finger, belatedly, as though waking from a nightmare. *I know*, she wanted to say. But then she realized he wasn't pointing at the fires, but at the battlefield, lit by torchlight.

At two riders dressed in desert garb, halfway up the center of the battlefield between the two main battles raging on either end, streaking toward the Citadel on white stallions.

She fumbled for the glass, lifted it, craning to see through a rising waft of smoke.

She didn't recognize the first rider. She panned a fraction of an inch and homed in on the other rider. Gray hair, long and unkempt. She knew the line of that cheek, the set of that mouth.

Saric!

She watched in horror as they flew for her gates, seemingly unseen by her own forces. Only two, but one of them was Saric, and Saric did not know the meaning of failure.

"They've come," Rom said with strange wonder. "They've come to save us."

She felt the blood drain from her face.

"They've come to kill me," she heard herself say.

In a sudden uncontrolled rage, she slammed the looking glass into the window. It crashed through, sending glass shards out into the night.

The servant outside threw open the door.

"My liege?"

She took one last look at the white stallions halfway to her gate, swept up the hem of her gown, and strode toward the servant. She spun at the door and glared back at Rom.

"Tell Corban to execute our prisoner," she said. "Take him down!"

CHAPTER TWENTY-NINE

JORDIN LEANED over her horse's neck, knees tight against its flanks, feeling the roll of its muscles against her thighs, the Citadel gate less than a half mile before her. Saric rode to her left, their two stallions racing down the field like a streak of light.

From beyond the city border, they'd seen the glow around the distant Citadel and known that the battle was under way. Even from there, they'd been able to see the clouds shrouding Byzantium. *Maker.* Had they ever been so ominous, so low? As they had entered the city, speeding down streets and alleyways gone silent, the roiling darkness had hit her, lifting the hair off her shoulders, sheathing her in chills.

They had flown past the barricade, thundering toward the gate, the battlefield before them divided, strewn with bodies of the fallen. On either side, she could see the tens of thousands of Dark Bloods...the battered and shrinking Immortals, their white and gore-smattered skin like flotsam in a sea of black.

Overhead, lightning illuminated the sky, throwing the clouds in stark, negative relief against the electric light of the Citadel itself. This wasn't a typical Byzantium storm.

It was darker. Deadlier. As though evil itself had come in one last bid for those who would be left.

"Ride!" Saric roared. "Ride!"

Jordin leaned low, loosened her grip on the reins, and let the horse have its head.

They were a quarter mile away when sections of Bloods began to break from their main bodies on either side, two black hands reaching to seize them before they gained the gate.

Twelve hundred warriors, Roland had said. A quick glance right and left told her that more than half, perhaps many more, had been cut to strips. She searched for a sign of Roland...prayed he wasn't among the fallen.

Lightning streaked to the east, a jagged finger piercing the darkness. The thunder, when it followed, rumbled up through the ground, jarring mount and rider to the bone.

Another day, she would have reached for bow or sword.

But *being* was Jordin's greatest weapon now.

A hundred lengths. Eighty.

Their stallions' hooves rumbled above the din of clashing steel and death cries. The dust of battle. The metallic bite of blood in the air.

Jonathan's last words after kissing her whispered through her heart. "Remember," he'd said gently. "The flesh and blood you see is like a dream. Don't let your mind play tricks that lead to fear and rage. See light. Be light. I am with you always." He'd placed his hand on her chest. "Always."

She'd spent an eternity with him beyond the veil. Together they'd plunged deep into his waters and breathed its elixir of raw love. She had laughed with unrestrained delight, unknown in the world of dreams where she'd dwelled for far too long.

They'd walked the shore, hand in hand, as Jonathan spoke more secrets than she could possibly remember.

Even now, blazing toward death, his words bubbled up from deep inside her being. "A lake *within* you. An eternal spring of life-giving water as vast as an endless ocean."

Fifty lengths. Jordin scanned the battlefield again, searching for Roland. How she would be able to pick him out in such a furious sea of bodies, she didn't know. Only that he would come; a way would be made.

Ahead of them, the Dark Bloods were closing to cut them off, and for a brief moment, Jordin felt an instinctual stab of fear. But the moment the emotion cut her mind, she recognized it. Remembered the truth. Jonathan, smiling at what could not hurt him. Jonathan with her. Jonathan, impervious.

With the memory of Jonathan's kiss, she leaned forward and chuckled beneath her breath.

Saric glanced at her, but only for a moment, intent on his own mission. He'd met her on the other side of her waking, two horses saddled, prepared, and waiting for a mission he'd been saved to complete.

Twenty lengths.

The time had come.

Strange how such peace embraced her. No shred of concern for her own life—only for those she must save. If, in her attempt, her body was cut down as Jonathan's had once been, she knew she would wake in his lake once more.

A part of her dared—invited—any to make an attempt on her life. She knew her reward! But then they were nearly on the Citadel, the battlefield open ahead.

Ahead and far to her right, a red-chested Immortal

raced along the front edge of the Dark Bloods, leaping up onto a riderless horse. His black hair whipped the air as he raced forward, sword flashing. With one vicious swing of the blade, the Ripper took the heads from two Dark Bloods before arching his back to narrowly avoid a spear slicing in from another.

Roland!

She couldn't see his face at this distance, but she could hardly mistake the movement that lived up to the Immortal name.

"There," she said.

Saric followed her eyes.

No fewer than fifty Bloods broke from the main line behind Roland, rushing to cut him off. She knew that he could sense them coming after their Immortal prize. Knew also that he would escape the obvious trap.

With a blood-chilling roar, he twisted to the side and buried his blade into the head of a horse pulling abreast. Rider and mount crashed heavily to the ground, tripping up two others directly behind.

The Citadel gates loomed ahead, thrown open to give Feyn's hounds easy access in either direction.

This prince wasn't backing down. He might very well fight his way clear of the Bloods sweeping in behind him, and on another day, she would have watched him evade and cut them down in awe, but she wasn't taking any chances.

"I go," she said.

"Do what you must."

She veered to the right, angling directly for the Bloods closing on Roland, who was fully intent on taking advantage of the distraction.

Or was his intent to save her?

He charged his mount into four Bloods on foot, knocking two on their backs. Then, dropping over the side of his saddle, he took the leg off another with a low sweep of his blade.

Fifty meters.

She pounded toward him.

Thirty meters.

Roland was in a dash for the gate. But the Bloods ahead of him were too thick.

When she was only ten meters from him she turned into the outer line of Dark Bloods. Only when the first spun and roared his warning did she scream her own.

Jordin wasn't prepared for what happened at the sound of that cry. She *saw* it, a slight distortion in the energy field rippling out before her into a shock wave sent out by her entire being.

It struck the closest Bloods like an invisible wall, sending them flying back into those behind them.

She saw it in real time, but her mind saw more slowly— not as an Immortal would see, but with even greater clarity. The force slammed into Bloods five meters from her horse as she swept in behind Roland. She cut through the edge of the surging horde, passing only paces to Roland's right flank. She cut short her scream and threw a command over her shoulder. "Follow!" She then veered back into the battlefield, leaving a mass of stunned Bloods behind her scrambling to their feet.

Roland hesitated a moment, obviously shocked. And then he kicked his mount and tore after her, five horse lengths to her rear. Saric, to their left, had nearly gained the Citadel. Dark Bloods swarmed toward the gates.

The battlefield had turned its focus on the race to those gates. Jordin gained Saric's side, her head low, seat off the saddle, dress streaming behind. Roland, gore-smattered and bloodthirsty, caught up as Dark Bloods roared in from both sides.

Three lances destined to reach the point of entry at the same time.

A dozen Bloods were frantically rushing to close the gates as the hordes closed with a full-throated roar, faces reddened and knotted with rage.

They were going to collide, all of them. The gates moved to shut. The swarming Bloods, too fast. Their white lance was a second too late to avoid crushing impact, horse on horse, flesh on steel, scream on scream.

And yet she felt only surreal calm. It would be as it was meant to be. She no longer saw Dark Bloods, but a rushing sea of night come to block the light.

Could darkness dispel light?

She was aware of Saric on her left, of Roland on her heels, the Bloods converging before her, but she was far more aware of something closer. Of something inside of her.

Of the presence that was one with her.

It was Jonathan who commanded this battle—not the desperate forms attempting to be seen as shapers of their world, oblivious to the far greater reality brimming with inexhaustible power behind the veil of mind and temporal sight.

She didn't scream. Didn't panic. Did nothing, in fact, except fix her eyes beyond the gates and ride.

At the last possible moment, she felt a single whisper of fear. What if this was her end?

A blur of mounted Dark Bloods reached the gate with her. Her stallion collided with the Dark Blood leading the western charge.

But it wasn't her horse that made contact with the other. It was her presence. A wave of raw energy threw the horse aside as if it were an ant. From the corner of her eye, she saw Saric slam through a dozen mounted Bloods. Light struck the Bloods head-on, sending them flying back, flinging wide the half-closed gates, parting the Dark Bloods like a black sea.

Then they were through, and by the sound of his stallion thundering behind her, Jordin knew that Roland had followed in their wake.

She raced up the grand walk to the palace itself, taking marble stairs at a full run, a stride in front of Saric. She hadn't considered the sealed doors but she was in such a state of assurance that it hardly occurred to her that they could be a problem until they loomed, tall and thick, before her.

She didn't slow.

"Jordin!"

Roland's warning from behind.

Fear spiked in her consciousness at his cry—a moment of panic that flashed in her mind and cut off her breath.

She was going to crash into the doors!

But just as Jordin was sure her horse would make contact, they blew open with a loud boom. Not just open, but off their hinges and thirty feet into the palace where they struck a far wall and toppled to the floor.

Her horse sailed through the entrance, landed on the marble floor, and slid to a whinnying stop next to one of the doors, a full ten paces into the palace.

Jordin pulled hard at the air, momentarily taken off guard by the ease with which they'd breached Feyn's stronghold.

She scanned the rotunda. Gold glinted down from the

domed ceiling like an inverted sun. Atop the grand staircase, high arched walkways split in either direction to run
down the far length of the palace.

Roland sat on his horse, looking wildly about and then
staring, at last, at her. Saric sat more serenely. No other
soul in sight.

Those without souls, however, had recovered from
the scene at the gates and were surging into the Citadel
grounds, like oil flowing through a funnel.

Roland dropped from his horse, blade in hand, and
crossed the main floor of the rotunda to the stair. He
pointed to the western corridor above, toward the senate
wing. "This way. I can smell her."

Smell her? Jordin didn't know that she smelled any different from other Dark Bloods.

A way will be made.

Saric was already dismounting. He tugged his mount
to face the onslaught of Bloods outside and slapped its
rump. The horse snorted and walked to the door, where
Jordin's stallion joined it. The sight of the white horses
that had plowed so effortlessly through those Dark Blood
ranks would at least give the minions pause.

And then she was striding up the stairs, two at a time,
after Roland, Saric at her side. "We have to find Rom."

"I go for Feyn."

"And I brought you in."

He cast a look over his shoulder as he turned down
the western hall. Below, the horses reared, a wild whinny
echoing up to the domed ceiling. Their hooves crashed to
the marble, shattering it, and then they were bolting down
the stairs of the palace. Their fate was no longer Jordin's
concern.

She caught Roland. "She stays alive."

He remained silent, face intent, blinded by rage even after the display of power he'd only just witnessed.

"Alive, Roland. Alive!"

They ran the length of the walk, past the end of the rotunda court where it turned into a grand hall—past office doors, the flags of the nations, until they reached the senate atrium. Four Dark Bloods stood guard outside the doors, which meant someone worth protecting was inside. Roland sprinted for them, having never answered Jordin.

The Senate Hall. And so Feyn had retreated to the place of her resurrection at the hands of Saric six years earlier. Here, she had returned to life. Here, she would make her final stand or breathe her last breath.

Jordin slowed to a stop as two of the guards stepped out to intercept Roland. Both left their heads on the floor. Their bodies collapsed nearby. The other two circled for better position, fear straining their faces.

Roland threw open the doors of the atrium and vanished inside.

Saric lifted his right hand at the two standing Bloods as he slowed to a brisk walk. "Stay!"

They blinked. They also stayed. Jordin gave Saric a glance as she passed by him into the atrium. She crossed to the great inner doors of the Senate Hall just as Roland was flinging them wide.

They strode in together, but halted as one barely three meters inside the hall.

The sight that greeted her sent a chill down her spine.

Feyn stood on the dais, long golden robe draped over a midnight gown. Her hair fell to her waist in long black waves, unbound. Her arms were at her sides, the ring of office glinting from her hand. Her stare was hard as stone, face chiseled with bitterness. A knife was in her hand. This did not concern Jordin. Nor did the fifty Dark Bloods divided to Feyn's left and her right, glaring with as much vitriol.

What alarmed her was the absence of Rom.

The door thudded shut behind her. The latch clanked in place. Saric stepped up on Roland's far side and calmly took in the scene.

The end could come here.

CHAPTER THIRTY

FOR SEVERAL LONG seconds silence reigned in the Senate Hall. No one moved. Overhead, the electric lights were on—Jordin had seen them go dark at their approach. Apparently only the supply to the wall had been cut.

Jordin could not parse a full spectrum of enhanced senses the way Roland surely could in that moment, but she knew the look of hatred. Could see the utter defiance on the prince's face. The wrath flashing from Feyn's black eyes.

The knife in her hand.

Feyn drew her other hand into a clenched fist.

"This is your time, Jordin," Saric said softly. "See what you must see."

Jordin looked from Feyn to the Dark Bloods spanning the sides of the dais.

See...

"I know who you are," Feyn cried out, eyes locked on her. "Jordin, lover of Jonathan, the would-be Sovereign who spawned a deviant race by that name. And you, Roland, so-called Immortal. You will find your death here." She strode toward the edge of the dais. "And my *dear* brother. Come to see me die where you brought me back to life, have you? How quaint, how poetic. A former Sovereign, one who calls herself Sovereign, one who would be prince... and yet you stand before the true and only Sovereign of the world!"

A deep calm settled over Jordin. At one time she might have trembled before such words. But now... she saw only a woman who had forgotten who she was. Who appeared absurd standing in the midst of her own rage and self-righteousness.

Life was a cycle of remembering and forgetting, Jonathan had told her beside the lake—of remembering that flesh and blood are only a dream next to the reality behind them. Of forgetting the same truth again, after only minutes or hours of realizing it. It was why Sovereigns had had such clarity of knowing—even snippets of the future—immediately after taking Jonathan's blood six years ago... only to forget the way of that knowing.

"If this is what you want, this is what I will give you," Feyn cried. "Death and more death until not even a single Immortal robs the earth of my air!"

Perfect love casts out fear, Jonathan had told her—and anger and jealousy and malice with it.

She'd understood then that the world that enslaved itself to the Order had left behind the one antidote to the evils that had plagued it an age before.

Love. How clearly she saw it!

Stained head to foot with his victims' blood, however, Roland did not.

Dragging the tip of his sword along the floor behind him, he strode forward, up the center aisle, eyes fixed on Feyn.

Let him go, Jordin.

She breathed with ease and held back.

"Kill him," Feyn snarled.

Six Dark Bloods on either side bounded from the dais and stormed forward, blades ready. Loyal to the end, surely aware that Roland could best them.

But he would have a hard time besting the ten others in their wake, or the ten that suddenly moved to either flank and rushed up the side aisles.

Roland strode evenly, as if he'd been truly blinded, in both mind and sight.

The Dark Bloods converged, rushing with a speed that defied their bulk.

Jordin held her place. But Feyn wasn't as resolute.

"Kill him! Cut off his head, you pathetic worms!"

Roland didn't even lift his sword from the long mark it had left along the floor until the first Dark Blood reached him and brought his blade to bear.

Then he moved with stunning speed. He dropped to a crouch as the blade sung overhead and then sprang up into a head butt that landed on the Blood's chin with a loud crack. The Blood staggered into the man behind him.

Roland flowed with his momentum, leaping onto the long senate bench to his right before they could recover. He raced across the tops of the tiered benches with the agility of a cat, a far better judge of distance and weight than his Dark Blood pursuers.

The Dark Bloods cleared the center aisle and cut into the tiers, running along the benches with devastating speed to intercept him.

But Roland had timed his outing perfectly, waiting until all but ten had vacated the platform in pursuit. In one last bound, narrowly avoiding twin blades that clashed where his legs had been, he cleared the last bench, took two long running strides, and leaped onto the platform, not five paces from Feyn.

Hold...hold...

She held and she saw.

Only now did Roland use his blade, slashing across his body right into the necks of the two nearest Bloods on stage. Throwing it like a knife into the face of a third. Rolling past the rush of three others to come up behind and to the left of Feyn with a large carving blade in his fist.

He was going to reach her, but to what end? The Bloods on the senate floor were already storming the dais from all sides.

Jordin began to walk toward the dais, eyes on Roland. But he had no time to notice her. He threw himself behind Feyn, sidestepping the wicked stab of her knife. He slapped the knife away, spun her around, grabbed her hair with one hand, and tugged her head back at an obscene angle.

His blade was pressed against her jugular.

"Call them off," he growled.

She struggled, and he pressed the blade against her with enough force to draw blood.

"Off!"

"Back!" Feyn cried.

The Dark Bloods pulled up sharply—all but one. He launched up the front of the dais with a growl. Roland kicked in his teeth with an audible crunch of heel against jaw. The warrior dropped with a hard thump.

The Senate Hall stilled to silence.

Jordin continued down the hall, eyes locked on Roland, who was dragging Feyn back toward the exit behind the dais. That he meant to leave through that door was clear. That he would not leave her alive before he did was a given.

And then he would go out to the battlefield and fight to the end.

Now, Jordin. See. Do what you know to do.

"Roland."

Her voice was gentle but not without power. She watched the wave of energy leaving her, rushing to meet Roland where he stood. He turned his eyes and stared at her over Feyn's head, as if remembering for the first time that she was even in the chamber.

"No, Roland." The words left her mouth as silent, concussive ripples like heat on a blistering road. As they folded around him, he paused, appeared confused.

"No, Roland. Not now."

His movement stalled, one knotted fist full of Feyn's hair, one hand pressing his knife against her panting throat. Feyn's face had paled to bleached bone, lips drawn back as much in fury as fear.

"Not ever," Jordin said.

She was acutely aware of every eye on her. That they stood transfixed in the grasp of a power that they couldn't possibly understand, much less resist. As for her, the entire room had become a waking vision far more real than the stage play that had just unfolded with all of its screaming and leaping and swinging of swords.

Spoiled, angry child's play. Insanity.

And she, the bearer of serenity.

Of true Sovereignty.

She mounted the steps and rose to the platform, eyes locked on Roland's. For several long breaths, she rested in the presence within her. Jonathan's presence, humming through her veins. Of water, tree, trunk, and branch...

Life beyond the veil.

She stepped forward, hardly feeling the floor beneath her feet.

"You, Roland, are destined for the throne. You will

rule in a kingdom far greater than the one you seek. In a realm filled with more power than you realize."

He blinked, eyes squinting in consternation.

She stopped three paces before him. Compassion swept through her like a hot breeze. Roland stood as the Prince of Immortals, waging war on principle, bound by an honor that was as much his identity as the brawn of his frame. He was a man who could snap his fingers to call a thousand Rippers into battle or issue a single word to bring them all to their knees.

And yet here he stood, struggling to hold his own over an orphan girl he himself had once saved to serve him.

One who had come to show him salvation.

She closed the distance between them, only vaguely aware of Feyn's frantic breath, her long white neck bleeding under his blade.

Jordin lifted her hand to Roland's face, brushed his cheek with her thumb.

"I love you, Roland."

The words were borne on white light. It flowed into his eyes, through his skin, washed over the top of his head. And she knew then that she spoke with wholeness, void of posturing or position for gain.

This, too, Jonathan had told her: that she would truly love Roland. That it was Jonathan's gift to her, to them both.

His brows drew together. A tear broke from his right eye and slipped down his cheek. The misguided bonds of loyalty to his realm resisted unconditional love—a love that knew no status or position. And for his resistance, she only felt more compassion.

"I love you," she repeated, her own eyes filling with tears.

She lowered her hand.

"It's time to surrender your suffering. To embrace new power and life."

He started to speak, but whatever he meant to say came out only as a stutter.

She offered him a shallow nod. "You will see. You already do. You feel my love washing away your deepest fears. Surrender, my love. Surrender and live."

His face slowly strained with emotion. Surrender didn't reside in Roland's world. He knew no such word, knew it only as weakness—never as power.

"Let Jonathan save you, Roland. From this. From yourself."

His lips parted as tears spilled from his eyes to trail through the spattered blood staining his cheeks.

"Rule with me in a realm where all sit on the thrones of love. Let Feyn go. She will be Sovereign of this world. It will be her burden to bear, not yours." And then, "Let her go."

She knew it was not her but the truth in his own heart that he obeyed as he relaxed the blade at Feyn's throat. He lowered his knife, released his grip on her hair.

Feyn jerked forward and spun out of Roland's grip.

Jordin's glance lingered a second longer on Roland. "You will see, my prince. I promise, you will see."

"Kill them!" Feyn cried, voice filled with wretched dread.

But her Dark Bloods were either too confounded by the strange power in the room or struck by the sight of their maker so twisted by terror to move.

"No," Jordin said, turning to Feyn. Her deception was deeper than Roland's, flowing to every cell in her body through veins blackened by alchemy. But the life she had tasted once many years ago still lived behind that darkness, a tiny ember waiting on only a breath of love to fan it into flame.

"No," she said again. Waves of light streamed between them.

Feyn was lost to rage. She shoved a trembling finger at Roland and spewed her demand, spittle flying past her lips.

"You will kill them!"

"No!" The force of Jordin's shout filled the room with a thundering echo that surprised even her.

Feyn's face knotted in confusion. She slowly lowered her arms and took another step back. She was visibly shaking. "You have no right..." Her voice was thin and desperate. "You..." She seemed to lose track of her intention, so taken off guard by the one crushing word hurled in her face.

"No, Feyn," Jordin repeated more quietly. "The time for death is done." She stepped closer. "I've come to give you the power you were born to possess. As Sovereign."

"I..." Feyn looked around her, lost.

"You were born Sovereign, the seventh chosen by time in the Cycle of Rebirth. You are to reign over the world, not as Dark Blood or Corpse, but as Sovereign." Jordin watched the truth of her words flow out to Feyn.

"Hear me. Jonathan came to be Sovereign, but not in this realm. He came to bring a new realm to a world lost in death. And he died so you could bring Sovereign light to them all."

"I...I'm going to die," she said softly.

"No. You aren't. Saric knows this now. I know it. You, too, must know it."

"I am the world's maker."

"Maker only of your own pathetic dream. A dream that leads to misery and death. But that's not what you were chosen to do from the beginning."

Her lips spread wide in a silent, desperate plea.

Jordin moved toward her, reached out for that trembling hand. She took it gently in her own. Lifted it, eyes piercing the veil of confusion thick in the Sovereign's eyes.

She spoke in a low, sure tone. "You must allow Jonathan's blood to bring you life. The ancient blood that Rom gave you made a way. Only then can you awaken to the Sovereign Realm where Jonathan rules, alive."

She reached into her pocket and withdrew the object inside it, given her by Saric. Two simple stents connected by an arm's length of tubing and a rubber bladder pump. Feyn went rigid.

Jordin held her hand firmly.

"Everything has happened as it was meant to, Feyn." Still grasping Feyn's hand in her left, she slid her right hand to one of the stents and lifted it to her own arm.

"Everything."

She slid the sharp metal tube into the vein on her arm, welcoming the prick of pain.

Feyn began to whimper. Her body shook from head to foot as the dark blood in her screamed with revulsion. Tears streamed down her cheeks to drop from her chin.

Across the Senate Hall, Saric stood, unmoving...tears glimmering on his cheeks.

The darkness in her mind will resist, Jonathan had said. *But Feyn is far stronger than even she knows. Bring her to life, Jordin. You have my blood. Bring her to life!*

"Surrender," Jordin said, gazing into Feyn's bloodshot eyes. The agony in them broke her heart, and she briefly wondered if she would have the strength it took to climb out of such a deep well of despair.

"Surrender."

Feyn closed her eyes and began to whimper as the tears streamed down her face. Then a wail—a piercing keen that pushed her Dark Bloods back in terror.

Her trembling legs lost their strength; she dropped to her knees before Jordin. Mouth open in an anguished cry, she opened her eyelids to slits. Her body was rebelling, but her dark eyes were begging for life. For a spark of light. For rescue from the torment that wracked her soul.

"Take Jonathan's blood. Find life," Jordin said, pushing the velvet sleeve of her gown up her arm. And then she shoved the stent deep into the inky black vein in its crook.

She wrapped her fingers around the bulb halfway down the tube and pumped. Saw her own blood, crimson red, flow into the tube, through the pump itself, then down the tube and into Feyn's arm.

Feyn's wail swelled to a piercing shriek. She jerked back in recoil, but Jordin held her arm with a firm hand.

"Find life, my Sovereign. Find life."

The words streamed as white light, flowing over Feyn's face and chest, even as she screamed as one being flayed alive.

Because she was.

"Life," Jordin whispered gently.

But the wave of light from her last word was not gentle. It slammed into Feyn and smothered her cries of pain.

The Sovereign's body shut down, and she crumpled to the floor as one dead.

Chapter Thirty-one

FEYN'S PULSE exploded in her ears, unbearably loud and growing impossibly louder by the second. Fire seared her veins, ignited her nerves. Somewhere in the distance, someone screamed.

I die, she thought.

At least it would be for the last time.

She gave herself to the blackness when it enveloped her, to the excruciating pain that dragged her from that oblivion. To the terror.

It came on her like a black wave, filled her lungs and darkened her eyes. Fear, guilt, shame, pride, anger—all at once. She sucked for breath, found there was none. In the drone behind the drumming of her heart, a distant chuckle, slow and ominous. The screaming again, rising up over the laughter, too loud to be human.

Let me die. Let it end.

The accusation of her every failure. Of the blood on her hands. The deaths added to her conscience. Their faces were before her—Seth, Dominic, countless thousands. The Corpses in Byzantium, fleeing, begging, pleading for their lives. The women ruined by her Dark Bloods. The Corpses condemned by her domination. She could never repay it. The burden of pride, of eclipsing the Maker, of aspiring to a seat she could never fill with even her greatest hate, ambition, or desires. Futile. Empty. Black.

She couldn't bear it.

Screams again, unending screams. Her own.

Maker, take my life!

Hades could be no worse than this.

But then it was worse. Her body was on fire. She clawed but found nothing, not even air, blind in a sea of tar.

And utterly alone.

There was only this—an endless space populated by her own grief over what could not be undone. A price that could never be repaid.

The drums began to fade. The laughter had already rumbled to nothing.

Silence and darkness settled over her like a blanket.

Even her thoughts, her pleas to die, were gone.

Silence. Darkness—for how long, she did not know.

Only when a bare drone edged into the silence did she become aware of anything. It began as a vibration somewhere in the distance, flat and as unending as a line, stretching in either direction, never meeting east or west. Never ending. A hum, growing in undulation until it was not one note but two. A broadening ribbon of sound in a space otherwise empty—no, not empty at all but filled with a spectrum of sound.

Bands of light. Color. Filling the void, impossibly full, doubling on itself. East. West—never ending.

And now, an explosion of light! It blinded her, though she knew she did not see with her eyes. Impossibly bright.

Drums in the distance. They came, faint as a pattering step, thrumming as a pulse. As a heart pounding to rapid and dizzying life.

She was waiting for the laughter. It didn't come. It would never come. The guilt, the shame...where were they? The wish for death, the pain of it. Where was the sting?

She sucked in a breath, felt it rush into her lungs, *felt* it enter her very cells, the minute workings within them vibrating with it.

Time to wake.

No.

I will be with you.

Never leave me.

She blinked her eyes open. An electric fixture, glowing overhead. Something remembered and distant. The hum was fading, and she closed her eyes.

Don't let me go.

I will never let you go.

As though in answer, fingers clasped her arm.

"Feyn."

No...

Hard flooring beneath her back, sweat trapped within the heavy velvet of her gown, plastering her hair to her neck, a web of it over her face.

A face obscured her vision.

Jordin.

She started to push up, fell back, rolled to her shoulder along the floor. Her sleeve was pushed up, a wound bleeding from her arm. The blood was still wet, and she realized that somehow an eternity of terror had passed in the space of moments.

She was still staring at the wound when she realized the veins beneath her skin were fading. There, before her eyes, as though retreating behind a scrim. Her skin—hadn't it been white? But now color flooded it.

She grabbed her sleeve, pulled it higher. The golden hue darkened her flesh before her very eyes. Not as pale as it had been in her life as a royal—genetically engineered by the virus to breed bloodless beauty in its royals—but the color of skin as it had been *before*.

She lifted her gaze with wonder. There was Jordin, standing at arms' reach. And behind her...

Roland, on a knee, face wet with tears.

Had either of them ever been so lovely to her? Even bloodied and blackened from the fire of battle, had she ever seen a soul so tortured and beautifully broken? Roland, whom she had hated. But her heart rent at the sight of him now.

She looked at Jordin. At this woman with wisdom she could not even now comprehend. This woman endowed with more power than Feyn could have ever claimed.

"I'm..." Her voice faltered. She looked around at the Dark Bloods staring at her in confusion. They were hers once...no more. For a brief moment she pitied them.

Back to Jordin. "I'm alive?"

"Alive." Jordin smiled. "Very alive."

"Like you?"

Jordin took her hand. "Yes. And not quite. It may take some time."

Roland, five feet away, lifted his head, lashes wet, his cheeks smeared with tears and blood. "Jordin. I'm ready."

"Yes. You are, my prince. You are."

He rose and moved toward her, glancing at Feyn and then staring into Jordin's eyes. There was a tenderness to his look that Feyn had never seen before—a lion bowing to a power greater than its own.

"Forgive me—"

"Shh, shh..." Jordin put a finger to his lips.

"Give me this," he said.

"I will." Jordin appeared luminous, not with light but with the same life that flowed through her own veins. A small smile touched her lips. "I will."

Feyn twisted and looked at the senate doors where he'd stood. Saric. He was gone. She glanced around the chamber, but there was no sign of him.

"Where's my brother? He has to know!"

"He does, Feyn. He knows." Jordin's voice was soft, as if her words held great meaning to her. "You'll see him soon enough. There are more urgent concerns on his mind right now."

Memory of the battle suddenly came storming back, shoving aside the surreal scene before her.

"The battle! We have to stop it."

Roland glanced toward the entrance, as though only now remembering the war waging outside himself.

Feyn pushed up onto her knees, turned to the Dark Bloods.

"Stop the battle. Send word to the commanders. Pull back. The battle is won. I need the remaining Immortals alive!"

They glanced around as though lost. Had she not just spoken, given a command?

"They were loyal to you, bound by blood," Jordin said quietly.

Bound by blood no more.

Feyn rose unsteadily to her feet, tugged at the clasp of her cloak, which had twisted around her neck, let it fall to the floor. She straightened and addressed the Bloods still shifting on their feet.

"You will go to the field and stop the war," she ordered pointedly, shoving her finger at the door.

Some made as if to go, but others stood dumbstruck.

"Go!" Feyn shouted.

Casting glances over their shoulders, they began to file out, gaining momentum in their strides as they went. She watched until the last of them had gone and then glanced at Roland.

"You have no assurance they'll obey," Roland said, springing for his knife. He quickly sheathed it. "I don't know how many of my men are still alive, but there's still time. They, too, will take the blood."

"My Bloods won't follow your orders. I have to go."

"Then go. I go for my men."

Her eyes lit on the knife Roland had knocked from her hand. She moved toward it and slipped it into the sheath slung against her hip, praying she wouldn't need it.

"The other Dark Bloods will all be dead within twenty-four hours," Jordin said. "After that, you won't need to worry about anything other than burning the bodies."

Dead. Every Dark Blood engineered or converted. She drew a slow breath of unexpected relief until—

"Rom!" she cried.

Jordin spun. "What of him?"

"I have to save him. I condemned him."

Jordin took a moment. As she did, calm seemed to settle over her—the same serenity she'd shown earlier.

"Then you must save him." To Roland: "I'm with you. Too many Immortals have given their lives today. No more."

Roland took her hand by the fingertips, his gaze level as he lifted it to his lips. "Thank you," he said and kissed her hand. "Thank you."

And then he was turning on his heel, flying down the stairs, and striding up the aisle, Jordin close behind.

They would stop the battle, but Feyn's mind was no longer on thousands of men. Only one.

Rom. The man who had first shown her life so many years ago...the man whom she had sentenced to die a bare hour ago. Her heart was pounding. The memory of those bleak faces, that utter condemnation, returned to her.

But where had Corban taken him?

Maker, let me not be too late!

Feyn ran for the door, her mind spinning.

THE ENTRANCE to the laboratories had been left guarded by a single Dark Blood. He gave her a strange glance as she reached him, and for a moment she wondered if he would stand aside.

She brushed past him without a word, and he didn't move to challenge her.

Only inside the great laboratory, lit by low work lights, did she realize she'd been holding her breath. She strode past the first row of workstations before grabbing her skirts and breaking into a run.

Maker, let me not be too late. She'd found new life. But she didn't know how she could live with herself if she found Rom dead.

When she reached the dungeon cells, she found no sign of him. Her heart went cold. She grabbed the bars of the last cell and glanced at the lock. No, they wouldn't have brought him here. Not to kill him.

She hurried back out to the great chamber, ran through the maze of tables and then back to the chamber that held the glass sarcophagi filled with Bloods in the making. The sight of those bodies had once filled her with pride. She'd once thought them a thing of beauty. Seeing their lifeless forms now, she was filled with revulsion. This was a place of horrors.

She turned, looked around, momentarily lost. And then she was moving with long, swift strides toward Corban's private laboratory.

She slipped inside. The tables were full of dark vials, discarded trash, stents and tubing, crumpled notes, some strewn on the floor. She passed by the main lab toward the observation suite.

Even from outside, she could see light shining beneath the door. Her heart surged, daring hope. She opened the door to the outer room and stepped inside, breath quick.

There—movement through the window to the inner room: Corban, in a dark tunic without his lab coat, standing over the bench with his back toward her. His acolyte stood in the corner of the chamber, scribbling notes. And strapped to the chair...

Rom.

His head had fallen back, and he appeared to be bleeding from a fresh gash in his face. His sleeves were rolled up, a stent buried in his arm, tube dangling toward the floor and dripping blood.

As she watched, he lifted his head and opened his left eye. His other was nearly swollen shut. Feyn gasped, rushed to the inner door, and threw it open.

Corban spun from his worktable, startled.

"My liege! I was just..." He paused, cocked his head.

"Release him!" Feyn ordered. She would have done it herself, but the sight of Corban arrested her attention.

His skin, pale as hers had once been, had begun to peel from his face. It lay open and ragged around sores that oozed pus. His hands, normally gloved, were bare, blackened in spots. The flesh was peeling from them as well.

He was squinting at her strangely, stepping toward her.

"Your face," she said.

"Yes. My face. And my back. And my hands." He held them up, backs to her, for her to see. "They're rotting away even as I live. The result of prolonged exposure to the virus as I've slaved to find an antidote to save you. My gift is an early death."

So he'd seen the difference in her. Felt the loss of connection between them, had already turned against her—she could see it in his eyes. And now she saw that he'd been in the throes of madness—working frantically to extract answers from Rom before killing him.

"Cut him free," she said.

"Your lover? You care more for this *thing* than for me, the one who's toiled at the cost of his skin to save your life! Never mind the cost to myself, I did it for loyalty. Because I must—we were bound by blood. But now I sense that you, my liege, are much changed."

He crossed the distance between them in two long steps. Now she could smell the rot in his flesh. Could see that when he opened his mouth to speak, his teeth were edged in black.

His nose wrinkled in disgust. She realized for the first time that he could smell her—that the same offensive odor she'd associated with Rom and any Sovereign before came from her own skin.

"Your skin has lost its Brahmin pallor. And your eyes…" He reached toward her, as though to turn her cheek this way or that, but she slapped his hand away.

"Stay back!"

He made no show of hearing, much less obeying, her. "How did you do it? How did you manage it when I have found no solution?" He stepped closer, his breath foul in her face. "How is it possible that you find salvation and leave me to die?"

She gazed at him in silence. Hatred filled his eyes as the full truth settled into his rotting mind.

"Then it's true. He said you knew the pollution of that ancient vial once."

He turned away, slowly. Then, in a sudden fit of rage, he swept his arm across the table, sending vials and instruments and syringes and collection tubes crashing to the floor. The Corpse, Ammon, backed to the wall, eyes wide at the sight of his enraged master, notes clutched against his chest.

"You've abandoned us all!"

"Forgive me," Feyn said, very quietly.

He spun and stared at her. It was the look of the damned staring the living in the face.

"Forgive me," she said again.

The sound that came up out of him started as a keen. He grabbed his head, pulled at his hair, as it deepened into a guttural cry.

Ammon slid into the far corner.

"I created your army!" Corban raged. "I made your lovers, custom-built your minions—for what? Is this my reward? You have sent me to my grave!"

He spun back and launched himself at her. She threw herself against the wall, but he was on her, bleeding forearm pressing into her throat.

Behind him, Rom was straining against the leather straps, veins bulging from his neck, lips pulled back from his teeth.

"You did this!" Corban roared. "You've killed us all!"

Feyn struggled against his wiry weight. He was deceptively strong, as she once was. Her uncanny strength gone, she felt his forearm crushing her windpipe, her weight coming off her feet, her body being shoved up along the wall. Pinpricks dotted her sight. She reached for his face, but he twisted away. She grabbed again for his hair, one of her thumbs stretching toward his eye.

Her lungs struggled in vain. Her body began to spasm for air. Desperate, she shoved her finger into his eye. The arm at her throat answered with crushing pressure.

She heard a growl in her ears, rumbling like the coming of a train. A low and rage-filled cry gaining in pitch from behind the master alchemist until it became a loud scream.

Something snapped. She wondered if it was her windpipe breaking, or her neck.

Another guttural roar filled her ears, this one from beyond Corban. In her failing vision she saw the movement behind him, sweeping in like a dark shadow. Rom, rising up.

Corban tried to snap his head round, but her thumb was buried in his eye.

Consciousness was failing her...

Corban jerked back, as if hit by a hammer. He crashed into the side table as Feyn slumped to the floor, gasping for air through lungs that refused to work fast enough.

Face bleeding badly, Corban flew at Rom, who ducked a swinging fist. He dropped to a knee, lunged toward Feyn, and grabbed the knife at her waist.

With a loud cry, Rom twisted and shoved the blade up under the alchemist's ribs. Jerked the knife back out. Grabbing Corban by the front of his bloody tunic, he slashed the knife across the alchemist's neck, slicing through throat and bone and larynx.

Corban stiffened for a moment, expression incredulous at the spray of red, before toppling forward.

Rom dropped to his knees, breathing heavily, bleeding from the stent still in his arm. He lowered the knife.

Feyn scrambled across the floor toward him.

"You were right," she said, struggling to speak. "You...were right, my love." She reached for his head, which had dropped forward as he sagged. "There's still time. Here...Here..." She fumbled with her sleeve, and then looked at the instruments strewn around them.

"Don't..."

"Hush. Let me just find..." Where was it? Where was Corban's stent? She had seen one here. "You'll take my blood. This will be over."

Rom laid a hand on her arm.

"Feyn. It won't work."

"What do you mean? I'm Sovereign now. You were right! And I *see*." She straightened, drew a long breath into her lungs. "For the first time, I know it. I know *life*."

"You're still converting. There hasn't been enough time. Feyn...it won't work."

"Then come with me. Jordin's here. We'll find her. Get up. Rom, get up!" Tears were streaming down her face, and she didn't know why.

"The Immortals need it."

"You do as I say, Rom Sebastian. I will not see you killed for my actions, for saving me. Corban was right. I've consigned enough to death as it is!"

"They were never meant for life, your Dark Bloods. They could never have known life. They hardly knew it as they lived...and knew nothing of true goodness."

"For all I know Roland might have been too late to save any of them. Get up—we have to find Jordin!" She slid her arm beneath his shoulder.

"No." A voice from behind her. "Take mine."

Feyn swiveled to the voice behind her. Saric stood in the open doorway, eyes on Rom.

"Take my blood," he said.

Hope sailed up through her chest, but then faltered at something in his eyes. It was the look of them...resolute. At utter peace.

She stood slowly, gripped by the look on his face.

"Saric..."

She'd looked into Jordin's eyes and seen utter peace too...but there was more in Saric's expression. An otherworldliness, as if already retreating from this reality.

A gentle smile curved his mouth. Tears filled his eyes. "It is so good to see you *alive*."

Feyn crossed to him quickly, suddenly overwhelmed. "Thank you, brother." She sank to her knee and grasped his hand, looking up at his face. Her brother, not the Sovereign he had once been, but one who had risen from the ashes to show them all a truer way.

"Thank you," she whispered.

He gently eased her to her feet. "This is the way it was always meant to be. Where I once brought death, I now bring life. I am the grateful one."

"Then we all find life."

He went on as if he hadn't heard.

"Jonathan's blood has given me life, replacing the Dark Blood in me that took a thousand lives. Ten thousand... more."

Something—some unnamed resolution in his voice— sent a chill down her neck.

"But it doesn't matter now, you see? We are alive, and you can save Rom. You will reign with me, at my side."

"No, Feyn." He lifted her hand in both of his own. A tear escaped his eye. "This is no longer my realm to rule."

"But of course it is! Now more than ever."

He gently let go of her hands and then slowly crossed to the chair.

"Saric?" she said.

"My journey here is over, Feyn. I have taken many lives. But now I will save Rom and the remaining Immortals."

"You and Jordin, you mean."

"No, Feyn. There are more than thirty to be saved. One of us must give all that we have."

She felt the heat drain from her face. "No. That can't be true." She went to him and fell to her knees, grabbing his hand. "You've just come back to me. Saric. Brother. There has to be another way."

He quietly stroked her hair. "No. There isn't. But this is my gift to give, and a small one at that. One that I've waited long years to give, knowing this day would come. Didn't you yourself die once, for the sake of hope?"

"Yes, but—"

"Then allow me to do the same. Not only for the sake of those who I save, but for mine. For Jonathan. For you. For Rom. For the Immortals who may live through my blood."

She glanced at Rom to find his eyes resting on her.

"Tell him. Tell him there's another way!"

Rom quietly shook his head. "He's right."

"No! It can't be! I finally have life—true life—with my brother, for the first time! Why will you take the years to come away from me?" She was weeping as she said it.

"We have the gift of this time. This moment will live, Feyn."

"But you won't."

"Yes, I will," he said, tipping up her chin. "Just not in this realm. Join me in my joy for that which awaits."

He glanced up and nodded at Rom, who began to look around him.

No! she wanted to scream. But even here, there was beauty. She had never seen Saric so radiant in her life.

Rom was searching among Corban's things. Feyn looked from him to the corner. Ammon was gone. No matter. Rom found the stent and a large basin. He quietly crossed to the chair. Kneeling beside the chair, he took up the stent as Saric drew back his tattered sleeve.

Saric took a deep breath and let it out slowly, face settled with a deep contentment.

He leaned back and laid his head against the top of the chair so often used as a device for interrogation and torture. But in that moment, it looked like a throne.

Feyn reached for both his hands as Rom shoved the stent deep into Saric's vein. She closed her fingers over his, tears coursing over her cheeks.

As the blood began to trickle into the jar, he turned his eyes upward and stared at the ceiling, lips softened in a quiet smile. She laid her cheek against his knee.

She watched as her brother's life slowly drained from his body.

"Now I go," he said, voice barely more than a whisper.

She lifted her head. "Where?" But she already knew.

"To be with Jonathan," he said, and closed his eyes.

CHAPTER THIRTY-TWO

Three Weeks Later

THERE WERE SEVEN primary continents in the world. Seven houses that governed them. Seven, the number of perfection. Seven, the seal of the Maker.

The Sovereign who'd proclaimed herself Maker ruled them all from her seat in the Citadel, rising above the ancient city of Byzantium—such was the way of her Order.

But Byzantium had been ravaged by death and war and Order had fallen. Feyn was no longer Maker; she was simply a new Sovereign yet unknown to the sea of citizens who'd been urgently summoned to witness the new inauguration along the old processional way at the Citadel basilica. Among them, prelates, each of the continental rulers, and nearly half of the world's twenty-five thousand royals.

Feyn sat on the stage staring out at the throngs gathered in fear to hear her words. Fear, because it was all they yet knew. Fear, because they unwittingly breathed death each day without realizing even that they were dead.

Today they would learn the truth.

She looked at Rom, seated in a chair beside her, watching her with the same gentle eyes that had once wooed her in a field north of Byzantium. The blood he'd given her that day had awakened her to life, but she had never known how abundant that life could be until three weeks ago.

He laid his hand on hers—a simple gesture of assurance. To say that she wasn't concerned would be to lie. Not for herself, but for those who would hear words spoken that hadn't been voiced in nearly five hundred years.

Her eyes flitted to Jordin, seated next to Rom, and Roland, who stood across the platform with his back to them, issuing final instructions to three servants who shifted nervously, casting glances her way every so often. How strange she must appear to those Corpses who'd once served under her iron fist. Today, their tyrannical Sovereign had shed her regal robes for a simple white dress. Her eyes, once black, had turned bright blue; her skin, once white, was now the color of living flesh.

Feyn smiled at the thought.

So much had changed.

Fifteen years earlier she'd stood on this very platform, anticipating her inauguration as Sovereign of the world. By the law of the Order, she'd been chosen from among eligible candidates not by peer or by merit, but by the hand of the Maker himself, according to the twelve-year Cycle of Rebirth, which had been completed three times in her father's forty-year reign. The births of those royals born closest to the tolling of the seventh hour on the seventh day of the seventh month of each new cycle had all been recorded. And she had been born closest of all.

Was it chance or fate that Talus, the first Keeper, had

predicted that a Sovereign with pure blood would be born to rule the world? Jonathan had been that Sovereign and he ruled today, but it was she who would rule this world of flesh and blood—"this dream," as Jordin was fond of calling it.

It all made such perfect sense in hindsight. The order of Keepers, guarding the blood for so many centuries; Rom's giving the blood to her; her own death and stasis that paved Jonathan's succession to the throne; her resurrection that seized it back. Even Saric's alchemy and her own dark reign. Would she be standing here today if any of it had been different? Would life—true life—now be seated as Sovereign if even one piece of history had not played itself out as it had?

Saric...

Her throat still knotted at the image of him yielding his blood to save the thirty-seven Immortals who'd taken it following his death. Having found life in the desert, he had delivered that life to save not one but many—founding a new race of humans who would in turn offer their blood to the world.

There were fifty-three in total now, having been judicious in the process of seroconverting others, taking the time to think through the massive undertaking before them. They'd agreed to call themselves Mortals once again, to avoid confusion with her office, despite knowing they truly were Sovereign, each and every one of them.

They would never manipulate or force any to take the blood. Never offer clever words of persuasion. Masses regaining the full range of emotions could wreak havoc in a society that had no tradition of dealing with those emotions.

She turned her eyes to the huge crowd gathered before

the inaugural platform. They waited in fearful silence—waiting to hear what their transformed Sovereign had in store for them.

With Rom, Roland, and Jordin, she'd carefully laid plans for this day, agreeing not to thrust the truth on the world with too much haste. As a result, she'd told none of the governing body yet.

They would hear it all today. All of them. Across the globe, the blue light of television screens illuminated the city centers of every continent, broadcasting images of New Byzantium.

Traditionally, the observance of Rebirth was required to be witnessed by all. The passing of authority from one Sovereign to another was among the holiest of events. To Feyn's way of thinking, today was no different; after all, she had truly been birthed to new life, the first ruling Sovereign to find that life. And so across the world, throughout the continents of Asiana and Greater Europa, of Nova Albion and Abyssinia, Sumeria, Russe, and Qin, the loyal gathered in the hundreds of thousands in every city to watch.

Roland turned and crossed the stage, dressed with Nomadic flare in leather and light wool, his hair braided with dark-blue beads.

Nearby, Kaya sat on a mat, running her hands over the back of Talia's lion. Having stayed behind with Kaya and four others who did not fight in Byzantium and faced with the prospect of certain death from the virus, Talia had vanished into the desert to face her fate with her lion. The lion had returned alone.

"All will be ready in a few minutes," Roland said, inclining his head to Feyn.

"I'm your Sovereign, not your queen," Feyn said with raised brow.

He stared at her for a moment. His eyes shifted to Jordin. "No, that would be another."

Jordin smiled and stood. Stepping toward him, she brushed aside a loose strand of hair hanging over his right eye.

"And such a proud queen she is," she said.

He lifted her hand and placed a kiss on her knuckles. "Always."

"Always," she replied.

Feyn glanced at Rom and winked. The look in his eyes had nothing to do with Jordin and Roland's display of tenderness. In close circles it was already known that she and Rom shared a profound love that would surely require a breaking of the tradition that sitting Sovereigns did not marry.

"Consider the stage secure, my Sovereign," Roland said.

He was still the Nomadic Prince, still the warrior with battle-hardened hands, but in so many other ways he was a completely new man, his strength displayed in love and composure.

If Rom were to lead the new senate, a matter still undecided, Roland would take matters of security in hand. The world would soon know full emotion as Sovereign blood reversed the death that had kept ambition and anger at bay. Conflicts were bound to erupt. Feyn would need a principled man of Roland's strength and skill to navigate the dangerous passages of awakened emotions in a raw world.

The prince took his seat next to Jordin and draped his arm over the chair, legs spread out as one who possessed all he could see and more. Once a ruler, always a ruler.

Their first order of business following seroconversion

of the Immortals had been to rid the city of the stench of death. Reaper had ravaged the fifteen thousand Dark Bloods who'd survived the Immortals' onslaught. They'd gone mad with the disease, many of them fleeing into the wasteland, where they died. Thankfully, only two citizens had been killed; Feyn had feared far worse.

Clearing the battlefield had required the work of two thousand men. They'd loaded the Dark Blood carcasses on carts and hauled them into a canyon just east of Byzantium, where they had been burned along with every trace of Dark Blood alchemy, including the samples, the equipment, sarcophagi, and even the papers chronicling their making. The fires had burned for days, illuminating the horizon. When the last of them had burned out, the canyon had been filled with earth, forever sealing in the remains of darkness.

Roland and the other survivors had carefully laid the bodies of the fallen Immortals on a funeral pyre. Together, they'd paid their respects to the dead in Nomadic fashion—with stories, tears, and hope.

It had taken two full weeks to clear the rubble left from the homes of those unfortunate enough to have been summarily displaced by her orders. The mile-wide swath of leveled ground surrounding the Citadel was a stark sight to the royals who'd traveled for today's re-inauguration. One she regretted. One she would rebuild.

For now, the grounds before the basilica had been planted with trees and strewn with flowers leading all the way up to the bleachers of the royals—if only to present a less shocking image to those who viewed the broadcast around the world.

Today, the sky over New Byzantium was clear and brilliant blue. Gone were the oppressive clouds that had hovered over the capital for centuries; strangely, not even a wisp had been seen in her skies for weeks.

The affair administrator, a blond woman named Brandice whom Feyn had known since school, hurried up the steps and took a knee before Feyn, head slightly bowed.

"We are ready, my Sovereign."

"Stand up, my friend. Please don't kneel before me again."

The woman lifted her head, saw Feyn's smile, and stood. "The broadcast is scheduled to begin in three minutes."

"Thank you, Brandice."

The woman dipped her head and stepped to the side of the stage to direct a nearby servant.

"Are you ready?" Rom said.

"As much as I can be."

Roland leaned forward. "Remember who you are."

"Who I am or who I was?" She sighed. "I don't feel like a Sovereign."

"Which will only make you a better one."

Her identity had shifted so dramatically that she didn't know how she should rule, particularly as a Sovereign responsible for ushering in a new age. She was only just beginning to understand her new self. Gone was the rage. Gone, the bitterness, deceit, ambition, and hatred. In its place lay an undercurrent of peace and love greater than any she had ever known.

Among them, Jordin's transformation remained the greatest. Rom lived in a constant state of grace and peace, but he hadn't encountered the same mystery except in small pieces. Neither had Roland, Kaya, or her.

But their eyes had all been opened, even if not as wildly as one plunging through a lake, breathing Jonathan's love as if it were water. Feyn had teased the younger woman that she had probably just been dehydrated—a joke they all shared in every time they heard the story—but every one of them knew her transformation was undeniable, and they longed in their hearts for the same.

Brandice caught her attention and held up one finger. One minute. Feyn acknowledged the signal with a nod.

"Tell me again, Jordin," she said. "What is the secret to fully living in the Sovereign Realm? I would hear it before taking the stand."

"Surrender," Jordin said.

She knew this, of course. So simple. So easy to forget. She would ask to be reminded again and again, the rest of her life.

She considered the woman with the deeply settled countenance. The gentle smile on her face was now a permanent feature. She was more their leader than Rom, Roland, or even Feyn herself, if only in matters concerning Jonathan's realm.

"Surrender to what?" she asked, though she knew the answer.

"Surrender to Jonathan," she said. "To unconditional love. To what is. To the awareness that beyond all you see with the eyes in your head, there is a greater reality full of love that knows no suffering. Surrender to that knowing, and the fear in this life will always vanish."

"It's that simple."

"Yes. It's that simple."

"Surrender to love," Rom said, gazing out at the royals in the bleachers.

"Love without judgment," Jordin said.

"Surrender to the fact that you are Sovereign of the world," Roland said with a wry smile. "And to the knowing that you were chosen to take this stage and abolish five hundred years of tyranny under an Order of fear."

He paused.

"Set them free, Feyn."

She glanced up at the blue sky. A small, gray cloud hung on the distant horizon. The first in weeks. And then she nodded and pushed herself to her feet.

Thunderous applause erupted spontaneously, filling the air with what might be the first true expression of freedom in so many years. They didn't yet know truth, but truth knew them.

"For you, my Sovereign," she whispered.

"For Jonathan," Jordin said.

"For Jonathan," Roland and Rom repeated in unison.

Then Feyn Cerelia, Sovereign among Sovereigns, walked to the stand and lifted her hands to the roaring throng.

It was time to change the world.

EPILOGUE

THE LONE figure knelt at the base of a cliff deep in the desert, staring at the small pack he'd carried for three weeks, one of two, the other containing the remains of his food supply.

It was nearly sundown. He didn't like being in the wasteland after dark; terror lurked there, images of the Citadel's dungeons, of battle.

The time had come—he'd waited too long already.

He unbuckled the pack and carefully dug out the metal box inside. Flicking open the latch, he withdrew a carefully wrapped parcel. Lifted a small scroll bound by a single leather twine.

With trembling hands, he removed the string, opened Corban's scroll, and read the words written in the Dark Alchemist's hand.

My dear Ammon,
You are the last vestige of Order as it was … as it was
meant to become. Escape with your life. Establish an
Order of Keepers. Guard this precious remnant for
the Day of Reckoning.

The Dark Blood herein destroys or grants the power to live.

—Corban

Ammon carefully set down the note, tucked it inside, and then unwrapped the thing inside the box.

A vial of blood.

ABOUT THE AUTHORS

TED DEKKER is a *New York Times* bestselling author with more than five million books in print. He is known for stories that combine adrenaline-laced plots with incredible confrontations between unforgettable characters. He lives in Austin, Texas, with his wife and children.

TOSCA LEE is the *New York Times* bestselling author of *Demon: A Memoir, Havah: The Story of Eve, Iscariot,* and the Books of Mortals series with *New York Times* bestselling author Ted Dekker. She is best known for haunting prose and humanizing portraits of maligned characters. A former international business consultant and lifelong adventure traveler, she makes her home in the Midwest.

"The Books of Mortals rocks with the same level of intensity and brilliance as Dekker's Circle Series. Riveting, resounding, and a magnificent blend of Dekker's and Lee's styles."

—*Library Journal* starred review

Book 1

Book 2

Available Now in The Books of Mortals Series